To Dan,

With best wishes

reading. *Frank Dur* June, 2012

THE WHITE CROW

Frank Durham

authorHOUSE®

AuthorHouse™ UK Ltd.
500 Avebury Boulevard
Central Milton Keynes, MK9 2BE
www.authorhouse.co.uk
Phone: 08001974150

First published by AuthorHouse 06/21/2011

ISBN: 978-1-4567-7035-8 (sc)
ISBN: 978-1-4567-7034-1 (ebk)

'I feel that it is my vocation to save Germany—
I cannot and may not evade it . . .

I cannot love any woman until I have
completed my task.'

Adolf Hitler

This book is dedicated to:

Jane—for believing in me

*The late R.S.M Ernie Bennett M.M.—and
all his chums from the trenches*

The late Andre Becquart—the inspiration for this book

With special thanks to:

Major Ian Jones (ret'd) MBE

for his invaluable help in sharing his expertise in explosives

Original cover idea: Jane Ball

CHAPTER ONE

June 17, 2000

Lowly reporter Adam Cornish, pint of bitter ale in hand, stood at his retirement party, like a slowly collapsing sand castle amid a beery tide of newspaper men and women.

They brushed past him in the packed bar of the Nine Bells pub, laughing and joking, paying little heed to the man who should by rights be the star of the occasion. But not even by a long stretch of anybody's imagination at the "local rag", the Kentish World, could Adam be described as anything as bright as a star.

None of these boozy revellers could have foreseen, even in their wildest dreams that, by an amazing stroke of fate, he would soon be strutting the world stage. Never in a thousand alcohol-sodden blue moons, could they have imagined that this down-at-heel joke, Adam Cornish, would metamorphose into a monster of the history books.

Back in the mundane here and now, the journalist, with his untidy beard and greying hair, cut a sad figure as he waited for the inevitable stock goodbye speeches and presentation. He wore a crumpled check shirt, brown corduroy trousers, shiny with wear, and a stained grey sport jacket. His once-black shoes, cracked from years' lack of polish, partly hid hole-riddled socks.

The only things of note about Adam were his vividly piercing blue eyes. These, set above bruised and puffy bags, seemed strangely and unsettlingly familiar.

At times, women found them hypnotic. Occasionally, both men and women found them frightening. Their depths were deeply unforgettable.

During Adam's intermittent and barely-suppressed fits of rage, when the teasing became too insistent, those eyes sparked to a blaze. They became the eyes of the monster.

People shuddered and again wondered where they had seen the like of those remarkable eyes before.

They were to find out only too soon.

Colleagues slapped Adam on the back with indifferent bonhomie as they pushed through the drink-fuelled crowd to the bar. He knew they thought of him as some sort of pet poodle.

His lack of talent, his old-fashioned, spiral-backed reporter's notebook and his notable absence of promotion during years of undistinguished service had rendered Adam Cornish partly invisible.

He was regarded as a piece of the office furniture. A mildly funny joke.

If only they had known what was going on behind Adam's half-closed eyes that festive night in the pub. The eyes had become chips of blue ice, as Adam stood swaying and secretly fuming among them.

"Fuck these morons and fuck their piss-taking over the past 40 years. I have a Voice inside my head that tells me I'm a universe better than them. When I achieve the greatness and power that my Voice says is my divine destiny, they will become less than a dog's mess on the sole of my shoe."

Adam tasted rage like an acid, burning the back of his throat and stomach. He watched with contempt as tipsy reporters, photographers, sub-editors and all the other Kentish World toilers shrieked and roared under the ancient, blackened beams of the old pub.

"Let them piss it up while they can. They are the stupid bastards, who have always held me back. One day they will be singing a different tune. I promise that. They will pay. The whole sodding world will pay. In blood.

"Everybody will want to know me then. I will put the fear of God into them. They will be only too eager to pay me the respect I deserve.

"There will be rivers of blood . . ."

Meanwhile, the Kentish World revellers, oblivious to Adam's inner fury, stoked the party towards its climax.

Outside the Nine Bells pub, a gentle rain fell on Southdown, a ripe fruit of a town set in the Kentish "Garden of England". It created soft, golden halos round the streetlamps that fringed the market square, on the edge of which the ancient inn crouched.

This sedate town had been the centre of Adam Cornish's humble empire. His lacklustre career had raised scarcely a ripple outside his rural beat.

No international scoops or Pulitzer prizes for Adam. No tempting offers from the bright lights of Fleet Street, just 25 miles or so to the north.

Over the years, the World's readers had become used to seeing his name above reports on jumble sales, petty court cases, unremarkable deaths and chip-pan kitchen fires.

The bosses at the posh, "mahogany end" of the offices decided that Adam didn't rate a car, as did the more

3

important members of the staff. They handed him the keys of a humble motor-scooter, which had become yet another office joke.

Adam was something of an institution in Southdown and the scattering of surrounding villages. He was the well-worn slipper that fitted comfortably on to the feet of local people's lives.

Now even this modicum of fame was coming to an end. At his leaving party at the Nine Bells, he was going out with more of a hiccough than a bang.

But, in his bitter heart of hearts, Adam believed that bang would surely come some day. It would be a mighty explosion that would rock the world. Then he would ride in a chauffeured limousine, graciously saluting the adoring crowds.

Suddenly, Adam was brought back to the present. He was hauled to the front of the bar and the World's staff formed a semicircle round him. This was to be the main event of the evening, carefully timed by the powers-that-be to take place before a tsunami of booze overwhelmed proceedings.

Silence fell. Protocol had to be observed. In time-honoured newspaper tradition the Editor, balding, rotund "Curly" Capon, handed Adam a framed, mocked-up front page of the newspaper he had served so long.

It was emblazoned with a picture of Adam, wearing his usual shabby, ex-Royal Air Force greatcoat, astride his motor-scooter. Across the top of the page, a sub-editor had chuckled as he dreamed up the headline: "ADAM'S SCOOTING OFF AT LAST!"

Amid drunken cheers, Curly presented Adam with the fruits of this afternoon's last-minute office collection. This was a cheap pewter tankard, engraved with Adam's name and the dates of his service at the Kentish World.

Adam noticed the family owners of the World, and its lucrative parent group, standing on the fringe of the crowd. The Goldsteins—the Old Man and his sons, Mr. Leon and Mr. Oliver—were expensively barbered and wearing sharp suits and hand-made shoes.

They took polite sips of Perrier water before setting down their half-finished drinks. Then each in turn, they clapped their departing employee on the shoulder. Duty done, the Goldsteins gratefully slipped out into the drizzle, bound for their country mansions.

"Smug bastards. Jew boys, Here and now, I decide that they will be the first to pay for putting me down. Hitler had the right idea about the Chosen People."

Curly was making a speech, full of insincere praise. The crowd hooted with laughter at the thinly-veiled and well-worn jibes showered on the now-swaying Adam.

Tears of rage coursed down his cheeks, which onlookers mistakenly thought were a rare exhibition of gratitude and emotion.

Wiping his eyes, Adam burbled and slurred a rambling reply to the Editor's homily. Amid the rowdy cheers and applause that followed, pint after pint of beer was lined up on the bar in front of him.

As the retiring reporter downed them manfully, he again became the invisible guest at the party. The roisterers, aflame with alcohol, pushed past him, jostled him and yelled pleasantries at one another round him.

No-one spoke to him.

Suddenly, the party was all over. Adam's life crashed, like a thousand of his old news stories, smack into a full stop.

The newspaper people spilled out into the night, vanishing like snowflakes on a hot shovel.

To them, Adam was already a misty memory.

The aging reporter drained the last pint from his presentation tankard. Jim, the florid, heavy-set barman, grabbed it and plunged it into the sink beneath the bar. Adam leaned over and snatched it back with a growl.

Jim didn't even bother to look up as the retiring reporter found the bar door handle with difficulty and staggered into the deserted, late-night streets of Southdown.

Adam paused and caught hold of the fence in a nearby garden. The rain was easing off, and he tried to focus on the stars beginning to peep through the mist.

He offered up a drunken plea to Whoever Is Up There:

"Punish the bastards, O Lord. And give me the power and the glory I know is mine."

In the shadows, eyes were watching.

The next morning, Adam awoke slowly and painfully in his tiny flat, situated above one of Southdown's many newly-minted coffee bars. He was suffering from a crashing hangover and an acute case of boozer's gloom.

The black dog of depression lay heavily across his chest. The reporter's eyes felt as though somebody had tried to glue them shut. Lurking behind the other afflictions was the bitter residue of last night's fury.

As he prised sticky eyes open, blinking as the sunlight poked its finger through the grubby window of his bedroom, Adam suddenly recalled that his old life had ended.

He asked himself:

"What have I got to show for it . . . for all those years working on that poxy newspaper?"

He had only to turn his head painfully to one side to find the answer. It stood on his cluttered bedside table, next to the knocked-over alarm clock.

The sole fruit of his professional life was a cheap pewter tankard, engraved with his name. It smelled sourly of last night's excesses at the Nine Bells.

Adam groaned and levered himself to the edge of the bed, where he could look out the window. Below him, was the high street of the town, which had for so long been his life and his living.

His life had changed overnight, but Southdown's hadn't. People were going about their business in the same way as on any other day. Vans delivered to the shops, and a road-sweeper manoeuvred his noisome machine along the pavement.

Wallowing in gloom, Adam told himself that his passing from the Kentish World amounted to a non-event. His going would be mildly remarked upon with a few lines in next week's edition.

He would sink into the sub-life of Southdown's retired and unemployed. He would join the idlers, sitting on bar stools, waiting to don wooden overcoats for their last sad journey to St. Luke's graveyard at the top of the town.

Just for a while his hate, his bravado and his certainty of impending greatness deserted him.

Adam passed a hand over throbbing temples. His soul felt the first nibble of loneliness at its edges, like a mouse discovering the cheese.

His wife, Anna had divorced him five years ago. For 41 years of marriage, she had endured his lack of success,

7

bizarre sexual demands and affairs with the bottle and a series of gullible girl reporters.

Worst of all, were Adam's sudden, violent bouts of white-hot rage. These "turns", as Anna euphemistically called them, had terrified her and the children. They were the final reason she left him.

Adam's remarkable blue eyes, that had once cast a spell over Anna, gradually lost their magic for her. Suddenly, the Sixties dolly bird turned grey-haired matron, made a life-changing decision.

She bought new clothes and a new hair-do, and went to the gym to sweat her way to a new body. Anna began forging a social life that excluded her drab, philandering husband. With their children grown up and a trim, sparkling new self, she dumped her loveless marriage and moved into a flat in South London.

Anna maintained a close relationship with the children—41-year-old son Grant and daughters Victoria, aged 39, and Zoe, 37. They, too, rejected their father, blaming him for the break-up of the family.

Adam heard rumours of a new man in Anna's life. These stung him to jealousy and anger.

"He'll pay, just like the others. That man is on my list."

Now the Kentish World had turned its back on him, too. They had even taken back his motor-scooter—his much-derided but sole means of transport.

It had been handed over, with much hilarity and in a mock ceremony, to one of the World's new breed of reporters. Her name was Ros Litherland. She had long, blonde hair, major breasts and a degree in philosophy or some such nonsense.

Ros had never had to serve a dreary apprenticeship, like reporters in Adam's day. As a junior, he spent many a draughty hour, propping open a church door with his foot so that he could list the name of each mourner at a local dignitary's funeral.

Then it was out into the rain-soaked churchyard to examine each and every "floral tribute" wreath and bunch of flowers for the names on the labels. Weekends were usually spent at village flower shows.

Then there was translating into pseudo stories the forms people filled in for their daughter's weddings:

"The bride wore a full-length dress in white brocade . . ."

As Adam stared gloomily out the window, he gave a contemptuous snort, which made the ache behind his eyes stab savagely.

Kids on newspapers had it too easy these days. They didn't know they were born. In an age of new-fangled public relations hand-outs, they were given half their stories on a plate.

The rest of the time, they seemed welded to their telephones.

Adam reflected that, at 65 years old, bookies would lay good odds that his future would be less than bright. Theoretically, short of contracting a terminal disease, he had years of loneliness and sterile indolence stretching before him.

Then, with a rush, his old feeling of destiny reasserted itself, like a cork bobbing to the top of water in a bucket. Adam cracked a secret smile and those blue eyes leapt to vivid life.

The Fates had obviously been waiting for just this sort of opportunity . . . a pause in his life. Soon, very soon, they would reach down to touch him . . . to anoint him. Then his would be the power and the glory.

It was so close, he could taste it.

Adam staggered into the confusion of his kitchen. Every surface was piled with dirty plates, mugs and congealed take-away food containers. He rinsed a cup briefly under the tap, spooned in instant coffee and boiled the kettle.

He carried the scalding liquid back to the bedroom and, throwing a pile of dirty clothes on the floor, sat down on the only chair.

Adam trembled as one of his "turns" possessed him.

Mentally, he began to draw up a "hit list" of all the people who had wronged him. At the top were the villains who, although recognising his genius, had jealously held him back.

He remembered the Goldsteins in the pub last night. Cool and patronising bastards. They were dressed by the wealth generated by his and other people's sweat. They, of course, headed his list.

The reporter, wearing only yesterday's dingy underpants, sipped his coffee and lapsed into one of his favourite fantasies. It was based on a photograph in one of the World War Two Nazi propaganda books that were his constant bedtime reading.

The Old Man and his two sons are on their hands and knees in Southdown High Street, their heads bowed in humiliation, their expensive suits stained and torn.

Storm-troopers stand over them, hands on hips. Adam and other gleeful townsfolk jeer. They urge the Jew boys to clean up every speck of dust and every dog turd on the pavement.

Bliss. Adolf would have loved it.

The "turn" passed, dumping Adam into the bitter and lonely present. He looked round at the flat's chipped woodwork, shabby Fifties furniture and antique cobwebs.

He must get out of here. There was only one place for a journalist to go on the first day of his retirement. And that was the nearest pub. In the world of newspapers, booze is the answer to everything.

Adam swilled his tankard under the tap and shook the remaining drops of cold water into the sink. He prepared to face the day.

Yesterday's underpants would have to do for now. So would the checked shirt and trousers, with their faint aroma of perspiration, and the greying handkerchief.

He "shone" his shoes by rubbing each in turn on the back of his trousers. Adam looked at the new stains on his jacket and decided that it would have to do.

Blearily, he padded into the bathroom and peered into the damp-speckled mirror. He was confronted by a grey, untidy ghost of himself. Hurriedly, he looked away.

Adam winced as he sloshed cold water on his face, and "combed" his beard and hair with shaking fingers. Now he was ready to face the world of retirement.

Adam took his old Air Force greatcoat from the hook behind the door, shrugged into it and clomped down the bare boards of the stairs he had always intended to have carpeted.

He let himself out his front door, sandwiched between the coffee bar and old Ted Barnes' soft furnishings shop. Ted, a local councillor, gave Adam a desultory wave and went on rearranging the curtains displayed in his window.

Adam trudged towards the market square, fitful sunlight making him blink painfully. He reflected on how the town had changed for the worse during his lifetime.

Its old market-town personality had been suffocated by chain coffee bars, chain clothing stores, chain estate agents and chain supermarkets. Gone were the sweet-smelling grocery emporiums, hardware shops and corn chandlers, often owned by generations of the same family.

Adam cut through a cobbled alleyway where once the Three Horseshoes, a thriving pub owned first by his grandfather, Ernie Cornish, and then by Adam's late father, Albert, had stood in all its Victorian splendour. The site was now occupied by a chic Italian restaurant, with chrome furniture and waiters with tight, black trousers and phony accents.

He was sorry his mother, Polly, who outlived Albert, had seen the swinging demolition ball cruelly destroy their home and its memories. Adam's step-grandmother, Maud, had long since gone to her rest before the vandalism occurred.

Adam came to the market square. Outside the Nine Bells, pensioners sat chatting, clutching their shopping bags, on a scarred old wooden bench. In olden days, when the Nine Bells doubled as a courthouse, condemned prisoners sat on this seat, supping their last bowl of ale.

He stepped into the pub's cool interior. It smelled of two centuries of tippling and a lingering memory of last night's revels. He put his tankard on the counter and Jim filled it with a couple of practised tugs of the beer pump.

As Adam's eyes adjusted to the gloom, he saw there was a lone customer at this early hour, slumped over the bar. Harry Connor was such a dyed-in-the-wool "regular", he was jokingly referred to by the locals as a Nine Bells' "fixture and fitting".

Harry was dressed in his customary "military" style. He wore a faded, red paratrooper's beret, a threadbare blazer with a regimental badge on the breast pocket and stained flannel trousers, with the faint remnants of a soldier's crease.

Adam could see an assortment of medals glittering on Harry's chest. He wore these daily with a certain panache, and they attracted many a free drink from gullible tourists. Adam moved closer for a better look.

Harry seized the opportunity . . . "The going price for a look at my gongs is a pint, old mate."

Adam reluctantly pulled a fiver from his wallet and placed it on the bar. Jim, guessing the approaching scenario, had already refilled Harry's glass.

Adam ruefully picked up his change before peering at the medals. Two of them, with frayed and stained ribbons, seemed familiar. He pointed to them and asked "I seem to know these, Harry, what are they?"

But, before the old man could wipe his beer-sodden moustache and concoct a lie, the answer flashed into Adam's mind. He snapped angrily: "You bloody old fraud! You must have nicked these in some jumble sale.

"They're the same as my grandfather's from the Fourteen-Eighteen war . . . the British War Medal and the Victory Medal. You're nowhere near old enough to have earned them.

"You'll be telling me next that Princess Alexandra sent you one of her brass boxes, full of tobacco, as a present for Christmas, 1914. That was when you were up to your neck in muck and bullets—I don't think. You lying old bugger!"

Adam's anger mounted. He had always had a sentimental place in his heart for his grandfather, Ernie Cornish, a sergeant on the Western Front in the Great War. This fraud was a desecration of Ernie's memory.

He had framed his grandfather's medals, which included the Military Medal for bravery, and fixed them to his sitting-room wall. Inside the glass-fronted case were other treasured mementos of Ernie's service.

Harry, hugging the secret that he was long ago rejected for military service because of flat feet, decided the best form of defence was attack. He sneered: "What the bloody hell would you know about medals, son?

"Let me guess, you were a schoolboy National Serviceman with nothing but bum fluff on your cheeks. You were a mummy's boy whose only battle was to get to the front of the queue for a cup of tea.

"Kids like you need to get some service in. You make me sick."

Harry picked up his glass and drank urgently, as though it might be snatched away at any moment. He went on: "Everyone knows these two are World War One medals. You're not clever to spot that

"These were my grand-dad's—same as yours. If you knew the least piddling thing about military customs, you would know that people are allowed to wear their relative's medals on the right-hand side of their chests.

"That's what I've always intended to do. I just haven't got around to changing them round from the left. So stop wasting your breath when you don't know what you're talking about."

Adam was momentarily taken aback. He *did* have some vague inkling about the custom of wearing a relative's medals . . . although he thought it applied only to one's father or husband. And Harry had come close to hitting the bull's-eye about Adam's own service in the Royal Air Force.

He had been called up as a callow youth of 18, later becoming an acting/unpaid corporal. His job was personnel selection at a basic training camp, perched way up on the bleak moors of Northumberland.

Adam ticked boxes on the forms recruits had filled in. These were theoretically designed to see for which trade the men were most suited. What a joke? Brawny butchers became pen-pushers and gentlemenly bank-clerks found themselves roaring obscenities as drill instructors.

In the rare moments that he was honest with himself, Adam admitted his military service had been just about as undistinguished as his journalistic career.

He gulped down his beer and pushed the empty tankard across to Jim. He ordered: "Wash that and hang it on one of the hooks above the counter for me, please. I must rush— things to do."

The sun was warmer and higher in the sky as Adam stood moodily on the market square, something tugging at the corner of his mind. It was a momentous idea he couldn't quite grasp.

From behind the window of a coffee shop across the square and among the people thronging a market fruit and vegetable stall, eyes were watching.

Back in his flat, musty with old dust, Adam was still seething after his confrontation with Harry Connor in the Nine Bells. Was this the sort of pathetic company he would be compelled to keep during long years of retirement?

That germ of an idea was still tugging at his mind, like a fretful child at its mother's skirts. What on earth was it? Adam remembered it had been sparked by the mention of his grandfather.

He walked to where Ernie's three medals, lovingly cleaned and mounted, gleamed behind the glass in their wooden frame. They provided the sole splash of colour and personal touch to the shabby apartment.

Above the medals was the red and white enamelled badge of the North Kent's Old Comrades' Association.

Below them, a buff Army form set out the bare bones of the sergeant's life in the "war to end all wars".

The strangely titled "Certificate of Disembodiment on Demobilisation" recorded starkly: "Regt. No. 865387; Rank: Sgt; Names in full: Cornish—Ernest Frederick.

"Unit or Corps from which discharged: 1/9th. Battn. North Kent Regt.; Enlisted on the 10th. August, 1914; Medals and decorations awarded during the present engagement: Military Medal.

"Place of rejoining in case of emergency: Maidstone; Medical category: C4."

Adam the journalist always felt compelled to try to put flesh on those bones. Although he had spent hours talking to his grandfather about life in the trenches, he instinctively felt the old man was holding back something important.

Ernie, whose colourful turn of phrase would have done a journalist proud, conjured up graphic descriptions of his days in the killing ground of the Ypres salient. He painted word pictures of the tortured landscape around the martyred Belgian town of "Wipers" and of men surviving like rats in their holes.

The old soldier sometimes paused and blew his nose loudly as he spoke of chums who had "gone West", the Tommy's euphemism for death. Then he chuckled over some comic event or other that happened during the war.

Ernie spoke, too, of the historic battle of Passchendale, whose name was forever afterwards written in blood in the annals of the Great War. He told of gas, of enemy artillery barrages so terrible that they sent men mad. He described deeds of valour and kindness amid the carnage.

But Sergeant Ernie Cornish MM, afraid of being labelled what he termed "a sprucer", would never tell young Adam how he came to win his Military Medal for gallantry.

The memory of his grandfather's modest, Edwardian reticence sparked even more anger in Adam as he thought of Harry Connor's phony medals in the Nine Bells this morning.

Harry's name went on the list. Oh, yes.

Ernie did, however, tell of the wound that caused him to plunge from A1 medical category—being at the peak of fitness as an athlete in Civvy Street—down to the lowly grade of C4.

He told the wide-eyed schoolboy: "I was one of the lucky ones. I got away with a touch of gas and a piece of shrapnel inside me. It was what we used to call 'a blighty wound' because it got us home.

"That bit of metal was a lovely souvenir from dear old Fritz. Doctors were afraid to try to get it out. It was too close to me vitals, you see. It's sitting there, nice and quiet, to this day.

"It's that bit of gas that'll do for me in the end. It's the cough that'll carry me off, all right."

Ernie was wrong. It was the scrap of metal, courtesy of one of Herr Krupp's artillery shells, that did for him.

When the old soldier was 60 years old, he suddenly dropped dead in his public bar at the Three Horseshoes.

At Ernie's inquest, the pathologist reported that the shrapnel had inexplicably moved. It had kissed Ernie's "vitals", sending him off to join his comrades, already lying row on row in Flanders fields.

As Adam grew older, his interest in the Great War became more intense. He found from military records that Ernie's battalion had served in the epic 1917 attack on the Messines Ridge.

This battle, one of the most famous on the Western Front, had always fascinated Adam. He pored for hours over maps and documents, and studied the strategy that gave the Allies one of their first victories.

He even recreated the battle in a *papier mache* diorama of the battlefield, in the loft of his flat. It was a work of art, complete with hand-painted model soldiers, trenches, barbed wire and artillery pieces.

Ernie must have been in the thick of it. He probably went "over the top" of the trench with his chums in the shadow of that ridge.

But all Adam's eager questions about Messines were met with what seemed to be an embarrassed silence. Then the old soldier would abruptly say: "Time to brew up, my boy", before retreating to the kitchen.

Did Ernie Cornish have a deep secret from those dramatic days? Was there something about which he daren't speak? Instinctively, Adam felt this could be something vital to his own life.

What had happened to Sergeant Ernie Cornish at Messines?

Adam went into the bedroom and reached down a cardboard box from the top of the wardrobe. It contained his grandfather's treasured possessions from the war.

Was the answer in here? He carried the dust-covered box to the kitchen table, pushed aside some dirty crocks, set it down and began to sort through its contents. Every item brought back a memory of the old Tommy.

First, there came a pair of identity discs on a piece of rough string. One disc was to go to Regimental Headquarters if Ernie fell in battle, so that the dreaded telegram announcing his death could be sent to his parents. The other would remain on his body, enabling them to bury him according to his "C of E"—Church of England—religion.

Then there were Ernie's sergeant's stripes, faded with age and still a little mud-stained. Beneath these in the box were four dark blue chevrons, surmounted by a red one. These, once worn at the bottom of Ernie's tunic sleeve, were his pride and joy.

He used to tell Adam: "Every blue one represents a year's service. It's the red one that's special. It showed everyone that I joined up during the first week of the war.

"I was one of thousands who lined up at the recruiting offices every day. We couldn't wait to sign on for what we imagined would be the great adventure of our lives. I thought what a wonderful change a battle or two would be for a plumber from boring old Southdown.

"We might not have been so eager to go, had we known what was in store for us."

Ernie would stroke the chevrons like old friends . . . "Not many of these red ones about, my boy. Most of the lads who joined up when I did are still out in Flanders—sleeping under gravestones.

"Or their remains were scattered to the four winds by the guns. God bless 'em. God bless 'em all. I think of them every day of my life."

Ernie blew his nose and wiped his eyes. He said: "Getting old and soft these days, my boy. I'm lucky to be here . . . so many never marched home.

"I was a bit of a middle-distance runner before the war, you know. I was quite a star of the Kentish Harriers athletic club. I sent out letters after the war, suggesting a reunion.

"Only two other blokes turned up. The rest had all gone West. We just shook hands and went home."

Adam lifted out his grandfather's brass gift box from Princess Alexandra, and a souvenir pencil made from a 303 calibre cartridge case. Right at the bottom of the cardboard box was a leather-bound photograph album.

He pulled up a kitchen chair and started slowly thumbing through the book. Here was a picture of Ernie in his Harriers running kit, a number pinned to his chest. There was another with his mother and father, uneasy in their Sunday best clothes, posing in a stiff family group.

Here was Ernie again, proudly displaying his new uniform, one hand resting on a pedestal on which stood a potted aspidistra.

As Adam turned the pages, the photographs charted Ernie's progress through the war. There were groups of grinning chums, some with souvenir German helmets perched jauntily on their heads.

First, Ernie wore the single stripe of a lance-corporal. Then, in a snap where he was sitting in a trench, toasting the camera with a mug of tea, Ernie sported a corporal's tapes.

A later photo showed Ernie, with three stripes sewn on to what were obviously hospital "blues", sitting with a group of men bound with bandages or leaning on crutches.

In each successive photograph, the horrors of war were more deeply etched on Ernie's face. At the hospital, the camera had caught a glimpse of torment in his eyes.

Adam closed the album and went to put it back in the box. A photograph, lodged loosely between its pages fluttered to the floor, landing face down. Its edges were ragged and it had paste marks on the back, as though someone had torn it out and then thought better of throwing it away.

He picked up the photograph and turned it over. There was a smiling Ernie, standing with his arm round a vivacious, dark-haired girl. She was looking up at him impishly. The couple was standing outside a low brick building. A sign over the front door read "Estaminet".

Adam gasped. This must be Marie LeBrun, the scandalous, scarlet woman who had so shocked the good folk of Southdown. She was Ernie's French wife, who was significantly missing when the wounded hero came marching home just before Christmas, 1917.

Adam's Gallic grandmother caused quite a stir when she finally arrived in the sleepy Kentish town early the following April. The young and gorgeous French beauty was carrying in her arms a month-old baby. He was Adam's father, Albert Ernest Cornish.

There were soon more scandals for people to savour. When Albert was just six years old, the love of Ernie's life suddenly and mysteriously vanished.

She returned a month later, wearing the latest French fashions, and demanded a divorce—the first anyone in town could remember.

After a distraught and bewildered Ernie surrendered and granted Marie her wish, she disappeared again. This time *la belle Marie* vanished forever.

Strangely, not long after Marie LeBrun Cornish had shaken the dust of Southdown off her daintily-shod feet, Ernie came into money. The amount was so substantial, he was able to lay down his plumber's tools for ever and buy the Three Horseshoes public house.

There was enough, too, to pay for Albert's expensive education at a local minor public school. Mysteriously, from that time onwards, there always seemed to be plenty of money in the Cornish coffers.

The day after Marie left, Ernie retired into his garden shed with several bottles of whisky. When he emerged three days later, he looked as shell-shocked as if he had been through Passchendaele all over again.

Then, as people did in those days, he quietly got on with his life. That generation was well used to losing loved ones.

Ernie eventually married Maud, a shepherd's daughter, who had been his sweetheart before the war. Maud always treated her stepson—a boy with strikingly vivid blue eyes—as though he were her own flesh and blood.

It was Maud who stepped into the role of bridegroom's mother when Albert married a local beauty called Polly. The couple's son, Adam, was born on March 11, 1935

That elusive idea suddenly struck Adam. Here was a goldmine. Here was his destiny.

Ernie's life had all the makings of a Hollywood blockbuster. War . . . heroism . . . sex . . . heartbreak. All it needed was a bit of research, and Adam had plenty of time for that.

This was a story that would knock Steven Spielberg's film, Saving Private Ryan, into a cocked hat! It would make The Deerhunter look as tame as a vicarage tea party.

Adam could imagine Nicole Kidman and Catherine Zeta-Jones fighting for the Oscar-winning part of Marie. Brad Pitt and Matt Damon would duke it out to play dashing Sergeant Ernie Cornish, battlefield hero and lover.

There is greatness to be had here.

Adam's head spun with excitement. He would become rich and famous. With the millions would come power . . . and power enough to make his fantasies become reality.

He would breathe new life into the wonderful old Nazi political party, the National Socialists, that was his nightly study and lifetime obsession. He would assume his rightful place in the world at last.

Then they would pay. Oh, yes.

But, not even in his most frenzied fantasies, could Adam picture the dark forces he was about to unleash.

CHAPTER TWO

May 3, 1917

Marie LeBrun and her lover were lying naked, tangled amid sweat-damp sheets on an ancient brass bed in a room over a café called Au Fossoyeur—the Gravedigger—in the Franco-Belgian border town of Comines.

The girl forced herself to lie completely still. This prevented the bed's internal organs from creaking and groaning—embarrassing sounds she knew could be heard only too clearly by the soldiers in the bar below.

For once Marie's man was silent and relaxed, his mesmerising blue eyes closed in sleep. He was exhausted from their weird lovemaking and his impassioned speeches, which inevitably followed.

The girl reached out tentatively to touch her lover's drooping moustache. She giggled, considering this dark appendage ridiculous . . . but, at the same time, faintly appealing.

On second thoughts, Marie hurriedly withdrew her hand, afraid of disturbing the sleeping man. Her soldier was having a few hours respite from the killing ground just a few kilometres up the road.

She studied her lover as though he were one of the paintings she loved. The sheets had slipped from his gaunt body. The sunlight, peeping between chinks in the bedroom curtains, threw into sharp relief skeletal ribs, and protruding collar bones and pelvis.

The soldier's face was a study in exhaustion. Dark brush-strokes of fatigue under the man's eyes contrasted with his Western Front trench pallor.

Marie winced, noting the livid scar on her lover's left leg. This was a grim reminder of the wound that, last year, had snatched him from her. An ambulance train had born him, jolting and rattling, back to his beloved Germany.

She had prayed for her man's return. For Marie feared his native land would seduce him into staying. Germany was his other mistress, and she knew it was useless to try to compete

But the wound had healed and Marie's unlikely-looking warrior was soon back in her arms . . . then into the perils of the trenches, in which he appeared to revel.

At this stage of the war, the first surge of patriotism that had inspired the men on both sides had long melted away. Both Fritz and Tommy yearned for the guns to fall silent so that they could go home.

But Marie's little *gefreiter* still gloried in the fight. His patriotism was as brightly burnished as the day he enlisted on August 18, 1914.

He told his mistress:

"I sank down on my knees to thank Heaven for the favour, on being permitted to live in such a time."

Marie was pleased but puzzled that her soldier never seemed to go home on leave. Then a comrade explained that the eccentric little corporal amazed them all by gifting them his leaves. He seemed happier amid the danger and squalor of the trenches.

The girl knew that men were dying in tens of thousands on the battlefield, where the guns growled and thundered night and day. But her man assured her that she had no need to worry. God was saving him for a great destiny.

He assured a still-fearful Marie:

"Bullets, bayonets and shells cannot kill Adolf Hitler."

Lying on their brass bed or in the sweet grass of a Flemish meadow, Hitler would explain how Fate had proved, again and again, that he could never die in battle.

For example, one day he was eating stew from a mess tin with a group of comrades in a trench when a Voice in his head told him to move immediately. Hitler sprang to his feet and ran, slipping and sliding over the wet duckboards, to a spot 50 yards away.

He had just seated himself on the fire-step and was about to dip his spoon into the cooling food when there was a terrible explosion. A British shell had landed on the exact spot where he had been just minutes earlier.

Hitler told Marie it had been his sad task to collect the pieces of his former comrades and load them into sandbags.

Lying next to her lover this early summer afternoon, Marie shuddered at the thought. She felt a chill, too, as she remembered the name of the café which was their haven of love.

Why would anyone call a place, built for enjoyment, "The Gravedigger"?

The naked girl leaned over her soldier and tenderly brushed aside the tendril of dark hair that habitually fell over his forehead. She cherished these moments alone with Dolphie, but they came at a price.

The French girl was only too aware she was sleeping with the enemy. And she paid for this "treason" in the coin of humiliation.

She hated the knowing way the estaminet's patronne, Chantelle, stared at her, the blowsy, thirty-something woman's ten-year-old daughter, Marguerite, peeping round the door.

Madam's thoughts were written clearly across her sharp features:

"Here's yet another French slut opening her legs for the Boche. Just wait until the Hun is thrashed and runs home with his tail between his legs and his dick as limp as last year's cabbage.

"Then these whores will get what is coming to them. And so will the fruits of their wanton loins—their fils and filles de Boche—bastard sons and daughters."

Chantelle would spit contemptuously into the sawdust and dried trench mud powdering the floor of the café as Marie, cheeks aflame, pushed between the tables where soldiers in field grey downed tumblers of rough white wine.

They whistled appreciatively at her full breasts, striking, high-cheek-boned face, framed by dark, bobbed hair, and her long, long legs. Marie was tanned and bloomed with health from working in the fields.

Gratefully, Marie would reach the beaded curtain that divided the café from the living quarters. She pushed through it and climbed the dusty wooden stairs leading to the sanctuary of their bedroom.

Downstairs, the soldiers spoke disparagingly about the little corporal, slaking his lust in the room above their heads.

However had that runty little loser, Adolf Hitler, managed to win the heart of such a beauty?

What an odd one he was . . . staying up all night, spearing rats with his bayonet Then there were his constant barmy rantings about politics and founding a new Reich.

Was he suffering from shell-shock? Gefreiter Hitler's eyes weren't normal, and that was a fact. Perhaps he had been out here too long.

Hardest of all to stomach was his toadying to the officers. Why, that shitty little messenger boy even offered to do their laundry.

What a weirdo! What a creep!

Hitler, only too conscious that the university-educated Bavarians of the 16th Reserve Infantry Regiment (List) sniggered at him and his uneducated ways, took refuge in secret fantasies.

Soon, these arrogant fools will be held to account. They are on a long list I have compiled of fools who take my name in vain or stifle my true greatness.

They are listed with Jews and Freemasons, men who have been sucking the lifeblood out of us for centuries.

On the day I become Fuhrer of all Germany, as the first step of my destiny, punishments will begin. These will be swift and righteous.

I can see it now . . . my men stand ready to do their Fuhrer's bidding with guns, gas and nooses. I watch as they go to work to wipe this sub-human excrement from my boots.

Bliss.

In the estaminet, as Hitler slept, the soldiers were still discussing him. Reluctantly, they had to admit that the buffoon didn't lack courage. He may be away with the fairies, but he had guts.

Firstly—unlike most of them—he was decorated with the Iron Cross Second Class for valour. And they had all seen him unflinchingly do his duty as a *meldegange*—regimental runner. By common consent, this was one of the most dangerous jobs on the battlefield.

Time and time again, Adolf Hitler defied shot and shell to deliver vital information from the front line to regimental headquarters, in the crypt of the church at Messines.

Sometimes things were so bad, they sent two runners with the same message, in the hope that one would get through.

But, despite Hitler's courage, and as thousands fell around him, the regiment's Jewish adjutant, Hauptman Engelman, constantly reported to his superiors that this soldier was unfit to lead men.

In the trenches, the little *gefreiter* was such an oddball that the soldiers coined a special name for him.

They called him the White Crow.

The sunlight began to fade in the bedroom and still Hitler slept. Marie savoured every minute they spent together. For Hitler, who seemed to know far more than a common soldier could be expected to, warned her that a massive Allied blow was soon to fall.

Then she would lose him again to the demons of war. Marie prayed to her schoolgirl Catholic Mary to keep her Dolphie safe.

She carefully turned on to her back and stared at the damp-stained ceiling. The patches of dark brown looked like continents in a sepia map of a world that didn't exist.

Marie thought back, with a twinge of nausea, to their recent love-making. "Love-making" seemed too tender a name for their bizarre coupling.

She had been a virgin when she and Dolphie met last year. But, even in her sexual innocence, Marie realised there was something strange about her lover's demands.

This was confirmed when, naively, she confided in her more experienced female workmates.

They giggled as they sipped their evening soup round the farmhouse table and whispered that Dolphie was something of a freak in bed. He was making Marie suffer indignities *they* would not permit for an instant. And, the girls added, she wasn't even satisfied herself at the end of it all.

"What was she getting out of this relationship?" they asked. Not even hard cash. Corporals didn't have enough money to pay for this sort of service.

"Get rid of him," they advised. "With your looks, you could snare an officer. Now *that* would be a prize worth a little play-acting in bed."

But, Marie reflected, she would do anything in the world her Dolphie asked of her. He was her first and only love, and her life.

It had taken many—for her—embarrassing experiments before they had settled into a successful bedroom charade.

Now sex followed a strict pattern. They would strip and climb on the bed. Then Hitler, eyes ablaze, would harangue his audience of one bare girl as though addressing a great political rally.

Today's well-worn theme had been the iniquities of the Jews. By now, Marie knew the speech by heart. She waited patiently until she heard the familiar cue:

"The Yids are less than vermin. They are lower than the rats who feed on the corpses of brave men. I deal with the rats. I shall deal with the Jews."

Marie reached over and seized his flaccid member, and the weird drama began.

Hitler roared:

"What are the Jews? Say, 'Scum and vermin'."

Marie repeated obediently:

"Scum and vermin, Dolphie."

- "Don't say, 'Dolphie'. I am the Fuhrer!"

- "I am sorry, my Fuhrer."

- "What shall we do with the Yids? Say, 'Exterminate them like the rats they are'."
- "Exter . . . er . . . kill them like the rats they are."

She could feel his penis beginning to stir.

- "No mercy. No mercy. Say it!"

- "No mercy. No mercy"

- "Wipe them out. Shoot them like our brave soldiers are being shot. Gas them like our brave soldiers are being gassed. Starve them. Don't give them so much as a rotting cabbage. See them suffer."

- *"I can't remember all that, my Fuhrer."*

- *"Say it! I command you!"*

His penis throbbed under her slender fingers. She mustn't lose him at this critical moment.

- *"They must all be gassed . . . shot . . . er . . . and given nothing to eat."*

- *"Kill the Yids by the million."*

- *"Kill them by the million."*

Some instinct told Marie that she must somehow delay the moment. She loosened her grip slightly. Unknown to the girl, Hitler was slipping into one of his favourite fantasies:

He is watching as that accursed Jew boy, regimental adjutant Hauptman Engleman—the man Hitler realises is stifling his genius—dies very, very slowly.

The officer is suspended from a beam by piano wire. The cruel noose is cutting deep into his neck, so that his eyes protrude and his tongue lolls from blue lips. The hauptman's legs kick convulsively, as though riding an invisible bicycle.

It was time. His cock rampant, Hitler ordered the girl to leap astride him. She thrust him into her and rode him wildly, like an unbroken horse in the fields of her native France.

Hitler, those blue eyes upturned in ecstasy, groaned: *"Oh, oh, oh!"*

Marie, thinking of tomorrow's mundane household chores, repeated by reflex: *"Oh, oh, oh!"*

She felt him spurt deep within her. It was over.

For her, it hadn't even begun.

※

Now, lying next to her sleeping Dolphie, Marie was happy because he was happy. She pushed her sexual frustration into the deep recesses of her mind.

Careful not to disturb him, she slipped out of bed and crept softly to her clothes, lying in an impatient tangle on a cheap, wooden chair. Marie picked up her petticoat and mopped herself between her legs.

She felt soiled by their love-making, and wished she could bathe in the cleansing waters of a cool stream. His jacket was thrown across the back of the chair. Marie reverently touched the ribbon it bore.

Her gallant soldier often recounted how, just ten kilometres from here, he had won the Iron Cross, Second Class. Still naked, she sat on the chair, recalling the story, so dramatic in the telling.

In years to come, there would be many versions of how Adolf Hitler won this decoration. But Marie, listening with rapt attention in their dusty bedroom, would always remember these extravagant words:

"It was in the winter of 1914 that I was forged into an iron hero of the Fatherland. This happened in the white heat of the battle for Axle Wood, near the Flemish village of Wytschaete.

"I was shivering in the cruel November cold, along with my surviving comrades of the 16th R.I.R (List). List, incidentally, was the name of our colonel. We were lying exhausted on the frozen ground after the slaughter of a night attack.

"There were more dead here than living. But we had the satisfaction of knowing that we had done our duty. We had

gallantly captured Axle Wood, so named because its shape was that of an axle from a homely farm wagon."

It was here Hitler always paused, as if gathering his thoughts to dictate a historic story to a scribbling secretary.

Before recounting the drama of winning the Iron Cross, he would meticulously set the scene.

"The German staff officers obviously believed our bitter sacrifice was a price worth paying. For the shattered trees, tangled undergrowth and human flotsam of Axle Wood marked a vital spot on their maps.

"It sat on a gentle rise of 130 feet, strategically placed at the foot of the Messines ridge, rising from the flat Flanders plain. From here, we battle-weary Bavarians could look down on the martyred city of Ypres, so doggedly held by the British.

"We would dig in, and the enemy would have the lethal disadvantage of attacking uphill. That is why every knob and pimple of high ground here is fought over by the armies, like two dogs with a bone.

"We still hold that little patch of ground—renamed Bavarian Wood in our honour. But the Tommies constantly plot to snatch it back. I must warn you, my dear Marie, that they will attack here in force this very summer.

"I may be only a gefreiter, *but I can read tactics and strategy better than the highest general.*

"When I take messages to headquarters, I study the maps on the walls of the crypt and listen to the officers' conversations. Then I draw my own conclusions. These are always correct. One day, I will be higher than a field-marshal.

"I can tell you this, girl. First, the blow will fall on Messines. Then, in the autumn, there will be another battle for high ground, probably somewhere to the North East of Ypres.

"This will be on another ridge—my guess is the village of Passchendaele."

After assuring himself that Marie knew the military background to his story, Hitler would go on to describe his act of courage. Again, it was as if he were dictating for a history book.

The story was always the same, almost word for word:

"In the grey light of that December morning in 1914, we are occupying hastily-dug trenches in the wood. Bullets snarl about us like angry hornets, and wounded men scream for their mothers.

"Minute by minute, the Grim Reaper wields his scythe, gathering a rich harvest of young lives. Most of the infantrymen slump in the crumbling soil of the trench, eyes glazed with exhaustion.

"But this day, as every day, I am different from the rest. That is why I am proud when they call me the White Crow. To me, that name is a badge of honour.

"I am still very much awake. As usual, I am constantly watching, evaluating and calculating. Suddenly, I tense. I see my commanding officer, Colonel List, is standing in the shell hole in which he has set up headquarters.

"I love the colonel like a brother. I am not ashamed to do little chores to make his life easier, no matter what the others say. He is a soldier's soldier. I realise that the colonel, a true leader of men, doesn't want to cower in the safety of his hole.

"He wants to evaluate the battle ground, That is why he has decided to stand tall, even though bullets are flying. He is also showing us he is not afraid.

"But I can see something vital that Colonel List has obviously missed.

"By standing in his present position, he has only seconds to live."

Adolf Hitler paused for effect before resuming:

"A French machine-gun is dug into the rising ground below us. My soldier's eye sees that it has a fixed arc of fire. Every few minutes, the gun traverses to its right, men falling to its bullets, like mown corn.

"It pauses briefly before traversing left, claiming more German lives. At present, the gun is silent. I calculate it will open up in less than 20 seconds. My Colonel will be standing in its field of fire.

"Right on cue, the machine-gun begins to spit death. I leap out of the trench and race to where my commanding officer is lethally exposed. I shield him with my own body before pushing him roughly back into the shell-hole.

"We tumble down together and stare at each other as, just seconds later, the machine-gun's bullets whistle over our heads."

Hitler gazed intensely at Marie, making sure she had grasped the full extent of his soldier's instinct and bravery.

"At that instant, both officer and corporal realise that the lowly one has saved the other. But both are true soldiers and brush aside fear and danger. The colonel pulls himself slowly to his knees, checks that his moustache is still trim and undisturbed and brushes soil from his uniform.

"I jump to my feet and, despite the danger, stand to attention before my commanding officer. I request that I may return to my post. The colonel drags me back into safety.

"His voice is gruff as he orders, 'Keep down, you idiot! Give me your details—smartly now!' He pulls a notebook and

35

pencil from his tunic pocket and writes down my name, rank and number.

"'That was well done, soldier. You will be hearing from me. Off you go . . . and let's see if we can both stay alive.'

"On December 2, 1914, I had the honour to be decorated with the Iron Cross, Second Class. It was presented to me by Colonel List himself, in front of the whole regiment.

"That made those so-called intellectuals from Munich sit up and take notice, I can tell you. The White Crow had flown high above their heads. It was the proudest moment of my life.

"It was the first of what will be many proud moments. For everything I do and say will one day become history."

In the estaminet at Comines, the town that could never make up its mind whether it was French or Belgian, Marie LeBrun slipped back into bed. Hitler slept on. Sometimes his eyelids flickered and he groaned and twisted restlessly.

The low evening sunlight caused golden dust motes to play above her head in the bedroom. For once, she thought, their little nest looked pretty rather than shabby.

Marie closed her eyes, and thought back to her early life. Then, a smile lighting her young, unlined face, she moved on to memories of the romance which now ruled every moment of her life.

Her first years were scarred by misery. Marie was born into an unhappy household in the Picardy village of Seboncourt, in the St. Quentin region of France.

Her father, Pierre Lebrun, was a heavily-built butcher and a loud-mouthed bully.

Marie's attractive, dark-haired mother, Violette, was frail, gentle and cowed. As Marie grew into gangling girlhood, she and her mother were unquestioningly subservient to the swaggering, violent man of the house.

Pierre, heavy-jowled and unshaven, beat his wife often and enthusiastically. As the years passed, he began to slip off his heavy leather belt and thrash his daughter, too.

Marie cringed from her father's violence and often ran to hide in the surrounding countryside. Pierre always found her, dragged her home and punished her. Her mother never dared to intercede.

Marie eventually found solace in an unexpected way. When her father was busy in his shop, festooned with the corpses of the animals he slaughtered, and her mother was occupied in the kitchen, she would slip upstairs to her bedroom.

There, the girl would indulge her secret love of art. She would paste into a scrapbook, copies of classical paintings published in magazines, thrown out by the local newspaper and book store.

She kept the precious book hidden under her truckle bed, away from the prying eyes of Pierre LeBrun. Marie knew he would take great enjoyment in tearing to shreds her only treasure.

When the girl's spirits were at their lowest, she would bring out her book of second-hand masterpieces. She greeted each picture like an old friend, drinking its beauty.

The works of art, cut out so painstakingly, brought vibrant colour into Marie's drab, sad life. Downstairs, she would hear her father—nicknamed "Pere Boulette" because of the famous meatballs he made—ranting and raving. Upstairs, all was peace and beauty.

When the invading Germans came marching into Seboncourt in 1914, Marie was fast blossoming into a beautiful young woman.

As Pierre hurriedly ingratiated himself with the enemy, she and her mother had to endure the scornful stares of neighbours, patriotic people angered by stories of raped nuns and bayoneted babies.

Worse, Marie's father turned his treachery into hard cash. His new Hun friends paid him to travel with them through the occupied area of Northern France. He slaughtered pigs, sheep and cattle before the very eyes of the farmers from whom they had been stolen.

Pierre made his famous meatballs for the Germans. They enjoyed them so much, he slyly and little by little, increased their price.

Pere Boulette, desperate to keep control of his ripening, 15-year-old daughter, insisted she travelled everywhere with him. But, after a few weeks, he was happy to swallow his principles in return for money.

Marie's father accepted, on her behalf, the offer of a job sweeping and cleaning the soldiers' quarters. He also insisted on accepting her wages.

But, at least, her beatings had stopped.

Then, suddenly and unexpectedly, young Marie escaped from her life of drudgery. The Germans drafted her, along with hundreds of other French women, to work the fields deserted by French and Belgian menfolk when they went off to war.

Her father tried to seize her meagre wages. But these Germans were not the Boche friends for whom he usually worked. They refused to pay anybody but his voluptuous French daughter.

Although the toil was backbreaking, Marie tasted freedom for the first time in her life. She even had money enough to walk into the nearest village and buy the red and white spotted kerchief she had long coveted.

She spent the days in the sweet-smelling open air, sowing, scything the golden corn and gathering in the harvest.

In the evenings, after dinner in the little stone cottage in which they were billeted, the women took the naïve teenager's education in hand. They sat round the stove, glasses of rough wine in hand, and delightedly taught Marie the facts of life.

But, for all her new friends' graphic and salacious lessons about sex, Marie remained ignorant of the facts of love.

Little did she know she was soon to discover those for herself.

At Au Fossoyeur, Marie lifted herself on to an elbow and watched fondly as her man tossed restlessly on the grubby mattress. Was he reliving the horrors of battle? Or was he tormented by the flame of the unrecognised greatness he told her was burning within him?

The girl sank back on to the feather pillow and slipped happily into her favourite memory.

She remembered it all so vividly. It was a beautiful late summer's day, and Marie and six other women were haymaking near the village of Fournes-en-Weppes, close to the town of Lille, on the Franco-Belgian border.

Marie, sporting her new kerchief to protect her head from the sun, loved feeling the warmth on her bare arms and legs. She was expertly tossing hay into a farm wagon, its horse chomping into its nose bag, when she caught sight of a solitary figure in the next field.

Shielding her eyes with her hand, she saw it was a German soldier, perched on a milking stool. Her eyes sparkled with interest as she saw he was painting at a rough easel, made from pieces of packing case.

An artist! The first she had ever seen. Amazingly, the painter was daubing his paints out here in the middle of nowhere. Marie, the covert art lover, knew at once she couldn't rest until she had met him.

She laid down her pitchfork and walked towards the soldier. Marie closed her ears to the catcalls and whistles from the other girls. They shouted:

"Give him one for me, darling! Don't drop your drawers until you see the colour of his money! Share and share alike . . . don't forget your friends. We're all panting for it!"

As Marie neared the man, totally absorbed in his work, she saw he was painting in oils on a piece of hessian, cut from a sandbag. It was truly a soldier's picture.

She stood silently behind his shoulder and peered at the painting. Under the soldier's brushes, the landscape in front of him was springing to life.

Marie, with all the experience of her scrap-book paintings, looked at the half-finished picture with a critical eye.

A pleasant enough picture, but this fellow isn't a true artist. He is only playing at it. He is an amateur with a small amount of talent. I wouldn't paste this painting into my book, alongside the Great Ones.

"But, he IS an artist. And his absorption in his work is appealing. I don't want to disturb him, but I can't let the opportunity of meeting my first artist slip through my fingers."

Marie spoke, diffidently and respectfully, as the man on the stool continued to paint: "Congratulations, m'sieur. You have caught the scene exactly."

He ignored her.

Marie stood patiently, watching the man fill in the sky of his landscape with bold strokes. She tried again, using words of German she had picked up in the cafes and barracks: "Forgive me for interrupting your work, m'sieur, but I feel compelled to say . . ."

Abruptly, the artist turned. She was taken aback. Startling blue eyes stared at Marie from a pinched, intense face, adorned with luxuriant moustache and a tumbling black forelock

He silently surveyed the attractive young girl with the red spotted kerchief and cheap matching dress.

There was an embarrassing silence, which Marie felt compelled to fill. She went on, breathlessly: "I am sorry to spoil the concentration of such a skilled artist. But your work was so accomplished that I felt . . ."

The soldier laid down his brush and his gaze softened. When he at last spoke, she noted that his voice was slightly throaty. Marie found its deep timbre exciting.

This was the voice of a man who could thrill simply by using words. He was not handsome as the men pictured in her magazines were handsome. But he exuded an unsettling magnetism.

And those eyes! My God, those hypnotic blue eyes! A girl would die for eyes like that. She could drown in them!

The artist, his eyes roving over Marie's tanned face and full body, told her: "You have a good eye for art, mademoiselle. That is unusual in a peasant girl who labours in the fields.

"I can assure you that, one day soon, this masterpiece you have rightly seen fit to praise will become a valuable collector's piece."

Marie made the mistake of asking candidly: "Is it *that* good, m'sieur?"

The man scowled as though he had just swallowed some rusty nails and his eyes blazed with fury. Her implied criticism had touched a raw nerve.

The artist felt bile rise in his throat as he thought back to those pathetic, know-nothing professors at the art school in Vienna, who had so cruelly rejected him.

Then he looked again at this innocent beauty standing before him, obviously entranced by his talent. The soldier's mood softened and he replied: "Certainly, my girl, the painting is *that good* artistically.

"But it is not only its merit which will send its price soaring. Collectors all over the world will seek it out, if only for the signature in the corner. It is only a matter of time until I become the most famous man on the planet."

Marie was stunned. She watched in silence as this strange little German soldier loaded a brush, this time with white. He began to create fleecy clouds, floating above the Flanders countryside.

Although this man attracted her in a damp and embarrassing way, she told herself that, in all honesty, his painting was worth just two bottles of cheap white wine in a local estaminet.

But the dark-haired man in field-grey enthralled her. The 15-year-old girl was enough of a woman to know instinctively how to set a romantic trap. She simpered: "I am lucky to be the first to see such an accomplished work of art, m'sieur, and to meet the artist in person.

"Please tell me what you call this masterpiece, so that I can one day pick it out in the Louvre."

The German soldier was beginning to tire of this conversation with the peasant girl. He pointedly concentrated on his work before tossing words over his shoulder like spilled salt: "Coup d'Oeil vers Fournes."

The girls in the next field began calling Marie back to work. But even though the artist was so dismissive, she was reluctant not to seize the opportunity to cement this contact.

She couldn't believe her own daring as she gasped, heart racing: "I can see you have a master's touch. I myself am very interested in art, in a poor and modest way. It would be wonderful if you could spare a few minutes to teach me about painting.

"You must know so much and I so little. But I thirst to know much, much more, m'sieur. Could you bestow on me a gift of a few moments of your time, just to tell me about art . . . ?"

There! It was done! Marie felt her cheeks burning at her impudence, her unaccustomed forwardness. She ignored the cries of the girls.

The artist hunched over the painting for three long minutes without replying He instinctively knew the power of keeping an audience waiting on his words. Eventually, just when Marie was about to turn away in disappointment, he spoke.

"It is my duty to pass on knowledge and fragments of my great skills. One day, the world may expect this. I may tell you that my genius isn't restricted to mere painting."

Marie took the bull by the horns and asked: "Will you be off-duty this evening m'sieur?"

"Perhaps."

"Do you know the Café Canon in Fournes?"

"Maybe"

The artist began to add trees to his landscape.

Marie, the moisture between her legs becoming more insistent, spoke in a great rush, like a runaway farm cart clattering down a lane.

"My name is Marie LeBrun. Would you do me the honour of telling me yours?"

Again he made her wait before replying: "*Gefreiter* Adolf Hitler of the 16th Reserve Infantry Regiment List. I am a regimental *meldegange* and holder of the Iron Cross, Second Class. I am a hero of the Fatherland."

She whispered: "Au revoir, Herr Hitler. I sincerely hope to see you this evening. Shall we say eight o'clock?"

Hitler didn't reply. He had already decided to pay a visit to the Café Canon."

CHAPTER THREE

June 19, 2000

Monday greeted Southdown sombrely, performing a rain dance on its roofs, streets and pavements. Adam, his old Air Force greatcoat stained darkly by the wet, was inside a brightly-lit store called World Electronics. He wandered, bewildered, up and down the rows of equipment.

Huge televisions screens mouthed silently and car radios, stacked shelf on shelf, burbled a constant cacophony of pop music.

A beanpole youth, hair gelled into spikes and face pimpled with acne, came to the rescue. The youngster, whose breast tag introduced him as "Wayne", greeted Adam warmly in computer-speak. He had all the fervour of an evangelist.

Wayne's inner-London patois was intricately laced with such exotica as booting, megabytes and hard and soft discs. As far as new-minted retiree Adam was concerned, the youngster might as well have been speaking in tongues.

Adam crumbled under the relentless onslaught of technology. He cravenly asked Wayne, still garrulous with enthusiasm, to choose a computer for him. Then he marched over to the nearest till, ears closed and credit card in hand.

The youth selected a laptop computer, slipped it into a box and placed it into a plastic carrier bag. Adam paid without looking at the price, and escaped into the downpour.

Back in his flat, the computer stood dark and silent on the kitchen table. It seemed to be challenging him to make it perform.

At last, greatly daring, Adam leaned forward to locate the power button, and pressed it firmly. Sure enough, the laptop sprang, beeping, to life.

Like Wayne, it spewed out a stream of incomprehensible information before settling down to a meaningless message on its screen.

Adam reached for the phone, desperate to find somebody fluent in computer-speak. He punched in the number of the Kentish World's Information Technology wizard, Rod Russell.

Adam spoke ingratiatingly—a reporter courting a favour: "Hi, Rod, how are you this soggy morning? How about brightening it for me—there's a couple of beers in it? Could you pop round to my place? I have a problem of the computer kind? It'll take just a couple of minutes for a man of your calibre."

Half an hour later, the flat's entry-phone buzzed and Adam released the front door. Rod came clattering up the uncarpeted stairs. Although he was in the middle of a working morning, he took a relaxed view of his duties at the Kentish World. He knew the bosses couldn't manage without him.

Rod came into the kitchen and ousted Adam from his chair. The computer expert was scruffy, but lean and fit under his outfit of frayed jeans, cracked leather bomber jacket and T-shirt, bearing a faded picture of Superman.

His trainers were so worn, his big toe poked out the left-hand shoe.

Rod, sporting a fashionable three days' growth of stubble, swept long, dark hair from sharp, intelligent eyes.

When he spoke, it was with an accent smacking of an inner-city upbringing and education.

"What seems to be the trouble, squire?"

"No trouble, Rod. I've just bought a laptop and don't know how to work it."

"*Nada problema.* Watch and learn."

Rod's fingers flew over the keyboard, the computer obediently obeying their commands. He gave a running commentary to Adam, who began making notes. The I.T. expert spoke down to the reporter as though to a slightly bewildered inmate of an old folk's home.

He got Adam on to the Internet, linked him with a server and fixed him up with an e-mail address. Then Rod showed the writer how to do research using the Google search engine.

Slowly, it all began to make sense to Adam. Rod wasn't satisfied that his lesson had sunk in until the reporter went through everything for himself. Adam felt the glow of achievement.

At the World, he had treated his office computer as a super typewriter. He learned to write his mundane reports, save them and, with the press of a button, magic the words to invisible sub-editors in some far-flung office.

Now he was beginning to realise that he could command his computer to do useful tasks. These included chores such as researching an epic book.

Today, Adam Cornish had a world of knowledge at his fingertips.

Rod felt he had done everything necessary to drag the retired reporter, smelling of stale beer from the day before, into the 21st Century. He scribbled himself copious notes, which he slid into the back pocket of his jeans.

Rod switched off the lap-top, stood up and stretched.

He said: "Time to collect me wages, old son. I've made myself a record of everything I've done to your computer, in case you forget. If you need me, just give me a bell."

Unknown to Adam, Rod had done far more to the laptop than the reporter could ever imagine. Now Adam could never so much as depress a single key without the computer expert, at some remote hideaway, knowing about it.

Rod hinted heavily: "Christ, all this work has given me a throat as dry as a lime kiln."

To Adam, too, the Nine Bells beckoned with an irresistible siren call. The two men left the computer sleeping on the kitchen table and made their way through the rain to the pub.

In the accustomed gloom of the bar, Adam saw that it was "press day", when the newspaper was "put to bed"— finished for the week. Traditionally, the editorial staff held an alcohol-fuelled celebration in a local pub.

The World's veteran chief photographer, Arthur Burfield, was standing at the bar, nursing a pint of bitter ale. Adam and Arthur had been friends and contemporaries for more or less a working lifetime.

Ruddy-faced Arthur, doyen of his department, was a caricature of an old-time local newspaper snapper. He wore the traditional uniform of crumpled herringbone sport jacket, concertina flannel trousers, un-ironed check shirt and a tie bearing traces of a week's eating and imbibing.

Arthur was telling journalistic war stories to two young reporters. Adam saw with a twinge of anger that one of them was Ros Litherland, the over-educated, toffee—nosed bitch who had pinched his scooter. He peered across and took a better look

He could see that the girl, who was in her mid-twenties, was struggling to keep up with the men by downing pint for pint. As Arthur reached the punch-line of his story, she threw back her head and roared with laughter.

This sent her long, blonde hair spilling down her back, and her full breasts jouncing under the tight blue sweater. Adam saw the trace of a naked knee poking from her trendily-torn jeans. The girl wore high-heeled boots that accentuated the length of her slim legs. The over-the-hill reporter felt a twinge of lust.

In the old days, I would have bought her a couple of gin and tonics and given her a quick tumble. Ah, those were the days, until Anna refused to put up with it.

This Ros girl is one of the new breed of reporter . . . the sort who knows nothing and cares less. She sniggers about me behind my back. I know they all call me an old fart, who can't find his arse with his hand.

She'd better be very, very careful, or she will go on my shit list.

Hitler knew how to deal with people who were a waste of space. He gave them suits of pyjamas and a warm reception. Soon, they didn't take up any space at all.

Arthur spotted Adam and Rod and waved them over. The photographer thumped his old colleague on the back and bellowed: "Good leaving do, Adam

"Got well bladdered. We all did. You mustn't lose touch. You're the only one left who speaks the same language."

Adam felt in his pocket for the money to buy a round of drinks. This was more like it. He had warm memories of him and Arthur standing at this very bar, looking at life through the bottoms of rose-tinted beer glasses.

He bought pints for Arthur and Rod, pointedly ignoring Ros and the boy wonder reporter to whom she was chatting. They got the message, buying their own drinks.

Adam couldn't help noticing that Ros kept within earshot. She was probably hoping to learn something at last, he thought, burying his nose in the beery foam.

The "press day" lunchtime surfed on a tide of alcohol. Writers, photographers and sub-editors packed into the bar, red-faced with the stuffy atmosphere and Kentish beer.

Adam, fired by eight pints, was chatting, reminiscing and unknowingly proving to the youngsters yet again that he was adept at playing the old fart. In fact, they agreed, the ex-reporter had refined his act into an art form.

Even in his drunken state, Adam began to realise that his listeners' faces were glazing with boredom. So he decided to play his ace card . . . one that would impress the pants off them.

He slurred: "I don't expect you'll see me in here much more. I'm working on an epic story that is going to take the world by storm. And that includes Hollywood, my friends. Look out for me on the red carpet on Oscars night."

Arthur, suddenly sober, declared: "By God, you're a dark horse, Adam. Give us a clue. What's this blockbuster all about?"

Ros Litherland edged nearer and Rod Russell put down his pint pot and listened intently.

Adam was in full flood; He drained his pint, grasped the bar for support and declaimed: "It's a war story that will make Steven Spielberg's movie Saving Private Ryan look like a vicarage tea party."

Arthur urged Adam: "Go on, don't keep us dangling . . . tell us a bit more, old pal."

Adam, who hadn't given the book more than a passing thought, felt trapped into replying. He blustered: "It's huge! This is a sweeping story of love, courage and betrayal . . . all set in the inferno of the Western Front in World War One.

"The big star is my granddad, Sergeant Ernie Cornish. He cheated death a thousand times in battle, and became a decorated hero. This brave Tommy fell in love with a beautiful French girl After a battlefield marriage, she broke his heart.

"Ernie was a victim of war, just like the wounded and the shell-shocked But he was given one great reward. When his girl ran away, she left him with a wonderful son.

"So, like all good Hollywood stories, there's a happy ending."

Adam slurped some more beer and warmed to his theme: "Bloody hell, my story's got everything—tons of sex and violence and towering central characters. It's never been told before. Everyone's bound to go barmy over it.

"The big stars will be fighting over who will play my granddad, Ernie Cornish, and his beautiful but fickle wife, Marie.

"I just have to do a little research. Then I will put my arse firmly on the chair and start writing. Soon, I'll be rich and famous. When that happens, I'll buy you all two pints for the one you're going to get me now."

Arthur, Ros and Rod, slipped from the pub.

"Mean sods," grumped Adam, "They'll do anything to get out of paying for a round of drinks."

He bought a refill for his tankard and gulped it down, beating the barman's "last orders" call by seconds. Adam and the Kentish World staffers spilled on to the market square.

The newspaper people, chatting merrily, strolled back to the office, planning to while away the time until they could decently slope off home.

Suddenly, Adam was alone on the pavement. For the first time in 40 years, he was not a working part of The World. The newspaper had consigned him, like last week's edition, to the dustbin.

The ex-reporter experienced a bitter taste of loneliness. He felt the first chill trace of rain fall on to his greying head. Raindrops began to spatter the pavement.

The copious booze he had consumed began to hit Adam hard.

He staggered home and, after half a dozen attempts, managed to get the key into the lock of his front door. Adam climbed the stairs, hanging on to the hand rail, and found his way into the bedroom.

Still dressed in his old greatcoat, he collapsed on the bed amid a cacophony of springs. Within seconds, he was snoring lustily.

The virgin computer sat lifeless on the kitchen table.

Adam slept, oblivious to the waves which, because of his Ernie Cornish project, were washing on to secret shores.

The first wave on the shore:

Photographer Arthur Burfield was making an untraceable call from one of the red telephone boxes in Southdown High Street. He shivered in the dank air of the confined space, redolent with urine and damp clothing.

This was Arthur Burfield as nobody in Southdown had ever seen him. His crumpled clothes were the same. But his affable, avuncular persona had melted away, like bottles of Scotch at a reporters' party.

The little, damp-speckled mirror in the booth reflected the face of a cold, efficient leader. This wasn't cheery Kentish born-and-bred Arthur Burfield. These were the features of an arrogant Belgian called Andre Lacroix.

The veteran photographer, speaking Flemish, a Belgian patois of Dutch, snapped down the phone: "After all these years of watching and waiting, it looks as though The Time may finally have come.

"My years of baby-sitting the soak Cornish, and of enduring the inanity of life on this stupid little English paper are coming to an end. Best of all, I will no longer have to soil my hands with their filthy Jewish money."

Lacroix's's face contorted with fury. He went on: "Yes, sir, I have been forced to smile and shake the greedy hands of the Tribe Goldstein.

"Now it seems as though our precautions over the years were necessary. Great danger could strike us. That oaf Cornish has decided to track down the origins of his grandfather, Ernie Cornish. So he will be researching his grandmother, too.

"Stupid though he is, Cornish is a reporter and knows how to dig and delve. He could discover the Great Secret. Just as we have always feared and, if I may I say so sir, sometimes hoped?"

Lacroix mopped his forehead with a large, red-spotted handkerchief. In spite of the chill, he was sweating at the thought of the wonderful cataclysm that could engulf the world.

He knew he must keep a firm grip on himself. Discipline was all. That was one of the Fuhrer's watchwords.

Lacroix's voice remained steady as he continued: "We have a major decision to make. Do we erase this problem immediately? That will present no difficulty. Cornish's drunkenness is legendary.

"He has a steep, uncarpeted flight of stairs at his home . . . need I say more? Or he could stagger in front of a car one dark night and have a fatal accident. There are a dozen ways, sir.

"On the other hand, we could turn this minor problem into a great opportunity. Perhaps *Der Tag*—The Day—has at last come. Maybe we could manipulate this shabby loser to lead us to our long-awaited destiny.

"He has the Blood. He has the Eyes. That is all we need. Our iron brotherhood will supply the rest. In my long years of shadowing the oaf, I have detected in him absurd delusions of grandeur.

"These, sir, should make him putty in our hands. We could give a nobody a chance to be a very big somebody. Puppet Cornish would never realise we were pulling his strings.

"I will report again soon. After all, he is supposed to be my friend and drinking buddy. If Adam Cornish can't confide in me, who the hell can he pour out his heart to? Remember, sir, an urgent decision is required."

Andre Lecroix replaced the receiver, stepped into the fresh air, and rapidly turned into Arthur Burfield.

He muttered to himself: "So, is it to be death or glory for Adam?"

Andre's transformation wasn't quite complete. For his words were still Flemish—his native tongue and that of his wartime Nazi father.

The rain had stopped. Arthur sat down on a wooden seat and plunged himself into a warm bath of nostalgia.

Children played round him and cars came and went in Southdown market square, but the photographer was back in a different place and a golden time.

Andre Lecroix was just a lad during the German occupation of Belgium. The boy basked in the power and fear surrounding his father, Wilfred. Wilfred was a dark and surly man, quick with his fists who, before the Second World War, had toiled in a menial job at a local timber yard.

People joked that the thickset labourer had such a big chip on his shoulder because he sawed so many planks. As far as Wilfred was concerned, the world was a deeply unfair place. It was peopled by milksop cheats and liars, who enjoyed a soft, cosseted life that should have been his.

But the Germans didn't see Wilfred as a joke, but as someone ideal for their purposes. Here was a bully with a grudge—a malcontent who would revel in wielding power over those who ridiculed him.

So they gave Wilfred a Nazi uniform, complete with jackboots, and made him *gauleiter*—Czar of the Ypres area. The strutting ex-labourer, pistol on hip and whip in hand, was answerable to no-one but his Nazi bosses.

For Andre, these were the barely-remembered glory days. One sour look from his father could make anyone—from land-owning baron to humble shop-girl—cower in fear of their lives.

Wilfred ruled by the carrot and the stick. He rewarded cronies and crawlers with coveted work, ration and travel permits. He punished others at whim, often by the stroke of his clumsily-wielded pen.

One note from the *gauleiter* to his Nazi overlords could lead to the sinister slamming of car doors in the depths of the night outside his victim's home. This sound chilled the very soul, for only the Germans had cars.

If they came for you in the night, it could mean anything from deportation for forced labour to torture and death. People watched from behind curtains in darkened rooms as neighbours were dragged from their homes.

They saw the men in the long, leather coats of the Gestapo orchestrating arrests. They watched, too, as *Gauleiter* Lacroix gave the enemy brutal assistance.

The Germans were pleased with the choice they had made. Wilfred crushed the local population—apart from a few crazy Resistance hotheads—into fearful submission.

Hitler, who had fought gallantly here in the Great War, even promised to grant the area a great honour. The Fuhrer planned to raise a tribute to his thousand-year Reich—a gigantic statue of himself—at his old battleground, Bavarian Wood. This was close to Wilfred and Andre's modest workman's cottage.

But, before the first stone could be laid, the dark clouds of peace gathered. The guns of the second war fell silent. The Germans fled.

Canadians marched into Ypres. Their boots echoed under the Menin Gate, soaring First World War memorial to 54,896 men of the Allied armies with no known grave.

Since then, life was never the same for the Flanders Nazis. But, happily for them, some of the old fear lingered on. Locals always kept their mouths shut about the wartime activities of Wilfred and his comrades-in-terror.

The shameful principles of Wilfred's generation of Nazis—West Flanders even raised its own S.S. division—are still woven into the fabric of life in the area.

As death thins their ranks, there are always plenty of like-minded younger men, such as Andre Lecroix, who are eager to step into the vacant jack boots.

Like Andre, these men keep their uniforms, their pistols, their whips and their swastikas hidden away in cupboards and sheds . . . ready for *Der Tag*.

Arthur, the bench pressing uncomfortably into his buttocks, came reluctantly back to the lack-lustre here and now. He looked around at the soft, Jew-ridden world that was the cross he had to bear.

He sighed.

God willing, the good times will return to Flanders. It could happen soon, thanks to that buffoon Adam Cornish.

Baggy jacket flapping in the damp Kentish wind, Arthur made his way to the office. That evening, he would meet Cornish, sink a few pints, feel his flesh crawl and do his duty.

The second wave on the shore:

Rod Russell was making a secure telephone call in a rambling, six-roomed mansion, two miles south of Southdown. His colleagues at the World believed he rented a room here.

In reality, the computer wizard and six underlings had the run of the whole place, thanks to the British taxpayer.

For this was where Rod Russell—a.k.a. Captain Hamish Sinclair of the Scots Guards—ran a high-tech intelligence centre. Its sole purpose was to keep a strict eye on Adam Cornish, grandson of jilted Ernie Cornish and deceitful Marie Cornish.

British Intelligence had long known the Big Secret. They knew, too, that the late flighty Marie LeBrun was the key to an old scandal that could rock the world.

Now Cornish was, unknowingly, threatening to expose that secret. So a British emergency plan, drawn up many years ago, was kicking in.

Hamish made his phone call in a cut-glass public school accent. Just as Arthur Burfield's Kentish brogue had vanished, Rod Russell's nasal, down-market speech melted away.

Aristocratic Captain Sinclair MC and Bar, had the gift of being a social and professional chameleon. This ability was highly valued by secret service bosses, who often called on him.

When working undercover, Hamish missed donning his fancy Guards mess kit to enjoy a convivial, candle-lit dining-in night with his colonel and brother officers.

While playing the scruffy IT expert in Southdown, Hamish looked back nostalgically on his old, tally-ho life. He just loved giving assorted insurgents a hard time.

Over the years, Hamish had transformed himself into a Midland car worker, an East European refugee, a Lincolnshire potato picker and a Northern Irish barman.

Sometimes, it was only his skill at mimicking accents and speaking foreign languages that saved him from a body bag. He never spoke of how he won his medals, even to his closest friends.

It had been strongly impressed on Hamish that the watch on Adam Cornish, which had apparently been going on for years, was of prime importance.

So now the World's erstwhile scruffy computer guru was reporting over the phone with clipped efficiency. "Yes, sir, it looks as though that silly bastard Cornish is about to put the cat among the pigeons.

"He has announced this project to dig up his grandfather's World War One past. We know what ructions that could cause . . . especially in the case of his grandmother of blessed memory, that devious sex bomb Marie LeBrun.

"Adam Ernest Cornish has the eyes and he has the blood. That, as we have always feared, could prove an explosive mixture.

"Cornish is pretty dim, sir—he only made acting corporal in the Royal Air Force—but he is enough of a journalist to do simple research. History teaches us to beware of little corporals."

At the other end of the line, a leathery-faced, straight-backed man in a tweed jacket and immaculately-pressed flannels, thoughtfully stirred a cup of Darjeeling tea.

Outside the window, street-lights flared into life on Horse Guards' Parade. The tweedy man grunted: "Go on, captain . . . give me everything. This is vital."

Hamish continued: "We've had a stroke of luck, sir. Cornish bought himself a laptop computer for his research and, typically, didn't know how to use it.

"So he called me and, of course, I was only too willing to lend a hand. Without boring you, colonel, with all the technical guff, I rigged him with a fixed IP.

"This means that, whenever he dials out on his laptop, his call will also automatically go through to both you and me. So we will always know what Cornish is up to. Neat, eh? He'll never suspect we are tapping his communications."

The man in Horse Guards spoke again, and Hamish listened with a respect that would have astonished colleagues at the World. He replied: "Yes, sir. Thank you, sir. Of course, I will keep him under even stricter surveillance.

"It won't be difficult. He thinks I'm his friend and his new computer buddy. The worst thing about this job is having to down that appalling pig swill the Kentish call beer.

"You definitely owe me a pink gin in the mess when this is all over, colonel. Just a moment . . ."

With an electronic beep, the monitor on Hamish's desk burst into life. He began to read the words as they scrolled across his screen. He again picked up the phone.

"Cornish has come out of his alcoholic haze and is starting work on the Marie Lebrun project. He is doing a

Google search to find out how to research the record of a World War One soldier.

"It's begun, sir. Goodbye for the present. I'll report back shortly."

Hamish put down the receiver. He swung thoughtfully on his antique swivel chair, doodling with a ballpoint pen on his blotting pad. He muttered to himself: "I'll let him run for now. He might lead us to something interesting.

"After that . . . we'll see. If it comes to the worst, I'll have to take him out. No problem there. I've always been rather good at that sort of thing."

It was Hamish Sinclair rather than Rod Russell who plunged the point of his pen savagely into the pad.

The third wave on the shore:

Ros Litherland was sitting cross-legged on the bed in her modest flat, a white, fluffy dressing-gown hiding her generous curves, and a towel wrapped round her long, blonde hair.

Ros, too, was speaking on the phone. She said in Hebrew: "How are things in Tel Aviv, captain? I should have known the answer before you said it, 'We never rest here at Mossad!'

"You set me to watch Adam Cornish, sir, because of his dangerous family history. I regret to tell you that a crisis has arisen. He is set on a notion to research the First World War story of his grandfather, Ernest Frederick Cornish, and his grandmother, nee Marie LeBrun.

"The result could be catastrophic, captain, as you well know. No, sir, Cornish doesn't have a clue about the Great Secret. But he could well stumble across it . . . or it could be pointed out to him for the worst of reasons."

At the other end of the line, the captain spoke, brusquely and urgently. Ros, her hands absently drying her hair, listened intently. Suddenly, she froze.

"Surely, sir I don't have to get THAT close to the odious bugger! Yes, sir, of course, sir. I do know my duty. Yes, sir, it would be a sacrifice well worth making for the security of my country.

"I have sworn to do everything in my power for Israel, sir. Yes. I DO know that life as an agent is not always a picnic. I will therefore obediently carry out this duty, and will buy mountain of soap at Mossad's expense.

"Let's hope it doesn't come to my doing this horrible duty. If it does, captain, perhaps my reward will be to conduct Adam Cornish's extreme termination. I'll keep constantly in touch."

Ros Litherland, a.k.a. Ros Goldstein, shuddered as she put down the phone. She decided to take a second shower.

Adam, stomach sour from pre-nap drinking, stepped into the welcoming fug of the Nine Bells. He was pleased to find Arthur Burfield already comfortably ensconced, one foot resting on the bar's brass rail

Arthur pushed Adam's already foaming tankard towards the reporter. He greeted Adam bluffly: "Knew you'd be in about now, me old mate. I can almost set my watch by the urgency of your thirst."

The photographer waited respectfully while Adam drained half a pint of the dark liquid in two or three grateful gulps.

Then he asked: "What have you been up to since you left us? Working on your great work—the one that's going to outsell the Bible and make you as rich as a bunch of rock stars?

"What is it with your family past? What did your granddad and grandma get up to that makes them fascinating enough to be worth a Hollywood fortune? You can trust me, old mate, I won't tell a dicky bird . . . ."

Adam, who still hadn't written a word, was trying to hide his embarrassment by burying his face in his tankard when the door opened and Rod Russell loped into the bar.

Arthur exercised iron restraint as fury scalded the back of his throat.

Just as I was hoping to get some vital information from one idiot, another idiot walks in. I suppose this computer nut wasn't to know I wanted a private chat with Cornish. But his interference is infuriating, nevertheless.

Discipline. Discipline. Remember the Fuhrer's watchword. By a great effort of will, Arthur calmed himself down.

But there was still an edge to the photographer's voice as he snapped: "If you want to join the club, my lad, the admission fee is a pint all round. Anyway, you IT whiz-kids all have money running out of your ears."

Rod pulled a tatty wallet from the back pocket of his jeans and tried to catch the eye of Jim the barman.

Arthur nudged Adam and urged: "Come on, spill the beans. What's so special about dear old Grandad? Did he have a dark secret, back in the days he was up to his waist in muck and bullets?"

Before Adam could frame a reply, the door opened again. Ros Litherland walked in and peered around the bar. Spotting the three men, she waved and walked over.

She asked sweetly: Is this a private boys' club, or can anyone join?"

Arthur, veins of fury pulsing on his forehead, snarled: "Beers all round . . . and they're on you, miss, if you please."

The girl reporter appeared unfazed and ordered the drinks . . . beers for the men and a vodka and tonic for herself. She undid her coat and edged closer to Adam.

Jim put the glasses on to the beer-ringed mahogany counter. The two interruptions had given Adam time to frame an answer to Arthur's questions. He hoped it would serve as a distraction.

He said: "*Grandma* is going to be just as important to the story as Grandpa. What she gets up to is going to wow people big-time When Marie LeBrun was around, it was never all quiet on the Western Front.

"Keep it under your hats, but I'm going to take a *very close* look at my sexy grandmother."

Rod and Arthur hurriedly downed their pints, made their excuses and left.

Ros leaned against Adam so that he could feel her erect nipples through her sweater. She whispered: "It's a tragedy, but I really have to go, too—this time anyway.

"I'm sure we'll be seeing a lot more of each other." She pressed her chest against him as a goodbye.

The door slammed behind her and Adam was left alone in the bar.

Soon, the waves were beating.

CHAPTER FOUR

September 8, 1940

The black velvet darkness was studded with countless diamonds. Every second, more were sprinkled, flaring, sparkling, winking.

Ten thousand feet up in the night sky, Oberleutnant Otto Muller, gloved hands gripping the comfortingly familiar controls of his Dornier Do. 17 medium bomber, stared down at the myriad bomb bursts.

Heinrich, the bomb aimer, pressed the release button to stoke up the fires. The crew felt the aircraft jolt and lift as a stick of incendiaries, mixed with high explosive, fell away.

Although the crew of the Dornier could never have known, one of those bombs was to change the course of history . . . and transform Adam Cornish's life.

Otto, tense in the bomber's cramped cockpit, looked down on a suffering city. He instinctively crossed himself and said softly: "My God, we're burning London to death. So this is how the Fuhrer's promised *blitz*—lightning— looks when it strikes."

The Dornier's bombs joined thousands of others, whistling down in a banshee of death and destruction. Otto recalled the Fuhrer's promise that this agony would bring England to its knees . . . and its senses.

But as the Dorniers—nicknamed "Flying Pencils" because of their long, slim shape—and the stolid Heinkels droned overhead, people in the burning city were taking it on the chin.

Londoners, armed with thermos flasks, full of hot, sweet tea, and packets of sandwiches, huddled in hastily-dug Anderson shelters in their back gardens. They heard the crump of bombs falling around them and the clamour of fire-engine and ambulance bells,

But, like children covering their eyes in a vain attempt to protect themselves against danger, they felt safe in their flimsy refuges—soil-covered arches of corrugated iron. Many died as high explosive bombs blew their shelters into fragments.

Other families clattered down cobbled streets from their homes, pushing prams and barrows, piled high with their most treasured possessions. They set up makeshift beds under nearby railway arches.

Deep below the capital's streets, Londoners were sheltering in Underground railway stations. As babies wailed, fathers, mothers, grandfathers, grandmothers and soldiers on leave defiantly sang the latest songs.

Their taste this night was for the jaunty and the jolly.

We're going to hang out the washing on the Siegfried line, have you any dirty washing, mother dear?

Roll out the barrel, let's have a barrel of fun . . .

Run rabbit, run rabbit, run, run run, don't give the farmer
His fun, fun, fun . . .

My old man's a dustman, he wears a dustman's hat,

He killed 5,000 Germans—so waddya think of that?

Mothers, giggling, covered their children's ears as the soldiers chanted the bawdy punch-line to the song, which described how those Germans were shot in a particularly painful place.

The mothers' hands remained firmly in place as the men in khaki, dark and light blue roared:

Hitler's only got one ball,
Goebbels has none at all!

The nonsensical songs lifted the spirits on this night of death and destruction. For a while, people forgot the danger as they swayed in time to the familiar songs.

In the grey light of dawn, they would emerge from their burrows. Many would find gaping holes and piles of rubble where their houses had once stood. Friends and neighbours, who had stayed at home to brave the bombs, were sometimes dead or missing.

This night, Otto, in his brown flying suit and helmet, found it hard to tear his eyes from the tapestry of destruction he and his fellow flyers from the Luftwaffe's Kampfgruppen 2 were weaving.

He imagined the horror the bombers were visiting on the London streets, docks, schools, homes and hospitals. Surely the British must soon surrender.

Not only did commonsense dictate it, but the Fuhrer had promised the German nation that the collapse of Britain was imminent. The Englanders' morale would shatter like the glass in the windows of their blitzed homes.

Otto should be feeling no pity. He and the other aircrews had been told they were avenging the bombs the Royal

Air Force had dropped on Berlin, on the express orders of warmonger Winston Churchill.

The blitz on London had been ordered because the Fuhrer himself was furious. Goering had promised Hitler, and Hitler had promised the German people that not a single bomb would fall on the German capital.

Then the impudent R.A.F. had somehow sneaked through the air defences and proved the Nazi leaders wrong.

Now the sinister, unsynchronised beating of hundreds of Luftwaffe engines sang a hymn of revenge.

Otto remembered that, only four days ago, the Fuhrer had addressed a rally of nurses and social workers in Berlin. The newspapers, as usual, reported his words verbatim.

"When the British Air Force drops two, three or four thousand kilograms of bombs, then we will, in one night, drop 150, 230, 300 or 400,000 kilograms.

"When they declare that they will increase their attacks on our cities, then we will raze their cities to the ground. We will stop the handiwork of these air pirates, so help us God!"

Back in Britain, Churchill and his military leaders were also thanking God. Hitler's decision to attack London had, miraculously, taken the pressure off the R.A.F. By diverting his bombers from attacking British airfields, the Fuhrer had granted Britain a vital reprieve.

One more week of airfield attacks would have finished the R.A.F. and won the war for Germany.

Otto gratefully turned his Dornier on a course for home. God willing, they would soon be crossing the Channel.

Minutes after sighting the French coast they would touch down on the sanctuary of their airfield. There would be a carefree breakfast with the other crews, each trying to outdo the others with extravagant gestures and tales of derring-do.

Then Otto would make his weary way to his quarters, to be rewarded for his night's work with the blessing of sleep.

But, the pilot reminded himself, he was still over enemy territory. Danger could lurk behind every cloud. He snapped an order over the intercom for his crew to remain vigilant.

They smiled to themselves. Otto, at 24 the oldest of them, was a bit of an old fuss-pot. Although the Luftwaffe had suffered grievous losses at the hands of the Spitfires and Hurricanes only yesterday, that was when they were naked in daylight.

Now the German flyers had the cloak of night cosily wrapped around them. Everyone knew the British pilots hadn't mastered the art of fighting in the dark. Mess rumour claimed that the R.A.F. possessed only a handful of puny night-fighters.

These were twin-engined Beaufighters, equipped with ramshackle detection equipment. Tonight, the British would be overwhelmed by the sheer weight of the attacking hordes.

The British anti-aircraft defences were just a bunch of useless pop-guns. They were hardly worth thinking about.

Otto's crew were lulled by the comforting throb of the two 1,000 horse power BMW radial engines as the twin-tailed aircraft left the fires behind and sped towards home.

But Otto shifted uneasily in his seat as searchlights probed the sky around them on this late summer night. He saw in his mind's eye yesterday's burning German aircraft, spiralling down to their crews' deaths.

Around him, the British guns grumbled like toothless guard dogs. Not a single flaming aircraft fell from the sky. They were as good as home. But why, Otto asked himself, did he feel this sense of dread?

Records say that, of the swarms of German aircraft that savaged London that night, only one was to die

Otto threw his forearm over his face as blinding light flooded the cockpit. Seconds later, a shell tore into the Dornier, turning it into an inferno.

The young pilot and his crew of four went to their deaths screaming, as their funeral pyre fell from the sky.

While the wreckage of the Dornier burned in a Kentish field, flames were licking round an anonymous office building in London. An incendiary bomb, meant by Otto's bomb aimer, Heinrich, to fall on nearby docks and marshalling yards, had instead hit the War Office Repository.

Inside the building, at Arnside Street, London, South East 19, was shelf after shelf of records. Mountains of paper charted the lives of five million soldiers from England, Ireland and Wales who fought in World War One.

The yellowing pages told of promotions, postings, illnesses, punishments, wounds and deaths. Some hid from families the shameful fact that their men had been shot at dawn as cowards.

The burning office was a low priority for the firemen, as they fought frantically to save their city. Hoses ran dry as bombs shattered water mains.

Fire-fighters tried to pump water from the Thames, but were shocked to find that the river was at a dangerously low ebb. The German planners had done their homework well.

So the bells of the racing fire-engines clanged past Arnside Street without stopping. For many hours, the fire consuming the old documents flared and spread unchecked.

When soot-blackened firemen finally arrived on the scene, water from their hoses added to the destruction.

69

Among the soldiers' records that turned to ash and blackened pulp that night were those of Sergeant Ernest Frederick Cornish M.M; regimental number 865387, of the 1/9th Battalion North Kent Regiment.

. . . .

July 2, 2000

It was Sunday morning in Southdown, and the sun was shining on the town's righteous. Bells chimed over the roofs of chi-chi restaurants, fragrant coffee bars and over-priced homes.

In St. Luke's, the organ thundered into a spirited version of Onward Christian Soldiers and the mostly-elderly congregation rose to add their voices to the martial hymn music.

Adam Cornish was not among their number. He was sitting in his flat across town, gloomily nursing yet another hangover. Adding to his Sunday-morning depression was the unsavoury news his computer had delivered.

He was beginning to hate the thing. It had hinted that, to research Ernie and Marie's story meant weeks, or even months, of hard work.

His foray into the website of the National Archives, where soldiers' records were stored, had not been the instant and labour-light success for which Adam craved.

Adam looked gloomily at his scribbled notes. It was even possible, according to the Archives, that his grandfather's records no longer existed.

Adam ran his fingers through his beard. It was less than fragrant from last night's industrial quantities of beer, consumed at the Nine Bells. A bitter ale hangover gnawed at his brain like a hungry rat.

The former reporter had to face the fact that, before he could write a word of his Hollywood blockbuster, he needed diligent research to be able to sketch out its bare bones.

There were dozens of questions that needed answering. And Ernie's service record was the obvious place to start.

Just where and when had Ernie served? How and where had he won his decoration for gallantry? When and where was each of his promotions? Where on the battlefield was he wounded?

What was the nature of his injuries, wounds severe enough to lead to his discharge—and possibly save his life—before the end of the war?

Was he at Messines? If so, did Ernie's records hold a clue as to why he would never talk about the battle? Just who was listed as his next of kin as the war progressed?

The list went on and on . . .

Hard work had never been Adam's forte. During his years at the Kentish World, he had ducked and dived, He had always avoided the more demanding assignments to free up time for forays into the Nine Bells and a dozen pubs in the surrounding villages.

Adam had always yearned for that well-deserved promotion. For he believed this would mean he could shed most of his work on to subordinates. But over the years, incomprehensibly, that promotion never came.

The Goldsteins were obviously at the bottom of it all . . . holding him back to save money. They knew his true value and, Jew-like, decided they wouldn't pay it. Bastards!

One day, they would be made to suffer as six million of their fellow Yids suffered in the last war. Adam Ernest Cornish would see to that . . . once he had the power and the money.

He could promise them that. And all the others . . .

But the unpalatable fact was that the money which would bring power now had to be earned.

Was it all going to be worth it?

Miserably, Adam took a sip of tepid coffee from the mug, emblazoned with the word "stress", which was stagnating at his elbow. He tried to ignore the thought that was tugging at his mind as insistently as a child at its mother's skirts.

It told him, as surely as an alarm clock, that it was precisely 27 minutes before the Nine Bells opened. Adam resisted the siren call—for the time being. He bent once more over his notes.

The pensioned-off reporter tried to forget his headache. He made a mental note to brave Wayne and World Electronics in the morning and buy a printer. This would save all this wearisome note-taking. He decided, too, to get hold of Rod Russell and ask him to install the new piece of kit.

Meanwhile, his spidery notes defeating him, Adam switched on the laptop and sought out the Google search engine. He inquired for "Soldiers' records in World War One", and up popped the National Archives site

Adam, yet again wearing yesterday's socks and underpants, padded into his kitchen, poured the cold coffee down the sink and made a new cup of instant. He hoped the caffeine would give him the boost he needed.

In his farm-house, two miles away, as Adam switched on his laptop, Rod Russell's monitor screen came to life. The undercover agent hurriedly pushed aside the remains of his Sunday breakfast—two fried eggs, three rashers of bacon, mushrooms, tomatoes and baked beans.

He muttered, wiping his mouth on a napkin: "Christ, he's at it again. I'd have hoped the idle old sod would have given up by now. Perhaps he's really going to do it after all.

72

"Then the shit will hit the fan big-time."

The officer pulled a scratch pad towards him and began to write urgently.

Hamish read along with Adam as the screen told its story.

"More than nine million men and women are estimated to have served in the British armed forces during the First World War. Many of the surviving records from this period can be found in the National Archives and can be used for tracing an ancestor who fought in the Great War."

Then, once again, came the depressing news. Adam took a sip of his coffee and massaged his aching forehead. He and Rod Russell read on:

"Records destroyed: When war broke out in August, 1914, the British Army numbered just 730,000 men . . . but the scale of the conflict between the Allies and the Central Powers demanded massive increases in Britain's military manpower resources. By the end of the war in 1918, more than seven million men and women had seen service in the British Army."

Adam took another gulp of coffee. The alarm clock in his aching head was counting down the time to when Jim would unbolt the pub's doors. The reporter rubbed his red-rimmed eyes and soldiered on:

"Unfortunately, more than half of their service records were destroyed in September, 1940, when a German bombing raid struck the War Office repository in Arnside, Street, London.

"However, an estimated 2.8million service records survived the bombing, or were reconstructed from the Ministry of

Pensions. *This means that there is a roughly 40 per cent chance of finding the service record of a soldier who was discharged at some time between 1914 and 1920."*

The Burnt Documents: *"The service records that survived the Arnside Street fire in 1940—the so-called 'Burnt Documents'—are located in the series WO 363. Due to fire and water damage, they are too delicate to be handled and are consequently only available to the public on microfilm . . .*

"The microfilm catalogues, which are mostly arranged alphabetically by surname, cover soldiers who completed their service between 1914 and 1920."

"Bloody terrible odds of finding Ernie for all the work involved, "Adam muttered. "Hello, what's this? Could this be light at the end of the tunnel . . . but a bloody dim light at that? And it seems to be shining on another great heap of work."

Adam scrolled down further. This was new territory, and it brought better news.

The "Unburnt Documents and other material. *"The service records in the series WO 364—the "Unburnt Documents"—were recovered by the War Office from the Ministry of Pensions and other government departments after the Second World War.*

"They mainly concern men who were discharged (with pensions) from the army because of sickness or wounds received in battle between 1914 and 1920. Aside from the usual military forms, most of the individual files in WO364 thus also contain detailed medical records."

Suddenly, Adam sat up and paid strict attention. Because of Ernie's wounds and "touch of gas", he had come marching home before millions of others. The sergeant had been discharged and back in Southdown around Christmas 1917. He had been trailing scandal like cordite fumes in his wake.

In later years, he used to joke as he sat Adam, his toddler grandson, on his knee: "That shell splinter in my insides turned out to be a Christmas present from old Fritz."

Adam leaned back in the kitchen chair and pictured Ernie as he was in those far-off days. The old man had never lost his sergeant's military smartness. His shoes always glistened with generous applications of spit and polish.

The creases in his trousers were so sharp, the little boy believed his granddad when he told him he sharpened pencils on them. Ernie wore his trademark bow tie with crisp, white shirts. His jackets were pressed into parade-ground order.

Even when" that old rascal age" was beginning to make the old soldier's legs waver, his back remained ramrod straight. At Southdown's annual Armistice Day parades, he marched unaided—almost to the very end—medals gleaming.

Adam thought: "Surely, with his wounds, Ernie must have been receiving a pension. That would place his records into the 'Unburnt' section, which were spared the blitz. The odds are improving."

Adam little knew the brutal way in which the wounded "heroes of the trenches" were treated by parsimonious authorities.

Ernie had sat with a dozen others in a bleak waiting room, ready to go before a pensions board. Two of the soldiers had missing limbs, one's face twitched uncontrollably, another coughed incessantly, holding a stained handkerchief to his mouth.

The first to be called was a corporal, his face terribly disfigured. He had a gaping dent in his forehead into which a man could put his fist. The door closed behind him. They heard his boots crash to attention.

There was the sound of voices. Some were brusque and hectoring. One was tremulous and pleading. After ten minutes, the corporal staggered into the waiting-room, head bowed and tears streaming down his face.

"Next! Sergeant Cornish!" roared a medical orderly, holding a clip-board and wearing an immaculate uniform that had clearly never seen either mud or blood.

Ernie marched in to the board room. He stamped to attention and saluted the Royal Army Medical Corps moustachioed colonel, flanked by two captains, who were sitting at a trestle table covered in files.

The officers left Ernie standing at attention. The colonel pulled a file towards him and studied it slowly. He looked up accusingly and snapped:

"I honestly don't know why you're here today, sergeant. I suppose you are after a handout, like most of the others."

Ernie swayed slightly and coughed.

The colonel shouted: "Stop the play-acting, Cornish. You can't fool us. We've seen hundreds of scroungers like you. Stand at ease, if you feel you have to."

The colonel, fleshy face made rosy by mess port, glanced again at Ernie's file: "Nothing down here but a whiff of gas and a miniscule fragment of shrapnel, which don't seem to be affecting you too much today."

Ernie, standing at ease, hands clasped behind his back, clenched his jaw in anger and said nothing.

The colonel started to write in Ernie's file. He told him: "Tell you what we'll do. Stop wasting everybody's time with this ludicrous claim for a pension, and we'll give you a present.

"If you agree to waive the pension, I'll discharge you from the service and put you down for a lump sum of £80.

More than you deserve, but it prevents a lot of paper work. Did I hear you say you agreed, sergeant?"

The colonel exaggeratedly cupped his hand to his ear. The captains permitted themselves a smile.

Ernie nodded dumbly. In later years, he tried to calculate how many hundreds of pounds his pension would have added up to had he not surrendered to the colonel's bullying.

"Right, sergeant, dismiss! Orderly, send in the next malingerer."

Back at the War Office, Ernie's service record remained with those of the uninjured and unrewarded. It gathered dust on the shelves of the War Office repository in Arnside Street until Otto's stray bomb reduced it to ashes.

Back in Southdown that sunny Sunday morning, Adam's memory of the plumber-turned-soldier began to fade and the reporter's gloom returned.

The prospect of all this research, without even a guaranteed result, served to make his booze-induced headache worse.

Work and the prospect of work had always depressed Adam Cornish.

The laptop's screen with its blinking cursor seemed to mock him. Adam felt as though he'd had enough for one day. Referring to Rod's notes, he managed to close down the machine.

In the farmhouse, Rod's monitor screen went blank. The captain stared at it, deep in thought, for a full five minutes. He was becoming seriously worried.

He wondered: "What was that stupid, drink-sodden, old fart Cornish going to do next? What damage might he do, stirring up the explosive past of Sergeant Ernest Frederick Cornish?"

Rod picked up the phone on his desk and dialled the highly-secret number of an office in Whitehall. After a brief conversation, he snapped smartly: "Yes, Colonel. I agree. I'll get straight on to it."

The undercover soldier shrugged into his shabby anorak. He knew just where to discover the source of the information he had just been ordered to find. He stepped out of the building's back door, into the disused farmyard, and made his way towards the Nine Bells.

Arthur Burfield had just completed one of his staple local newspaper tasks . . . photographing an elderly couple who were celebrating their golden wedding. As he automatically snapped the beaming couple cutting an amateurly-iced cake, surrounded by relatives, his mind wasn't on the job.

He, too, wondered what Adam Cornish was going to do next. A single decision could turn out to be lethal for the old soak. Or it could lead to him starring in an epic, world-wide drama.

"Only one way to find out," Arthur told himself, as he bade the golden couple goodbye at the door of their thatched cottage.

Arthur stowed his camera gear into the boot of his modest office estate car. Then he set off from the little Kentish village where the couple had lived all their married lives.

As he drove through the picturesque lanes, flanked by summertime orchards and hop fields, he reached for his car phone. He caught Adam, just as the writer was leaving for the pub.

Arthur said breezily: "Hello, me old mate. Fancy a pint?" The receiver quacked an assent.

The photographer put the phone back in its holder before he, too, set course for the Nine Bells.

Back in his Southdown flat, Adam was still securely in the grip of boozer's gloom. This temple-throbbing malaise was not helped by the fact that his once-glittering project was rapidly losing its lustre.

During the preceding week, Adam had phoned the National Archives office in Kew, Surrey, and tried to wheedle a woman there into doing his research for him. She promised only to send him a card so that he could do the job himself.

He now picked up that card, ringed by coffee cups and stained by food. It bore a detailed map of how to get to the centre. The thought of making multiple trips to Kew from Southdown depressed Adam even more.

Bloody hell! He would have to walk from his flat to Southdown station and catch a train to London. He would then change trains to get to Kew. After all this, according to the map, he would be faced with yet another weary walk, to the National Archives building.

After hours of tedious research, the seriously unfit and unwilling Adam would have to reverse the whole energy-sapping process to get home. Again and again.

Wearily, he asked himself: "Is it all going to be worth it?"

Adam had happily contemplated a retirement task consisting of bouts of inspiration, light research and dilettante writing. This would be swiftly followed by international acclaim and a Niagra Falls of money.

Now, staring at his notes and the laptop's blank screen, he felt himself recoil from the prospect of toiling on a research treadmill. After all, he had spent a non-working lifetime avoiding just this sort of thing.

Should he just junk the whole idea and write a best-seller from his fertile imagination and inspiration? No research involved?

The alarm clock in his aching head began to ring, preventing Adam from making a decision. In spite of the coffee, his throat felt as dry as the little-used towel in his bathroom.

It was pub opening time . . . an alarm call that couldn't be denied.

Adam nearly fell into the Nine Bells. He was pushing at the weathered oak door just as Jim slid back the bolts from the inside. The dank smell and gloom felt like home.

The reporter was alone at the bar, as Arthur was still on his way. Jim, disinclined to encourage conversation, pulled Adam a pint of bitter ale. Then he clattered down the steps to the cellar and noisily started to move metal kegs around.

Adam climbed on to a stool and took the first sip of the day from his tankard. His presentation gift was already beginning to fit into his hand with the familiarity of an old friend.

The cool liquid slid down his parched throat and eased his headache. By the second sip, Adam's conscience began pricking. For all his big talk of creating a Hollywood blockbuster, he had, in fact, achieved nothing.

He was, once again, frustrated to find himself victim of his own sloth.

Arthur was bound to ask how the Ernie Cornish project was going. And, being Sunday, it was likely that others from the Kentish World would drop into the Bells for a pre-lunch tipple. They would pose the same question.

Adam realised, in the cold light of day, that he should have kept his big mouth shut. This is where having a drink too many lands you, he told himself bitterly. Adam drained his tankard and pushed it over the bar to Jim for a refill.

The writer was halfway down the second pint when inspiration struck. Adam silently repeated his old mantra: "Booze is the answer to everything".

He would consign to the back burner any tedious research in the archives. He would replace it with something much, much more exciting . . . an "Ernie Cornish pilgrimage" to Flanders.

Adam looked forward to sinking a pint or two now, with a newly-eased conscience. When he got back to his flat this afternoon, he would jot down every place name from the old battlefields he could remember his grandfather mentioning.

He would take a ferry to the Continent and follow in Ernie's muddy footsteps. It would be a journey of respect, remembrance and research. He would savour the feeling of history, sacrifice . . . and the prospect of a rich reward to come.

True to his journalistic roots, he would pop into a few cafes on the way, and pump the drinkers there for their local and historical knowledge. This was sort of project Adam relished.

He pictured himself in a Flemish version of the Nine Bells, sinking the odd beer or three, tape-recorder turning, while the locals painted word pictures of life in the 1914-18 war. He would harvest gems from the mud.

A few hours writing would, inevitably, lead to fame and power. Perfect. He blanked out the fact that there would still be archives to research. That was for another day.

Adam's headache dissolved completely at the thought of a task that compelled him to drink his way across the old killing fields. He pushed his newly-emptied tankard over the bar.

A voice behind him boomed cheerily: "Hello, me old mate. I'll get that one!" Adam had been so absorbed by his thoughts, he hadn't noticed Arthur Burfield breeze into the bar

Jim plonked down the frothy beer and the pub door opened once more. This time Rod Russell, duffel coat flapping open to reveal an old T-shirt and holed jeans, entered. He slicked back his long hair and chuckled: "It looks like I'll have to get in the queue to buy the old bastard a noggin."

Ros Litherland hurried to catch the door before it swung shut behind Rod. She laughed: "Put me down on that list, guys. I'm in a buying mood this fine Sunday. It seems it's your lucky day, Adam."

The blonde was wearing jeans that fitted like a second skin, outlining trim calves and a tightly-curved bottom. Her sweater appeared to be several sizes too small. Ros sidled up, brushing Adam with her breasts. He felt an unaccustomed stirring in his crotch.

Did this young stunner really fancy him? Adam permitted himself a small hope that she did. After all, he *was* handsome, experienced and talented in an Ernest Hemingway sort of way.

Wrapped in fantasy, he leered at Ros's ripe boobs and failed to notice the expressions of annoyance and frustration on the faces of Arthur and Rod.

Arthur broke an uneasy silence. "I'm surprised you could find the time to hobnob with the likes of us. I expected you to be deep into writing your Hollywood blockbuster. How's it all going then, old chum?"

Adam, happy he could field the expected questions, kept his audience in suspense. He took a long swallow of his beer, and wiped his moustache and beard with the back of his hand. He dried the glistening hand on his trousers.

Ros barely concealed a shudder of distaste. Then, like Rod and Arthur, she pasted on an expression of admiration and intense interest.

Adam, happy that he had their undivided attention, announced: "All is going well. But there has been a change of plan. I will be doing field research for a week or two, instead of going straight to the archives.

"Tomorrow morning, I shall book myself on to a cross-Channel ferry at Dover and sail away to the Continent. I shall drive across the French border into Flanders and follow Ernie Cornish's trail across the battlefields."

Rod nodded to Jim, who silently refilled Adam's tankard. The photographer, the IT expert and the girl looked deeply thoughtful as they sipped their drinks.

Arthur made Adam splutter by suddenly slapping him heartily on the back. The photographer declared: "Well, me old mate, it so happens you will need a photographer to record your researches. Nothing like good, sharp pictures to refresh your memory when you come to do the writing.

"Who better to know what snaps you need than Uncle Arthur, your old pro from the World. It so happens I'm owed some holiday, so I am ready and willing to join you as and when.

"I hear they have hundreds of different sorts of beer in Belgium. You can pay my fee with the odd glass or two, just to oil the wheels, so to speak."

Adam, his feeling of wellbeing enhanced by alcohol and the camaraderie surrounding him, saw a monumental booze-up in the offing. He flung his arms wide, spilling his drink over Ros's sweater. He gulped as he saw her nipples thrust through the wet cashmere wool.

"Everyone's welcome," he roared. "Just so long as you pull your weight . . . and that applies to buying the good old Belgian beer as well."

Adam looked again at Ros, swallowing hard as she winked and ran her tongue over her lips meaningfully. She leaned close and whispered in his ear: "Is there room for little old me, too?"

Adam, rosy-faced with alcohol, gulped the top off his sixth pint. He slurred: "You're all welcome. It's going to be quite a party!"

He raised his tankard and shouted a toast: "Here's to Ernie Cornish."

They all raised their glasses and chorused: "To Ernie."

This was more like it.

CHAPTER FIVE

June 15, 1917

Marie's elfin face, framed by dark, bobbed hair, snuggled against the soft down covering the chest of Ernie Cornish. The naked couple had rolled together into the trough their sweat-slicked bodies had made in the soft Flemish "matrimonial bed".

The big iron bedstead upon which they lay had tarnished brass balls on each of its four corner posts. These frequently jangled noisily to the rhythm of their love-making.

The old bed had seen birth, sickness, death and innumerable couplings in its century of service. Now, in this time of war, it continued to do its duty.

Ernie slept the sleep of deep exhaustion. His youthful reserves of joy and energy had been drained by the sight of too much suffering, too much death, too much squalor.

Looking at his sleeping face, Marie found it hard to believe Ernie was still just a boy of 22 summers. The plumbing apprentice from those almost-forgotten days of peace had been made old by his constant acquaintance with death.

To add to his torment, the young sergeant nursed a terrifying secret. Every time the whistle blew in the trenches for the men to "go over the top" of the parapet, Ernie had to lead his men into the bullet-swept horror of No-man's Land.

As he sprinted through the moonscape of shattered trees and rotting corpses between the lines, only he knew just how close he was to breaking—to joining the disgraced men throwing away their weapons and bolting back to safety.

In his mind's eye, Ernie pictured the price he would pay for such cowardice. Stripped of his sergeant's stripes and blindfolded, he would die ignominiously before a firing squad, probably composed of the men he once led.

When Ernie charged towards the enemy barbed wire and spitting machine-guns, he knew he must never betray his fear by so much as a twitch of a muscle of his face or tremor of an eyelid.

His men looked upon the blond, finely-muscled senior non-commissioned officer as their fearless leader. Playing that role was a heavy burden that, daily, sapped the sergeant's resolve.

How much more could he take? Only God knew that, and He wasn't telling.

Even in sleep, Ernie couldn't find peace. He groaned and gasped as, in his nightmares, the bullets and creeping gas tried to seek him out.

Marie was wide awake. She, too, was in agony, suffering the pangs of a broken heart. With the Tommy's sperm still warm inside her, she thought hopelessly and helplessly of her lost German love.

Her yearning for her blue-eyed Dolphie was like a bayonet twisting in her guts. She took a small comfort in remembering that, although he was lost to her, she was still doing his bidding.

Surely that should be worth a smile from the strange *gefreiter* who had captured her heart and soul?

As Marie lay on what she thought of as her bed of sin, she could hear the clatter of booted feet in the street below the bedroom window. She knew these belonged to mud-caked Tommies, out of the line and seeking solace in this town they affectionately called "Pop".

Ernie had brought her here to Poperinge, a relatively safe ten miles from the killing ground of the notorious Ypres Salient. To the British, who jauntily nicknamed Ypres "Wipers", Pop was a sanctuary. Here, 250,000 of them forgot the war for a while.

But the windows of the bedroom above the Hotel de Tramway in the town square, where Marie and Ernie were playing out their romantic charade, still rattled to the distant thunder of the big guns.

The girl knew that, a little way down the road, there was a line of soldiers outside a house in whose window a red light constantly burned. But for a lucky twist of fate, she could well have ended up behind its ever-open door.

If Marie had not been taken under the wing of the soldier lying next to her, she would have had to make a living any way she could. She might well have solved that problem in the same way as the whores in the nearby brothel.

Those weary-eyed, ageing prostitutes, Marie reflected, were doing much more than earning a few francs lying on their backs. They were providing the comfort only a woman could give to traumatised fighting men.

Marie had seen, among the Tommies patiently forming a line on the pavement, fresh-faced soldiers, looking little more than the schoolboys they were just months ago. These youngsters, faces tense with apprehension, were desperate to sample their first—and perhaps only—carnal experience.

The dark-eyed French girl pictured those shy, virginal boys reaching embarrassing climaxes at their very first sight of a naked woman. Then the prostitute, probably not bothering to hide her boredom, would hand them a grubby towel and ring the hand-bell for her next customer.

In a side-street off the market square, officers slipped into a more discreet house of ill repute. While out shopping, Marie had seen them ringing the polished brass bell at the double doors of a three-storey building with drawn, heavy velvet curtains.

Gossips in the boulangerie reported that the girls in the officers' brothel were 20 years younger and more attractive than those who serviced the Tommies. They wore expensive dresses, slashed to the thigh and showing generous amounts of *decolletage*

Behind those heavy curtains there was dancing to gramophone records of the latest London musical's hit tunes. After a tactful time, the girls led their partners by the hand to tastefully-furnished upstairs rooms.

But all was not debauchery in Pop. Last Sunday Ernie, a former Southdown Sunday school scholar, and Marie, a lapsed Catholic, made their way to an imposing, white-fronted house at 43 Gasthuisstraat.

Ernie explained that, since the 11th of December, 1915, this many-roomed building had been the legendary domain of a redoubtable British Army chaplain, the Reverend Philip "Tubby" Clayton.

This cheery, monocled padre made it his holy mission to gift the troops precious moments of peace, by setting up what he "called the Soldiers' House". In the privacy of his upstairs den, he listened to their secrets and sorrows, pouring balm on war-torn lives.

As well as having healing chats with Tubby, the men could wash away the grime of the trenches, relax with a book in the house's library and sleep in the luxury of beds with clean sheets and blankets.

As Ernie and Marie entered what was once the home of wealthy brewer Maurice Coevoet, the sergeant pointed to a sign, boldly painted over the door: "Abandon rank all ye who enter here."

Ernie said: "That's typical of Tubby. He treats us all the same, from lowly private to field-marshal . . . although I don't suppose he gets many of them here.

"They're snug in their grand chateaux, safely behind the lines. Tubby calls this place Talbot House, named after a chap called Lieutenant Gilbert Talbot, who was killed in action in July, 1915.

"The Army signallers' code for the initial letters of Talbot House - "TH" - is "Toc H" And that is the name Tubby has given to a religious movement he has founded here. They reckon it's so popular, it will one day spread all over the world.

"That Tubby . . . he's a man and a half. You'll see him for yourself in a few minutes. I thought you'd like to go to one of his services."

The couple stepped into the cool interior of the building and into an oasis of serenity.

They little knew the major role this Soldiers' House and the charismatic padre who presided over it, was soon to play in their lives.

Marie was in turmoil as she climbed the stairs to where Tubby and a band of volunteers had rigged a chapel in the loft of the building. As a Catholic—even a lapsed one—the girl wasn't sure she should be worshiping here.

Added to that problem, was the question of unforgiven sins. She thought guiltily of her affairs with Dolphie and Ernie. And there was worse, much worse than that . . . there was her current terrible deception.

Ernie climbed purposefully upwards in front of her, his boots ringing on the wide, worn treads. Marie felt she had no option but to follow.

Marie's sergeant lover, too, was plagued by guilt. He came here most Sundays when he was in Pop, sometimes straight from the brothel down the road.

Then there was the guilty matter of his "best girl", waiting faithfully for him back in Southdown . . .

Marie and Ernie reached the top of the stairs and entered Tubby's attic chapel, where troops were already crowding on to home-made wooden pews. They turned to stare appreciatively at the attractive French girl.

A corporal shouted: "Shove up, you lot!", and the soldiers shuffled along to make room for Ernie and Marie.

She looked about her with curiosity. Everything here was makeshift, cobbled together from wood scavenged from ruined barns and farm houses on the battlefields. Even the cross on the altar was fashioned from second-hand timber.

By working some modern miracle, Tubby had conjured up an old harmonium. This wheezed into action, under the fingers of a burly Scottish Black Watch private, resplendent with kilt and two wound stripes.

Marie remained silent as the soldiers roared out old, favourite hymns from home. Afterwards, Tubby gave his khaki congregation a simple sermon, making it a message of hope.

His monocle glittering in the candle-light, the padre reminded them of the cause for which they were fighting the good fight. He blessed the souls of their comrades, who had made the Last Great March.

He silently blessed, too, the lives of many of the survivors. . . . the maimed and the disfigured. Soldiers feared this fate much more than a quick death by bullet or shell.

They knew there were special wards at military hospitals where the wounded were shut away from the world, their faces too awful for the general public to look upon.

Tubby scanned the youthful features of the Tommies in the pews. Some already bore the scars of wounds. There were few familiar worshippers here today. Sadly, his congregation was always changing.

The men were packed, shoulder to shoulder. He recalled the old saying: "There are no atheists in the trenches."

The padre knew only too well the temptations of Pop, and that many here today had surrendered to the siren call of the red light. But Tubby felt it would be impertinent of him to judge these men, who lived in the shadow of death.

His eyes filled as he whispered to himself: "God bless them all."

Tubby took comfort in the emblem of his new movement, Toc H, which was an eternally burning lamp. It symbolically provided a comforting light, even in this dark world.

After the service, Ernie led his young mistress into the beautiful garden. Tubby called this peaceful haven "the largest room in the house".

The couple sat on a bench and drank in the perfume of the fragrant bushes and flowers, still being tended by the ever-willing hands of Tubby's volunteers.

Ernie took her hand, and noted how it lay lifeless in his. He felt a stab of pain at the barrier that always seemed to divide them.

Marie was sinfully willing to do his bidding in bed. But Ernie was only too aware that she never let him into her heart. Sometimes, in their wildest moments of love-making, he saw tears coursing unaccountably down her cheeks.

Even now, sitting in this quiet garden, he knew his lover's mind was elsewhere.

But where? With whom?

Breaking his sombre mood, Ernie pointed out to Marie the old hop barn at the bottom of the garden. He chuckled as he described the riotous concert parties the troops staged there.

For an hour or so, Ernie and his comrades could forget the war in a magical world of music, dramatic monologues, jokes, and bawdy sketches. These often starred a comic "sergeant major" or effete "officers".

The troops always saved their biggest applause for the show's "chorus line". These "girls" were burly soldiers sporting grotesque make-up, skimpy costumes, ill-fitting wigs and—best of all—gigantic bosoms.

They cavorted on the makeshift stage to music pounded out on a looted, bullet-scarred piano by a Tommy, a Woodbine dangling from his lower lip.

Tough Sergeant Cornish was by no means alone in blowing his nose hard and brushing aside a tear in the darkness as he joined in the sentimental songs, so beloved of the soldiers far from home.

There's a long, long trail a-winding, to the Land of My Dreams . . .

Keep the home fires burning . . .

Roses are blooming in Picardy . . .

Take me back to dear old Blighty—soldiers' slang for home.

Finally, the dusty rafters of the old hop store, wreathed in tobacco smoke, rang to the mens' favourite. This song had become the anthem of the Ypres salient, the most lethal patch of land in the world.

"It's a long way to Tipperary . . .

Sitting in the peaceful garden of Talbot House, hand in hand with his enigmatic and beautiful French mistress, Ernie recalled experiencing a stab of conscience as he had joined in the chorus of another popular ditty:

If you were the only girl in the world, and I were the only boy . . .

For Ernie was keeping his great secret from Marie. Of course, she *wasn't* his only girl in the world.

The young sergeant closed his eyes and pretended to doze as his memory conjured up a poignant picture from his last day of leave in Southdown.

In his mind's eye, he was once again standing on the smoke-wreathed platform of the town's station, bright with carefully-tended flower beds. Clinging to his arm was Maud his "best girl", sobbing into a tiny handkerchief.

At just 17, Maud Waterman was blooming into full womanhood. Ernie's heart leaped as he remembers how shy, virginal and trusting she looked as the guard's whistle began to shrill.

She was scrubbed, healthy and as wholesome as the apples in the orchards of the nearby big manor house, where she worked as a "tweenie"—the most junior of a team of maids.

Ernie had met Maud when he called to fix a couple of dripping taps in the manor's vast, food-fragrant kitchen. He recalled that, on that memorable day, the vast room was a hive of industry, crowded with scurrying cooks and footmen.

He had made the simple task of fitting new washers to the taps last as long as possible as he gazed, moonstruck, at the girl with the trim figure and smiling face. That morning, she looked irresistible in her neat black dress, crisp, frilly apron and cap.

Maud paused in her duties and blushed prettily when she noticed the young plumber's apprentice staring admiringly at her. But she returned his gaze from modestly-lowered eyes.

So it had begun. Before reluctantly packing up his tools to leave, Ernie whispered in the tweenie's ear, arranging a rendezvous. Her cheeks still pink with embarrassment, Maud had agreed.

As they strolled in a Southdown park on her Wednesday evening off, the couple took a shine to each other straight away.

Soon Ernie, the master plumber's son, and Maud, daughter of a shepherd on the manor's estate, were "walking out". This led to the next formal, though unspoken, step in their relationship.

The folk of Southdown, nodding sagely, opined that the couple had "come to an arrangement". This was just one step away in the Edwardian courting ritual from the buying of an engagement ring.

Now, on Southdown station, it was time for Ernie to go to war, and the couple embraced desperately as the guard's whistle sounded urgently for the last time.

The train had already begun to move when Ernie disentangled himself, pulled open a carriage door and climbed in. He lowered the window and leaned far out, waving to Maud until a bend in the line blotted her slight figure from view.

As he settled into a seat, Ernie found the smoke from the engine was "irritating his eyes". He rubbed them roughly.

Two other soldiers in the compartment, who had seen the couple saying their goodbyes, looked politely out the window.

Maud, too, was wiping her eyes as she walked slowly back to the big house. The butler had "done his patriotic duty" by granting her an hour away from her duties to say goodbye to her soldier sweetheart.

As his train sped towards London, and as she walked through the sweetly-smelling lanes, the lovers both wondered if they would ever meet again.

Now, as he sat in the Talbot House garden, Ernie's hand unconsciously went to the pocket of his tunic that was closest to his heart. He felt, under the rough cloth, the shape of the latest post card to arrive from Maud.

Ernie knew the picture on the front and the copperplate writing on the back by heart. The postcard depicted a young girl, not unlike Maud, looking up at a bright full moon, sailing regally over the thatched cottages of an English village.

The words beneath the picture asked: "Is that the same moon that is shining down on him tonight?"

On the back of the postcard, Ernie's sweetheart had written simply: "Keep yourself safe, dearest. Come back soon. Yours affectionately—Maud." Her name was followed by three daring kisses.

The Flemish sun warm on his face, Ernie knew only too well that Maud and his parents must be living in dread of a visit from a telegraph boy. All too often, these messengers bore missives from the War Office.

These contained stark messages beginning: "It is my painful duty to inform you . . ." Then followed tidings of death, wounds or loved ones who had disappeared into muddy oblivion.

Marie's hand stirred in Ernie's like a small, trapped animal. He opened his eyes and told himself fiercely. "Bugger it all. I could be dead in a week. I'll grab what pleasure I can while I'm still in the land of the living."

These were desperate days on the Western Front. Christian husbands in uniform sought temporary relief from their terrors in adulterous fornication.

In the trenches, teetotallers, who had "signed the pledge" never to let alcohol pass their lips, eagerly gulped their ration of liquid courage from rum jars.

Staring into the face of death, the timid frequently became warriors and braggarts often turned into craven cowards.

For Ernie and Marie, the precious minutes of tranquillity were rapidly draining away. He pulled out his pocket watch, a 21st birthday present from his parents, Enoch and Emma.

"Nearly twelve. Time for me to get back, old thing."

The sergeant escorted his lover back to the Café de Tramway in the square. She gave him a quick peck on the cheek before hurrying inside. Again, Ernie felt the jolt of pain like a punch in the stomach.

Even though he was marching back to a probable death, she still kept that impenetrable barrier between them.

He asked himself for the first time: Was he falling in love?

A month later.

Ernie had sent word he would be back this morning. In the musty room over the café, Marie swung her legs out of bed and fought the nausea from which she had been suffering for the last week or so.

It was time to get ready to do her duty for Dolphie. Marie drew her thick, flannel nightdress over her head, padded across to a battered chest of drawers and took out a brief black, transparent chemise.

"My whore's uniform," she told herself bitterly. "I'm no better than the girls down the road."

Before putting on the chemise, Marie critically examined her nude body in a mildew-speckled mirror on the door of the bedroom's heavy armoire. She gazed at her curves intently, turning this way and that.

Marie whispered: "He still won't know. When he looks at me decked out like this, he will think of nothing but sex."

She knew, too, that Ernie, would—as usual—never take the time to notice that her eyes were red-rimmed by many hours' crying.

The girl gave a convulsive sob as she slipped between the sheets of the squeaking bed. She turned her face into the pillow that still smelled of his sweat and hair oil, and asked the question haunting her: "Dear Lord in Heaven, how did I come to this place?"

She clasped her hands together and added pitifully: "Forgive me, for I have sinned. Is there any help for me?"

Black memories of that last, cataclysmic day behind the lines with her German lover threatened to overwhelm her. Marie knew she must push them to the back of her mind. She had grieved too long and too often for her lost happiness,

Instead, as she waited for the Englishman with his hungry hands and mouth, the girl lay on her back and forced herself to slip into a happy reverie.

She drifted back to that sunny day in the fields of Fournes-en-Weppes, when she had shocked herself by boldly asking *Gefreiter* Adolf Hitler for a date.

How the other girls had laughed that evening as their favourite virgin made a careful toilette and put on her best red calico dress.

"He'll never turn up. You're tarting yourself up for nothing," they teased.

When Marie made her way nervously to the Café Canon in the nearby village, it took her several minutes to notice the girls were trailing along in a crocodile behind her.

They followed her into the café, crowding on to other tables, so that she sat alone, in the very centre. The minutes ticked past and, still giggling, they kept repeatedly and obviously looking at the clock on the nicotine-yellow wall.

They sent her over a glass of lemonade, calling: "We can't see him. Is your soldier the Invisible Man?" Eight o'clock came and went.

Marie's cheeks were aflame. To the delight of her friends, she had to keep fending off the advances of other soldiers in field-grey

Then the door opened and the girls fell silent. Hitler, his Iron Cross shining on his tunic, marched into the estaminet. His eyes immediately picked out the girl in the red dress.

He came to attention in front of Marie. Although only a humble *gefreiter*, Hitler exuded authority: He looked down at the blushing teenager, sitting with her drink untouched.

Hitler said: "I must take you out of this zoo, *fraulein*. You wish to speak with me of art, which is a serious matter. This is no place for that. We will walk together and I will begin the instruction you requested."

The farm girls screamed with laughter at this pompous, stilted speech from the German soldier, whose luxuriant moustache seemed too big for his pasty face.

Hitler turned the blaze of his vivid, blue eyes on them and they immediately fell silent. The farm-girls watched in wonder as their little virgin obediently rose, as though hypnotised, and followed the stranger out into the damp, Flanders night.

Hitler was silent at first, deep in thought, as he and Marie trudged through the village streets. As though obeying a silent order from the *gefreiter*, the moon dutifully appeared and silver-rimmed the windswept clouds.

The Austrian, walking with a strange and distinctly unmilitary gait, seemed to have forgotten his promise of an art lecture. Instead, when he at last spoke, he launched into a fierce diatribe—one that was to become familiar to Marie during the months to come.

Those dunderheads at the art colleges, obviously inspired by Jewish jealousy, had been deliberately blind to Hitler's unique talent. They slammed the doors in his face while letting in low-lifes and Yids.

Hitler, a lock of dark hair falling across his forehead, said this was a mere fragment of proof of the Jewish plot to look after their own and feather their filthy nests.

Passers-by turned to look with curiosity when the soldier's voice rose as he became yet more impassioned. Marie, pretending not to notice the stares, remained tactfully silent.

Hitler said the rejection in his early life was a symptom of a great international Jewish conspiracy to control everything and everybody. Already they were taking over the banks.

There wasn't a financial institution in the world that wasn't riddled with Yids. They knew where the true power lay . . . money, money and yet more money.

They were the scum, he assured the bemused girl, who were behind Marx-inspired communism and the back-scratching, Judeo-based Freemasons.

The couple came to a wooden park bench and Hitler gestured for Marie to sit. He continued his speech, eyes fired by his zeal.

He promised that, one day, this situation would change. He personally had been called by an Inner Voice to open the world's eyes to the insidious danger lurking in their midst.

Millions would come to acclaim him as their saviour . . . a man with a clear and sacred vision, who would sweep these Shylocks off the face of the earth.

Marie gazed wonderingly at her strange new friend as he declaimed to the night: "I will build a mighty and clean new world. I will not be afraid to use the bones of my enemies as its foundation.

"Those hook-nosed nobodies who rejected me from art school did me and the world a great favour. I went into the streets and, in my struggle to survive, learned invaluable lessons at the University of Life.

"While they taught people to create senseless daubs, I learned how to put my finger on the pulse of the people. When I become the great and invincible Fuhrer, I will take my revenge on those people who tried to stifle my genius."

Marie shivered in the night air, but dare not speak or move to shatter this man's bizarre vision. She instinctively knew this was how Adolf Hitler liked her to be.

As he came to the end of his tirade, Hitler pinned her like a rabbit in the hypnotic beam of his eyes: "Everything I do and say must be correct. For I am history!"

Marie thought of the amateurish brush-strokes she had seen on his sandbag "canvas" that afternoon, as Hitler painted the landscape he called *Coup d'Oeil vers Fournes,*

He was certainly deluded about his artistic talent. Was all the rest a delusion as well? Was this odd but compelling man a little strange in the head?

But the young French girl had to confess to herself that she was enthralled by his difference and his passion. Later, others were to use the word "besotted" about her.

This was a condition in which she would remain, through undreamt-of tragedies, for the rest of her life.

Hitler, at last silent, escorted her back to the Café Canon. Marie hoped with all her heart that he would come to like her. And perhaps, dear Lord, something more . . .

They stood outside the estaminet, its windows steamed up by the heat of the roistering troops and girls inside. Marie's heart fluttered like a summer butterfly as she felt his eyes on her.

She lifted her face expectantly, but Hitler just lightly touched her on the shoulder before turning to leave. Marie called after him, a note of desperation in her voice: "Shall I see you again m'sieur?

"I know I have much to learn. Perhaps tomorrow? Same place? Same time?"

Hitler was silent for one, two, three, four heartbeats. When he turned back, his face was in shadow, so that she couldn't read his expression.

At last, he replied: "That will be permitted, *fraulein*. But this place is not for us. There is nothing here for me. I don't drink alcohol, I don't eat meat and I don't smoke a pipe or cigarettes. I keep myself pure for my destiny.

"Be patient until I contact you. Meanwhile, I will find a room where we can be together and continue your instruction."

So her instruction began. She was to prove an obedient and willing pupil.

Now all this had brought her to the Tommies' town of Pop. In the bedroom above the raucous cafe, Marie ran her fingers through the dark silk of her hair.

The pain of her present shameful circumstances returned and, despite her best resolutions, she began to sob.

Dolphie was to blame. But, in spite of everything—from his weird and unsatisfying love-making to his apparent disregard for her feelings—she loved him.

Marie, tears streaming down her cheeks, confessed to herself that she was imprisoned by a love that was total and unconditional. She would worship her strange charismatic and dangerous man until the end of time.

She wondered what her bullying father, Pierre Boulette, would say if he could see her now, dressed as a cheap trollop, ready to couple with an unloved lover.

Unlike the other harlots in Pop, Marie, on this creaking iron bed, performed a labour of love. But, bizarrely, this was not love for the man between her sheets.

The Tommies in the bar below, fuelled by the cheap white wine they called *vang blonk*, launched into some of their more cynical songs.

The bells of hell go ting-a-ling-a-ling for you but not for me . . .

I know where the battalion is . . . hanging on the old barbed wire . . .

Oh, my, I don't want to die . . .

Gassed last night, gassed the night before . . .

Marie heard the café door open and shut for the hundredth time. Then she recognised a familiar, parade-ground voice that made her suddenly sit up and dry her eyes.

She heard Ernie, with his country burr, bellow over the noise: "Hello, lads. It's nice to hear your lovely voices.

Try singing in the trenches, and you'll scare old Fritz to death."

The sergeant's remark was met with a roar of laughter from the soldiers. One, bolder than the rest called out: "Hey, sarge, where you bin? Robbin' yet another Froggie girl of her innocence?"

Another Tommy, emboldened by booze, took up the tease: "Ain't one enough for yer? I bet that little sweetheart of yours is upstairs right now—ready and waiting wi' no drawers on!"

There was a gale of drunken laughter. Upstairs, Marie turned a distraught face into the pillow. Why was Ernie letting them do this to her? He must know she could hear them through the thin floorboards of their bedroom.

A voice with what she recognised as a thick Northern accent added to the hubbub: "You lucky bastard, sarge. Them with the stripes get all the luck *and* all the leg-overs.

"Want a *vang blonk*, sergeant, afore you race up yonder stairs? Just to get you in the mood for it, like?"

Ernie snapped at the roisterers with his sergeant's voice: "That's enough of that, men! I hope you're as brave as this when you next get the order to fix bayonets."

But one slurring voice persisted, bringing hope of a brief reprieve to the girl listening in the bedroom above. "Come on, sarge. Off parade's off parade. Loosen up a bit, why don't yer?

"No need to be all regimental now we're all cosy in Pop. Tell you what, here's my plate of egg and chips. I 'aven't touched it. See, it's all nice and 'ot. I'll ask madame to cook me another lot. 'Ere you are—take it."

Ernie began to waver at the smell of his favourite food, as the Tommy stuck the eggs and chips under his nose. His stomach, starved since his Spartan breakfast in the trench, growled hungrily.

Abruptly, he grabbed the food and sat down on a proffered chair. The girl heard him say grudgingly: "O.k., so I am a bit on the empty side, lads. But don't think this pally-pally stuff will get you anywhere when we're back on parade.

"I'm warning you that I will still be the horrible bastard you love to hate." He picked up a knife and fork and tucked into the dish so beloved of the Western Front Tommies.

Ernie's surrender was greeted with cheers. Emboldened, the soldiers began to serenade their sergeant as he speared a chip and dipped it into the yoke of one of his eggs.

Who were you with last night, out in the pale moonlight?

The pay-off line of the song made the floorboards tremble in the room above the bar:

Oh! Oh! Oh! I AM surprised at you!

Marie heard the clink of many glasses as the soldiers roared once more:

Hello, HELLO, Who's your lady friend,
Who's the little girlie by your side? . . .

An hour ticked past. Marie pulled the sheets up to her chin and waited. She noticed that Ernie's voice was becoming more slurred and his words muddled. He was obviously being plied with copious amounts of *vang blonk*.

Then she heard the inevitable, halting footsteps coming up the uncarpeted stairs. Marie hurriedly threw back the bedclothes and adopted a lewd pose, one leg bent at the knee to reveal her sex.

The bedroom door crashed open and Ernie staggered in, his tunic buttoned the wrong way. He belched loudly.

Marie forced a welcoming smile, which she hoped was seductive. She slipped off the shoulder straps of her chemise and cupped her full breasts in her hands, offering them to him.

But the girl's sexy gesture was wasted on the drunken sergeant.

His bloodshot eyes focused on the beautiful girl waiting for him on the bed. With a grunt, he shed his boots and tore off his trousers, fly buttons popping off in his haste. His Army-issue underpants still trapped round one ankle, he threw himself on top of the girl.

In his lust, Ernie never noticed the fear and horror contorting Marie's face as his weight crushed her. She turned her head away as, without the tenderness of foreplay, he penetrated her. Seconds later, he pumped his sperm into the girl, uttered a satisfied grunt and rolled off.

Within seconds, Sergeant Ernie Cornish fell into a deep sleep, snoring lustily.

Marie, lying wide awake beside him, ran her hands fearfully over her ripening belly.

CHAPTER SIX

July 10, 2000

Adam Cornish, blue eyes diluted by alcoholic emotion, slumped on his bar stool and propped up his face with his hands, the arms of his shabby jacket soaking in the beer-puddled counter. He took another swig of his pint and threw a chummy arm round the shoulders of Arthur Burfield, seated next to him in the Nine Bells.

The writer slurred: Would you really give up your holiday to help me out in Flanders, old son? Take a few snaps of the places and people for my great Ernie story? You won't go short of a few bevvies, I can promise you. That's a given."

Rod Russell, perched on the stool on the other side of the drunken reporter, the drink at his elbow ignored, listened intently. A few minutes later, unnoticed, he slipped out of the pub and into the shadow of a nearby shop doorway.

The undercover intelligence officer spoke into his mobile phone, reverting to his clipped, military tone. "Cornish is on the move, Colonel . . . and in the worst possible way.

"The piss-head extraordinaire is staggering off to Flanders to do some so-called research into Ernie Cornish's past. That's just what we didn't want him to do. Drunk though he is, the man might just stumble across something dangerous."

The phone quacked briefly in reply.

"Burfield, sir? Strange you should ask about him, because he is going with Cornish. So is that floozy reporter Ros Litherland . . . bizarrely, she seems to have taken a shine to the old soak. A drunken father figure, perhaps?"

The Colonel spoke again and Rod replied: "Yes, sir. I understand perfectly. I *will* go to Flanders to oversee our operation, but Cornish mustn't know I'm there. Yes, sir. It would look like too much of a coincidence if the whole office went."

The I.T. man chuckled and went on: "What a weird party this will be. The best scenario, sir, is that the whole thing will turn into a glorified booze cruise, and they'll learn nothing more important than that the Belgians make beer out of raspberries.

"The worst scenario . . . we know the Nazi bastards are on the march, Colonel. It only needs something like the advent of a new fuhrer to put a gale up their tails. Then there could be a bang as big as the start of World War Three."

At the other end of the phone the Colonel, hunching his shoulder to clamp the instrument under his left ear, accepted a cup of his favourite Darjeeling tea from his corporal orderly.

The burly, red-faced n.c.o, his ginger hair beginning to thin, placed it in the dead centre of the officer's pristine blotter, on the top of a walnut desk as bare as the Gobi Desert.

People were often fooled into thinking the Colonel was a Colonel Blimp, stuck in a Thirties world of grouse shooting, croquet and country house parties. But Rod and his fellow covert agents knew the reality was very different.

That crusty, Edwardian exterior was merely a mask. The Colonel had a mind as sharp as a squaddie's bayonet and a ruthless streak to go with it. He had been responsible for many a violent death . . . on both sides of the fence.

The Colonel gave a brief nod as the corporal silently placed a plate of digestive biscuits neatly to the right of the tea cup. The senior officer dunked one in the Darjeeling and listened carefully as Rod continued:

"Cornish and Burfield are in the local pub as I speak, pickling their livers in the local rot-gut brew. I've just been eavesdropping, sir. What I've heard seems to point to the fact that we have a decision to make about Cornish. What is your take on this, sir?"

The Colonel was already a light year ahead: "I want you to keep a very strict eye on Cornish in the Flemish boondocks. We'll see what, if anything, pops up. Then I'll make a decision as to whether to let him run or not.

"Maybe he can lead us to some useful information about these swastika gangsters. On the other hand, he might turn out to be a dangerous liability. In that event, you will have to close him down. Permanently.

"I suppose that, if you carry out an extreme termination, I must do the usual by sharing a bottle of rather good claret with you at the In-and-Out club.

"Keep in touch. This one looks tricky . . . very tricky indeed. I can smell blood. As you know, I'm never mistaken about that particular aroma."

Rod unthinkingly checked the little automatic pistol that made scarcely a bulge under the armpit of his sloppy, student-style sweater. He replied crisply: "Yes, sir. Understood, sir."

The Colonel concluded: "I don't like the feel of this Mr. Burfield. He seems to be cropping up at all the wrong times in all the wrong places. I don't believe in coincidences.

"I'm going to check up on the bugger. Phone again in 20 minutes and I'll let you know what I've found out."

The Colonel bellowed for his orderly. Seconds later, the corporal, wearing an ill-fitting but beautifully-cut blue suit that had once belonged to his boss, stood in front of the Colonel's desk.

The officer barked: "Arthur Burfield, Corporal! He's a photographer chappie on a local rag, the Kentish World, in Southdown. Find out about him, at the double."

The corporal spoke with a cockney twang: "Sir! Smell something fishy, sir?"

The Colonel snapped: Yes, I do. And it's not the usual aroma emanating from your underpants, either. I take it you know what to do, corporal?"

There was a tinge of insubordination in the orderly's reply: "I ought to, Colonel, after ten years dancin' attendance on you in this bloody pen-pusher's paradise.

"I enjoyed it a lot more when I was polishing your boots, and watching your back when the bullets were flying. When are you going to let me go, so's I can do a bit of real soldierin'?"

The Colonel fired a warning shot: "This *is* real soldiering, damn your insolence. We are still meting out death and confusion to our country's enemies, corporal. It's just that our battlefield is of a different nature. Even an n.c.o. of limited intelligence can see that, surely?"

The orderly stood silent and unbowed. The Colonel suddenly dropped his gaze. Although he would be the last to admit it, the corporal was the only man on this planet whom he would trust with his life.

He reflected he had already done just this a time or two in the past.

The corporal was the nearest thing to a friend the Colonel, isolated by his lonely and dangerous job, could call upon when the chips were down. There was a strange bond between this lowly man with two stripes and the senior officer with his crown and two pips.

When he spoke again, the Colonel's tone had mellowed: "You know you're too useful for me to let go. So you've been here ten years, have you, by God? Keep your nose clean, and I could be calling you 'sergeant' soon."

The corporal relaxed: "I'll get right on to finding out about Burfield, sir. Afterwards, shall I pop down to stores to see about that extra tape . . . the one you've been promising for the past 12 months, *sir*?"

His cocky manner belied an admiration for his boss bordering on hero worship. The corporal would never dream of serving another master while the Colonel lived and breathed.

The colonel snorted: "Stop being a barrack-room lawyer, or you'll lose the stripes you have already. Chop! Chop! I want that info yesterday."

After the corporal had marched out of his office, the Colonel pulled a leather-bound notebook from his pocket and made a note with a gold ballpoint pen. Yes, it *was* time for a spot of promotion for his friend."

Good man, the corporal. The very best.

Within five minutes, the orderly was back. He reported: "Easy one, sir. This so-called Arthur Burfield is already well known to us. Real name: Andre Lacroix. Born: 1942 in Zillebeke, West Flanders. Not far from Ypres, sir.

"Father: Wilfred Lacroix. He was a well-known collaborator during the last war. Wilfred is still alive and so is his wife, Denise, another rabid Nazi. They have an adopted son, Jacques, six years older than our Arthur/Andre.

"Wilfred is a nasty sod. He led a reign of terror during the war. It is pretty certain he sent several hundred Jews to their deaths, and packed off hundreds of men and women for forced labour."

The Colonel asked: "Why wasn't Lacroix brought to justice after the war?"

The corporal replied: "Because the locals wouldn't testify against him. They were shit scared of him, sir. And, even though he is now in his eighties, they still are. There are still plenty of Nazis in the area.

"The place has a long tradition of this sort of thing, sir. They even had their own S.S. division in the war. Now our Arthur has pulled on a pair of jackboots and is following in his dear old Dad's footsteps.

"He is a leading member of the local neo-Nazis. The records bods are sending us over a file on him, sir. There are snatched photographs of Arthur, all kitted-out in his storm-trooper gear, taking part in extreme right-wing rallies in Dixmuide, near Ypres.

"Our Arthur owns a cottage near Wipers. It's well buried in Polygon Wood, an old First World War battleground. Apparently, we've had a quiet look round, and found that our genial snapper stashes his Nazi gear there, including a Luger and ammunition.

"No known wife or partner, Colonel. He's probably too busy having wet dreams about Hitler to bother with that sort of thing."

Suddenly, the corporal's moon face, reddened by years of overseas service, cracked into a smile. He said: "Incidentally, the Nasties are planning to hold one of their jackboot rallies soon. Fancy hiring fancy dress and joining in the fun, sir?"

The Colonel scowled and growled: "Don't be ridiculous. That third stripe is by no means in the bag. Dismiss!"

He slid open a drawer in his desk, pulled out a pad, and made another neat note with his gold pen. He tore it off and signed it . . . just as he had put his name to death warrants before.

111

Rod snapped his mobile phone shut, assumed a vague, boffin-like air, and stepped back into the Nine Bells. He noted that Adam and Arthur had left their bar stools. They were now slurring at one another, seated in a huddle on a battered couch, its innards spilling out like grisly guts.

Imperceptibly, the computer buff edged to within earshot. Adam was holding forth: "Listen, me old mate, this Ernie stuff has got all the makings of a Hollywood biggie . . . sex and violence.

"Back here in the U.K. alone, it will rake in millions. The First World War is white hot. School-kids are going out to Flanders by the coach-load to learn all about it.

"The little bleeders even sit exams on the subject. Every day, a new magazine is launched about "Great-Grandad's war". It's nostalgia covered in dollar signs.

"There's a fortune to be made here. And I'm the one who's going to make it!"

Adam, his face crimson with booze and enthusiasm, went on: "Hollywood is going to eat this up, Arthur. Big time.

"They've always loved a good war film. Perhaps I can drop in a few Yank heroes, like Sergeant York and that pilot chap Eddie Rickenbacker, to make the thing more transatlantic.

"I'm getting a hard on just thinking about all those lovely dollars pouring into my bank account. Ernie is going to be the hero of the age. He fits the image to a 'T'. He had bags of guts, was a bit of a lad and good-looking with it.

"Matt Damon and Russell Crowe are going to fight each other to play my old granddad."

Arthur's eyes were wide with feigned admiration. He hiccoughed and took another mouthful of tepid beer before asking: "Where does the sex bit come in, Adam? I can't wait to hear about the X-rated stuff."

The couch creaked as the writer shifted his weight. He didn't notice the beer dribbling over the edge of his tankard as he leaned closer to Arthur Burfield. He confided: "Sex? It's there by the bucketful, chum.

"Ernie's sex life was the scandal of Southdown. I can tell you. They couldn't believe their eyes when he came back from Flanders, followed by a tasty French bit as his bride. What a looker!

"I've seen a picture of her in the family album. She had lovely dark, bobbed hair, boobs like a movie star and legs that went on forever. Her gorgeous looks were the first thing the Southdown women had against her.

"Worse, as far as the local biddies were concerned, the girl brought a little baby with her. It was obvious just what Granddad had been up to when they thought he was over there fighting for King and country.

"The couple strolled down the High Street, bold as brass—him wearing his uniform, although he was officially discharged, and she in a flouncy French gown.

"*Quelle scandale!* Ernie quickly put it around that they were legally hitched. But the gossips just nodded and whispered about a wedding that had a whiff of the shotgun about it.

"The men-folk envied our Ernie his French tart. They secretly lusted after her and tried to peek on her washing line to see if she had some of the oo-la-la knickers they'd seen in pictures of the Moulin Rouge.

"But all they saw were rows of nappies. Marie was ahead of them, and aired her undies indoors. Their next-door neighbours swore they heard the springs in the Cornishes' bed going ten to the dozen all night, every night."

Arthur exclaimed: "Bloody hell, Adam—that baby must have been your dad, Albert Cornish. I remember him well. He and his wife, Polly, used to run the old Three Horseshoes.

"They were a lovely couple . . . a real old-fashioned landlord and landlady. He had a proper-sized corporation with waistcoat and gold watch-chain to go with it. She was dressed up behind the bar, as though about to do a music hall turn.

"Everyone knew old Albert was good for a few bob if any of his customers fell on hard times. Your Dad had a heart of gold, young Adam."

Arthur nudged the reporter playfully, winking and making him spill yet more beer. He went on: "Just like you, eh? Think of all those young girl reporters you've helped over the years

"There'll be plenty more nookie to come when you're rolling in dough, you old rascal. And I hope you'll spare a bit for your old snapper buddy."

Rod sipping his pint, edged yet closer. He continued, unnoticed, to listen into the increasingly drunken conversation. Adam had passed boozer's high and was now sinking into boozer's gloom.

His blue eyes filled with tears and he gripped Arthur's arm. The reporter said sadly: "My dear old granddad, too, had the proverbial 1,000-carat heart. They must run in our family. But he was too wonderful for his own good.

"After all that he'd done for that Froggie wife of his—marrying her when he got her in the family way, even though he was gassed and wounded—she turned round and did the dirty on him.

"One day, Marie simply dumped Ernie. She walked out on him without a second thought . . . just fucked off, leaving my granddad with a young kid to bring up all by himself.

"That was a French slapper's way of saying 'thank you' for standing by her, bringing her home and waiting on her hand and foot. She never wanted for anything in the short time she was in Southdown, I can tell you."

Adam, spilt ale flecking his unruly beard, wiped his sleeve across his eyes and went on: "So my lousy French grandmother never saw her English grandson—poor little me.

"Forget birthday and Christmas presents, I never got so much as a card from her in all those years. And all my dear granddad got was a set of divorce papers through the post.

"Marie Lebrun Cornish must be dead by now. Good riddance to her. I hope the bitch is burning in hell."

Arthur put his hand over Adam's and gently but insistently probed for more information about this old scandal. Rod leant over, straining to hear above the hubbub of the crowded pub.

But Adam had slipped out of the world of the Nine Bells into one of his explosive "turns", a reddish mist blurring his faltering vision. His vividly blue eyes were ablaze with rage.

I'd have made the filthy, foreign whore pay, just as Hitler made the scum with the hooked-noses pay. She'd soon have wished she'd never shat on my granddad, my dad and me.

One of Adam's favourite wartime scenes flashed into his head. He saw a Nazi concentration camp with its wire, dogs, watch-towers and black-uniformed SS guards going about their cruel business.

They were herding, whips rising and falling, dozens of naked, cowering women down an avenue of barbed wire. At the end of this road of misery were the doors of what Adam knew to be waiting gas chambers.

There's my grandmother, stripped naked like the rest. She doesn't look so cocky now, her back, buttocks and legs striped by the lashes. She's running the gauntlet to a well-deserved choking

"Oh, how she'll scream when those doors clang shut behind her and the gas comes pouring in. That's the price evil Marie should pay. Hitler would have loved that sort of retribution, all right.

He would know how to deal with the likes of less-than-human Marie LeBrun.

"Hey! Wake up! You all right, Adam, me old son?"

Adam was startled to realise that Arthur was shaking him gently by the shoulder, mock concern written over his ruddy, farm-boy features. Dizzily, the reporter shook his head, slowly emerging from his juicy vision.

Arthur peered closely at him, saying: "For a minute, I thought you were going to pass out there. Was somebody walking across your grave, or were you dead scared at the thought of buying the next round?"

When Adam, swaying, stood up and pushed through the drinkers to the bar, he was surprised to find his fantasy had given him a rare erection. His cock was as stiff as when he looked at those smuggled magazines he kept under his bed.

He reached the bar and, waiting to buy two more pints, noticed Ros Litherland standing a few feet away. He could hardly miss her, with her long, blonde hair tumbling down her shoulders and trademark tight, blue sweater straining over her breasts.

She seemed to have an inexhaustible supply of these markedly undersized garments. He wondered what she would look like without a bra. Or even without a stitch on.

The girl was part of a group of young male reporters from the World. They were noisily downing cocktails with silly names such as Slow Screw Against The Wall, Slippery Nipple and Sex on the Beach.

Adam grabbed hold of the bar to steady himself and gazed at the 25-year-old girl and her tempting 25-year-old melons. Unusually, his erection persisted.

Ross caught him in mid-stare. Even in his befuddled state, the ageing writer noticed she didn't drop her eyes. They looked into his with an expression that seemed damn close to invitation.

Was he imagining things? No, the girl was definitely signaling that she fancied him. He was not too pissed or too past it to recognise that look. Anyway, Adam had to admit he was a bloody sight more interesting than those spotty-faced nobodies she was hanging around with.

With his distinguished beard and lived-in face, he believed he *could* appear to be that latter-day Hemingway.

The young male reporters were all looking at Adam now, sneering and smirking . . . letting him know they thought he was nothing but a dirty, old man.

A flash of inner fury: *A few more for the gas chambers.*

Ros smiled a faint, enigmatic smile, turned away and bent to retrieve her hand-bag, ready to pay for the next drinks. Her short skirt rode up high, revealing an expanse of firm and inviting thighs. Surely that couldn't be accidental?

In spite of the fog of alcohol that swirled round Adam's brain, scarcely-remembered reflexes from the mating ritual kicked in. He said thickly: "Hi, there, Ros, let me buy you that one. After all, we're soon going to be shipmates."

She turned and flicked back her hair in a gesture that made the sweater pull even tighter over her boobs. "O.k.,

Adam. Never let it be said that I turned down the chance of drinking with one of the World's legends."

Adam looked at the girl suspiciously, but could detect no trace of sarcasm. Was she for real?

He tried a joke: "Would you like a Screw Against the Wall?"

Ros replied archly: "That depends . . ."

He ordered the strangely exotic drink from Jim, whose face remained professionally impassive. As a barman in a newspaper's local pub, he had seen it all before.

Adam took a tighter grip on the bar. Ros didn't seem to be fazed by his inebriated state. Just as well, he thought, she would have to get used to it in Flanders. Now he had to pull himself together, or a great opportunity would be lost.

All thoughts of buying a beer for Arthur Burford vanished as he moved on to the next step in the ritual. He suggested: "Let's sit down."

Ros replied: "That seems like a good idea."

The reporter again studied her closely, but she didn't seem to be taking the piss. They sat on one of the wooden settles, which seemed to have come from a sale of surplus church property.

Adam said: "When we're away, you should watch me at work. There's a lot you can learn."

Coolly: "I bet there is, maestro."

There was no mistaking it. This gorgeous girl, less than half his age, was definitely giving him the come-on. Adam felt a rush of elation, swiftly followed by a bout of dizziness.

That old magic, which had beguiled a multitude of eager young girl reporters into his bed, was obviously still at work here. He stroked his Hemingway beard suggestively.

Adam wondered how this one would perform. Most of the girls left him, a look of horror on their pretty faces, when his bedroom demands became more than they could stomach.

Every girl, like wife Anna, left him in the end. That, of course, would change when he had the heady aphrodisiac of power and money to offer them.

Adam looked at Ros, calmly sipping her strange concoction. He wondered: "Will she be the one who likes it all? I mustn't frighten her until I've got her hooked. Flanders will be the place for that. We'll be thrown together there. I'll play her like a fish."

Adam noticed with alarm that the booze had at last made a flop of him. That Old Rascal Time was up to his tricks. But, if it came to the prospect of sex, he would give it his best shot.

He clinked glasses with Ros, now regarding him quizzically. He drank a silent toast to himself: "Upwards and onwards. And, if I get lucky tonight, inwards, as well."

The reporters jeered as Adam staggered from the Nine Bells with the discreet support of Ros. He was well past rising to the bait. As she steered the ageing drunk into the Southdown night, Ros had her own reasons to ignore the jibes.

Barely minutes later, Rod and then Arthur left the pub.

Rod, speaking once again into his mobile phone in the doorway, spelled out Ros Litherland's name. At the other end of the call, the Colonel and the Corporal went to work.

There was a three-minute pause before the phone quacked back to life. Rod gave a whistle of surprise before snapping the phone shut.

"Christ . . . Mossad, Heavy stuff here," he said softly.

Adam opened a bleary eye as sunlight poked the same cruel finger on his face through a gap in the bedroom curtains. His mouth tasted like the proverbial Greek wrestler's genital-wear and his head pounded.

He steeled himself to open the other eye. The reporter discovered he was lying naked in bed. His clothes were neatly piled on a chair.

On top of them was selection of garments, obviously belonging to a young female. He focused with difficulty on a minimal thong, minimal bra and minimal skirt.

There was also a sexy blue sweater, which looked familiar.

Adam painfully turned his head and discovered he was sharing the pillow with a tangle of long, blonde hair. He slid his hand under the bedclothes and encountered firm, naked flesh.

He decided he was in bed with the delectable Ros Litherland. In spite of his crippling hangover, he felt a jolt of sexual electricity. Adam, barely suppressing a groan, raised himself slowly to a sitting position.

Ros turned towards him. He noticed for the first time that she had large, grey eyes. They were blank . . . without the slightest trace of emotion.

Her expression didn't change and she lay passively as he pulled down the bed-clothes, revealing her nudity. Her breasts were even better than in his heated imaginings.

Adam gazed at their inviting fullness, the nipples perking in the morning air. He accepted their invitation and slowly kissed each in turn. Ros neither objected nor responded.

Finally, he kissed her on the lips and asked: "Was I any good?"

She replied in a neutral tone: "Good at what?"

Adam smiled at what he thought was a jest with a slight edge. But Ros's eyes and lips remained expressionless. He felt a tug of worry and shame. A chill gripped his heart.

"Sorry. I'd had a lot to drink last night. I . . ."

"Don't be."

"I've got some coffee in the kitchen . . ."

Ros pointed to a cup on her bedside table. "You have. It's of the instant variety. And there's no milk."

Adam propped himself up against the yellowing pillow and asked: "Would you like some more? I'll go . . ."

She interrupted: "Is coffee all you have to offer a naked girl in your bed? It looks as though I'm in for a boring trip to Flanders, doesn't it?"

The writer, head throbbing and cock inert, felt panic rising. It was a long time since he'd performed. And that hadn't exactly been a roaring success. He decided it was better not to make the attempt than to be humiliated by failure.

Ros lay calmly gazing at him, running her hands slowly over her breasts. Waiting. She could guess what the problem was, seeing the state and age of him.

But the Mossad agent knew she must hook him here and now. She had to forge a bond to keep them close. It was a vital part of her assignment.

Adam said desperately: "Honestly, Ros, much though I want to, I'm still hammered by last night's booze. I just don't feel up to it this minute . . . brewer's droop and all that.

"Let's wait until we get away. We'll go at it like rabbits. I can promise you that. I fancy you like crazy. It's just that . . ."

Adam bought himself time by climbing out of bed and padding into the kitchen, his dangling member mocking him As he put the battered kettle under the tap, his mind came up with a possible solution to his problem.

It reminded him of advertisements in his secret magazines for so-called miraculous "little blue pills". He had always dismissed these absurdly-priced tablets as probably being made of coloured chalk.

Now Adam gave them serious thought. He could buy these without a doctor's prescription.

The reporter spooned coffee from a jar, sticky with age. He thought of the advertisements, illustrated by pictures of passionately-embracing and obviously well satisfied, couples.

Could he and Ros be like them in a day or two? He went to the fridge and, sure enough, there was no milk. The kettle boiled and he filled the cups with black coffee.

Adam wondered how long would it take for the pills to reach him if he posted his order today. He hoped the postman would bring them before he left for Flanders.

Adam felt better as he carried the two steaming cups into the bedroom.

Ros sat up and stretched before taking her coffee. The effect was both dramatic and erotic. But, to Adam's dismay, it had no visible effect on him.

She told him: "Come on, get back into bed. I haven't given up hope yet." She looked at his flaccid penis and asked it: "What do I have to do to make you stand to attention and salute, Private Member?

"Perhaps you are in need of a helping hand?"

The naked girl reached across, held it between the fingers and thumb of her right hand and gently massaged it. There was no effect.

Ros delved into her memory, conjuring up those training sessions that had stripped her of every shred of feminine modesty.

Adam's cheeks were aflame with humiliation and frustration as Ros continued to address the unresponsive cock: "What would it take to wake you up, I wonder? Wait while I have a word with the man to whom you are attached."

She asked the reporter: "Come on, you must have a way of making Mr. Member do his duty? Obviously it's not a wank under the bedclothes. Shall I talk dirty to you? I can do filthy.

"Or perhaps you like a girl to give you a golden shower and pee all over you. Would that do the trick? I can be a stern Miss Whiplash, too. Just show me a leather belt and I'll turn you into a happy slave."

Ros looked at the penis lolling between her fingers, soft as a boiled prawn. She went on: "You can tell Ros. She's not a shrinking violet, especially when she is feeling as randy as she is right now."

Adam couldn't believe these words were coming from the lips of the innocent-looking reporter, who routinely called on vicars in the course of her duties.

The reporter, making a vain effort to hide his sagging belly with his hands, turned away. Should he reveal the dark secret that had cost him his wife and most of his girlfriends?

Ros was relentless: "Come on, Adam, help me out here, like I'm trying to help you. We both want a good time, don't we? Talk to me. What turns you on?"

He stammered: "I like to think about the terrible things I'd do to people who are stopping me achieving my true destiny."

Ros looked at those vivid blue eyes, now beginning to spark up, and felt a surge of nausea. This was one nasty weirdo all right. But, she supposed, that was only to be expected.

She had solemnly sworn to do her duty to her country, and that was just what she would do. She told herself what was happening in this bedroom was more important than commanding a tank or flying a jet fighter.

Ros fought down the sickness and asked matter-of-factly: "How does that work then? What do I have to do and say to turn you into the Southdown Stallion?" She wiped fear and repugnance from her face.

His reply was so incomprehensible and unexpected, it stunned her.

"I think about the Goldsteins a lot."

"*The Goldsteins!* Why on earth would they turn you on?"

Now it came out in a rush: "Those bastards have held me back all the years I've been at the World. They were afraid of being outshone by my talent. They know I am cleverer than they are.

"They secretly fear me because I'm not only better than them, but better than the poxy Editor and everyone else on that pathetic rag. Yes, the Goldsteins detest me because of my talent.

"If they had promoted me and let me realise my real potential, I would have been an embarrassment. Yet I am the one with a Voice that tells me that I have greatness."

Adam was now sitting bolt upright in the bed, his blue eyes flaming. Ros was ashen-faced with shock.

The ageing journalist went on, his voice harsh: "I hate those bloody Yids I hate all Yids. Hitler was right. They're all part of the Jewish conspiracy to take over the world.

"I'd like to send those Goldsteins to a Nazi concentration camp and see how they liked those apples! Give 'em a whiff of the old Zyclon B."

Ros whispered hoarsely: "Is that what you imagine when you want an orgasm? What do I have to do in all this?"

He commanded: "Repeat everything I tell you, and play with my cock. You *did* ask."

The girl turned her face away as she began to masturbate him. She felt near to fainting, but managed to whisper: "I'm ready to start."

Suddenly, the pathetic old loser was transformed into a towering tyrant. He snapped: "The Goldsteins are scum and must be punished."

Ros stifled a dry heave and repeated obediently: "The Goldsteins are scum and must be punished."

"They should be hung with piano wire from meat-hooks—just like Hitler hung his traitors."

"I can't remember all that, Adam . . ."

He shouted, spittle dripping from his chin, blue eyes raging: "Say it! You must say it! I command you!"

Fear gripped Ros by the throat. This man was definitely dangerous. With a gut-wrenching effort she managed to croak: "They should be hung . . . er . . . like Hitler's enemies."

"Hang the fucking Jews"

Her voice was failing as her mouth dried. She croaked: "Hang the fucking Jews."

"Again! Again!"

Ros tried to pretend to herself that this was all happening to somebody else. She felt his penis harden in her hand. She knew his climax must be near.

Adam writhed on the bed and roared: "Get astride me! Ride me! Now! Quickly! Quickly!"

The girl obeyed, her face whiter than the grubby sheets on the odorous bed. Within seconds, Adam bucked and orgasmed inside her.

It was over.

He lay panting. He wondered if she would desert him after this first lesson. Ros climbed off his sweat-slick body and quickly began to dress, her stomach and mind in turmoil.

Adam called to her, his voice normal now: "Ros, I want to see you again. After this morning, I know we can be terrific together. And, with my guidance, you can be a brilliant reporter.

"With your looks, there could even be a part for you in the film."

The girl was shaking so much her fingers fumbled with the buttons and clips. She knew this disgusting act was her duty. The first part of her mission was successfully accomplished.

Ros daren't, in her present state, contemplate what horrors lay ahead. She pulled on her sweater and made for the door. Ros steeled herself to call over her shoulder: "Let me know the arrangements for Flanders."

Adam relaxed. She was still o.k. with him. His life was already taking a turn for the better. He heard her high heels clatter down the stairs. The front door slammed.

In the street, Ros Litherland, a.k.a. Ros Goldstein, vomited into the gutter.

CHAPTER SEVEN

August 2, 1917

The young Bavarian soldiers of the 16th Reserve Infantry Regiment, packed tightly together in a cattle truck, laughed and joked as the train wheezed asthmatically through a ravaged landscape.

Each turn of the wheels took the boisterous students in uniform, still caked in the mud of the trenches, farther from the killing ground surrounding the Ypres salient.

Despite the jollity, the soldiers' eyes betrayed the horrors they had seen. The men's voices were a little too shrill, their laughter smacked of the desperate.

The youths' relief at this reprieve from death and danger was writ large on their young-old faces.

Hitler propped himself in a corner, squatting on the mouldering straw that covered the floor of the truck. His lip curled in contempt beneath his heavy moustache at his comrades' levity. He steadfastly refused to join in.

The untidy *gefreiter* dismissed these so-called soldiers as stupid schoolboys, let out of the classroom for their summer holiday. University students? More like over-educated idiots! He was glad he wasn't one of them.

These were the pathetic, over-privileged few he had never been able to join. So-called academics and cunning, conniving Jews and Jew-lovers. Communists and Freemasons had seen to that.

They'd sensed his latent genius and pulled up the drawbridges at their castles of learning. But now Adolf Hitler was above the petty humiliations that had once stabbed his heart.

He had learned at the University of Life. Those street-level lessons would enable him to achieve the greatness his Voice assured him would be his. That was why Fate had protected him for these past three dangerous years.

When he is Fuhrer, these people, who think they are so superior, will dance to his tune. A pretty lively one it will be, too. He promised himself that.

Hitler continued to ignore the lively soldiers in field—grey. A non-smoker, he sniffed disapprovingly as they lit pipes and cigarettes, filling the wagon with tobacco smoke.

The scruffy *gefreiter* seemed all but invisible to the former students. In spite of his Iron Cross Second Class, it appeared that, to them, he was a person of no account.

They chattered around him like starlings on the spree. Men who had fought in hell since the autumn of 1914, regarded their new posting as the most wonderful stroke of luck.

A mole at regimental headquarters had told them they were about to enjoy several weeks of paradise. They were bound, in this elderly piece of rolling stock, for a Shangri La, far from the war.

The youngsters let their imaginations roam happily over the joys that might lie at the end of this rumbling line. They called back and forth about scalding hot baths and bars of rich soap.

They would dine on food that wasn't cold from its often-lethal journey from the cookers to the front line. My God! There might even be women who weren't whores . . . girls who smiled, chatted and fucked for the pleasure of their company.

These dream girls' bodies would have the heady scent of soap and perfume instead of the rancid sweat of a thousand joyless couplings.

The Bavarians bathed in a warm glow of anticipation. The filthy, louse-ridden troops who, just hours ago, daren't tempt fate by thinking of tomorrow, looked forward to weeks of bliss.

The headquarters spy, in return for a couple of cigars, had given them the magic name of this heaven-on-earth. The soldiers rolled it round their tongues like a fine brandy . . . Hochstadt, near Muhlhausen, in Alsace.

A few hours into the journey, they rolled back the sliding doors of the wagon and peered out. Yes, they were definitely rattling southwards. It looked as though the mole's information was correct. God bless him!

They gazed in wonder at the passing countryside, as though it were a strange and exotic land. There were green fields, unscarred by shell holes, and trees, untouched leaves fluttering in a caressing breeze.

The soldiers stared at cottages, thatched roofs as neat and intact as the day the reeds were laid. Women and girls were hanging out washing and working the fields. The only sign of war was the absence of men.

They were either dead, wounded or still at the Front.

The Bavarians sniffed the fresh air wafting into their fetid cattle wagon as though it were a rare wine. There was no trace of poison gas, shell-hole latrines or rotting bodies.

This was the life!

A corporal delved into his pack and pulled out a mouth organ. Soon its sweet notes were evoking pictures of faithful sweethearts and cosy welcomes awaiting returning heroes.

Like the Tommies they faced daily across No-Man's Land, the German boys dreamed of home. They, too, didn't want to die . . . to lie under wooden crosses in the sea of mud.

They wanted to return, limbs and lungs intact, to run races, jump high and long and play on the sports fields of their Munich university.

The buckles on the Bavarians' uniform belts spelled out "God Is With Us". But sometimes, amid the horrors of an artillery barrage or gas attack, it seemed He had deserted them. Why did He permit this carnage?

The mouth organ played sad and sentimental airs, and the troops' eyes moistened as memories crowded in.

One of the soldiers wiped his eyes with the back of his hand and shouted to the musician: "Play something cheerful, for God's sake, Hans. You'll give us all a nervous breakdown.

"Cut out the mournful crap and cheer us up with some jolly marches."

Another voice roared: "Balls to the marches! Keep those for when the Kaiser pays us a visit. By the way, has anyone seen our esteemed Emperor in the Front Line trenches lately?"

The corporal, in a huff, put the mouth organ back in his pack, muttering: "There's no pleasing anybody these days."

Speculation about their destination began again. One of the young soldiers, a student like the others, called out respectfully to a portly, middle-aged private.

The man was sitting in the corner opposite Hitler. He was leaning comfortably on his pack, legs stretched out in a narrow gap amid the press of bodies. The soldier had pulled off his boots and was airing his feet in the breeze from the open door.

The student asked: "Hey, Professor Solomons, You were the fount of all knowledge in Munich. Can you give us students a little lecture on Hochstadt and Muhlhausen?"

The wagon fell silent. Professor Isaac Solomons commanded more respect than any of the officers of the regiment. Rumour had it that he had thrice refused a commission in the 16th. R.I.R.

The Professor pulled a pipe from his tunic pocket and filled it slowly and methodically from a pouch. His former students waited patiently, as always, for his measured words.

As the ageing private lit the pipe and puffed yet more tobacco smoke into the general fug, his sharp eyes noticed *Gefreiter* Hitler giving an exaggerated wince. The Professor stored away the information for later.

Isaac Solomons, once a rabbi, promised himself it would soon be pay-back time for that nasty, loud-mouthed Jew-hater. But first, he would deliver his lecture. His former students settled down, prepared to hang on his every word.

The Professor, who had secretly primed himself, assumed his lecture-room manner: "The name Hochstadt, my unlearned friends, is apparently derived from 'Staette des Hoho, meaning 'places of the Hoho'. Hoho would have been the name of a tribe."

This information was received with catcalls.

"Ho! Ho! Bloody ho! This is pretty boring stuff, sir. Do you know if the girls there are pretty and willing? Do they forget their knickers? That's what we *really* want to know."

The Professor was unperturbed. He stroked his prominent nose, and his pipe emitted yet another large cloud of smoke. He noticed with amusement that Hitler mimicked a coughing fit.

Inside the little *gefreiter's* head angry thoughts were building like a thunder-cloud. This was just the sort of airy-fairy, superior kind of Yid intellectual who was poisoning the world.

Professor Solomons continued: "Hochstadt has been devastated by countless armies through the centuries. In 1813, the area was occupied by the French."

Boos.

"In 1814, they were replaced by the Russians."

Boos.

"In 1815 the Russians, in their turn, were replaced by the Bavarians."

Loud and prolonged cheers.

"In 1849, it was the turn of the Prussians . . ."

Restrained applause.

A fresh-faced youth, dirt-spattered tunic unbuttoned, shouted: "We'll be glad when we've had enough of this boring stuff, Prof. What about Muhlhausen? Is that more interesting. Can we dip our wicks there, *sir.*"

The Professor poked around in the bowl of his pipe before relighting it. He was pleased to see the draught from the open door wafted the smoke straight towards *Gefreiter* Hitler.

Solomons noted that the lullaby of the train's wheels had already sent some of the exhausted soldiers to sleep. But Hitler's vivid blue, hate-filled eyes were riveted on him.

The academic droned on: "Muhlhausen is an interesting place, situated in the picturesque Unstrut River Valley. A certain Johann Sebastian Bach was the organist of the Divi Blasii Church . . ."

Hitler tensed in his corner as the word 'Muhlhausen' triggered a weird premonition. Instinctively, he knew this was one of the secluded places he would choose to visit vengeance on Jews and other scum.

The crowded railway wagon faded from his vision. Instead, Hitler saw a strange and sinister camp, which he knew was called Muhlhausen. It was ringed by barbed wire and watch-towers.

Guards in black uniforms strutted between rows of wooden huts. They paused from time to time, savagely to whip the camp's cowering, emaciated inmates.

Hitler knew without doubt that these human skeletons were Jews. Every one of them bore the mark of death. In his vision, he was the Fuhrer and this place belonged to him. Other camps, just like it, were his, too.

The scene faded and the *gefreiter* was compelled to shift his position on the wagon floor. He had to ease the embarrassing erection that threatened to explode in his trousers.

Hitler hurriedly switched his thoughts from his sado-erotic fantasy to a problem he had recently so neatly solved. He had cured the hiccough in his life caused by that clingy French peasant girl.

Although she was not a Jewess, thank God, she could have been a stone in his shoe on his journey to greatness.

On reflection, Hitler congratulated himself on the masterly fashion in which he had dealt with Marie LeBrun. He had been prompted, as usual, by his infallible Voice.

She had not complained about his unpalatable orders. Therefore, although LeBrun was a potential embarrassment, he would allow her to survive. For now.

This was a soft-hearted gamble on his part. After all, he was planning to tell future adoring millions that Germany was his only mistress.

Hitler's thoughts were interrupted by the Professor. The fat Yid was addressing him directly, his tone both teasing and insulting. This arrogant private was still speaking as though in a university lecture room.

Solomon's student audience sniggered as he said: "Now let us turn to the strange case of our patriot *par excellence*, *Gefreiter* Adolf Hitler. That is him over there in the corner, wincing this very second at the smoke from my pipe.

"He is probably wincing also because, as he has so often and so loudly declared, he can't stand Jews and Freemasons. And I, gentlemen, I am both. I tick two important boxes of Hitler's hates.

"But, to my mind, his worst offence is of bombarding us with his boring lectures on how he would rule the world. So let me now give Herr Hitler something of a counter barrage."

The students settled back to enjoy the baiting. To most of them, Adolf Hitler was a figure of fun and an outsider. He wore the same uniform, ate the same food and fought the same battles.

But scruffy, eccentric, ill-educated *Gefreiter* Hitler would never be one of them. He was so radically different to the other men of the 16th R.I.R. that they had derisively nicknamed him the "White Crow".

The Professor warmed to his theme: "Our humble comrade has dreams, my students, dreams so great you can hardly imagine them. He dreams of being Fuhrer of all Germany . . . even though he can't even make sergeant when all around are falling.

"What a comic picture this delusion conjures up! Let us hope he will shave off that ridiculous moustache before goose-stepping through a Jew-less Germany to glory."

The soldiers laughed loudly at their professor's stinging words. The private reached into a breast pocket of his tunic and unfolded a sheet of paper. He made a great show of relighting his pipe while pretending closely to examine the note.

Solomons went on: "I shall now demonstrate the value of research. For my fellow Freemasons in Vienna and Munich have sent me information our patriotic and vociferous Fuhrer-to-be would rather forget."

In his corner, Hitler remained silent. His eyes flamed with fury and his hands clenched so tightly the nails bit into his palms. He mentally blocked the private's ludicrous words, words which amounted to blasphemy.

He took refuge in his thoughts: "No-one must *ever* question my words, my actions, my life! Never! Whatever I do and say will one day become history. I will follow the dictates of my Voice and become the greatest German of all time.

"People who mock me and people who stand in my way will pay the price. This Jew will be the first."

Hitler glanced around the crowded cattle wagon. There were a select few who were not under the professor's thrall. Hitler had secretly recruited them as knights for his holy crusade.

Authoritative, muscular Regimental Sergeant-Major Max Amann caught Hitler's eye and, understanding, gave a barely perceptible nod. Feldwebel Johann Karlatz and Corporal Franz Muller followed suit.

These men had listened, entranced, to the *gefreiter's* impassioned speeches in Black Marie's café at Fournes-en-Weppe. They, like Marie Lebrun and millions to come, had fallen under the spell of his hypnotic eyes.

Although Hitler was of lower Army rank, these soldiers had gratefully accepted promises of plum appointments when the *gefreiter* came to power. They had sworn him an oath of allegiance. To them, the bicycling messenger was a man of destiny.

Now, in this dawdling train, their Fuhrer is silently giving them their first task. He wants this lard-like Jew dealt with. Hitler's men were eager to obey. There are many ways for a man to die on the battlefield.

Professor Isaac Solomons continued his attack on Hitler, oblivious to the fact that he was signing his own death warrant.

He referred to his note and went on: "Now, let us see . . . our great German is actually not a German at all. He is an Austrian.

"I wonder why he hates those whom he calls 'university intellectuals'? Let me give you a clue. In 1907, young Herr Hitler failed the entrance examination to Vienna Academy of Fine Arts.

"He was also turned down for the School of Architecture. Reason? He didn't even have a school leaving certificate."

Solomons glanced across to Hitler and was delighted to see his face was ashen. The man appeared to be almost catatonic with anger.

The Professor read on to his captivated audience: "After these humiliating rejections, our friend is said to have sunk lower and lower. From 1908 until 1913, he was reduced to living in a flophouse.

"Existing in a slum trench is something of a step up for him. It is of interest that, even in the flophouse, Herr Hitler's political speeches were considered something of a joke. Things haven't changed much, have they gentlemen?"

The soldiers sniggered. Hitler seethed.

His tormentor went on relentlessly: "Now we come to his patriotism; in 1913, Hitler fled from Vienna to Munich to escape military service. The following year, police tracked him down.

"But he wriggled out of the Army by saying he wasn't fit enough to be a soldier."

Solomons pointed at Hitler and declared: "He looks fit enough to me. Doesn't he to you, gentlemen? He is fit enough to toady to the officers. I hear our great Fuhrer-to-be even washes their underclothes. Our next leader is a washerwoman!"

Referring once more to his piece of paper, Solomons went on: "Hitler, apparently, was still feeling poorly on February

5, 1914. That was when he was dragged before a board at Salzberg and pleaded for his call-up to be postponed.

"Those Austrians swallowed everything sickly Adolf said, and they declared him unfit for military service. No wonder that, when war broke out that August, Hitler didn't want anything to do with his native land.

"The people there, gentlemen, knew too much about Hitler 'the patriot'. Feeling that call-up was inevitable anyway, he made a grand gesture. He wrote to no less a personage that our own Bavarian monarch, King Ludwig 111, asking to join his army.

"His Majesty must have said, 'I'd be honoured to have you, Adolf.' So here he is gentlemen, sitting in his small corner among the despised intellectuals of Colonel List's finest."

The sergeant-major shouted: "The Colonel wouldn't be alive now, if it wasn't for *Gefreiter* Hitler. Take a look at that Iron Cross! Do you have one of those, Solomons?"

But Max Amann's words were drowned in a chorus of laughter and catcalls. Solomons tucked the paper back into his pocket and continued with his baiting.

"I now come to a familiar theme of Hitler's boring rants . . . that the sexual urge makes fools of weak men. Yet we all know that he has a child mistress tucked away above the Café Au Fossoyeur.

"We all wonder at what this tender youngster sees in this pitiful White Crow. Do they spend their nights together discussing the iniquity of Jews, Marxists and Freemasons? Does she orgasm when Adolf tells her how he will rule the world?

"Those only-too-audible bed springs tell another story. Shame on the man who has always told us that Germany will be his only mistress! Or perhaps he is practising his goose-step on the bed?"

The Bavarians roared. This was the stuff to give the troops, bored out of their wits by this seemingly endless train journey

The Professor said: "Now that girl-child has suddenly and mysteriously vanished. Where has she gone? What did she do to be kicked out of Hitler's bed and life?

"Did she have the temerity to tell him he wasn't the greatest German of all time? Did he find out that she was a Jew, a Marxist or, even worse, a female Freemason?"

Solomons pointed once more at Hitler: "Tell us, my mighty *gefeiter*, what have you done with your tasty French tart? Where have you hidden her? And why?"

Hitler hugged his knees and said nothing.

This insolent nobody had signed his own death warrant for a second time. He had now touched on the very secret that Hitler was keeping close to his breast.

In a flash of memory, he saw Marie, sobbing in their Comines bedroom.

She had just delivered the nauseating news, and her hands were clasped protectively across her guilty belly. Hitler felt again the white heat of his anger. But when it had come to solving that problem, he had acted coolly, calmly and efficiently.

With a few, deft brush strokes, he had painted Marie LeBrun out of the picture of his life. Now here was this slimy Yid picking at his secret like a scab on a wound.

Hitler decided that Private Solomon's death was not only imminent, but would be infinitely painful.

People must learn never to speak of Marie LeBrun.

October 4, 1917

Paradise was lost. The nightmare had returned. A restless darkness cloaked Lizy in the battle of the Aisne River. From time to time, the gloom was torn apart by the pitiless light of flares. They revealed sprawled bodies, stunted trees and, all too often, writhing wounded.

In the trenches of the 16th R.I.R., running with water from a recent downpour, a small patrol was assembling. A gap had already been cut in the wire for them to creep into No-Man's Land.

The men had been told that the staff needed information about the enemy troops facing them. Those arrogant, be-medalled generals, living in luxury far behind the German lines, wanted these details at any cost . . . except to themselves.

Regimental Sergeant-Major Max Amann had already given instructions to the men who were to accompany him on this mission. Now, in a low, rasping voice, he called their names:

"Corporal Muller."

- *"Present, sir."*

"Sergeant Karlatz."

- *"Present, Sergeant-Major."*

Private Solomons."

"I'm here."

"SIR!"

"I'm here, SIR."

At a softly-spoken word of command, the little group clambered over the sandbags on the parapet of the trench. The soldiers remaining watched the dark figures melt away. Each guiltily thanked his god he was not among them.

The patrol's comrades waited anxiously, checking their pocket watches and peering out into the wasteland in front of the Bavarian lines.

Machine-guns suddenly rattled in the darkness, sounding like a summer hail storm on a corrugated iron shelter. Lone rifles cracked. Desultory shelling began from the French lines, to be answered by German guns.

To the watching eyes, occasional flares failed to find the men of the patrol. The troops reassured themselves that their comrades were all experienced men, who knew that freezing like statues all but made them invisible.

There was a long, menacing silence, suddenly shattered by a single shot. Silence again wrapped the battlefield, as though in a funeral shroud.

Dawn began to paint the sky a dirty grey. On both sides of the lines, the men stood-to on their trenches' fire-steps, peering apprehensively into No-Man's Land.

For the half-light at the beginning and end of each day were the best times for an attack. As the sky lightened, Germans and Frenchmen relaxed and stood down.

The men of the 16th R.I.R. still watched through the wire for the patrol. As the minutes ticked by and full daylight was about to blossom, hope faded. The Bavarians began to boil water for their breakfast coffee.

Just as the sun rimmed the murky horizon, crouched figures wriggled through the gap in the wire. Elated, the soldiers in the trench saw that the returning men were dragging a prisoner with them.

The patrol handed the quaking *poilu* over to a sergeant. Then they collapsed, panting, on the trenches' streaming duckboards, backs resting against the mud.

Minutes later, List himself came splashing down the trench and clapped Amann on the shoulder. He said: "Congratulations, sergeant-major. And that goes for all your men, too. I shall see headquarters are informed of your excellent conduct."

The Colonel looked down at the exhausted men and demanded: "Are they all here, Sergeant Major? Any casualties?"

The men in the trench had already carried out a silent roll-call. They knew one soldier was missing. And that man was one of the most loved and respected in the regiment.

Amann wearily pulled himself to his feet and stood to attention. He reported: "I regret to tell you, sir, that one man has given his life for the Fatherland . . . Private Solomons. He was a good soldier, sir, and bravely did his duty last night.

"He was with us right up to the enemy's wire. Then a sniper got him. I saw Solomons fall, sir. We had no choice but to go on without him, grab the prisoner and get back. That was our duty. I regret there is little hope for him."

List stood silently for a moment, eyes downcast, as though praying.

When he finally spoke, there was a catch in his voice. He regarded his soldiers as family. Even after all these deaths, he had never got used to losing them.

The Colonel said: "We have to pay a heavy price, Sergeant-Major. I shall make sure this man is not forgotten. Let us hope we will eventually find his body and give him the burial he deserves."

The Colonel turned away abruptly and walked down the trench, his boots sucking in the liquid mud. The troops watched him admiringly. Their colonel was no shrinking poo-bah. The C.O. was never afraid to share their dangers.

List was reputed to know the name and record of every man in his regiment. More important, he knew their strengths and weaknesses; who should be promoted and who should not.

Soon a *hauptman* appeared and pulled a pair of powerful field glasses from its leather case. Gingerly, he raised his head over the parapet and methodically swept the ground with the binoculars.

After a minute or two, the officer stiffened and adjusted the focus. He exclaimed: "My God! I think that must be Solomons out there!"

The glasses had revealed a soldier in field-grey, spread-eagled on the enemy barbed wire. To the horrified *Hauptman*, it looked almost as though the man was crucified, arms outstretched in agony.

Peering intently for several seconds, ignoring the risk from snipers, the officer was certain he saw the soldier move, slump, then move again. He shouted: "My God, he is still alive!"

The Bavarian private, hanging like a scarecrow on the rusty wire, was suffering a terrible death. The cruel barbs were slowly torturing the life out of him. The h*auptman* and Solomons himself must realise there could be no reprieve.

The French must by now know exactly where Solomons was. In fact, they had listened to his screams all night.

Any attempt to rescue the ensnared soldier would be certain suicide. The German officer wondered whether he could order a sniper to end a comrade's agony. He lowered the glasses and slowly wiped the lenses with his handkerchief.

Would such an order be legal, or even moral? Would it be right to ask any man to kill a comrade who had done no wrong?

As the *hauptman* mentally picked his way through the moral maze, he felt a tug on his sleeve. He turned to see that strange *gefreiter* messenger with the Iron Cross and combat wound medal standing beside him.

The officer snapped: "Yes, what is it?"

Hitler jumped to attention. "Sir, Private Solomons is my greatest friend. May I look through your field-glasses, sir, to see if there is any way I might go out and bring him in."

The *hauptman* softened and looked at the messenger with a new respect. "I am afraid there is no hope for your friend, although I appreciate your courageous offer. But I wouldn't want to throw away another life.

"Here, take the glasses and see for yourself. He is hung up on the wire. There is no way he can be rescued—even by the enemy."

Hitler stared long and hard at the outstretched body, noting the ever-lessening convulsions. To the officer, the messenger seemed to find it difficult to tear his gaze away.

At length, Hitler handed back the binoculars with a strange expression on his face. He said hoarsely: "I can see that you are correct, *Herr Hauptman.* I was being foolish. I trust my friend's torment will soon be over."

"Amen," said the officer. He put the field-glasses back in their case, and left to break the sad news of Private Solomons to Colonel List.

In the French trench, the soldiers, already ground down by the war to the point of mutiny, tried in vain not to listen to the agonised cries of the German. The horror had gone on hour after terrible hour.

As it became light, they saw the man had suffered one of the most dreaded of wounds. The blood staining the front of his tunic told them he had been shot in the guts.

The French soldiers' nerves were cracking under the strain. They asked themselves: "How much more of this can we stand? Why doesn't the bastard die? Die, you bastard! Die!"

The Boche soldier was only yards away, so close they could even see the anguish on his face. The *poilus,* too, knew it would be impossible to extricate this man and bring him in.

An hour passed. Then another. Although the screams were becoming weaker, they persisted, on and on, like somebody continually running their fingernails down a blackboard.

One *poilu*, in desperation, raised his rifle and sighted it on the man's chest. The dying German, close enough to see what was happening, suddenly fell silent. The French soldier thought he detected a look of relief and resignation on his face.

The *poilu* flicked off the safety catch and cocked his weapon. Then his nerve failed and he lowered it, crossed himself and prayed to the Blessed Virgin for forgiveness. The soldier had shot many a man in battle, but this was more like cold-blooded murder.

Then the French soldier told himself this would be an act of mercy. In one swift movement, he again raised and aimed the rifle and squeezed the trigger. The soldier closed his eyes as there was a sharp *crack!,* and the butt kicked into his shoulder.

When the *poilu* opened his eyes again, the German was slumped, like a broken doll, on the unforgiving wire. The lifeless eyes were still open, and appeared to be gazing accusingly at the *poilu*.

The Frenchman successfully pleaded with his sergeant to be posted to another part of the trench. The body hung there for several days, until it was blown to pieces by a German artillery shell.

Back in the German trench, the little group of Hitler's faithful gathered in Regimental Sergeant Major Max Amann's dug-out. A candle guttered, stuck in the neck of a bottle, which stood on a table made of an ammunition box.

Items of equipment hung from pegs driven into the timbers lining the mud walls.

Hitler's latest recruit, aristocratic *Gefreiter* Ernst von Reinholdt, was posted outside the heavy gas blanket shielding the dug-out's entrance.

Adolf Hitler's new Military Service Cross, Third Class With Swords, awarded for having been wounded in combat, glittered in the candle-light. The scruffy *gefreiter* immediately took charge.

He looked round appraisingly at his assassins—Amann, Muller and Karlatz—and told them: "You have done well, ridding us of this slimy and dangerous Yid. You will be well rewarded when the time comes . . . . and that, I promise you, will be soon."

The acolytes' faces warmed in the sun of their leader's praise. How were they to know they were being manipulated by a master of the art?

Hitler carefully delivered his speech: "You have had the honour of striking the first blow. That bullet you put into the Yid's guts was the beginning of a battle to cleanse our country.

"Solomons paid a just and painful price for being what he was. He will be the first of millions. They will all pay.

"You made history out there on the battlefield last night. You won the honour of spearheading my holy crusade. Together, we will cut out the canker of Zionism, Marxism and the Freemasonry. We are a new generation of Teutonic knights."

These were brave words, designed to spur on his followers. Only Hitler knew that these soldiers weren't the first to kill one of his enemies. They would never suspect that his own hands already had Jewish blood on them.

He went on: "When I was on leave in Berlin recently, I saw the huge extent of the work that must be done. The city was full of profiteers, shirkers and defeatists. I was glad to cut short my vacation and come back to the comradeship of the trenches.

"I am privileged to be among you.

"The death of Solomons is symbolic. He mocked me, and that meant he mocked us and all we stand for. We will not be mocked. When we march, we will be hailed as saviours. People will worship us."

Hitler, eyes blazing, arms folded across his chest, had the men's rapt attention. He went on to paint a vision of rank after rank of the Faithful, banners flying, bands playing, marching gloriously through the streets of Germany. The pavements were lined with cheering men, women and children.

These, of course, were Aryan men, women and children. Their uplifted faces were smiling and happy, their eyes alight with zeal for their cause.

Hitler rasped: "Yid Solomons was the first. Soon we will have the task of dealing with millions of his ilk. But we will not shrink from the immensity of our duty.

"We will kill, swiftly and methodically, so that others can live a clean and fulfilling life. No more will we fear a conspiracy to bring us to our knees. We will never forget the oath we have sworn."

He raised his arm in the stiff salute they had secretly practised in the back-room of Black Marie's café at Fournes-en-Weppe. The other three soldiers saluted in their turn, shouting above the rumble of the guns: "Heil, Hitler!"

It had begun.

CHAPTER EIGHT

July/August, 2000

The news that Ernie Cornish's grandson, Adam, was to go digging into the past in Flanders sparked feverish activity in the murky world of international intelligence.

Ros Litherland, a.k.a. Ros Goldstein, received an urgent phone call from Tel Aviv. Its content shocked her. She immediately began to pack sexy underwear and a PPK Walther semi-automatic pistol.

Arthur Burfield, a.k.a. Andre Lacroix, was contacted on a matter of urgency from Dixmuide, Belgium. As he replaced the receiver, his eyes glittered with anticipation, and adrenaline tingled round his body.

Rod Russell, a.k.a. Captain Hamish Sinclair of the Scots Guards, received a terse briefing at an office overlooking Horse Guards' Parade, London. Swiftly, with military precision, he formed his plan of campaign.

The orders of all three agents boiled down to the same thing: "Let Cornish run for now. He may lead you to the mainspring of a great Nazi revival. Beware! There are others, willing to kill, in the race."

Then came the bombshell: "The prize here includes Hitler's secret treasure.

"This was systematically looted from Europe during World War Two, and is worth countless billions of dollars . . . enough to finance a Fourth Reich twice over.

"The loot was hidden during the war and its hiding place has never been found. Cornish may lead you to it."

September 3, 2000

The English Channel was in angry mood. Spitefully, it lifted the bulky car ferry to the crest of a giant wave, only to drop it into a trough with a crash like thunder. Spray ran like countless teardrops outside the windows of the bar in the bows.

Inside, three people, gathered round the Formica-topped table, hanging grimly on to their slopping drinks. Down in the cavernous hold, where cars, lorries and coaches huddled together as though for comfort, the jarring impact set off a wailing of anti-theft alarms.

Arthur Burfield grimly gripped the table with his free hand, his ruddy face paling in the storm He was studiously ignoring Ros, in the seat next to him, attempting to down a gin and tonic.

The photographer had been venting his disapproval of the girl ever since Adam had invited her. Arthur demanded of the former reporter: "Why invite that slutty waste of space?

"Was it the drink talking, or were you talking through your cock? She'll only get in our way. Her dainty feet won't be able to teeter across the muddy fields and old trenches we'll need to explore.

"In fact, although I haven't mentioned it before, I'm something of an expert on the Salient. It's fascinated me since I was a kid. I can assure you, it's no place for a tarty girl. She'll only whinge to go home."

Arthur's words fell on deaf ears. Adam told the photographer: "She's not a bad reporter, and I can use her for some of the leg work. I've been on the Net and seen there are a lot of museums around the Salient.

"Ros can go and do some research in those, for example. That'll leave us free to do our battlefield thing and visit a few cafes. A pretty girl will brighten up our evenings."

Even now, as Adam struggled to down his third pint of lager in the swaying bar, he enjoyed heated thoughts of having sex on tap every night.

What exciting sex that will be! The girl was eminently teachable and durable. She had already demonstrated that. His member twitched.

Adam managed to raise the glass to his lips, just as the ferry made a sickening corkscrew. The lager shot upwards, soaking his face and beard.

Ros immediately produced a tissue from the pocket of her sturdy, blue anorak and mopped away the liquid. Arthur scowled darkly when he saw the female possessive gesture.

Adam gallantly kissed Ros's hand. Again, he was disturbed to notice that, in spite of the girl's affectionate action, her ashen and sweating face remained impassive. Just what was going on in her head?

In a moment of honesty, Adam asked himself: "What would an attractive, 25-year-old girl with big boobs see in a 65-year-old man who had let himself somewhat go to seed?

"What was in this for Ros Litherland?"

The boat took another sickening lurch, causing several of the surrounding passengers to reach for the waterproof bags scattered over their tables. Others, lurching like Saturday night drunks, made hurriedly for the toilets.

Adam, unaffected by the ship's violent movement, pushed disturbing questions about the delectable Ros to the back-burner of his mind.

Surely, the answer was obvious. The girl fancied him like hell. She recognised what glories might lay ahead. She confirmed Adam Cornish's long-held belief that he emanated a sexual aura.

This was reassuringly confirmed when Ros staggered to the bar and returned carrying a replacement for his spilled drink and a bag of peanuts.

As Adam took the glass and nuts from her, the blonde allowed her fingers to linger on his for several, suggestive, seconds.

They were now in mid-Channel and the ferry's motion was becoming ever more violent. Adam slumped back in his seat, eyes closed, enjoying the powerful turbulence.

When he opened them again, he was alone. Obviously, *mal de mer* had claimed both Arthur and Ros. The other tables were deserted. Adam tore open his bag of peanuts and poured a liberal portion into his palm.

The writer, chewing busily, let himself relax. He was surprised to see an attractive, middle-aged woman staggering across the heaving floor towards him

She was clutching a glass of brandy in one hand and a plastic package of ham sandwiches in the other. The woman, abundant red hair swept fetchingly on top of her head, was smiling. Large, grey eyes twinkled at Adam.

The woman arrived at the seat next to the writer and looked at him inquiringly. He nodded eager assent for her to join him. She sank down carefully, judging the action with the pitching of the ferry.

When she spoke, the woman had an attractive, slightly guttural accent. Adam decided it was either Dutch or German. She said: "It seems, *m'sieur*, that we are the only good sailors here. It is fitting we should keep one another company."

The woman had the confident, sexy manner often exhibited by Continental women of a certain age. Like fine wines, they appeared to mature with the passing years.

Her red raincoat was unbuttoned and Adam noted that, beneath it, she was wearing a black, woollen, figure-hugging dress. This was set off by a simple gold chain necklace.

Adam had always loved women in black and women with big breasts. Those on display were not only ample but firm. The woman placed her packet of sandwiches on the table.

She reached up to adjust a wisp of unruly hair, revealing a heavy, gold wedding ring. The coat gaped open yet more, to show a ripe figure. Was that action accidental? Christ! His sexual magic seemed to be working yet again.

Adam returned the woman's flirtatious smile, saying: "You are very welcome, *madame*. I was feeling lonely. Everyone else seems to have fallen victim to the storm. There is nothing I enjoy more than the company of a beautiful woman."

"Thank you, *m'sieur*, you are very *galant*."

Her eyes held his as she slowly bit into the soft, brown bread and pink meat of a sandwich. She somehow made it into an erotic act. Adam's pulses quickened.

He couldn't be imagining things. This great-looking woman was sending him a clear sexual message. The writer's chest swelled under his cheap, leather jacket. He attempted to pull in the muscles of his belly.

She slowly brushed a crumb from full, scarlet lips and went on: "It is a privilege to be in the company of so interesting-looking an Englishman. I am but a boring Flemish housewoman who has been shopping in Canterbury."

The woman sighed and added: "I hate to travel alone. But my husband, as usual, is busy with his business. He spends his days and nights making love to his fat rows of figures. His books of accounts are as his mistresses."

Adam was entranced. He loved the way she said "housewoman" instead of the currently politically incorrect "housewife". Was she signalling she was a bored one at that?

He was also intrigued by the way this woman demolished her ham sandwiches. He loved women with healthy appetites. He loved the promise she exuded.

She extended her hand. Her fingers were long and elegant, the carefully-manicured nails varnished scarlet to match her lips. "Permit me to introduce myself, *m'sieur*. I am Fabienne Boulanger, from Ieper, in Belgium."

Adam's heart leaped. He took the proffered hand and held it for several heartbeats exclaiming: "I am Adam Cornish. What an amazing coincidence, *madame*! I, too, am on my way to Ypres."

Spurred on by the alcohol, he continued: "I shall be staying in the area for several days. Perhaps we could meet sometime?

"I am researching my grandfather's life in Flanders during the 1914-18 war. Then I shall write a book and a film on the subject. It will be a huge Hollywood success."

Fabienne's grey eyes sparkled with enthusiasm. She declared: "Ooooh! That is *tres formidable!* How exciting! I have never met a real writer before. But, now that I look at you more closely, I can see you could be scarcely anything else.

"You are *tres distingue and tres interessant.* Fate has brought us together in this storm. How romantic! It is like a Hollywood film. We must, of course, rendezvous in Ieper.

I can greatly help you in your researches into *Quatorze—Dixhuit.*"

She took his hand once more and said breathlessly: "From tomorrow, I shall be at your service, Mr. Writer."

He protested: "But I don't know yet where I shall be staying."

"I shall soon find you. Ieper is a small town. I will show you many things. I shall be your courier. It will be an honour, and will help to fill the empty days of my life."

Adam protested: "I am afraid I haven't included the price of a courier in my budget . . ."

- "Your smile, *mon brave,* is all the payment I shall require."

He glanced at her wedding ring and asked: "Won't your husband object if I borrow you, Fabienne?"

She shook her head emphatically, replying: "He will not even notice I am gone, with his head buried in his precious books like a silly ostrich in the sand."

The message seemed clear and unequivocal. Adam smiled and said: "Then I would be delighted if you would accompany me. I will be most grateful for your expertise and charming company."

She laughed gaily: "Then it is settled. I will seek you out tomorrow. We shall have a wonderful time, working one with another for your writing."

- "I love your accent, Fabienne."

- "I love yours, too, Adam."

She leaned forward, her eyes serious now, and said: "I saw you with others. Perhaps I shall not be welcome. There was a girl who was young and pretty. Will she say you must not spend so much time with this old woman?"

Adam's hypnotic blue eyes looked into Fabienne's. His were chips of ice. He said harshly: "The girl must obey my orders. When I want to be with you, I shall be with you. No-one must question me. I am the leader."

The Flemish girl breathed: "I love a masterful man. I, too, will be happy for you to be my leader."

Without breaking her gaze, she again took his hand, turned it over and scratched his palm with a long, scarlet fingernail. Adam shuddered deliciously.

Handkerchief to her mouth, Ros slipped and slithered past a deserted coffee bar and an equally empty duty-free shop. She pushed open the door to the ladies' toilet and stopped abruptly.

The sights and smells of a shipload of women being violently sea-sick sent Ros's already delicate stomach into spasm. She retreated hurriedly and ran towards a door leading to the outside deck.

Ros was pushing at the heavy door when a thick-set member of the ship's crew stepped in front of her. The ruddy-faced officer, gold bars of rank on the epaulettes of his heavy blue sweater, spoke politely but firmly: "Sorry, Miss, no-one is allowed outside in this weather.

"It's all down to health and safety. It's far too dangerous for people to go wandering about on deck in a Force Nine gale. We wouldn't like to lose a pretty girl like you over the side, would we?"

This was sound sense but, as the ferry lurched again, Ros's need became desperate. She thrust the startled officer aside, pushed open the door and stepped into the storm.

He swore, looked at the rain and spray driving against the windows, and hurried off for his foul weather gear. He just hoped that bloody stupid girl wouldn't be swept away in the meantime.

On deck, the storm seized Ros with icy fingers. Screaming wind clutched fiercely at her clothes, sent her long, blonde hair streaming and doused her in torrents of spray.

The big ship buried its nose in a wave, and the jarring motion proved the final straw for Ros. She reeled across the pitching deck and clasped the brine-slicked teak rail with both hands.

She turned her head away from the wind, braced her feet firmly on the streaming deck and bent over the rail. Then, high above the white-capped waves, Ros was violently and helplessly ill.

As she retched, she felt somebody pinning her arms to her sides, lifting her and pushing her powerfully forward. Ros fought to regain her balance, but the pressure from behind was relentless.

She was forced to tip-toe, leaning farther and farther over the rail. Her feet left the deck. Ros, legs flailing, knew her attacker was preparing for a final effort, to pitch her into the sea.

The girl kicked out behind but the man had positioned himself to be out of her reach. He shouted in her ear, his words pitched above the roar of the storm.

Ros recognised the voice of Arthur Burfield. But, instead of its usual cheery, country tone, it was heavy with malevolence. He snarled: "I know who you are, you Yid bitch and what you're after. You think you can rob us of what is rightfully ours. What a joke!

"This is what happens to Jew scum who cross us. Hitler tried to teach you a lesson, but you haven't learned it yet. Six million of you went up the chimney. Now a filthy Yid is going to feed the fishes."

Arthur, spray streaming off a face contorted with hate, had the helpless girl bent over the rail. He prepared to deliver the *coup de grace*.

Suddenly, Ros felt the pressure ease, so that her feet slid back to the deck. Arthur wrapped an arm round her shoulders in what, to a casual onlooker, would appear an avuncular embrace.

She looked round, still speechless with terror, and saw the burly ferry officer, water streaming from his oil-skins, looming next to them. Shouting angrily against the wind, he admonished: "I told both of you not to go on deck.

"Don't you idiots listen? Do you want to end up in the drink? You wouldn't last a second in this lot. We couldn't save you. Get back inside and don't try this stupid stunt again.

"If you feel ill, do what everybody else does and grab a sick bag, or go to the toilet. Be warm. Be safe. Now get a hot cup of tea inside you."

The officer took them each by an arm, as though arresting them, and marched the girl and the middle-aged man back into the ferry. Passengers, feeling better enough to have returned to their seats, stared curiously at the streaming pair and their escort.

With a final glare, the officer marched off. Arthur and Ros, dripping water on to the polished wooden floor of the saloon, glared venomously at each other

Without breaking her gaze, Ros distributed her weight evenly and flattened her hands into karate mode. Arthur reached inside his soaking overcoat. Then they both simultaneously realised nothing could be done in front of dozens of witnesses.

The couple faced each other in a Mexican stand-off.

Ros hissed: "So you've been one of them all this time. We guessed you Nazi bastards couldn't be far away. Now I know who you are, I shall be ready for you. You won't take me by surprise next time.

"I'm warning you Burfield, or whatever your real name is, that I shall get what we're after. Nothing and nobody will stand in my way. As for you *Sturmbannfuhrer* Burfield, you are a dead man walking."

Arthur laughed mirthlessly and dropped into the language of the playground to ask: "Going to rub me out, are you? You and whose army?"

She snapped: "Yes, we *do* have an army nowadays. Unlike the time you sent six million helpless people up those chimneys."

The storm was abating, and the coast of France appeared as a dark smudge outside the bow windows. The motion of the ferry calmed.

Ros and Arthur slipped back into character for their return to Adam and, clothes still soaked, made for the bar.

They were amazed to find the writer deep in conversation with a stylishly-dressed, red-headed woman. Adam's fingers were entwined with the woman's and the couple was gazing into each other's eyes.

Ros and Arthur stood, stunned and unnoticed, next to the couple's table. Both agents realised another had joined the game. Judging by the progress the woman had made with Adam, she was obviously a professional.

The battle-zone was becoming crowded . . . and ever more dangerous. The Mossad agent and the Nazi slipped their hands inside their coats to check their guns.

Ros swiftly adopted the role of jealous lover. She snapped: "Hello, Adam, what have we here? We can't leave you alone for a minute, can we, darling? We've been gone only a few minutes and already you've fallen in love.

"Aren't you going to introduce me to your new girlfriend?"

Adam tore his eyes from Fabienne and gazed, amazed, at the dripping couple standing beside him. He chuckled:

"Been for a swim, have you? This is a perfectly good ship, capable of getting us all the way to France.

"There was absolutely no need to go it alone, you two. What on earth have you been doing, apart from the breast-stroke?"

Ros, assuming an expression of anger, said: "We felt queasy and thought we'd get some fresh air on deck. It was a bit damp out there."

She looked pointedly at the woman's figure, amply displayed by her gaping coat, and went on: "It looks as though I should have stayed here, used the sick bags like everyone else, and kept an eye on you.

"I'll ask you once more, darling . . . who *is* your lady friend?"

Before Adam, alcohol blunting his senses, could get his thoughts in order, Fabienne answered for him. Her voice was soft, but had a touch of steel.

She told the younger woman: "Permit me to introduce myself . . . I am Fabienne Boulanger. M'sieur Adam kindly allowed me to share his table because I was a lone woman in the storm

"Most of the other people were, like you and your companion, indisposed by the motion of the vessel. Adam and myself were the only *voyageurs* left in the bar. I am sure you understand."

Fabienne slowly buttoned her coat and, ignoring venomous glances from Ros and Arthur, went on calmly: "We chatted and found we had much in common.

"*M'sieur* has come to Ieper to look into the life of his *grand-pere in Quatorze-Dixhuite.* I am a Flanders girl, born and bred. All of us living *en Flandres* know much of the old battlefields.

"I am eager to help an English gentleman with a project close to both our hearts. I have offered to be his helpmate—

his personal courier. I am honoured that Adam has accepted that humble offer."

While Fabienne was speaking, Adam's head had nodded to his chest and he began to snore gently. Arthur took the opportunity to snarl to Fabienne: "Give yourself a pat on the back, whoever you really are. You've wormed your way into the game in record time. Bitch!"

He turned his furious glare on Ros and snapped: "She was even quicker than you were, Sunshine. Perhaps you ought to look and learn . . . while you can."

Adam woke with a start, oblivious of the bitterness raging over his head. He looked at the three people standing round the table and chortled: "Yes, this is going to be quite a party!

"Now there are four of us. The more the merrier, I say. Can't have too many willing hands making light work of old Ernie's tale."

He pointed to his empty glass and announced: "I think there's time for one more before we hit *La Belle France*."

Ros and Fabienne both reached for the glass. Ros won the tussle, picked it up, and strode angrily to the bar. She just managed to get it replenished before the bartender slammed down the grill with a crash.

Adam, besotted by his latest "conquest", failed to notice Ros had pointedly failed to buy drinks for Arthur and Fabienne. Ros seated herself beside the journalist and rested her head on his shoulder

Within minutes, the Calais quayside slid past the ferry's windows. The passengers stood up and gratefully gathered their belongings, ready to leave the nightmare voyage behind them.

Adam drained the beer with a series of deep and practised gulps and unsteadily got to his feet. He drew Fabienne into a close embrace and beerily kissed her full on the lips, his hands blatantly reaching inside her coat.

Ros shuddered. She guessed the old soak was sliding his tongue deep into the woman's mouth and groping her breasts. Rather her than me. However, this was but a horror delayed.

Adam released Fabienne, who dabbed at her lips with a tissue and deftly adjusted her clothes. Her face was flushed, and Ros noted that, although the ferry had come to rest, the woman appeared to be fighting a bout of retching.

The elderly writer, reluctant to break off contact, asked: "Can we give you a lift, Fabienne? We are going to Ieper, and there is a spare seat."

She answered quickly, still working at her mouth with the tissue: "You are most kind . . . a true English gentleman. But my husband has torn himself from his duties to meet me here. So I must say, *'au revoir'.*

"I will seek you out. Until then . . ."

Fabienne blew Adam a kiss from the palm of her hand, which he gallantly pretended to catch in his.

He told her: "See you soon."

Arthur snarled under his breath: "You can bet on that, old boy."

Adam, Ros and Arthur watched as Fabienne walked away, hips swinging. She made for the pedestrian exit from the ferry.

As he watched her go, Adam thought happily: "Not a bad trip, so far."

His two companions' thoughts were dark and homicidal.

The three of them were swept away by the crowd of pale-faced drivers and their passengers, eager to get to the roped off companionways leading to the car, coach and lorry decks.

Soon Ros, Arthur and Adam were tramping down the stairs and seeking out Arthur's silver Volvo estate car among the lines of parked vehicles. The ferry's ramp rumbled down.

Ten minutes later, they drove into the port . . . and whatever was awaiting them in Flanders.

Fabienne walked into Calais, head down against the driving wind and drizzle, legacy of the Channel storm. She turned into a side street, where a welcoming light spilled across the wet pavement from the windows of a café.

She hurried towards the promise of warmth, a hot, strong coffee and a cognac. Just as Fabienne reached the condensation-misted door, a figure slipped from the shadows and laid a restraining hand on her arm.

A clipped, military voice ordered: "Not in there, sergeant. Come with me. I have a set of wheels waiting. Better to get out of town where none of the nasties is likely to run into us. That would never do, would it?"

Rod Russell took Fabienne's arm and guided her to a black Land Rover with French licence plates, parked at the kerb nearby. As he opened the passenger door the interior light sprang on, and she saw an immaculately turned-out, off-duty Guards officer.

Rod Russell, the Kentish World's shabby computer buff, had morphed back into his real self - Captain Hamish Sinclair, Military Cross. He wore a dark blue blazer, starched white shirt with military tie, sharply-creased grey flannel trousers and highly-polished black brogues.

The couple slipped into their seats and Hamish started the engine, which gave a throaty roar. He switched on the headlights, stabbing the clammy darkness, put the Land Rover into gear and pulled smoothly away.

Fabienne, a.k.a. Sergeant Verity Vincent, undid the top two buttons of her coat as the heater blasted into life. She couldn't resist a giggle as she glanced across at the British agent.

When she spoke, Verity had a posh, Home Counties voice, without a trace of her foreign accent: "What a perfect disguise, Captain! Nobody would ever peg you as an off-duty British officer.

"All you need to complete your outfit is a bowler hat, a rolled umbrella and a Daily Telegraph tucked under your arm, *sir*."

Hamish snorted as, following the blue and white signs, he swung on to the road to Dunkirk. He snapped: "Don't be impertinent to a superior officer, sergeant.

"Although I'm not obliged to explain anything to you, I will merely state that I am on my way to an important meeting in Brussels about the current operation. They're all going ape-shit about the Nazi connection and, of course, the lucre.

"Lots of top brass will be there, so I can't go looking like a tramp. That would be pretty bad form. I would expect even a lowly girl like you to understand that."

Verity felt her cheeks burning. For a while she said nothing, watching as Hamish tucked the Land Rover behind a line of lumbering lorries in the slow lane of the coast road. The wipers carved clear arcs in the spray beading the windscreen.

Then, sitting to attention, she said softly: "There's no need to be patronising, Captain Sinclair, sir. Although I'm not wearing my stripes for obvious reasons, I am a serving senior non-commissioned officer in the British Army.

"I may be a *girl*, but I won those stripes the hard way. I did square-bashing at Catterick, in Yorkshire, assault courses included. Then I spent a year at Intelligence Special Forces School, which was no picnic."

When the captain replied, his tone was contrite. "Sorry, old girl. I was well out of line there. Strain of the job, you know. Forgot myself for a second or two. Sit at ease, Sarge.

"I don't have to tell you that you're one of the best we have at this sort of thing. Fill me in as we go along on what you've gleaned. I'll drop you at the Belgian border, where your 'husband' will pick you up.

"What I need now is a quick situation report to put the brass in the picture at the Brussels meeting. Did anything significant occur when that ferry was rocking and rolling?"

Verity told him: "Only that I bumped into that bloody murderous Nazi Burfield, who made me straight away. He was just looking for a chance to put my lights out. Adam Cornish was mostly drunk, and putty in my hands."

She proceeded to give Hamish a swift and highly professional account of her voyage from Dover to Calais.

Verity concluded: "So you should be aware that there are at least *two* other players in this game. There's this Nazi Arthur Burfield, posing as a photographer, whom we knew about already.

"But you may not know that a girl reporter from the same newspaper is obviously a serious threat. I don't know who is pulling her strings, but I smell Mossad.

"She is called Ros, and is a real professional. She has wormed her way in with our target in a big way. And she is obviously going to make like a limpet with Cornish over the next few days."

Hamish pulled into the centre lane and accelerated past the trucks before asking: "Sorry, old bean, I forgot to tell you . . . we've already checked on Miss Ros Litherland. She is really Ros Goldstein.

"And your instincts are, as always, brilliant. She *is* Mossad. Is Cornish fucking her, do you think?"

"I'm certain he is, sir . . . as best as he is able."

"Then you'll have to fuck him better than she does. Do you think you can do that, sergeant?"

"Yes, sir. Of course, sir."

"It is a matter of doing your duty. I know I can rely on you to carry out those repugnant orders in your customarily efficient manner."

"Thank you, sir! I won't let you down. I'm trained for this sort of thing. I know the mission is vital for our country and, possibly, the free world."

"No need to get too carried away, sergeant. Leave the speeches for the brass. Let us just say that a lot of things hinge on this trip to Flanders. You have a heavy burden of responsibility."

Verity stared unseeingly at the traffic flicking past as they headed towards Belgium.

She shuddered and felt a wave of nausea as she conjured up Adam Cornish's disturbing blue eyes, his dissolute face and the bulging body puffing out his crumpled and stained clothes.

Verity remembered with revulsion his tongue probing her mouth and his hands mauling her breasts. But it was the hauntingly familiar blue eyes that worried her most. They were the chilling eyes from thousands of old posters, photographs and films.

She knew from her briefings that Adam Cornish might well be Adolf Hitler's grandson, although the man himself had no clue to his sinister heritage.

There was something else that made her skin crawl. Just what bedroom horrors would she have to suffer to do her duty to God and the Queen?

Hamish looked at Verity's grim face, dimly lit by the dashboard lights. He guessed what might be going through her head, and respected her silence. At Dunkirk, he saw the sign to Ypres.

He swung the Land Rover up an on-ramp and blended into the traffic on the busy Lille auto-route. The captain broke the silence, informing Verity: "We're not far from the drop-off point.

"We'll turn off at Steenvorde and I'll let you out at the border. Your 'husband' will be waiting there to take you to your cosy little Ypres 'home'. I believe you already know him—Corporal Sanderson?"

Verity snapped out of her sickening reverie and replied: "I certainly do, sir. We've done an assault course or two together. He has hairy thighs. I could never actually marry a man with hairy thighs."

Hamish chuckled: "You don't actually have to, Sergeant. Don't forget, this is all just pretend. But I needn't remind you that the danger is real. Keep your wits about you at all times.

"The vultures are gathering. They are all after the same juicy prizes, and they won't hesitate to kill to get them."

They arrived at the Franco-Belgium border. Lights burned in the windows of the guard and custom offices, but the place appeared deserted. Hamish pulled into a remote corner of a lorry park and stopped next to a little black Peugeot.

Verity recognised the man leaning against the car as her new 'husband', Corporal Jimmy Sanderson. He straightened and threw up a mock salute.

As Verity put her hand on the door handle, Hamish Sinclair leaned across and kissed her full on the lips. Breaking the lingering contact, he said: "Just one question, sergeant?"

"Yes, captain."

"When this is over, will you marry me?"

She grasped his crotch with a practised hand and replied: "Of course, sir. At the double sir."

Verity got out of the car, slamming the door. She stood for a moment, watching the red tail lights of the Land Rover dwindling into the distance.

CHAPTER NINE

July 14, 1944

The slightly-built lad, mop of dark, curly hair falling over his face, lay prone, nestling deep into the undergrowth of Bavarian Wood. He was shaking uncontrollably and wide-eyed with fear.

In the brambles beside eight-year-old Jacques Deberte lay the rod with which, just minutes before, he had been fishing in a nearby flooded World War One shell-hole.

Jacques was playing truant from the village school. He had been confident no-one would find him in this remote place, a mile from the nearest village.

Then the peace had been suddenly and dramatically shattered.

The boy heard the sound of trucks, labouring up the hill that led to the old battle-field, famous for its crumbling German trenches and flooded mine-shaft. He slipped into the wood and peered between the trees.

Two lorries, packed with troops, pulled into a clearing next to the wood. Soldiers spilled out, non-commissioned officers shouting orders.

Jacques froze with horror. These men were wearing the dreaded black uniforms with lightning-flash runes on their collars. He recognised them as Hitler's savage elite *Schutzstaffel*—S.S.

These troops, with their death's head cap badges and gleaming jack boots, were notorious for atrocities committed throughout occupied Europe. They brought terror with them wherever they went.

Jacques was a bright lad. Like many Flemish people, he was fluent in Dutch, French and German. He now listened intently as the soldiers were ordered to throw a cordon round the area

He threw himself face-down into the brambles. The soldiers made a cursory search of the apparently deserted wood. Two booted feet stopped within a foot of the quaking boy.

Then the soldier moved on, playfully kicking an old can he'd found in the undergrowth.

The boy was old enough to realise that, if he were discovered, he would die. He felt a shameful warmth spreading inside his trousers as he lost control of his bladder.

Jacques knew he must keep as still as possible until the S.S. went away. But, as he listened to their conversation, he realised he was in for a long, agonising wait.

A third truck arrived. The officer in charge, a slim man with black, lifeless eyes and an evil, narrow face, ordered his men to unload pieces of heavy equipment. Jacques recognised these as the sort of generators his father used on their farm.

Although it was not yet getting dark, a battery of flood lights was set up. Cables were attached to powerful pumps, and hoses run out to the flooded mine-shaft on the edge of the wood.

Generators throbbed into life, and the pumps began sucking greedily at the water down the shaft. Hundreds of gallons flooded into nearby fields.

A previous generation of German soldiers had dug this deep shaft with its underground galleries. They christened it with the soft, feminine name, "Frauenlob"—"Praise of Women".

Now, 26 years after the guns had fallen silent, soldiers of another war were working here. Jacques wondered what it was they wanted so badly at the bottom of the shaft.

The Belgian lad's eyes pricked with tears. When he didn't come home to tea, his parents would be frantic with worry. He prayed they wouldn't come looking for him here. If they did, they would surely die.

Darkness fell and ants nipped at his bare knees. An owl hooted eerily. Jacques shivered with fear. He remembered a chilling ghost story told by the old locals, their breath heavy with cheap pincher beer.

They loved to frighten the boy by telling of a spectre that had haunted this very wood since the First World War. They said the ghost, a bullet hole clearly visible in his pale forehead, wandered among the trees, dressed in the mouldering uniform of a *hauptman*.

The German captain was, they said, eternally searching for his murderer, reputed to be one of his own soldiers. The ghost tramped restlessly round and round Bavarian wood, calling down a curse on his killer.

The restless spirit always disappeared into thin air at the same place—the entrance to the Fraulenlob mine-shaft.

Jacques' parents dismissed the ghost story as nonsense. But none of the local children would venture into this spooky wood after nightfall.

Now Jacques had no choice but to stay here in the dark. He watched as the troops tended the pumps in the brightly-lit clearing. Water spread like dark blood over the fields.

Shivering in his hiding place among the brambles, Jacques suddenly thought of a new danger. Perhaps a

Tommy bomber would spot these lights and unload a hail of death on them.

The boy wondered how many men had died violently on this haunted hillside. Were their shades flitting among the spectral trees?

If the old men in the cafes were to be believed, there could be bodies under where he lay, buried in the walls and floors of the dripping galleries.

During the Great War, the opposing troops were separated on this ridge—designated Hill 40 by the British—by just 750 lethal yards of No-Man's Land.

Germans and Tommies dug like human moles, trying to mine under each others' trenches. The front lines, packed with troops and weapons, made juicy targets.

The generals knew a chain of front-line explosions could be a winning prelude to a major attack. Their great ambition was to blow the opposing army off the face of the map.

Soldiers, stripped to the waist and slick with sweat, toiled below ground as silently as possible. They paused frequently to listen for sounds of nearby enemy mining.

Sometimes the Tommies or Germans would suddenly burst into each others' tunnels. Then there was hand-to-hand fighting, primeval in its savagery.

Lying in the chill darkness, Jacques recalled how the café sages said at least two great mines still lay unexploded on the Western Front. Records of their locations, buried deep under the rich Flanders soil, had been lost in the fortunes of war.

A new nightmare gripped him. Could a gigantic mine be lurking beneath him at this very moment? Would it take just a bolt of lightning to run down a tree, into the earth and set it off?

Then . . . whoosh! Perhaps he would join the ghost of the unhappy *hauptman*. His parents would never know what had happened to their son. The boy sobbed silently.

It began to rain, soft drops pattering on the leaves above him. Jacques listened fearfully for the first crack of thunder. The damp seeped into his very bones.

There was a sudden shout from the S.S. officer, who wore the badges of rank of a *sturmbannfuhrer*—major. The soldiers ran to join him at the mouth of the mine-shaft and peered downwards.

Jacques dared stealthily to raise his head, so that he could see the cause of the men's excitement. He listened to their chatter.

The officer ordered men to set up two powerful lights to shine directly down into the shaft. The water level had dropped, exposing a dozen or so copper electrical and water pipes, snaking down the sides.

The rungs of a steel ladder glinted. The new lights confirmed what the major thought he'd glimpsed. An object was wedged against the rungs of the ladder. He made a cut-throat motion to the troops manning the pumps, which obediently fell silent.

The major gestured brusquely for one of the S.S. men to climb down into the Frauenlob. There was a long pause. Then Jacques heard the men clustered round the dripping mouth of the shaft discussing the grisly object the soldier had brought up.

It was a skull, a bullet hole in the centre of its forehead. The soldier then reached inside his tunic and brought out several mud-encrusted bones.

The major examined the finds and then tossed them into the undergrowth. He barked an order, and the pumps throbbed back into life. Jacques watched from the shadows.

He wondered: "Were those the mortal remains of the *hauptman*? Will the S.S. officer now be cursed by the ghost of the woods?"

Sometime during that long, long night, Jacques heard the sound of more trucks climbing the steep incline. He knew they had just passed through his home village of Voormezeele and wished he were there at this moment, lying snugly in bed.

Three more canvas-covered lorries roared into the clearing. The engines died and the drivers jumped from their cabs and ran round to let down the tail-boards.

More S.S. men leaped out, and Jacques was terrified to see they were holding heavy whips. Then an army of scarecrows, skeletal men wearing ragged striped pyjamas, poured from the lorries.

The guards whipped the men into a straggling line and forced them to stand, swaying, to attention. Half an hour passed, during which several of the prisoners collapsed. Then a long convoy arrived.

There was room in the clearing only for the first three trucks. The rest waited in line down the hill. Amid shouts from the guards, the prisoners started to unload heavy metal boxes, marked "ammunition".

The frail men, who all appeared to be Jews, staggered painfully under their burdens. Whips rose and fell as the boxes were stacked next to the mine-shaft.

Meanwhile, men of the first S.S. contingent were busy assembling and erecting a crane over the Fraulenlob.

The rain became heavier, turning the prisoners into wraiths as they worked. One fell, and a guard walked over and kicked him savagely. The prisoner remained inert and the S.S. man drew his Luger and nonchalantly shot the Jew in the head.

Jacques gulped and placed his hands over his mouth as hot bile rose in his throat. He continued, as though hypnotised, to watch the bizarre scene unfolding.

Dawn broke mistily. No birds sang in this benighted wood. The heartbeat of the pumps died. S.S. men descended into the shaft, unreeling electric cables as they went.

After a while, there was a shout from below. Guards and prisoners climbed down the ladder, deep into the bowels of Flanders. For hour after hour, the heavy metal boxes were lowered by crane. As each lorry was unloaded, the Frauenlob swallowed its contents.

The ragged, underfed prisoners became exhausted. The rain stopped and the summer sun broke through the clouds, generating a shimmering summer heat.

One by one, the prisoners dropped. Each was summarily despatched by a guard and their body tossed aside.

The remaining Jews, mouths gaping, chests heaving, legs buckling, reached deep inside themselves for the strength they needed to save their lives.

The pace was relentless. It seemed that nothing must delay this strange military operation, taking place just yards from where *Gefreiter* Adolf Hitler won the Iron Cross, Second Class.

It was late in the afternoon when the last box was lowered into the shaft. Even the S.S. men were now beginning to flag, and had to be urged on by the curses of their corporals and sergeants.

The soldiers who had been working underground climbed wearily back to the surface, dripping with mud and slimy water. They sprawled on the ground, greedily gulping the fresh air.

One was detailed to stand guard, his machine-pistol pointed menacingly down the shaft. None of the prisoners climbed the ladder

The major, immaculate and seemingly indefatigable, strode among his men, handing out cigarettes, clapping them on the shoulder and cracking jokes.

He ordered cartons of food to be unloaded from the last truck and distributed to the men Soldiers squatted, munching biscuits and scooping cold stew with their fingers from cans.

The officer lit a small cigar and, puffing a plume of smoke, pointed to six S.S. men and ordered: "It is time for some military training. Today we shall practise shooting at moving targets.

"Round up the prisoners and make them face the field opposite."

The handful of remaining Jews, reeling with exhaustion, were roughly kicked and pushed into a line facing the distant city of Ypres.

The major stubbed out his cigar and ground it beneath the heel of his boot. He shouted to the prisoners: "This is your big chance of freedom! When, on the count of three, I fire my pistol, you will race for your lives.

"I promise that any man who passes that tree twenty metres away will be allowed to live and to go wherever he wishes. One . . . two . . . three . . . go!!"

He shot the prisoner at the extreme left of the line in the back.

At the sound, the Jews stumbled forward, their legs refusing to allow them to break even into a trot. The officer gestured to the six soldiers, armed with their Schmeissers. He raised his right arm and then dropped it to his side.

A fusillade of automatic fire crackled, and the prisoners fell to the ground. Two were still writhing and screaming. The S.S. major ordered: "Collect all the filth and throw it down the shaft."

The soldiers dragged all the fallen men at the site by the ankles to the mouth of the Frauenlob. Then, a pair of S.S. man taking each body's arms and legs, tossed the Jews one by one down the shaft.

Jacques heard a faint murmuring coming from underground. The guard pointed his Schmeisser down the shaft, and fired an echoing burst.

When the grisly task was completed, the major ordered his n.c.o.s to line up the S.S. men. Hands clasped behind his back, cigar smouldering between his fingers, he addressed them cheerfully.

He said: "We have one last job, men, and then we can go home. You must put a lid on our lovely Frauenlob and cover her up. I do not want you to even try to guess what is down there.

"Suffice to say, we are obeying the Fuhrer's express orders. He wishes our work here to remain a secret forever. If you are ever tempted to betray his trust, you must remember your sacred oaths.

"You, the men of the Fuhrer's elite, have sworn faithfully to serve our beloved Leader even unto death. The trust he places in you is more valuable than all the gold in the world.

"Right, get to it! The quicker you finish, the quicker you will get back to enjoy your suppers and a warm bed. We have even been able to provide a jew girl for every man who feels that way inclined."

The shaft was capped by sunken railway sleepers. The soldiers worked with a will, shovelling earth until no trace of the mineshaft remained. The lakes lying in the nearby fields were already soaking into the soil.

Hitler's secret treasure and the souls trapped with it were drowning.

In spite of the major's warning, the troops couldn't help conjecturing what might be contained in those weighty boxes. Most likely gold ingots, they guessed, just one of which would make a man rich

But the men of the lightning runes knew Hitler's trust and approbation were worth more than mere gold. In spite of their fatigue, they felt a charge of pride.

The major gave orders to call in the "ring of steel" cordoning off the area. Jacques watched the weary men come in from the fields, footpaths and lanes surrounding Bavarian wood.

They, too, were given biscuits and cold stew. The major walked among his men, humming a cheerful popular song. When the troops had finished their Spartan meal, he barked: "Line up, backs to the wood!"

The soldiers obeyed like a well-oiled machine and stood to attention, backs rigid, eyes front. The officer smiled approvingly. In spite of their muddy uniforms, they looked what they were—Hitler's finest.

He shouted: "From the right, number!"

The major took a black-bound notebook and a pencil from his tunic pocket and made a calculation. He nodded, satisfied at his arithmetic.

He barked : "Lay your weapons on the ground. Shultz! Braun! Collect them and stack them in front of me."

The soldiers looked puzzled, but obeyed immediately. Shultz and Braun made several journeys, piling the collected Scheissers and Lugers in front of the major's immaculate jackboots.

He snapped: "You two will retain your weapons. Stand next to me. When I give you the next order, you will obey at once and without question. The rest of you will remain at attention."

The major, flanked by the two soldiers, stood facing his comrades for a long moment. He reached into his pocket for another cigar. The scrape of his match broke the heavy silence.

Nonchalantly, the S.S. officer picked up one of the machine-pistols and pointed it at the line of S.S. men.

Suddenly, the major barked: "Shultz! Braun! Open fire!" His own Schmeisser was the first to spit death. Within seconds, the other two soldiers hosed their bullets up and down the black-clad troops.

The S.S. men went down like mown corn. Some lay in the stillness of death. Others groaned, screamed and thrashed on the ground.

The major addressed the two remaining soldiers, holding their empty weapons and staring, wide-eyed at the carnage: "Stay still! Don't move a muscle!"

He walked in front of them, drew his Luger and calmly shot each man between the eyes. Schultz and Braun crumpled to the ground. Then, cigar in mouth, he strolled to the line of fallen S.S. men, dispatching each with a *coup de grace* in the head.

The boy at the edge of the wood watched the slaughter aghast. He was bone-tired, painfully cramped and lying in his own filth. This nightmare scene would haunt him for the rest of his days.

The major stood alone on the killing ground. He threw away the stub of his cigar, holstered his Luger and permitted himself the luxury of taking off his cap. The wind, blowing from the Messines ridge, ruffled his blond hair.

With his finely-chiselled Aryan features, he looked like a heroic S.S. man on a propaganda poster.

From the direction of distant Ypres, the summer breeze bore the faint sound of approaching military vehicles. The major replaced his cap, straightening it to military correctness.

The next act in this bloody drama was about to begin.

Untersturmfuhrer Wernhe Konig lay prone in the long grass. His "hunter's hide" was in a field next to a stone farmhouse. The old building stood at the foot of the slope that rose gently to Bavarian Wood.

He expertly gauged the distance to the distant trees as 500 metres. A shot at this range was nursery work for a sniper of Wernhe's calibre. But he knew he must take every precaution against failure. This one shot had to be perfect.

It had been impressed on the S.S. sniper that this assignment was a matter of life and death. An accurate shot would be death for the target. A miss would result in death for himself.

Wernhe was confident. He had proved time and again that he was the best of the best. He had rarely been known to miss.

That was why he, the lowly equivalent to the Army rank of second lieutenant, had been entrusted with this top secret duty by no less a Nazi luminary than *Reichsfuhrer-S.S.* Heinrich Himmler himself.

When Wernhe was called to Berlin and told to report to the S.S. chief's office, he was filled with trepidation. Himmler was held in awe from the highest to the lowest in the S.S., an organization, which the *Reichsfuhrer* himself had founded.

His reputation struck chill into every man, woman and child in Nazi Europe. He was a bogeyman—sinister and without pity—who brought fear and death to millions.

Himmler, it was widely known, had marched shoulder-to-shoulder with Hitler back in 1923. The former fertiliser salesman and failed chicken farmer bore the Nazi standard through the turbulent streets of Munich during the failed Beer Hall Putsch.

Now everyone knew that 44-year-old Heinrich Himmler had the ear of Adolf Hitler himself.

Wernhe wondered what so elevated a Nazi could possibly want with himself. Had someone, perhaps, falsely denounced him as plotting against the Fuhrer?

He knew such things happened. As he waited outside the panelled oak door of Himmler's office, the 23-year-old lieutenant frenziedly ran through the names of jealous rivals.

A toxic whisper from any one of them could result in prolonged torture and the firing squad.

An immaculately-uniformed aide poked his head round Himmler's door and silently beckoned Wernhe inside.

The lieutenant marched to where the great man was working at his desk, stamped to a halt and came rigidly to attention. Himmler, monocle glinting, continued to flip through a heap of papers, occasionally scrawling his signature.

The sniper wondered whether this consummate clerk with the Hitler-type moustache was consigning millions of filthy Jews to their deaths.

It was well-known in the S.S. that Himmler and Reinhard Heydrich had orchestrated the Final Solution— the extermination of the Jewish race.

At last, the *Reichsfuhrer* looked up. When he spoke to his quaking junior officer, his face was bland and his tone reassuringly mild: "You may stand at ease *Untersturmfuhrer* Konig."

Wernher snapped to the approved parade ground "at ease" position.

Himmler told him: "On second thoughts, pull up a chair. I have important things to explain and I want your full attention."

The junior officer, looking round, saw an uncomfortable-looking, straight-backed chair standing against the wall. The *Reichsfuhrer* obviously didn't encourage visitors to linger.

Wernhe picked up the chair and placed it in front of Himmler's desk. He sat down, hands folded in his lap, back still rigidly to attention.

The S.S. chief fixed him with a piercing gaze, as though pinning a butterfly to a board. He said: "I take it for granted you are a loyal servant of our Fuhrer, of the third Reich, and of myself."

The lieutenant, bowels turning to water, replied: "Yes, *Herr Reichsfuhrer*, most certainly, *Herr Reichsfuhrer!*" Thinking quickly, he added diplomatically: "I would consider it a great privilege to give my life for you, personally, sir."

Himmler grunted and went on: "Many have, *untersturmfuhrer*. But that is beside the point at this moment."

He opened a folder lying in the exact centre of his blotter and went on: "I see you are a most accurate sniper. I have urgent need of a man with such a talent."

Himmler slid open a drawer of his desk and brought out a single sheet of paper. He offered it to the lieutenant, instructing him: "Read this extremely carefully Commit it to memory.

"Here are the date, place and exact timing of your mission. You must not deviate by a single second. Failure would have serious and—for you—fatal consequences.

"The Fuhrer himself has issued these orders. You will not fail him."

Wernher's hands, rock-steady on a rifle butt, were shaking as he read his orders. He assured Himmler: "You can rely on me, sir. I shall do my duty."

Himmler emphasised: "Everything must be carried out to the second. You will depart from the area the very instant your mission is accomplished. You will otherwise hear and see nothing."

The S.S. chief's words dripped ice, the threat naked: "Eyes will be watching, *untersturmfuhrer*. I shall know exactly what goes on in Flanders."

The *Reichsfuhrer* made Wernher repeat his orders three times. Then he produced a cigarette lighter, set a corner of the document on fire and dropped the flaming paper into a metal waste-paper bin.

He told the junior officer: "Those orders have never existed. You are dismissed."

Now, lying with the sweet scent of the meadow in his nostrils, the moment was fast approaching. A cricket chirped and, in the nearby farm's byre, a cow bellowed mournfully.

But the marksman was deaf to everything as he focused his sniper sight on the S.S. major, pacing restlessly at the edge of Bavarian Wood.

The magnification of the sight was so great, Wernhe almost felt he could reach out and touch his target.

The sniper ignored the sight of the bodies of the fellow S.S. men littering the clearing. They were irrelevant. His business was with the major who was, at this moment, lighting a small cigar.

The lieutenant raised his eye from the sight and checked his watch. It was nearly time. The rifle was loaded and the safety-catch off. He must not miss. His life depended on it.

Eyes were upon him . . . including those of Himmler and the Fuhrer.

The *untersturmfuhrer* began to sweat with the stress and concentration. But he held the weapon rock-steady, like the professional he was. The second hand of his watch swept steadily round the dial.

Wernhe looked once more through the sight. The man seemed instinctively to sense danger. He stopped pacing, took the cigar from his lips and turned to peer into the wood.

The sniper rested the cross hairs of his sight squarely between the man's shoulder blades. A last brief look at his watch, a pause, then he squeezed the trigger.

The single shot echoed across the peaceful fields, sending up a flock of cawing crows. The major slumped to the ground and lay still.

Wernhe knew at once that the target was dead. Wounded men instinctively throw out their arms to break their fall. Dead men collapse like a sack of coals.

His duty was done. Just as he had ignored the soldiers' bodies in the clearing, he thrust from his mind any question why this man—a fellow S.S. soldier—had to die.

Wernhe had obeyed orders and was content.

He slung his rifle across his back, and jogged to the BMW motor-cycle he had earlier parked behind a stone wall. The sniper kicked the machine into life and roared down the lane leading towards Voormezele and Ypres.

The young officer had gone only 50 yards when he was waved into the side and signalled to halt by an S.S. motor-cyclist coming in the opposite direction.

Werhne waved a casual greeting. But the man ignored him, the eyes behind his goggles expressionless.

Half a minute later, two motor-cycle combinations, soldiers armed with machine-guns in their side-cars, swept past. They were followed by a camouflaged, heavily-armoured staff car with tinted windows. A radio antenna whipped from its roof.

The sniper, sitting astride his BMW with its engine idling, guessed the car must contain somebody of the highest importance. What could such a person be doing out here in the boondocks?

A military truck drove past, its doors bare of regimental insignia. The driver, in familiar black S.S. uniform, stared woodenly ahead.

Wernhe, looking into one of the mirrors on his handlebars, saw the vehicles climb the hill and turn into the clearing in front of Bavarian Wood

He started with surprise as a gloved hand fell heavily on his shoulder. He looked up to see the S.S. motor-cyclist, his machine propped on its stand, gesturing for him to continue his journey.

Wernhe put his bike into gear and set off down the lane. He felt uneasy at the delay. But he told himself he had obeyed Himmler's orders to leave the scene of the shooting as quickly as possible.

As he roared towards the old Tommies' town of "Wipers", he wondered where those watching eyes were hidden.

The lieutenant took a sharp bend into the village of Voormezele, and was abruptly brought to a halt by a road block. He was surprised to see the soldiers manning it were from Hitler's elite S.S. bodyguard.

A sergeant stepped into the road, took a quick look at the rifle slung over Wernhe's back and waved him through. As the lieutenant rode away, the n.c.o. spoke urgently into the microphone of a field radio.

The sniper turned into a former Belgian Army camp on the outskirts of Ypres He propped his machine on to its stand by the red and white striped pole at the entrance and stomped imperiously into the guard-room.

An orderly *Wehrmacht* corporal, chair tilted comfortably back and feet on his desk, looked up from a pornographic novel. He took in his visitor's black uniform, with its lightning flashes and badges of rank, and snapped to attention.

He asked: "How may I be of help to the *untersturmfuhrer*?"

Wernher snapped: "I must use your telephone. Leave now. Don't return until I shout for you. If you or anyone else eavesdrops, I will shoot them. Go! Now!"

The lieutenant listened intently until the sound of the corporal's boots died away. Then he picked up the phone and snarled at the operator: "I wish to be put through to this number at once.

"This is a call of top importance to *Reichsfuhrer* Himmler himself. It will immediately be known if you listen, and you will be summarily dealt with. Quickly, now."

There was a click in the earpiece and then a mush of static. Werhne realised the call was being patched through to a radio frequency. The mild voice that spoke to him was unmistakably Himmler's.

"Well?"

"It is done, *mein Reichsfuhrer*, exactly as ordered."

"I already know that, Konig. You will now proceed to the Hotel de Ville, in Cassel, and report to a Colonel von Baum. He is expecting you."

Another click. Silence. Himmler had cut the line.

Werhne shouted for the corporal, who took his time coming.

"Give me precise directions to Cassel, corporal."

"It is on a hill just over the border with France, sir. It will take you just 20 minutes on your motor-cycle."

"I ordered you to give me *precise* directions, man. If you are incapable of that, fetch me a map."

The n.c.o. delved into a filing cabinet and produced a map of the area. The officer snatched it, spread the map on the desk and studied it. Satisfied, he screwed it into a ball and marched out of the guard-room.

As the motor-cycle throbbed into life, the corporal shut the door, made a rude gesture in the direction of the departing lieutenant, and went back to reading the novel.

Konig picked up speed and was half a mile down the road from the camp when a wire, stretched between two trees, took his head off.

A week later, a dozen hostages from nearby farms were rounded up by the Gestapo. They were executed for the atrocity, for which the local Resistance was blamed.

Jacques, eyes red-rimmed from trauma and fatigue, filthy and stinking, watched the next scene of the drama unfold. The armoured staff car parked next to the Frauenlob.

The truck stopped near to where the boy was hiding. S.S. troopers let down the tail-board and jumped out. They strolled up and down, stretching to remove the kinks of the journey from their muscles.

One unbuttoned his fly and urinated over one of the bodies, so close to the hidden boy that liquid splashed on to his face. Jacques lay so still that a passing fox sniffed his feet before slipping silently into the undergrowth.

A sergeant formed the men into three ranks and ordered them to come to attention. The soldiers stood amid the corpses and waited silently.

A *standartenfuhrer*—Colonel—climbed down from the cab of the lorry. He marched over to the staff car, opened a rear door and, throwing up a Nazi salute, also stood to attention.

A slight, bookish-looking officer stepped out and fastidiously adjusted his dress sword. The S.S. men gasped. This man was no other than their legendary leader and inspiration. This was the *Reichsfuhrer* in the flesh.

Himmler made his way to the front of the ranks of S.S. men. The sun broke through the banked summer clouds, as though cued to spotlight the Nazi superstar. When he spoke, his voice was the unassuming voice of a clerk.

Monocle sparkling in the sunlight, he told the soldiers: "Our sacred duty is to protect our Fuhrer from his enemies. We are also the sword of his vengeance. Today, others have justly wreaked that vengeance, as you can see.

"It saddens my heart that there were traitors within our own ranks—men who betrayed their solemn S.S. oaths to the Fuhrer. Last month, as you know, the impudent enemy came knocking at our door in Normandy.

"This was all part of the Fuhrer's carefully constructed plan. As our gallant soldiers were preparing to annihilate the invaders, certain of our men panicked."

Himmler drew his sword and, with a flourish, pointed at the body of the major. Appalled by the sight of blood leaking from the dead man, he hurriedly turned his head aside.

The *Reichsfuhrer* went on: "Thinking the war was lost, they threw in their lot with a treasonous movement called the White Rose. These despicable traitors plotted against the Fuhrer and the Fatherland.

"We sniffed them out like the stinking vermin they were. They were taken to this lonely spot and eliminated.

"Now you, our most trusted soldiers, will perform another task for our Fuhrer. He orders you to wipe the remains of these wretches off the face of the earth."

The S.S. leader raised his arm in a stiff Nazi salute and shouted: "Heil Hitler!" The soldiers returned the salute and chorused the shout. Himmler got back into the car and was swiftly driven away.

The sergeant barked orders and the men broke ranks. Jacques watched as they removed the earth and railway sleepers sealing the mouth of the Frauenlob. One by one, the bodies were tossed down the shaft, landing with a distant splash.

Swiftly, the S.S. men replaced the sleepers and resealed the shaft with soil. Then they climbed into the truck, which drove back down the hill.

Within a quarter of a mile of the spot where the S.S. sniper was murdered, the Resistance appeared to strike again. A series of bombs, exploded by a trip wire, wiped out the lorry and its occupants.

Back at Bavarian Wood, Jacques finally eased himself from his hiding place. He was a sorry sight, ashen face streaked with tears as, still clutching his fishing rod, he stumbled across the fields towards home.

The tousle-headed boy was passing a patch of trampled grass, where part of the S.S. "ring of steel" had been posted, when he heard footsteps swishing behind him.

He was caught in an iron grip and roughly spun round. Wilfred Lacroix, wearing the uniform of the local Nazis, thrust his face close to the boy's.

"Where have you been, my little man? Tell, or I'll break your arm . . . just for a start."

CHAPTER TEN

June 6, 1917

The couple lay together on the fetid battlefield. Bright moonlight revealed shell-holes, rotting corpses and the flotsam and jetsam of war. This was no lovers' tryst.

Marie, disguised as a German soldier in Hitler's second-best overcoat and cap, shivered uncontrollably. There was danger everywhere. Her ears rang to the unending British artillery barrage, the sort she knew sent soldiers mad.

A shell landed nearby, showering Marie and Hitler with clods of earth and other, decomposing and unspeakable things. There was another blast just yards away. Then came two more . . . each more terrible than the last.

Fumes assaulted the young girl's nose and grit stung her tear-filled eyes. A flare climbed lazily into the sky. Its bright light made Marie feel naked and vulnerable

A machine-gun stuttered. Shrapnel hissed around the couple like the Devil's hailstones. Death stalked this place.

Marie looked up at the Messines Ridge in front of them. Its dark shape seemed like a crouching, feral animal.

The teenaged French girl, used to working in peaceful fields far behind the lines, felt her nerves shredding like carrots being prepared for the pot.

Dolphie had made her bring a soldier's pack. There was nothing military about its exotic contents. They were part of his plan.

Bizarrely, in this ugly place of death, she was carrying filmy and seductive clothes. The sexy sort that turned men's heads and made them lose their senses. She had been ordered to forget her underwear.

Soon, she must play the shameful tart. She must be unfaithful to the man she loved to distraction. It was that very man who had ordered her infidelity and humiliation. She dared not disobey.

Marie knew that, at the least sign of reluctance, Dolphie would fly into one of his terrible rages. He had done this many times since she had told him her momentous news.

Later, he had hatched this scheme of debasement. Dolphie told her it was the only way she could please him now, after so nearly upsetting his sacred plans for the future.

She would do anything to earn a glint of approval from his beautiful blue eyes. She would even soil her Catholic soul by committing this sin

Marie had looked over this lethal battlefield before they started out, and she told Dolphie they must surely die. But he assured her they were immortal. His Voice told him so.

Fate was saving him for the role of a Colossus astride the world stage. Hadn't he, a *meldegange*—one of the most dangerous jobs in the war—survived, while millions perished?

Didn't his Voice, to quote just a single example, miraculously save his life one day in the trenches?

Lying in bed one afternoon in their Comines love nest, Hitler told Marie how he had been sitting on the trench's fire-step with some comrades, eating his dinner from a mess tin.

Suddenly, his Voice warned him to move immediately. He left his meal, ran down the trench and took shelter behind a revetment. Seconds later, a howitzer shell landed on the very spot he had been eating.

His comrades were blown to smithereens. He had helped to put what little was left of them into a couple of sandbags.

Now Hitler was lying on the battlefield next to his mistress, red-hot fragments of metal hissing round them. He was calmly studying his watch. All was going to plan. Amazingly, they hadn't even been challenged by a sentry.

Marie moved slightly to ease her position, and felt something uncomfortably sticking into her belly. She reached into the soil beneath her and recoiled with revulsion.

Her hand had met another, its fingers stiffened by death. She screamed and, as the guns had fallen briefly silent, Hitler heard her cry. He looked at her with contempt. He couldn't abide any sign of weakness.

He wondered whether, after all, he was being weak by allowing this girl to live. She could one day prove to be an obstacle on his road to greatness.

For, as Solomons had once contemptuously reported, Hitler planned to tell his adoring millions in the years to come that his only love, mistress and bride was Germany herself.

The *gefreiter* knew his followers from Black Marie's would keep their mouths shut about the girl. He had already let them sip a cocktail of power and vaulting ambition, and they wouldn't want to lose the taste of that heady brew.

As soon as that stupid peasant girl told him she was pregnant, Hitler knew the bitch mustn't be allowed to remain in Comines. Her swelling belly would broadcast their shameful secret.

Politics alone decreed she must vanish from the scene. First, he had wondered whether Marie should die with a bullet in the belly, just like that bastard Solomons. Like he had decreed the men who jeered at him in the railway carriage should be dealt with.

His Voice was silent on the subject of Marie's pregnancy. But the *gefreiter* felt instinctively that Marie was destined secretly to bear his baby.

The child would have the blood of the Fuhrer in his veins. There may come a day when the world would be in need of another White Crow. That would, in a way, make Adolf Hitler immortal.

So Marie LeBrun was allowed to live. But she would be watched until the end of her days.

Meanwhile, the fury of what was to become the Battle of Messines built around the strange couple lying among the dead.

Hitler, the secret strategic genius, had built the prospect of a German defeat this night into his plan. The fate of the trembling girl beside him was dependent on the Germans being blown up, then pushed off the ridge.

For, although Kaiser Wilhelm's generals were clapping one another optimistically on the back at this very moment, the lowly corporal believed he knew why they would lose the coming battle.

The Messines affair was to be very different to the set-piece battles that had gone before. This was not to be the usual grand but futile attempt at a major Allied breakthrough. The Tommies were planning only to land one solid, hefty punch to send the enemy reeling.

Hitler's brilliant grasp of the situation came from studying maps at the regimental headquarters, set up in the crypt of Messines church. Time and again, he pedalled his trusty bicycle there with messages.

Once inside, Hitler always begged a cup of ersatz coffee. He used the time he spent sipping it, in assessing the current strategic situation. Staff officers, busy with their futile plans, scarcely noticed the humble *gefreiter*. His expert blue eyes shrewdly drank in information.

The *gefreiter* could read a map and the story told by its little pinned flags, as easily as his comrades devoured their pornographic books.

Hitler knew the pompous staff nincompoops were mistaken in expecting the customary Allied attack at Messines. These officers thought the present heavy shelling would be followed by waves of infantry, advancing behind a creeping barrage.

The Tommies would be expected to walk into murderous machine-gun fire. Then the Germans would counter-attack to regain lost ground. The staff officers expected the battle to drag on for days.

They told themselves it was all a matter of attrition. Who would lose the most first? The defenders, they believed, would always have the upper hand.

Corporal Hitler believed the opposite. In his opinion, the Battle of Messines would be swift, deadly and different. This was because there was a brilliant new British general in charge.

Hitler had heard that General Herbert Plumer had a deep love of mining and explosives. So, Hitler calculated, the seeds of the approaching German defeat were, at this very moment, buried deep beneath their feet.

This was to be a unique victory, made possible by many tons of buried high-explosives.

What would Hitler himself have done to defeat the entrenched Germans at Messines? He would have set off a chain of mines, and then unleashed an infantry *blitzkrieg—lightning war*—on the dazed defenders.

192

That was the exact scenario Plumer, leader of the British Second Army, had painstakingly drawn up.

The avuncular, moustachioed general had begun planning his Explosive Surprise a year ago. He knew it was essential to wipe out the Messines strong-point that had dominated the British for two and a half years.

Just as Hitler surmised, Plumer's sappers had driven galleries under the war-torn soil of no-man's land. Some of these tunnels were amazing engineering feats—up to 2,160 feet long and 125 feet deep.

In all, the human moles burrowed more than 7,300 yards, heaving trolley-loads of high explosive behind them. To solve the problem of the wet soil, the tunnels were made in a layer of "blue clay".

Plumer, a stickler for meticulous planning, had issued orders that no less than 22 mines should be planted beneath the enemy. He was determined to blow the top right off the Messines-Wytschaete ridge.

First, he softened the Germans up. The barrage which Hitler and his mistress were at present enduring in No-Man's land had been thundering since May 21. The overture of shellfire built to a mighty crescendo this very night.

Behind the British lines gunners, stripped to the waist and bathed in sweat, slaved to feed 2,300 hungry guns and 300 heavy mortars. Even the humblest German private, hunched fearfully in his trench, hands clapped over his ears, knew this hail of steel must be the prelude to an attack.

A great blow was about to fall on the ridge. But, on the German side of the lines, Hitler was the only one to guess its magnitude and nature.

Marie sobbed and Hitler frequently consulted the watch given to him by his Munich landlady, Frau Popp. As they lay on the battle-field, Plumer was holding an eve-of-the-battle conference.

Pacing in front of a map on the wall of the ornate drawing-room of his chateau headquarters, the General appeared like the caricature Colonel Blimp. He sported an exuberant white moustache, bushy white hair and a burgeoning pot belly.

But he had one of the British Army's sharpest military minds, and was held in high esteem in the corridors of power.

Although Plumer was a strict disciplinarian, he was held in great affection by his men, who found his very presence reassuring. This night was to prove one of the pinnacles of his career.

And, unknown to the general, it was also to be of great benefit to the future Fuhrer of Germany.

Plumer regarded his red-tabbed staff officers as tobacco smoke wreathed in the room like a Flanders gas attack. Pointing with his cane to the Messines-Wytschaete Ridge on the map, he announced: with a chuckle: "Gentlemen, we may not make history tomorrow, but we will certainly change the geography!"

In the British trenches, more than 10,000 men waited for the attack to begin. They were dry-mouthed and their stomachs threatened to betray their fear. Some prayed for the first time since they were children at Sunday School.

Others scribbled notes to their loved ones in their field note-books, which they then replaced in their tunic pockets. They hoped that, if they "went West", some kindly stretcher-bearer would search their pockets and forward their final messages to Blighty.

Every Tommy, as he waited for the officers' shrill whistles, which would send him "over the top" of the trench's parapet, wondered whether he would live to see the dawn.

Among them was Sergeant Ernie Cornish of the North Kents. He little knew Fate was to single him out to survive and to carry out a special duty this night.

On the other side of the lines, Hitler took a last look at his watch and decided the time had come. He urged a reluctant Marie to her feet, and the couple ran through the bursting shells.

A farm-house loomed, the moonlight bleaching its whitewashed walls to the ashen pallor of old bones. This was the place where Hitler's lover would wait for one of the jigsaw pieces of his plan to fall into place.

The couple stumbled, ankle-deep, into a stinking pile of human and animal manure. This midden was in the middle of a traditional Flemish farm-yard, surrounded on three sides by animal and human living quarters.

The building's blown-out windows, dark as a skull's eye sockets, seemed to stare at the panting couple. Rafters, bare of tiles, reached like bony fingers towards the night sky The farm was deserted, its occupants having long since fled.

Suddenly, an emaciated fox terrier raced from one of the cattle byres, its frenzied barking rendered soundless by the shelling. The dog ran straight up to Hitler, tail thrashing, tongue lolling in joy.

He bent over the animal, scratching its ears and cooing. The man who had watched, unmoved, as hundreds of his fellow human beings died, was reduced to butter by this stray animal.

Hitler unslung his pack, reached into it and brought out some sausage, which he fed to the dog. It devoured the food ravenously. The corporal bent close to Marie's ear and shouted: "Meet Fox'l—Little Fox—my faithful friend.

"He and I met on the battlefield after he came over from the Tommy lines. Here we are again, alive and in one piece. Perhaps my Voice looks after all three of us."

Hitler patted Fox'l and gently shooed him away. The dog had no part to play in his plan.

The British gunners orchestrated their barrage to a Wagnerian thunder. The flashes of exploding shells constantly lit the farm's white walls. It was a scene straight from Hades.

The dog scuttled back to the comparative safety of the byre.

Marie huddled into the oversized great-coat, as though its flimsy fabric would shield her from harm. Hitler shouted in her ear, his voice calm and commanding: "You must take a grip on yourself. I have told you repeatedly, you will come to no harm.

"You may say 'hello' to my and Fox'l's old home, Bethlehem Farm. It is now to be *your* home, although I trust you won't be staying for long. I was billeted here for three comfortable months, so I know the place well.

"I will show you the cellar, where I used to sleep soundly. You will be as safe there as the King of England is in his palace in London. Stop snivelling, girl, and let me take you to safety.

"Then I must go. For tonight, I have a very special duty to perform. After I leave, you will carry out my orders to the letter. It will all work out perfectly. You will see, *mademoiselle*. I am never wrong.

"Now, follow me."

Marie trailed fearfully after her lover's dim figure as he went through a door, hanging by one hinge, and into the kitchen of the ruined farm-house.

For the hundredth time, she asked herself what sane girl would allow herself to take part in this dangerous and humiliating drama.

But she was *not* in command of her senses, any more than the men in the asylums for the shell-shocked. Marie admitted she was hopelessly and completely in the thrall of this odd and compelling man.

She felt she had no option but to obey Dolphie. She was, as ever, desperate to please him. Marie yearned to bask in approbation from those blue, blue eyes.

Here he was, ordering her to be unfaithful to him—this man who had become the whole reason for her being. Worse, to please him, she must sleep with a stranger she had yet to meet.

What would her father say? What would her mother say? What would her confessor say?

Hitler felt in his pocket and brought out a candle, which he lit with a match. He stuck the candle into the neck of a bottle, standing on a debris-strewn kitchen table. Shadows danced on the walls in time to the bellowing of the guns.

The German soldier seemed quite at home in this house of ghosts. He opened a drawer in the kitchen table and took out half a dozen more candles. Then he went to a huge country sideboard, its cups, saucers, jugs and plates long ago shattered.

From this, he picked up an oil lamp, lit it and pulled aside the kitchen table. The guttering flame revealed a large trap door in the floor, with an ancient brass ring set in the middle.

Hitler tugged the trap open. A flight of rickety stairs descended into darkness. Adolf Hitler told the quaking girl: "Now you'll see your snug little home. I'll light the way."

Marie climbed carefully downwards, her nose wrinkling at the musty smell of the cellar. At the bottom, they paused, their shadows thrown on rough walls.

So this was home. Marie peered round. A rough table stood on a square of mildewed carpet, with two milking stools serving as chairs. In the shadows, she could make out a truckle bed, pushed against a wall.

There was a large milk churn in one corner, obviously meant to contain the cellar's water supply, and a covered bucket in the other. Marie's mind shied from guessing its contents.

She thought hopelessly: "This isn't a home. It is a prison. Dolphie says a battle will soon begin. Will it bring the house crashing down over my head? Will this be my tomb?"

Frightened of sparking one of her lover's rages, Marie said nothing. Whatever happened, she would be a good girl. She would do anything to make Dolphie content. That would be her constant mission in whatever remained of her life.

All Marie had in the world now was Dolphie. And he was soon to leave her.

Hitler undid the straps of his pack and emptied it on to the table. Out tumbled three loaves of coarse bread, two large sausages and a full water bottle. These were followed by three candles and a box of British Lucifer matches.

He said to Marie: "Now let's see if you have obeyed orders. Turn out your pack and I will check its contents. Sharply, I haven't much time!"

Marie tipped out her pack, turning her face away. The gossamer-light contents floated gently to the table.

She made one last attempt to save herself. She pleaded: "Dolphie, do I really have to do this thing? Is there no other way? I cannot betray you like this . . ."

Hitler ignored her. He was already sorting through the underwear and checking it against a mental list. He picked up a flimsy petticoat, the hem of which would barely reach her thighs.

The neckline was daringly slashed to expose her breasts to the tops of her nipples. The material was so fine that, when Marie had tried it on, it hid nothing of her naked body. Even the triangle of her pubic hair was clearly visible.

Hitler laid the slip to one side and checked a pair of slinky black stockings. These were accompanied by frilly lace garters, each one embroidered with a delicate rose.

Last of all, he held up for examination a sheer, black night-dress. There were tiny forget-me-nots decorating the neckline, which plunged to a point just above her navel

The garment was so brief. Marie would be able neither to sit nor to bend without shamefully exposing herself. This was nothing more nor less than a whore's wardrobe. Even a good Catholic girl like Marie could recognise it as such.

Hitler looked at the wisps of lingerie approvingly. His appreciation was practical rather than sexual.

He smiled and told Marie: "You have done well. This is exactly what I had in mind. It would take a man of stone to resist you in these. Now, take off your clothes and put on the night-dress.

"Hurry! By my calculations, the British should be here soon. You must be ready and suitably adorned. I need you now to return my spare overcoat and cap, or I shall be in trouble with the quartermaster."

Hitler watched expressionlessly as Marie stripped naked, shivering in the dank cellar. He walked to the bed and thrust his hand among the rough, Army-issue blankets.

He announced: "A little damp. But that is to be expected after my long absence. You will soon warm them up. You must act like a true German soldier and smile at discomforts."

Marie slipped the night-dress over her dark curls, walked barefoot to the bed and climbed in. She lay shuddering with cold and fear, watching the man she loved preparing to leave her.

Since she had told him she was pregnant, he had never mentioned whether they would have a future together.

Hitler neatly folded the overcoat she had been wearing so that it wouldn't crease, and thrust it into his pack. He arranged his spare cap on top of it. Then he picked up Marie's empty pack and added it to the load.

He turned and, ignoring the tears trickling down her cheeks, told her curtly "You now have everything you should need. Play your part well, as I have instructed you. Goodbye."

Without a backward glance, Hitler climbed the stairs to the kitchen above. He left the trap-door open, as if in invitation to any callers, and vanished into the darkness.

Marie heard his boots clomp across the kitchen floor. Then she was alone with flickering candles, the sound of the guns and her turbulent thoughts.

With no Dolphie to chide her, she was at last able to surrender to her emotions. She buried her face in the filthy blankets, sobbing great, heaving gasps of despair, loneliness and shame.

Marie looked fearfully at the dark square of the open trap-door. Who would be the next man to come through it? Who would tramp down that old staircase? What would he do to her?

How could 17-year-old Marie LeBrun, once the dutiful daughter of a prosperous butcher and a respected resident of Seboncourt, in the region of St.Quentin, have come to this?

She was as much a victim of the war as the Tommies and Fritzes lying on their beds of pain in military hospitals.

Marie pulled the chilly blankets up to her chin and waited. Just as Dolphie had told her

It was one minute to midnight when Hitler slipped across the shell-torn moonscape of No-Man's land, moving like a sure-footed phantom.

As a veteran messenger, he knew every shell-hole, abandoned trench and length of rusting barbed wire.

The *meldegange's* knowledge of the battlefield rivalled that of Plumer's, on the other side of the lines. The general was said to know "every puddle in the Salient".

Hitler felt impervious to danger, even when exploding shells threw him roughly into the dirt. One landed within killing distance. It buried itself into the soil and failed to go off.

This was what the Tommies called a "dud". To Hitler, this latest escape from death was further proof that his Voice was always correct. He couldn't be killed.

The German soldier steered an unerring course to his old battleground, Axle Wood, now called Bavarian Wood after his valiant regiment. Tortured shapes of shattered trees were silhouetted against the moonlight.

Hitler saw carelessly exposed lights flickering from trenches and concrete strong points as soldiers lit cigars, heated their coffee and cooked their sparse rations.

He circled the spot where he had won his decoration for bravery, and melted into the bushes. Hitler opened the messenger's wallet on his belt and, by the light of the moon, checked it still contained a note, written on an official form.

Hitler, well-used to the phraseology of the military mind, believed he had forged the message to perfection. He ran over its contents in his mind:

From: Colonel List, Commanding Officer, 16th R.I.R.
To: Hauptman Engleman, Adjutant, 16th. R.I.R.
Dated: June 6, 1917.

You will immediately check the explosives below the Frauenlob mine-shaft and compile a situation report accordingly.

You will then, with all dispatch, hand this written information to the runner, who has been instructed to await your reply.

This matter is most urgent.

Signed: List, Colonel commanding 16th R.I.R

Hitler had seen the colonel's signature on orders a thousand times, and was able to forge it with ease.

In Bavarian Wood, Hitler delved farther into the pack. Groping into a secret pocket, his fingers met the cold metal of a British Army-issue Webley revolver.

Some weeks ago, he had eased this weapon from the fingers, not yet stiffened by death, of a British subaltern. The officer had been killed while leading a raid on the German trenches, close to where Hitler was peering over the parapet.

Now, crouching in the bushes, the *gefreiter* assured himself the revolver was fully loaded and the safety catch engaged.

He had previously examined the Webley—standard issue for British officers—with an expert eye. Hitler's loot turned out to be quite a treasure. The revolver was the Mark V1 version, which had gone into production only two years ago.

This Webley was a reliable and hardy weapon, well suited to the mud and filthy conditions of the battle-field.

Deep in Bavarian Wood, Hitler ran an approving finger down the cool metal of the barrel. The weapon was ideal for

Hitler's purpose tonight. It would enable the last part of his plan to click into place.

He stuck the Webley into his belt, revelling in the weight of it against his body. If he bumped into a vigilant sentry who challenged him, he would say he had the gun for protection while carrying out his dangerous duties.

He thought of the task he had set himself, and slipped into one of his frequent fantasies:

That bastard Jew, Hauptman Engelman, who has constantly denied me the promotion I so richly deserve, is about to be hung, as painfully as possible. As the man is led into the execution barn, Hitler sees gleefully that he has soiled his trousers in his fear.

The captain's braces have been removed and, with his hands tied behind him, he finds it difficult to keep his trousers from falling around his ankles He has been denied the mercy of a blindfold, and his eyes are stark with terror.

On Hitler's orders, there is no trap door. A length of piano wire is passed over a beam, a noose swinging menacingly from one end. Two S.S. men place this round Engleman's neck and pull it tight.

Then they tail on to the other end of the piano wire and haul it over the beam. The hauptman's stockinged feet leave the floor. His face turns purple and his tongue and eyes protrude.

He is dying in agony. Hitler is in ecstasy.

Lying in the bushes, Hitler feels an erection pressing against his trousers. The fantasy has succeeded where the sight of his naked mistress failed.

Soon that same German officer would die, but not by the agonising method of Hitler's imagination.

He would file that painful method of disposing of his enemies in his memory. It would no doubt come in useful in the years to come.

The *gefreiter* checked Frau Popp's watch yet again. It was time. He moved into the trench system, scarring the wood like open wounds. With a sure touch, he navigated his way along the trench walls, lined by woven willow branches.

The map of the wood Hitler kept in his head told him exactly where to find the concrete bunker that was his objective.

This bunker served as a first aid post when there were battles. During lulls in the action, the Adjutant used it as his office. Hitler knew the officer scribbled by candlelight there, hour after hour, on a desk made from two ammunition boxes.

Apart from writing recommendations for promotions— or otherwise—*Hauptman* Engleman devoted his life to such trivia as reporting the number of spare boots available, or what men had been a few minutes late reporting for duty.

In Hitler's opinion, the captain was nothing but a pathetic pen-pusher, not fit to be a member of the glorious army of the Fatherland.

While other men were fighting and dying, this Jew was sitting in safety, writing negative reports about Adolf Hitler, one of the bravest and most able men in the regiment.

If it weren't for Engleman holding him back, Hitler would be at least a sergeant-major by now, if not an officer. His comrades at Black Marie's frequently told him so. *They* knew a leader of men when they saw one.

The Yid deserved what was coming to him.

Hitler arrived at the bunker, pushed aside the thick blanket shielding the entrance, and entered the adjutant's stuffy domain. Engleman, annoyed by the interruption, looked up from the pile of papers he was reading.

His frown deepened as he saw the familiar *meldegange,* standing to attention before him and holding out a message.

Engleman couldn't stand this obnoxious man who, unfortunately, seemed to enjoy a charmed life.

He had heard about the *gefreiter's* diatribes against, among others, the Jews. This apology for a soldier was nothing but a rabble-rouser and trouble-maker. Word was that some of the other ranks were even beginning to listen to his poison.

Such barrack-room lawyers were dangerous, and had to be kept in their place . . . which was off the promotion list.

Engleman had read Hitler's records and noted that, before the war, he was a ne'er-do-well and a drifter. If the adjutant had had his way, the man would never have even been made *gefreiter.*

It was only because he daren't countermand the colonel's specific order, that Engleman had forwarded a recommendation for Hitler's Iron Cross, Second Class.

In the bunker, Hitler saluted, handed the captain the forged message, and waited at attention while he read it. The adjutant pointedly omitted to tell him to stand at ease.

Engleman tucked the message into a pocket and lit a storm lantern. He stood up abruptly, buckled on his belt and put on his cap. Picking up the lamp, he ordered: "You are to come with me."

Hitler, playing the good soldier, obediently followed the adjutant out of the bunker and into the moonlit trenches. The British guns continued to hammer the ridge as the two men made their way to the mouth of the Frauenlob mine shaft.

At this time of night, the shaft was deserted. Dim lights pierced the blackness of its depths and water and air pumps continued to throb. Engleman checked that he had the necessary pencil and notebook for his task.

Raising his voice above the roar of artillery, he ordered Hitler "Wait for me here. Don't move an inch. Understood? Not an inch!"

The officer placed a foot on the first metal rung of the ladder to begin his descent into the explosive-packed galleries.

Engelman thought to himself: "With a bit of luck, a fragment of Tommy shrapnel will come along while I'm safely below and take our trouble-maker's head clean off."

The adjutant's head and shoulders were still above ground level when Hitler drew his Webley and held it behind his back. He slipped off the safety catch and waited until the *hauptman* sank out of sight. Then Hitler peered down the mouth of the shaft.

He looked at the lamp-lit shape of the officer on the ladder just below him. Injecting a note of urgency into his voice, Hitler shouted: "Sir! Sir! Come quickly! There is an emergency! You are needed immediately!"

Hitler turned and addressed an imaginary audience: "It's o.k, sir. The adjutant is here. I caught him just in time. He will be with us in seconds."

The *hauptman*, startled, looked up inquiringly. Hitler shot him in the middle of the forehead. The officer's body slumped across the shaft, blocking it.

Hitler walked quickly into the darkness of the wood, rubbing the front of his trousers and giving a rare smile. He threw the Webley deep into the bushes.

The thunder of the guns rose to a new crescendo. Because of the intensity of the barrage, nobody ventured from their funk holes and dug-outs. An hour later, a British howitzer shell burst on the Frauenlob, sealing it.

Adolf Hitler, watching from the shadows, saw the satisfactory completion of his night's work.

Two more problems solved.

CHAPTER ELEVEN

April 22, 1945

Hitler lifted the slice of cake from a bone china plate, silently placed before him by one of his secretaries, and bit into it delicately. His hand trembled as he brushed crumbs from his black, uniform trousers.

The walls of the Fuhrerbunker shuddered from the explosions of nearby Russian shells. The Slav sub-humans were drawing ever nearer . . . street by bitterly-contested street in ruined Berlin.

The end was near.

Hitler's Voice had been silent for many, many months. His spiritual guide from the trenches had deserted him.

Here, alone in his subterranean study beneath the Chancellery, Hitler admitted he was no longer wrapped in a cloak of immortality. But, even though the Third Reich was in its death throes, the Fuhrer was confident he would beat them yet.

He would bequeath to the world an immortal legacy of National Socialism. There would be more Nuremburg-style glory days, more territorial conquests, more cleansings.

A new generation of Nazis would build a world-wide Fourth Reich, which would triumph through the millenniums. He could almost hear the roar of the crowds' *sieg heil*—hail to victory.

Hitler knew that soon he must die. But he had made sure his spirit and his powerful, shining crusade would march on.

He took another slice of cake, demolishing it hungrily. Although Hitler's world was falling apart, his appetite for cake and his favourite vegetable soup was undiminished.

The Fuhrer ran a finger beneath his famous moustache, sat back in his chair and surveyed the instrument of Nazi immortality which lay on his desk.

It took the form of a modest metal box, of a size that might serve as a container for a handful of large cigars. Hitler stared at the device as though hypnotised.

This box, so humble in appearance, represented the cutting edge of world technology. Only Nazi Germans, inspired by their great leader, could have created such a miracle.

Its potential was greater even than that of the "vengeance weapons"—rockets and flying bombs—he had sent to rain down on England. This box contained the future of his world.

Hitler reached out and ran a finger over the cold metal of the box's lid, stopping midway to caress a shuttered lens. The chill touch felt reassuring in this place of fear.

There was a knock on the door. Hitler slid the box into a drawer of his desk and pretended to be writing in his diary. Today's page contained nothing but a record of his daily diet of pills, potions and drops.

Before pressing the button on his desk to order the caller to enter, Hitler switched to his angry and optimistic mindset. He thrust all thoughts of imminent defeat into the darkest recesses of his mind.

An S.S. general entered. He stood before his Fuhrer, notebook and pen poised. He was immediately bombarded with a barrage of fury and useless orders.

Hitler, flecks of spittle flying, blue eyes blazing, issued "no surrender" exhortations to Army divisions that no longer existed.

He dictated a string of execution warrants, accusing generals already dead of treason. He went into precise but unlikely details of his forthcoming wedding to Eva Braun.

The S.S. general, thinking only of escape from the bunker, managed to keep his face impassive as he scribbled busily. Finally and explosively, Hitler was finished.

"Get out of my sight!" he roared, pointing at the door, a lock of hair falling over his eyes: "You're as bad as the rest. Defeatists! Cowards! Betrayers!"

The S.S. officer tucked the notebook and pen into a pocket and left. Hitler was alone with the cold reality of his thoughts.

The Fuhrer's eyes lost their fire and became dim and haunted. He could no longer control the tremors seizing his left arm and leg. He was physically disintegrating, like his world around him.

One last slice of cake remained. As he bit into it, Hitler decided that he had nothing with which to reproach himself. When he came to stand at the gates of death, the Aryan God Above would thank him for cleansing His world.

He would praise him for casting out the evils of Jews, Marxists, Slavs and Freemasons. Hitler could look forward to being reunited with the heroes with whom he had fought in the trenches.

The fallen Fuhrer would join them and countless other Teutonic heroes in Valhalla.

He shuddered. Surely, those Russian guns were nearer? They thundered a warning of impending doom. Icy fingers gripped his heart as he thought of the many people he had no wish to meet in the hereafter.

There was the Jewish *hauptman*, whose body was presently mouldering in the Frauenlob mine-shaft. Nearby, on the old battlefield, would be the grave of that Jewish professor, Solomons, who had mocked him on the train.

Hitler recalled the soft, clerk-like voice of Eichmann, reporting that—to date—six million Jews had gone up the chimneys of the concentration camps Also in that afterlife, there would be the marching shades of those who had died in his war.

The Fuhrer glanced at his diary with its litany of medications. No drug known to Man could quell the tumour of terror growing rapidly within him.

He would leave word he had died like a soldier, leading his troops in the battle for Berlin. But Hitler planned a softer, more private demise, by his own hand. He would take his bride, Eva, and his beloved dog, Blondi, into eternity with him.

Hitler knew only too well he would not live to see the funeral of the Third Reich. But he was making sure there would one day be the birth of a Fourth.

He slid open the drawer and once more placed the metal box on his desk. This device would ensure that the Blood of the Fuhrer pulsed once again through the veins of the world.

The lights in the bunker flickered like the eyelids of a dying man. Hitler's thoughts turned to Marie, who had for years been under the eyes of the Gestapo. He had followed her sad progress.

After she fled England and tried in vain to contact him, she had made two disastrous marriages. The once-beautiful and effervescent girl turned into a broken alcoholic, reduced to selling newspapers on a Parisian street corner.

Hitler pulled from his pocket the latest picture of Marie, taken by the Gestapo. It showed an old crone, bent, and dressed in many layers of tattered clothes.

Marie LeBrun had never betrayed their secret. Hitler's instinct had been correct there. He was glad he had let her live.

Their son, Albert, was a grown man. He was living in England, the owner of a public house in the Kentish town of Southdown. Hitler had secretly seen to it over the years that his son had wanted for nothing.

The Fuhrer's intelligence sources informed him that Albert had bequeathed to him an English grandson, ten-year-old Adam. Hitler's English family had so far escaped their father or grandfather's deadly bombs and rockets.

So the Blood of the Fuhrer lived on. It just needed the technical magic from Hitler's box to bring it to life.

Hitler had confided details of the box and his secret family to his closest friend and confidante, his private secretary and deputy Martin Bormann.

Within hours, Martin would slip away from this embattled bunker. He would disappear, through *Der Spinner*—The Spider escape route—into the jungles of South America.

The Nazi would take Hitler's box with him, together with strict instructions for its use. Bormann had been honoured by his Fuhrer with the task of sowing the seeds of a new Nazi empire.

Meanwhile, a *doppelganger*—look-alike—was standing by to lock himself into Bormann's office in the bunker, showing only glimpses of himself to the people remaining there.

Yes, those guns were definitely closer now.

The lights in the bunker constantly blinked. In a tray on Hitler's desk were situation reports, each containing disastrous news from the world above.

Deep in the bowels of his capital city, Hitler was now living in what Albert Speer, Reichminister for Munitions and War, had dubbed "The Isle of the Departed".

He could not deny, even to himself, that Berlin was a corpse. His aides, daring his wrath, described scenes straight from hell. Soldiers' bodies littered the streets like broken statues.

Civilians, dazed from the unending bombing and shelling, wandered as though sleepwalking among heaps of rubble. The bodies of defeatists, hung by the S.S., dangled from the remaining lamp-posts.

Schoolboys in oversized uniforms and carrying weapons meant for men, prepared to die for the Fuhrer.

This was the torment into which their charismatic leader had plunged them. And from which Hitler, sitting alone in his bunker, even now refused to deliver them. He would never surrender.

He pulled a sheet of notepaper, embossed with the Nazi crest, towards him and dipped his pen into an ornate inkwell. Hitler wrote in an unsteady hand: "If the war is lost, the people will be lost also. In any case, only those who are inferior will remain in this struggle."

The walls shook, as though trembling with fear. Hitler's Nemesis was approaching with heavy tread.

The air in the bunker was stale. The coterie of people remaining, whom Hitler still refused to allow to try to break out through the Russian lines, lived in a whirl of frenzied gaiety and debauchery.

In place of the sound of Nero fiddling, echoed the clamour of gramophone records and hysterical laughter.

Officers, party officials, secretaries and messengers drank heavily, played loud music and danced. Even as they fornicated, their brains were addled with terrors to come.

In his office, Hitler muttered to himself, getting the words into order that he planned soon to dictate.

"I myself, as founder and creator of the movement, have preferred death to cowardly abdication or even capitulation . . ."

He again stared at the metal box. When he was receiving acclaim in Valhalla, this would remain on earth to do his work.

❋

That box was the result of inspiration that exploded in August, 1943. This was engraved on Hitler's memory as the last time the Voice spoke to him.

The Fuhrer immediately ordered his rocket expert, Werner von Braun, to leave his headquarters at Peenemunde, on Germany's Baltic coast, and report to him in Berlin.

As the brilliant Prussian-born scientist, uncomfortable in his rarely-worn uniform of an S.S. *Sturmbannfuhrer* (major) waited outside Hitler's office, he wondered fearfully what the Fuhrer may want.

Von Braun was still basking in the praise heaped on him after the first V2 rocket had exploded on London last September. He and his team had fired the world's first ballistic missile just 21 months after the project had officially been commissioned.

But that was all in the past. Did the Fuhrer merely want a personal update on his work? Or did the Leader's summons presage something more sinister? The scientist had already had a taste of the Gestapo's dreaded knock on the door in the small hours.

Had someone again denounced him for a sin against the State, real or imagined? Treason was punishable by an unpleasant death.

Sitting in an uncomfortable, straight-backed chair outside the Fuhrer's study, the scientist experienced a stab of horror. Could Hitler, famous for his uncanny insight, have read his innermost thoughts?

For Von Braun's heart wasn't in creating vengeance weapons. He loved the rocket programme for its exciting scientific promise. The scientist wanted to use his gift to reach peacefully for the stars.

Sitting at his drawing board, he dreamed of sending Man far into the dark depths of space. Those V2 rockets, as far as Von Braun was concerned, were destined to land on the wrong planet . . . Earth.

He found the whole concept of his work being used to kill people extremely depressing.

The scientist's reverie was interrupted by the appearance of a blonde secretary. She whispered urgently: "The Fuhrer will see you immediately, major. He must not be kept waiting."

Von Braun, feeling as though he were wearing fancy dress, tried to adopt a military gait as he entered Hitler's inner sanctum. He halted smartly and gave a stiff-armed salute.

Hitler looked up from a file he was reading. He slipped some papers from it and placed them on the desk in front of him. Von Braun could make out that the top one was a clipping from the New York State Journal of Medicine.

He thought frantically: "Medicine? Medicine? The Fuhrer must surely know I am not that kind of a doctor. Has he summoned me here on a medical matter? Is what they are whispering about the Fuhrer losing his mind true?"

Hitler pushed back the famous lock of dark hair falling over his forehead and looked at the scientist as though examining a laboratory specimen on a slide. When he spoke, his voice was hoarse from the mustard gas that had attacked his lungs in World War One.

His words stunned Von Braun like a blow between the eyes. "You are standing here a free man because of my generosity. It was I who signed the order to release you from your prison cell last year.

"I made it clear to the Gestapo that your freedom remained conditional on your usefulness to the war effort. I don't trust you, Von Braun. You are a defeatist and, probably, a Communist, too.

"Maybe you have plans to flee to work for your fellow Marxists or perhaps the British or Americans. That is why I have taken away your private plane. You are still technically a prisoner of the Reich.

"Your continued freedom is dependent on your co-operation. I want to make this perfectly clear to you before I continue. Do you understand me, *Sturmbannfuhrer*?"

The scientist, his mind in turmoil, answered meekly: "Perfectly, *mein* Fuhrer."

Hitler pointed to the newspaper cutting and went on: "The clue to what I demand of you is in this article. It concerns iris and retinal identification.

"I have a task for you of the utmost importance and secrecy. You must give it precedence over the revenge weapons programme. Others can now take over that work for a while.

"First, I need an impregnable box made of an indestructible material. This container must be capable of being opened only by myself or a blood descendant. It will have no key or combination lock.

"I have already ordered some research in the subject of iris and retinal identification, with a view to using this technology to provide a 'lock' for such a box. The correct eye, staring into a lens, will provide the 'key' to open it.

"Believe me, I know what I am talking about. My genius doesn't extend only to military matters and the Arts. Present me with any complex subject, and I can analyse it within minutes.

"Time after time, I have proved so-called experts and academics wrong. I am a graduate of the University of Life. I have a degree in High Intelligence and Commonsense.

"Do you understand? Stand up straight, like the soldier you are not!"

Von Braun's muscles, more used to hunching over drawing boards and desks, screamed in protest. He replied: "Perfectly, *mein* Fuhrer."

Hitler tapped the folder and continued: "Listen carefully while I pass on to you what I have learned. The uniqueness of eye identification is well documented.

"No two irises are alike, even those of identical twins. In the iris alone are more than 400 distinguishing characteristics. These can be quantified and used to identify an individual.

"In short, the iris has six times more identifiable features than a fingerprint. Retinal identification is based on the blood vessel patterns found on the back of the eye's retina.

"Part of your project, Von Braun, is to isolate a genetic pattern, based solely on myself, which will work for my successive generations."

The Fuhrer, blue eyes ablaze with a messianic zeal, shaking left leg firmly clasped round the leg of his chair, roared on: "Work in this field has been going on in America since 1935. I now instruct you speedily to become an expert.

"You will take this technology to a high level the Americans would never dream possible. This must be achieved in six months.

"Fail, and you will be treated as a Jew and a defeatist. Succeed, and you will receive high rank, honours and financial security for life. I will even give you back your beloved airplane."

The scientist was staggered by the sheer magnitude of the task Hitler was setting him.

The Fuhrer banged his fist on the desk to ram home his points. He shouted: "You must pay the strictest attention. None of what I tell you must be committed to writing.

"In a nutshell, you will construct a small, imperishable box that can be opened only by eye identification. I want a system so sophisticated that only my eye, or that of a blood successor, can obtain entry.

"Six months. Dismiss. You will start work immediately."

Dazed, Von Braun picked up the file, left the presence of his Fuhrer and climbed into a waiting staff car. On the journey back to the Baltic coast, he turned the matter over in his mind.

Before even opening the file the Fuhrer had assembled on the subject of iris and retinal identification, he thought long and hard about the penalty of failing in this apparently impossible mission.

Von Braun had already had a sample of Nazi terror. He knew now that every citizen of the Third Reich, however illustrious, was only a hair's-breadth away from the torture chamber, the noose or the bullet. He remembered how he had been enjoying his privileged status as Germany's leading rocket scientist when the Gestapo knocked on his door in the early hours of March 14, 1944.

Von Braun was bundled into a car and thrown into a cell in Stettin. He was haunted to this day by the blood-curdling screams that echoed down the bleak corridors during his two-week incarceration.

Thinking back, the scientist believed he detected the source of his betrayal. He remembered going to a convivial party, where he met a vivacious woman dentist.

Over wine and canapés, he had confided that he would rather be working on peaceful space travel than killing people. He also spoke aloud what every German was thinking—that the war wasn't going well.

Obviously, that friendly dentist had been a Gestapo agent. Then a jealous Heinrich Himmler, head of The Gestapo and S.S., had seized the opportunity to try to dispose of Hitler's favourite scientist.

Himmler weighed in with false accusations that Von Braun was a Communist. A warrant was issued for his arrest.

The scientist, severely shaken, was released only because his input into the weapons programme was essential. But he knew he was being watched round the clock. Any future transgression would put him back in that cell.

He must succeed in this new project. His life depended on it.

As the chauffeur-driven car sped on its journey to the Baltic, Von Braun began carefully to read through the existing research into iris recognition.

Absorbed by the task, he began to make pencilled notes in the margins. The man with one of the most brilliant scientific minds in the world had already begun to solve the problem.

April 22, 1945

In the Fuhrer bunker, Hitler surveyed his precious box with deep satisfaction. Von Braun had delivered it—on time and exactly to specification—as Hitler had known he would.

The old carrot-and-stick method never failed. And, of course, fear of pain and death served to fine-focus the most brilliant of scientific brains.

After Von Braun, in fear of the big stick, was successful in carrying out Hitler's secret "magic box" project, he was given a large bite of the carrot.

While Heinrich Himmler seethed with rage, Von Braun was awarded a medal for unspecified services to the Fatherland. He also received a generous pay rise. His personal aircraft was, as promised, returned to him.

But Hitler shrewdly clipped his wings. Although Von Braun was an accomplished pilot, he wasn't allowed to fly the plane himself. He was allocated a Luftwaffe flyer for every trip.

No escape by air to the Allies was possible. It was made clear Von Braun was not trusted.

But, as the Russians now fought their way to the Chancellery, the danger of Von Braun defecting became irrelevant.

Hitler picked up a sheet of his personal stationery and began to write:

Berlin.
April, 22, 1945

"To whom it may concern,

"The fact that you have managed to open this device means that you are honoured by having the Blood of the Fuhrer in your veins.

"Possessing this precious blood is a heavy responsibility. For I now appoint you the chosen one who will carry on my great work. I hereby give you both permission and the means to create a Fourth Reich in my name.

"The man who keeps the museum at Bavarian Wood, in Wytschaete, Flanders—Jacques Deberte—will have seen you open this box and read this note. Therefore, he will know you are the new messiah of National Socialism.

"I order him to tell you the secret which is the key to untold wealth and power.

"You will use this to appoint yourself Fuhrer in my name. You will build a world of which I, Adolf Hitler, would be proud. This will be a true, Aryan world, free of the canker of Jews, Communists and Freemasons.

"Let nothing and nobody get in your way. This holy crusade demands that you will be as ruthless as I have been.

"Heil, new Fuhrer!

"Adolf Hitler"

The Fuhrer pushed aside the shutter on the box's lid and stared into the lens from a distance of about three feet, as Von Braun had instructed him. There was a click and the container sprang open.

Hitler picked up the note he had written, folded it carefully, and placed it into the box. He pushed the lid closed and covered the lens with its shutter. It was done.

The Fuhrer surprised himself by reverting to his long-abandoned Roman Catholic roots. Perhaps this was because his Voice had deserted him in his hour of need.

He crossed himself and prayed: "Father, bless the man who opens this with the strength and will to carry out my holy crusade.

"Bestow on him honour, glory and—above all—success. Amen".

Hitler pressed a button on his desk and Trudi, one of his secretaries, came into his study. He told her: "Send in Herr Bormann immediately."

"Yes, *mein* Fuhrer."

Within two minutes, Hitler's top aide appeared. The Fuhrer waved him to a chair in front of his desk. He looked with affection at the short, squat man who, by Machiavellian machinations over the years, had become Hitler's friend and deputy.

When Bormann spoke, it was in the coarse tones which had fooled his many detractors into thinking him a harmless lout: "The time has come, my Fuhrer?"

Hitler asked: "You are prepared? Your double is in place? You will carry out the vital Flanders assignment on your way to your new home?"

For Bormann, the ultimate administrator, these were rhetorical questions. His nondescript civilian clothes were already in the locker in his office. A guide stood ready to take him through war-torn Europe to Flanders.

After he had delivered the Fuhrer's box, Bormann would be delivered to the Vatican and then on to the safety of Argentina.

There, he would be welcomed into a safe and secure home. A plastic surgeon stood ready to alter his features.

He said, as the walls shook once more: "Yes, Adolf, all is ready. As you know, I am loathe to leave you after all these years. We are like brothers. Why can't we die together, like the warriors we are?"

Hitler replied: "You are my most loyal comrade, Martin. You are the only one I can trust with this last, vital mission. We have discussed this at length and I am adamant.

"I order you to put the interests of our nation before your own faithful feelings. You must save yourself to save Germany . . . and the future of National Socialism.

"I wish you goodbye. I will not say 'God speed', as I know how you hate the Church. Soon, I shall be in Valhalla. One day, I know you will join me there."

The two men, once the most powerful in occupied Europe, rose and solemnly shook hands. Hitler handed Bormann the precious box.

"It is the future. You know what you must do with it."

Hitler's deputy, a gleam of satisfaction in his eyes, gave the Nazi salute and left the study, closing the door quietly behind him.

The Russian guns sounded yet nearer. Hitler buried his head in his hands.

July 15, 1944

While Hitler was dreaming of posthumously playing his trump card, the ace in the pack was sitting at his desk in a school situated in the flat plains of Flanders. He was a bookish nine-year-old called Jacques Deberte.

A year previously, Jacques had witnessed heavy boxes being hidden down the Frauenlob mine-shaft, and the terrible slaughter that followed.

Hours after the last of many murders, and his subsequent torture in the hands of *Gauleiter* Wilfred Lacroix, the terrified boy had stood shivering in the kitchen of a cottage in Voormezele, a mile from the wood.

His hair was matted, his clothes pungently soiled, and his dirty cheeks streaked with tears. Jacques, who had been missing from home all night was clutching a broken arm across his chest and sobbing pitifully.

His distraught parents, Roger and Gilberte, showed no signs of giving him the smacked bottom he expected. Instead, they were standing aghast at the state of their son.

After they had hugged Jacques as though he had returned from the dead, they asked how he came to be in such a terrible state. Their son gazed at them with eyes glazed with horror, and remained mute.

Roger and Gilberte gave their son a cup of warm milk. They stripped the boy, plunged him into a hot bath and dressed him in warm clothes. Then they harnessed up their pony and trap and took him with all despatch to the family doctor in Ypres.

The elderly, white-haired physician, watch-chain straining across his ample belly, set the boy's broken arm and put it in a sling. Although Jacques screamed with pain, he never uttered a word.

Roger and Gilberte told the doctor how their son had gone missing yesterday afternoon and, in spite of searching for hours, they hadn't been able to find him. They couldn't make a thorough search, though, having been turned back by the S.S.

Jacques had just returned home, filthy and with a broken arm. Worst of all, he hadn't spoken. There was something wrong with his eyes. Jacques seemed to be watching a terrible dream inside his head.

The doctor, peering through his *pince-nez*, nodded sagely. He examined the boy and shone a torch into his eyes. Then he gently asked Jacques a few questions. The boy was apparently deaf to them . . . and to the outside world.

A grandfather clock ticked monotonously in the oak-panelled room. Jacques' parents waited anxiously for the doctor's verdict. Eventually, he cleared his throat portentously and told them: "Your son is in deep shock.

"He is in a state of trauma. Clearly, something has badly frightened him. Hopefully, his speech may eventually return. But he may never be able to speak of the event that has left him mute."

Roger and Gilberte paid the doctor a few francs and took Jacques home. His mother built a big fire, although it was high summer, and wrapped the boy in blankets. She sat up all night, holding his hand.

Instinctively, Gilberte knew she must keep a candle lit when night came. Darkness was part of her son's trauma. He screamed, he sobbed, he seemed to be suffering a nightmare sent by Satan himself.

Jacque's agony was breaking his mother's heart.

But there was much worse to come for the Deberte family.

The corporal in the guard room at the Ypres army camp barely bothered to look up from his pornographic book when Wilfred Lacroix stamped through the door. He thought: "Local Nazi . . . jumped up bully-boy and busybody. A load of shite. Could be dangerous, though."

Reluctantly, the *Wehrmacht* soldier laid down the book and asked: "Is there something you wanted . . . er . . . sir?"

Wilfred blustered: "I need to use your telephone on a very important and confidential matter."

The corporal deduced: "Another self-important bastard. This war seemed to breed them like flies." He pointed to the phone on the desk: "It is all yours, my friend."

Wilfred snapped: "I said this was a confidential matter. You must leave immediately!"

The corporal sighed deeply and made a big play of getting up from his chair, crossing to the door, and leaving the guard room. Once outside, he lit a cigarette and replayed the most graphic scenes from his book in his mind.

Wilfred picked up the phone and demanded to be put through to the local chief of Gestapo. Although he knew the officer couldn't see him, Wilfred stood to attention.

"Sir, I have the honour to report a local occurrence. It may be only a small matter, but I feel it my duty to mention it. Yesterday, the S. S. sealed off an area at Bavarian Wood.

"No-one was allowed into the area, and I assisted the troops who guarded the perimeter. After the S.S. left, I apprehended a small boy, carrying a fishing rod, coming from the direction of the wood.

"I questioned him rigorously, sir. But he made no reply. He seemed to me to be dumb."

The telephone spoke into the Nazi's ear. He had expected a mild, disinterested response. But his boss seemed to be taking the matter extremely seriously.

"His name is Jacques Deberte, sir. He is aged about eight years and lives with his parents, Gilberte and Roger Deberte, in the village of Voormezele. They are a farming couple, sir and have no criminal record."

The Gestapo boss ordered Wilfred: "You will go home immediately and stay there until my officers call on you. You will say nothing of this affair to anyone. Is that understood?

"I must now contact Berlin . . . that is how serious your 'small matter' is. This is not a secure line. Is anyone within earshot?"

"No, sir. I made very sure of that."

"Go straight home. Do not speak to the boy or his parents. Say nothing to your wife. Wait until you are contacted—however long that takes."

The corporal, lounging outside the guard-room, looked knowingly at the local *gauleiter* as he walked unseeingly past.

"Shitting himself, "the soldier said with satisfaction. "Got his knuckles rapped by teacher, I bet."

Meanwhile, the Gestapo chief, who had been informed of the strict secrecy of an S.S. operation at Bavarian Wood, picked up the phone in his office in Ypres. He was amazed to be passed to increasingly senior officers in Berlin.

Eventually, his bowels loosening, he was repeating Wilfred's report to Heinrich Himmler himself.

Within the hour, Hitler had decided that, when the time was ripe, this young lad, Deberte, would become the key to his secret. He again summoned Bormann to his office.

226

CHAPTER 12

July 18, 1944

An hour before dawn caressed the old battle-fields with grey fingers, there was a peremptory knock on the door of Wilfred and Denise Lacroix's cottage in the West Flanders village of Zillebeke.

A caller at this hour could mean only trouble. Wilfred lit a bedside oil lamp with trembling fingers, threw his military greatcoat over his nightshirt and hurried downstairs to open the door.

As he had expected, the two men standing impatiently on his doorstep wore long leather coats and the brims of their hats were pulled low over their eyes. They had no need to show their identifications.

The Gestapo men roughly pushed the Belgian Nazi in front of them into his sitting-room. Wilfred could hear the floorboards creak overhead as Denise got out of bed and paced fearfully in the bedroom.

One of the Gestapo agents, a man in his late twenties, a scar running from his right eye to the corner of his lips, pulled a document from his pocket and began to read: "You, Wilfred Andre Roger Lecroix, on July 15, 1944, detained a young boy named Jacques Deberte.

"You report you found him wandering in the area of Bavarian Wood, which had been sealed off for security reasons."

Wilfred's bare legs were shaking and he was close to tears. He pleaded: "Should I have killed him, sir? I thought it best that a superior officer should decide what should be done with him.

"I am a good and loyal Party member—anyone at headquarters will tell you this, sir. If I have made a mistake, I humbly apologise. Please don't be hasty . . . I have much still to give the cause. I am at present successfully rooting out defeatists . . ."

The other man, middle-aged, short and squat, his expression a permanent threat, snapped: "Stop babbling, you pathetic wretch. There is urgent work to do. It is the Fuhrer's personal work."

He produced a heavy envelope and handed it to the Flemish Nazi. Wilfred's eyes widened as he saw the red wax seal was that of the Fuhrer himself.

The Gestapo agent went on: "The Fuhrer has issued explicit orders that you and you alone are allowed to know the contents of this letter. You are to read it, memorise it and then destroy it in our presence.

"Do not waste time. We have been instructed to wait for a reply."

The Gestapo men were savouring the last vestiges of power. The Poles in their tanks, bent on vengeance, were reported to be fast approaching.

Wilfred was overcome by the immensity of the occasion. Adolf Hitler himself has sent him a letter! He pulled up a chair to the sitting-room table, moved the oil lamp close and, with fumbling fingers, broke the seal.

The letter, written by hand on the Fuhrer's personal notepaper, said: "You will read and obey this sheet before moving on to the next. First, you will shoot the two men bearing this document.

228

"Put their bodies in their car, drive it to Axle Wood and set fire to it. The remains will be disposed of in due course."

Wilfred's throat was so dry he could hardly speak. "You must excuse me while I get my spectacles, sirs. My eyes aren't as young as they used to be. I will be gone only a few seconds."

Leaving the oil lamp to shed its dim light over the room, Wilfred lit a candle and, tucking Hitler's letter into a pocket, stumbled up the stairs to the bedroom. His wife, angular and bony, cowered against the far wall. She asked, quavering: "Who are they? What do they want?"

Wilfred gestured impatiently for Denise to be quiet. He was on the verge of hyperventilating as he opened the door of a heavy wardrobe. His leather uniform belt and Luger hung from a peg inside.

He slipped the pistol from its holster, cocked it and applied the safety catch before thrusting it into a pocket of his greatcoat. Then, fighting to steady his breathing, he returned to the sitting-room.

The two men were fidgeting impatiently. The scarred one snarled: "Peasant idiot! You have forgotten to bring your precious spectacles. Hurry and get them. We are not in the business of dawdling. The Fuhrer hates time-wasters."

Wilfred produced the Luger, pushed off the safety catch and shot the man through the heart. Before the other could react, Wilfred killed him, too.

Denise, hearing the shots, came warily down the stairs. When she saw the two bodies, her hand flew to her mouth and she collapsed on the flagged floor. Wilfred crossed to his wife and slapped her brutally round the face.

"Come, woman. Hurry! There is the Fuhrer's work to be done! Help me get these bodies into the car outside."

Denise staggered to her feet and began to climb the stairs to find a coat to put over her nightdress. A boy's voice called fearfully from another bedroom.

She paused and said to her husband: "I cannot come with you, Wilfred. Andre is awake He is afraid of being alone."

The Belgian Nazi snarled: "So let him learn to be afraid. I need a second pair of hands. It is your duty to Adolf Hitler, the Reich and your husband to do this duty."

The couple laboured to haul the bodies out of the cottage and dump them in the back of a black Mercedes parked outside.

Curtains in nearby homes twitched but, as far as the Lecroixes' cautious neighbours were concerned, there was nothing to be seen.

When the couple returned on foot two hours later, the Gestapo men's funeral pyre lit the sky above Bavarian Wood. Nine-year-old Andre was wandering in the garden, hysterical, and Denise hurried to soothe him.

Wilfred pulled a chair up to the table, took Hitler's letter from his coat pocket and settled down to read the second sheet.

Again, the orders were written on the Fuhrer's notepaper. They said:

"*Gauleiter* Lacroix,

"I remind you of your S.S. blood oath to me. You will carry out the following instructions to the letter. Success will be rewarded with the knowledge that you have done your duty. Failure will mean death.

"Eyes will eternally be watching.

"You will despatch Jacque Deberte's parents, Roger and Gilberte, to Auschwitz immediately. Make it clear to the authorities that they must never return. You will legally adopt Jacques Deberte.

"I may have a sacred mission for him later. Bring him up as a true National Socialist, but ensure he keeps a low profile. Make him swear in my name to keep his secrets. He knows more than he told you.

"Jacques will be a sleeping Nazi, to awake only when my work is to be done. His secrets are the key to Social Nationalism's glorious future.

"When the boy is 18 years old, you will buy him Axle Wood, now known as Bavarian Wood. This is a sacred place for me. He will establish a German trench museum there.

"This is the place, when the glorious day of rebirth arrives, where you will oversee the building of a monument to me and to the Thousand-Year Reich. This has long been my dream.

"Money has been deposited for you in account no. 007788845/B at the National Bank in Ypres.

"I shall be handing on my torch. May it lead you and millions of others to glory.

"Adolf Hitler—July 17, 1944—Berlin

Wilfred, neglecting even to wash and shave, donned his uniform, slipping his recently-fired Luger into its holster on his belt.

He harnessed the trap and went at an urgent clip into Ypres. There Wilfred went into his *gauleiter's* office, where he began scribbling orders. Soon, a closed van was on its way to the Debertes' farm.

By the time Wilfred returned home, a bewildered Jacques Deberte had been delivered by two Belgian S.S. men. He was standing in the kitchen, dumb and terrified.

***

Gradually and uncomfortably, Jacques settled into his new family. His was not a happy life. His adoptive father, Wilfred, was brusque and unfriendly, although he seemed strangely in awe of the boy.

Denise treated Jacques with shrewish harshness, stopping just short of physical chastisement. Although the Lacroix family had unaccountably come into money, she begrudged every crust Jacques ate.

Worst of them all was Andre. He was bigger and stronger than his new brother, whom he fiercely resented. He bullied the newcomer at every opportunity, blacking his eyes and splitting his lips.

Andre's parents turned a blind eye to the abuse.

Over the months, Jacques, a nervous child with a sharp intelligence, slowly regained the power of speech. His questions regarding his parents' sudden and mysterious disappearance went frostily unanswered.

Eventually the boy gave up asking. But his unhappy thoughts persisted.

Wilfred, in constant fear of "watching eyes", carried out his instructions to the letter. He taught his adoptive son about the glories of National Socialism, warning the boy to say nothing of this in public.

As the days passed, the news became blacker and blacker for Wilfred. On September 6, 1944, he watched from a café table in Ypres' market square as Polish armour roared victoriously through the town. The Nazis hid their uniforms, burnt incriminating documents and kept a low profile.

The local population, fearful of Fascist power still bubbling below the surface, never mentioned the dubious events that had occurred during the occupation.

The following year, on April 30, Wilfred's beloved Fuhrer courageously took his own life. A week later, the Belgian Nazi was devastated to hear over the radio that Germany had surrendered.

For the first time since he was a small child, Wilfred was moved to tears.

A few days after the war ended, an amazing thing happened. A stocky, middle-aged man, with a vaguely familiar face, half-hidden by a scarf, arrived at the Lecroix cottage late at night.

The caller, who addressed Wilfred in coarse German, carried a small suitcase. He refused to open this until the two men were alone in a stone outhouse. Then he unlocked the case and took from it a weighty package, wrapped in oilskin.

The man, who didn't identify himself, said: "I am a personal emissary of the late Fuhrer. My word is his word. Do as I say. Eyes are still watching you, in spite of this temporary peace.

"Within this package is a metal box, which was once the personal property of Adolf Hitler. He ordered that you should be its guardian.

"You will take the box to Voormezele cemetery under cover of darkness. The tomb of the Becquart family has been unsealed. Place the box inside and reseal it. No-one must see you do this.

"Tell only the boy, Jacques Deberte, who is the guardian of the Fuhrer's great secret, where the box is hidden. He may need to know. One day, a man may come who claims to be the Blood of the Fuhrer.

"If you are initially satisfied the man is genuine, you will retrieve the box. If you are dead, you should already have instructed the boy in this duty. The box must be placed in direct sunlight for a day to power it."

The man leaned close to Wilfred and went on in a hoarse whisper: "Jacques Deberte must be there when the box is presented to The Blood. There is a lens in the lid. The claimant must look directly into this from a distance of three feet.

"If the man is of The Blood, the box will unlock. There will be a note inside. At this point, you will leave, and Jacques will tell him the secret. This act will mark the birth of the Fourth Reich.

"I shall learn about these events and will return. Be very sure to do your duty."

The man gave the Fascist salute, and said softly: "Heil Hitler!"

Wilfred, too, stood to attention and echoed: "Heil, Hitler!" He stammered: "I would consider it an honour to know your name, sir."

The man, whose features still tugged at the edges of his memory, ignored him. He melted into the night, leaving Wilfred alone with the mysterious package.

That night, he crept like a thief into the moonlit village of Voormezele. Owls hooted eerily in the trees and small animals snuffled in the bushes as he hid the package in the tomb.

There the secret rested as the years of peace passed. Wilfred often looked at his reticent, academic son and wondered what cataclysmic memories were stored in his head.

Not that he ever dared to ask, and Jacques was forever silent on the subject. To be doubly careful, Wilfred expressly forbade his adopted son to speak of the time before he came to live with the Lacroix family.

Obedient to the Fuhrer's instructions, and much to Andre's rage, Wilfred bought Jacques Bavarian Wood as an eighteenth birthday present. The terrified owner of the property hastily agreed to the derisory price offered by the local Nazi.

Jacques, who had grown into a well-built, gentle and thoughtful young man, found happiness at last. He meticulously led a team that reconstructed the old trenches, dug out the concrete bunkers and uncovered the mouth of the flooded mine-shaft.

He studied reference books and numerous wartime documents to become an expert on the old strongpoint. Jacques called his museum by the mine-shaft's old name, Frauenlob, literally meaning "praise of women".

This genuine German landmark from the First World War, unique in Flanders, was soon attracting people from all over the world. Tour buses poured up the narrow lane from Ypres—now called by its Flemish name of Ieper—to the Frauenlob.

Its curator conducted visitors round in a courteous, scholarly manner, switching languages with ease. A few of the tourists were sensitive enough to notice that no birds sung in Hitler's wood.

Old German marching songs echoed from loudspeakers among the trees.

Jacques, the mop-headed, studious museum owner, never gave the slightest hint of his rabid Nazi convictions.

He was careful to say he regarded the site, where so many died, as a lesson in the folly of war. To press home the point, he refused to charge admission for children.

He was also cautious in the way he spoke of the wood's most famous soldier—*Gefreiter* Adolf Hitler. Jacques quietly and impartially told how the Fuhrer won his Iron Cross, Second Class here.

Jacques referred in passing to Hitler's early ambitions to be an artist and architect. He hung copies of two of Hitler's local World War One paintings—"The Hollow Way" and

"Messines Church"—in the atmospheric bar and canteen he built next to the museum.

Also on the wall was a photograph of a triumphant Hitler, waving a proprietorial arm over Bavarian Wood, soon after the fall of Belgium in 1940. Jacques pointed out that this was one of the first places the Fuhrer visited after the German conquest.

No-one taking the Frauenlob tour would ever have guessed that their mild-mannered guide was eagerly awaiting the spiritual reincarnation of the White Crow, who once paced these very trenches.

The camera-clicking, polythene-clad hordes, chattering during yet another picture opportunity, never suspected that a time-bomb was ticking beneath their neatly-shod feet.

Now that bomb was soon to explode, and its thunder would shake the world to its foundations.

CHAPTER 13

Tuesday, September 5, 2000

Ros Goldstein was sitting on the king-sized bed in her room at the Sword Hotel and Tea-Room, in Ieper's market square. A shaft of sunlight gilded a halo round her blonde head. Fabienne Boulanger, red locks piled high, sat in a deep, overstuffed armchair, looking fondly at the younger woman.

Fabienne casually crossed her long legs, aware that her skirt was riding high. She said, without a trace of accent: "Isn't it delicious being secret friends like this?

"Even Hamish doesn't have a clue. Every day I thank the Lord we met on that job in Kiev. I thank Him also that we were both on the side of the angels on that assignment—you for Mossad and me for the good old Brits.

"I'd have hated to have had to kill you, Rosie. That would have really upset me."

Ros chuckled and stretched, pulling her sweater even tighter. She felt the other woman's eyes on her breasts as she replied: "Who'd have thought Fate would throw us together again so soon . . . and still with the angels.

"My betters—and yours, too, I'll bet—seem to think there are rich pickings in this one, and they want to scoop them up. But we, like the sisters we are, must look out for ourselves. I'm sure we can both do our duty *and* sneak off with some of the sweeties."

A loud snore reverberated through the wall of the next-door bedroom. Adam Cornish was sleeping off the tsunami of strong Duvel beer that had overwhelmed him last night.

Fabienne smiled sympathetically at the other woman. She commiserated: "I don't envy you your sick-making, sexual chore, Rosie. I'm only too aware I might have a similar duty to endure later in the trip. I take it the beer won over the bedsprings last night?"

The blonde girl shuddered and nodded: "Just a short reprieve, I'm afraid. He's hinting at afternoon sex sessions so that he can drink himself impotent in the evenings."

Fabienne crossed to the bed and put an arm round Ros's shoulders. She said softly: "While the man for whom we're all here is oblivious of his importance, let's do a little swapping of information. . . . just as we did at the cosy Hotel Kreshchatik, while the snow fell in Kiev.

"We both know Cornish is Hitler's grandson, although the slob doesn't yet realise it. You and Hamish have been keeping a strict eye on him.

"When my pillow-talk pal, Hamish, said Cornish was on the move in a significant kind of way, I was delighted when you joined the party . . . here, in soggy old Flanders.

"This loser of a journalist may very soon become a major player in a global game. Tel Aviv and Whitehall know there's more to this than power politics. What's your info on the goodies, Rosie?"

Although the snoring next door continued unabated, Ros lowered her voice as she confided: "We know that Hitler looted treasure worth billions from occupied Europe during the Second World War.

"We believe he converted this into gold bullion and hid it away. That much information leaked out of the bunker to our agents during the last days. But there has never been a whisper as to where this Aladdin's cave is located.

"A Nazi, wriggling to get off the hook when we caught up with him in South America, told us that the key to the loot would be someone who could prove he was of the Blood of the Fuhrer.

"That puts lover-boy in the next room, Adam Cornish, firmly in the frame. And, lo! here he is in his grandfather's old stamping ground in the First World War. He is accidentally on the brink of discovering who he really is."

Ros went on: "Perhaps Cornish will do the first useful thing in his sad life and lead us to Hitler's treasure. We must keep each other informed on this. Both Mossad and British Intelligence want to prevent the Nazis from being lavishly funded in this way, and thus resurrected.

"The Israelis want to give back the money to Holocaust survivors and their families. And we all know the British Government could do with a bob or two to help make its books balance.

"Maybe, just maybe, the two of us can find some means of siphoning off a *soupcon* of that loot for ourselves. A million or two, say, wouldn't be missed."

Fabienne whispered: "But there is somebody in particular who stands in our way . . . nasty Arthur Burfield, a.k.a. storm-trooper Andre Lecroix. I hear he tried to send you for a swim during the ferry trip."

Ros kissed the older woman lightly on the cheek: "There's no need to worry your pretty titian head about that. My masters in Tel Aviv have given me a potion to administer to anybody who upsets me.

"I'm planning to put a drop or two into his favourite beer. It will appear that the evil old snapper has had a heart attack. I am assured that, even if there is an autopsy, the stuff is undetectable."

Fabienne began gently to massage her friend's neck. She pleaded: "Please do the deed soon, Rosie. I think our local, neighbourhood Nazi has plans that aren't good for your health.

"I only wish you could spare some of your potion for that English pervert, snoring like a little piggie next door. What we girls do for our countries!

"However, for the moment, we need that creepy grandson alive and kicking. While he slumbers, I'll nip downstairs and get us a couple of coffees and some breakfast. Don't go away!"

The snoring in the next room stopped abruptly and was followed by a burst of coughing. The women listened attentively, then relaxed as the walls vibrated to a new concerto for sinus and larynx.

The redhead slipped out of the bedroom and hurried down the wide, linoleum-covered stairs. She followed the smell of freshly-brewed coffee into a deserted dining-room.

A plump waitress, her face inexplicably pale and taut, hurried through the swing door from the kitchen. She took Fabienne's breakfast order and scurried back.

Within minutes the girl returned, carrying a tray on which was arranged a coffee pot, cups, plates, a jug of cream, fresh bread rolls and a selection of thinly-cut ham and cheese.

She thrust it at Fabienne, paused as though about to speak, and ran back into the kitchen. Fabienne, faintly puzzled, carried the tray up to Ros's bedroom.

The blonde poured two cups of the fragrant coffee and topped them with cream. The women spread rolls with butter, added bland Belgian cheese, and hungrily bit into them

They emptied their cups and poured refills. Ros wrinkled her nose and said: "I find this coffee too bitter. It must be

240

all the chicory the Belgians love to put in. It tends to leave me with a dry throat."

The snoring stopped again. This time, although there was another bout of coughing, it didn't resume. Ros said urgently: "The old goat mustn't wander in here in search of early-morning nookie and find the two of us together.

"I'll probably bump into you later today. Enjoy your spell of horizontal callisthenics next door. Rather you than me, Rosie."

Ros replied: "It'll be your turn to twang his bed-springs soon enough. Did you remember to take some sick bags from the boat?"

As Fabienne made her way noiselessly downstairs, Ros pushed open the door of the neighbouring bedroom. She quickly covered her mouth and nose with a handkerchief, as though suppressing a sneeze.

The air in the room was a rank cocktail of male sweat, bad breath and stale alcohol. Adam Cornish was sitting up in bed, wearing a grubby vest. His eyes were rimmed by a hangover shade of red and his face was a puffy and unhealthy grey.

The seedy journalist once more coughed long and hard, making no attempt to shield his mouth with his hand.

The beautiful Mossad agent, fighting her sharp distaste, thought: "So this is the man certain people think should rule the world."

Dutifully, she leaned close to Adam, her breasts inches from his face. He ignored the invitation and, scratching under an armpit, said: "I could murder a cup of tea. Any chance?

"By the way, has that delicious tart, Fabienne, been here asking for me yet? She promised to show me round today. That'll give me some colour for the Ernie project. Work before pleasure, that's my motto.

"You can have a look round the Flanders Fields museum here in Ypres. See if there's anything useful for me. That'll keep you occupied until I get back. Then we'll have a little rest and relaxation, eh?

"Any chance of that cuppa?"

With a surge of relief, Ros stood back from the bed. Sentence postponed. She pretended to suffer a flash of jealousy.

"In answer to your question, Adam, there has been no sign of the woman who was all over you like a rash. I expect the whole thing will turn out to be the world's shortest shipboard romance.

"Anyway, Arthur says he knows this area like the back of his grubby hand. He told me he is staying with friends nearby, and I expect he'll be here soon.

"Unlike that red-headed tart, he knows how to take professional pictures to help with the Ernie research. Why do you need the services of that Belgian slapper . . . as if I didn't know?

"I'll just pop downstairs and get you a cup of tea. By the time you've drunk it and got yourself into gear, good old faithful Arthur will be here. Then we'll get going."

As Ros left Adam's room, taking deep breaths of fresh air, he was seized by another coughing fit. She heard bed-springs groan in sympathy.

The girl reporter clacked downstairs and pushed open the door to the empty dining-room. She looked round at the tables, already set neatly for lunch. The scene suddenly went badly out of focus.

Ros collapsed, her body falling limply like a soldier shot dead in battle.

Wilfred Lecroix marched out of the kitchen, where he had been orchestrating the scenario. The waitress, close to fainting, poured the rest of the coffee down the sink.

242

With it went the evidence of murder—the poison Wilfred had found while searching Ros's room as she drank downstairs last night. It was so much tidier than the gun or the knife.

The old Nazi supervised as Arthur Burfield and Jacques Deberte dragged Ros's body through the kitchen and into an outhouse in the Sword's back-yard.

They dropped it on to the stone floor, where Fabienne's corpse was already lying. Lecroix grunted with satisfaction. Two down. The lethal coffee had done its work well.

How the hell had these two thought they could get away with it? The Nazis' intelligence system was second to none—Mossad included.

The two men covered the women's bodies with a builder's paint-spattered tarpaulin. Wilfred barked: "Wait until dark, and then get rid of this rubbish. Discreetly. Make sure anyone who sees you realises that they have seen and heard nothing."

Ten minutes later, the three men were sitting round a table in a café, Aux Trois Savoyards, nestling near the market square. Their cups of coffee were cooling and untouched. They had about them an air of barely-suppressed excitement.

This might be *the day*.

After 45 years of watching and waiting, this could be the time of The Blood.

If the drunken, bearded stranger, presently staying at the Sword, proved himself, it would herald the Great Awakening

The three Flemish Nazis could almost hear the marching jack-boots, the martial bands and the roar of the multitude.

Housewives hurried past the café's windows, intent on mundane shopping trips. Inside Aux Trois Savoyards, the men savoured the power they may soon be wielding over these people . . . and millions of others like them.

Wilfred Lacroix's eyes glittered with anticipation. But his face, lined by more than eighty years of brutal living, remained set in a sceptical scowl. Would this Englishman convince the old *gaulieter* he was the new Fuhrer?

Wilfred's son Andre, toying with his teaspoon, had shed his bluff, Arthur Burfield persona like skin from a snake. The usual genial smile was replaced by an expression of cruel arrogance.

Andre thought of the storm-trooper uniform, waiting in its polythene cover in his wardrobe at home. He pictured, too, the plaited whip hanging beside it. Soon it would taste blood. His loins stirred.

The years had been kind to Jacques Deberte. At 64, his hair was still abundant, although greying at the temples. He sat deep in troubled thought.

He may at long last be permitted to tell of that terrifying day when, as an eight-year-old schoolboy truant, he had gone fishing in the mine crater at Bavarian Wood.

Jacques shrank from unlocking terrible memories of the slaughter surrounding the hiding of those precious boxes down the Frauenlob mine-shaft.

This might be the day when he could reveal the great secret of those boxes . . . a secret he kept all these years on the orders of the late Fuhrer.

As boy, hidden in the bushes, he had listened to the gossip of the S.S. soldiers as they worked. They said only gold could weigh so heavily.

Jacques wondered whether revealing his innermost secret would prove to be so traumatic he would again be struck dumb. Or would it be cathartic, and prove to be an enormous relief?

To Jacques, the wartime events at the wood had always been inextricably linked with the terrifying and mysterious disappearance of his parents

He looked unseeingly as a middle-aged couple came into the café, sat at a table and each ordered an Oxo hot drink. His thoughts ran around like mice in a maze.

To the outside world, expensively-educated Jacques appeared a gentle academic and historian. But of the men sitting round this table, he was the most rabid Nazi.

Wilfred had seen to that over the years, with constant instruction in the glories of National Socialism.

But, haunted by the sinister riddle of his parents' disappearance, doubts gnawed at Jacques. Were the Nazis, perhaps, responsible for the demise of Roger and Gilberte Deberte?

His old home was now a ruin. The skeletal farm-house, with its tile-less roof and gaping windows, was a constant reminder to Jacques of a family inexplicably and brutally torn apart.

The Nazis at Aux Trois Savoyards knew the Blood would bring untold riches. Wilfred and Andre had long suspected that Jacques held the key to Hitler's looted billions.

As the late summer sun turned the town's cobbles to gold, they wondered how they could, undetected, cream off some of the Fuhrer's riches for themselves. God only knew they had earned some sort of reward over the years.

Power and money. A heady cocktail. Just within their grasp. They could taste it.

Across the square at The Sword, Ros and Fabienne's bodies had grown cold. There were fewer in the race now.

Wilfred looked at his watch and gestured it was time to leave. The Nazis didn't pay for their coffees. The attractive, brunette patroness, watching fearfully from behind the bar, wasn't fool enough to ask for the money.

Adam arrived downstairs at The Sword in a foul mood. There had been no cup of tea, no Fabienne and no Ros. He found Arthur Burfield, sprawled comfortably in one of the restaurant's wheel-back chairs, pouring tea from a pewter pot.

The photographer pulled another cup towards him and filled it for Adam. He pointed to two empty coffee cups, bearing lipstick traces, and two plates, covered with crumbs and daubs of strawberry jam.

Arthur, dropping back easily into his good-natured Englishman role, told the disgruntled writer: "You've missed them both, old son. Fabienne turned up, chummed up with Ros and the two of them decided to go off shopping.

"Women! Who can make 'em out? No sense of responsibility. Still, you've always got me . . . and I know everything you need to know about these parts. You'll see. I suggest we take off without them.

"By the time those bints will have pawed over the knickers in the local shops, we will have done a day's work. When women are enjoying retail therapy, they lose all sense of time.

"It wouldn't surprise me if they decided to up sticks and take their carrier bags back to Blighty without telling us."

Arthur sipped his tea and went on: "Just to cheer you up, I have some good news. Last night, I cast around my local yokels and came up with a gem of a contact for your Ernie story. It'll turn out to be nearly as good as booze and sex, believe me, old mate.

"Trust Arthur to look after you. I'm glad Ros and Fabienne have gone absent without leave, as I want to keep this contact a secret for now. I won't tell you who the person is, as I want them to be a surprise

"I'll just tease your journalist's taste buds by warning you to stand by for someone who will put a rocket up your arse. In a nice way, of course. Now finish that tea. Chop, chop."

Adam, who had been looking forward to a sex session with Ros, followed by a day of alcoholic dalliance with Fabienne, said grumpily: "Blast those girls! Women are never there when you want them.

"I hope this lead of yours turns out to be as good as you say. I'd planned rather a different timetable for today."

Arthur chuckled, brushed crumbs from his wrinkled flannels, and stood up. He clapped Adam on the shoulder and told him cheerily: "What could be better than a great story, followed by a gallon of Duvel beer?

"I know, I know . . . . But you can't have a roll in the hay whenever you feel the urge. Think of the money you're going to make in Tinsel Town. Think of all the starlets it'll buy. Let's go, boss!"

The two men left the hotel and climbed into a yellow Porsche, parked outside. Arthur explained: "I borrowed this jam jar from a friend. We might as well travel in style."

The plump waitress, a tissue held to her lips, watched the sports car roar out of the market square. A black Landrover, with French licence plates, pulled out of a parking slot and followed at a discreet distance.

Arthur was expansive as he drove along roads that wandered through First World War killing grounds. Playing tour guide, he pointed out front-line positions and the scenes of famous actions. The photographer studiously ignored his passenger's silence.

The ruddy-faced Nazi, looking more farmer than storm-trooper, needed no map as he wound through the lanes leading to the nearby Franco-Belgian border.

Here and there, the car dipped into shallow troughs, where the tarmac had collapsed into the tops of old trenches. A soft breeze rippled water in shell-holes. Rusting stakes, made for cruel barbed wire entanglements, held up fences between peaceful fields.

Nature had done her best to wipe out the scars of a conflict that had destroyed a generation of young men. Their squandered lives were marked by cemetery after cemetery, trim military gravestones glinting white against "country garden" flowers.

Adam was paying a bitter price for yesterday's binge. He nursed a pounding headache, a burning gut, and a simmering resentment at having to work.

The Porsche's passenger seat was cramped, and the car's hard springing proved unforgiving on the country roads. Although it was only eleven in the morning, Adam looked longingly at every cafe they passed.

Beefy women were busy swabbing down pavements outside their businesses, foamy warm water spilling into the gutters. Customers' bicycles were already propped against the café windows.

A signpost flicked by, pointing to "Komen". The photographer chatted on: "We're on our way to Comines, old chap, which is astride the Franco-Belgian border. Spelt the French way it's 'Comines'.

"But the Flemish call it 'Komen'. It's all a bit confusing. Belgium, although a country only the size of a pocket handkerchief, has two main rival communities. They are the French-speaking Walloons and the Dutch-speaking Flemish.

"The Walloons, in the North, used to call the shots. Now the Flemish, in the South are fighting back. It's all a crazy puzzle of pride, politics and economics."

During Arthur's lecture, Adam's head drooped, and a dribble of saliva trickled down his beard. The photographer woke him with a start by sounding his horn at a startled cyclist.

The photographer joked: "Pay attention! I'll be asking questions later. We shall soon be in Komen. The town is on the Belgian side of the River Lys, which divides it.

"Komen was behind the German lines in '14-'18, and it was where Corporal Adolf Hitler used to spend his rest and recuperation time. It's here that I'll be revealing a great secret about your grand-dad, Ernie."

Adam shook his aching head in bewilderment. He thought: "Hitler? Big secret? Has old Arthur finally gone off his rocker? What are we doing bumping along at the back of nowhere when we could be doing something useful, like having a drink or a shag?"

Arthur steered carefully round a slow-moving farm cart, loaded with sugar beet, He asked casually: "What do you think of Hitler, old mate?"

The reporter snapped fully awake as the outlying houses of Comines came into sight. He replied, vivid blue eyes alight: "I think Hitler was just the sort of man we could do with today. He had all the right ideas, but lesser men let him down.

"The world's been going downhill since Hitler. In spite of his wonderful efforts in the war, the Jews are again running and ruining everything. Just look at those bastard Goldsteins at the Kentish World.

"They held me back for years, just because I was cleverer than them. Hitler would have known how to deal with the likes of the bloody Goldsteins. Today, the Lefties are also bossing everybody about . . . just as Hitler feared.

"Then there are those conniving sods the Freemasons, in league with the Yids. God only knows what evil damage they're doing behind the scenes . . ."

Arthur gave a secret sigh of relief at Adam's diatribe. This was the right sort of man for the job.

He pulled up outside a modest house in a cobbled side-street. The Porsche made a vivid splash of colour against the drab terraces.

Arthur turned to the reporter and said: "You don't know how glad I am to hear how much you admire the Fuhrer. I totally agree with everything you say. So do many of my friends."

The glitzy car was already attracting a crowd of urchins. They gazed at it as though a UFO had landed in their midst. Arthur climbed out of the Porsche and chased them away.

Adam, easing his cramped body from the passenger seat, noticed the photographer was speaking fluent Flemish. The two men walked up to the blue-painted front door, with its highly polished brass knocker and letter-box. Arthur clapped Adam on the back.

He whispered: "Get ready for the big surprise."

The photographer gave three peremptory bangs on the knocker, sounding like a secret policeman in the night.

A woman's high-heeled footsteps echoed inside the house. The door was opened by a comfortably robust, middle-aged woman, hair set in the old-fashioned corrugations of a permanent wave

When she saw the burly form of Arthur, recognition and alarm flared in dark eyes, set like raisins in her puffy face. Without waiting for an invitation, the photographer pushed brusquely past her and into the house.

He snapped: "Anne-Marie Vonneste?" The woman nodded wordlessly. "I sent someone to tell you we were coming to see your grandmother, Marguerite Vonneste.

"I hope she is ready to receive myself and my important friend here, and knows exactly what she must show and tell us

"Don't just stand there gawping, woman. Our time is precious. Take us to your grandmother immediately."

The woman, head bowed submissively, led them down the tiled hallway, Adam realised with a jolt that Arthur, the friendly photographer, was suddenly transformed. He was acting just like a storm-trooper of old.

Adam liked the new Arthur Burfield. This man obviously had hidden depths. The writer admired Arthur's demonstration of power. It showed how lesser mortals should be treated.

He watched the woman's ample bottom, swaying within her straining dress as she showed them to a sitting-room. Although a coal fire burned in the hearth, the place felt damp, as though rarely used.

The furniture was a dark, heavy, echo from the Twenties. A framed photograph of a young man in First World War Belgian uniform had pride of place on the mantelpiece. A single flower in a vase stood in front of it.

A grandfather clock ticked majestically in a corner. Otherwise, the room was laden with silence.

A very old lady, face like parchment, white hair scraped ruthlessly back to form a bun, sat in a worn leather arm-chair, close to the fire. Her clothes hung loosely on her skeletal body.

The woman's purple-veined hands clutched a heavy photograph album, resting across her lap. The woman didn't look up as the two men entered, but continued staring into the leaping flames.

Anne-Marie said: "This is my *grandmere*, sirs. Please try not to disturb her too much. She is 93 years old and is partially deaf and very frail. You see ... she has looked out the photographs, just as you ordered, sir.

"Grandma is trying to remember those events in which you are so interested. But they happened so long ago. She was just a young girl, sirs. I hope you understand."

Anne-Marie bent and shouted in her grandmother's ear: "*Grandmere,* These are the men I told you about. They would like to look at your photographs and ask some questions about the first war.

"Please help them as much as you can. Try to remember. These are important men."

The old woman looked up at her visitors for the first time, and stared straight into the vivid, blue eyes of Adam Cornish. She screamed, convulsing in her chair as though hit by a fierce electrical current.

The album fell to the floor with a thud. Anne-Marie wrapped her arms round her grandmother's thin shoulders. She shouted: "Whatever is it, *grandmere*?

"What is frightening you? These men have come to talk, not to hurt you. They are not here because you have done anything wrong."

The grandmother, trembling and fighting for breath, continued staring into the face of Adam Cornish. She gasped: "Those eyes! Those eyes! They are *his* eyes. They are the eyes that have haunted me all these years.

"They looked down on me from posters. They were always in the newspapers. I can never forget them. Never. They said he was dead. Now I see his eyes. Is he back from the grave?"

Marguerite, trembling, crossed herself. She went on, staring as though hypnotised at Adam: "God help me. I did the man with the eyes no harm. I was but a young child. When he came back in the next war, I hid.

"Those eyes! Yes, they are *his* eyes, blue as a bright summer sky. But they could strike like lightning. Oh, God. God, I pray to you to help me."

Adam ignored the old woman's ramblings and bent to pick up her photo album. It had fallen open at the page on which she had been looking.

It was now Adam's turn to gasp with shock. He stared at a sepia photograph, speckled with age and damp, as though he, too, had seen a ghost.

Adam was staring at the unmistakable features of his grandmother, Marie LeBrun. But there was a gut-wrenching difference here to the happy and affectionate scene in Ernie's album.

There could be no mistake that the girl was identical to Ernie's Marie. The camera had again captured her, flirting coquettishly with the camera, eyes sparkling with mischief.

The dark, bobbed hair and beautiful, high cheekbones were unmistakable. She was standing in bright sunshine, again in front of an estaminet. But this was a different drinking place.

Above the door, Adam could just make out the sign "Aux Fossoyeur". His grandmother wore a short summer dress that showed off her slender legs. She glowed with the same sun-kissed beauty.

But there was no smiling Sergeant Ernie Cornish in this picture.

She was resting her head affectionately on the shoulder of a moustachioed German soldier. His face was devoid of expression, but he clasped the girl possessively round the waist.

The whole world could see the couple were lovers.

The soldier in the photograph was Adolf Hitler.

Adam stared at it in disbelief.

The old woman muttered Hail Marys, a handkerchief clutched to her mouth. She pointed a trembling finger at the photograph and whispered: "She left it behind in her room.

"She called him Dolphie. I would know him anywhere. Those eyes! They pierced your soul!

"He came to my mother's estaminet many times with that French girl, Marie. I peeped at them round the door. They used to go upstairs to our spare bedroom. Mother took the money, even though she disapproved.

"I had no opinion, you understand, sirs, as I was only a child. I knew nothing of life. We could hear them up there. The soldiers in the estaminet used to laugh, but mother became very angry.

"She called the man's sweetheart bad names, which I didn't understand, for sleeping with the Boche. Mother said the girl would become pregnant and give birth to a *fils de Boche*, the baby boy of a German. I heard later that she had been right."

Marguerite covered her face in her hands and burst into uncontrollable sobbing. Anne-Marie put her arms round her grandmother and said: "It was all a long time ago. Calm yourself, *grandmere,* I am sure you have told these gentlemen all they want to know."

The old lady shook off her daughter, gasping: "There is more. Mama said the girl would pay for her sins. But, when the next war came, it was mother who paid.

"Somebody had reported her bad words about the *fils de Boche* to the Germans. They came and took my dear mama away and I never saw her again. She has no grave on which I can place flowers."

The old woman looked tearfully at Arthur and Adam. She told them: "That is all I know of the affair, gentlemen. I swear it. Please believe that I am not to blame for my mother's terrible words."

Anne-Marie pleaded: "Please leave her now, sirs. *Grandmere* is old and harmless. You can see she is very upset. She has helped you all she can. Now she must rest."

Arthur had no time for sympathy. He picked up the photograph album, tucked it under his arm, and told Adam: "Never forget how I found this vital contact for you.

"Now I will take you on to the next stage of your journey. This may shake you even more. In fact, Adam, it could change all our lives. Always remember how I have acted as your good guide and friend."

The two men strode out of the house, not bothering to close the door. Inside, the racking sobbing continued.

Back in the Porsche, this time wide awake, Adam opened the album at the picture of Marie and Hitler.

The truth began to dawn . . .

CHAPTER 14

June 6, 1917

There was no clock and Marie LeBrun had never known the luxury of owning a watch. Buried as she was, deep beneath the kitchen floor at Bethlehem Farm, time had become meaningless.

Lying in her damp, musty bed, as the British guns tore great holes in the walls and roof above her head, the girl felt the chill of loneliness and fear. She shivered in her whore's flimsy nightdress, its blatant sexual invitation a cruel joke in this lifeless place.

Marie knew something momentous was about to happen on the brooding ridge above Bethlehem Farm, its ruined buildings stark as rotten teeth in the moonlight.

She looked at the rickety ladder leading to the dark square above, where the trap-door had been left open. The uneasy silence was shattered every few seconds by the fury of exploding shells, echoing through the kitchen's glassless windows.

Dolphie had told her there was to be a great battle here tonight. Her lover was never wrong about military things. He had also assured her she couldn't be harmed . . . but the girl was not so sure about that.

Marie knew battles inevitably brought death. She was only 17 years old, and she didn't want to die. Neither did she want a second life, as yet unborn, to perish with her.

Her beautiful young face was pinched with fear as shells burst outside. It was as though the Grim Reaper was *knock, knock, knocking* on the farm-house door. Had he come for Marie LeBrun?

Was she now to pay for her sins?

Marie sobbed and pulled the old blankets over her head. The thunder of the prelude to battle was muffled, but still frighteningly insistent.

The girl had hoped the coarse bedclothes would still carry the scent of her soldier lover. But time and mildew had wiped away all trace of her beloved Dolphie.

There was only one comfort left . . . warm and happy memories.

❋

The sound of the angry guns and the smell of the mildewed blankets faded, and Marie was back in a bright and exciting world.

It is May Day, and the sun is shining as Marie and Dolphie stroll through the peaceful main street of Fournes-en-Weppe. She tries to take his hand, as lovers do, but he brusquely brushes it away.

But Marie still smiles. She understands he regards the impassioned speech he is making as far too important for him to be distracted by a young girl's trivial expression of affection.

Marie suspects Hitler is rehearsing for a meeting with his cronies later in Black Marie's café. At least when he is there, he seems to relish receiving the deference to which he feels entitled.

The girl, luxuriating in the sun's caress through her bright, bare-shouldered dress, listens with only half an

257

ear. She loves the blessing of the summer, gilding the rural landscape

Besides, she has heard variations on this theme of Dolphie's countless times. She is well-acquainted with the sins of the Jews, Marxists, Freemasons and even the Boy Scouts.

She waves happily as two of the girls from the fields pass by. They wave back, gazing with open curiosity at the ranting, gesticulating soldier by her side.

Marie smiles a sly, womanly smile. She plans to transfer some of Dolphie's passion into their dusty bedroom later. Perhaps this time, their lovemaking will be romantically different.

She guides him to a large, lush meadow, where there is music, dancing and singing to an accordionist. The people of Fournes-en-Weppe are trying to forget the war by holding their summer fiesta a little early this year.

The women are showing off their best summer dresses. But Marie sees there are no Frenchmen of military age among the merrymakers.

German soldiers, tunics unbuttoned and faces red with sun and drink, flirt with the girls, ignoring the flinty gaze of the village women. Now and again, couples slip away into a nearby wood.

Marie persuades Hitler, uncharacteristically, to try a glass of the dark, hop-bitter beer. He sips it, and starts to wave a finger in time to the music. As the *gefreiter* drains his glass, Marie slips another into his hand.

And another. Then a third and a fourth . . . Marie grins in triumph as her man, strangely relaxed, also unbuttons his tunic. Fired by the unaccustomed alcohol, he joins the dancers with rare gusto.

Marie and Hitler spin giddily round and round. Vivid blue eyes dancing, he laughs as he clumsily stumbles and trips. Adolf Hitler is a man transformed.

She presses more foaming glasses on him, which he downs eagerly. Then the accordionist breaks into a slow, romantic air. The girl dances more closely, pressing her full breasts against her lover.

One hand daringly slides over the front of his trousers. Marie is amazed to feel a bulge under the coarse, field-grey cloth. For the first time, her Dolphie is getting hard without their usual weird bedroom ritual.

Inflamed by the beer and the ripe body pressed to his, Hitler has become a man like any other. The White Crow of the trenches has suddenly grown black plumage.

The French girl decides that It Is Time. Hitler doesn't protest as she takes his hand and hurries him to Black Marie's café, where they rent a bedroom. This time, they enter openly as a couple, instead of arriving furtively and separately.

Marie defiantly clings to Hitler's hand as they weave between tables, packed with roistering soldiers and girls. The *gefreiter's* comrades-in-arms, whistling and cat-calling, stare in amazement as he waves to them cheerily.

One of the Bavarians takes a deep swig of beer, leans across the table, and shouts to a friend: "Perhaps the little turnip-head is human after all."

Marie and Hitler make for the stairs, and the chorus of bawdy shouts increases in volume. Hitler bows and dances a little jig before ushering Marie up to the bedroom.

In her farmhouse tomb, Marie smiled her woman's smile. This had been a time of rare romance. She was convinced this was the day *it* happened, and her life changed forever.

Her hands stole instinctively over her belly, clutching it protectively under the filmy silk. She shut her ears and eyes to the terrible present. Marie transported herself back to that day of sunshine and happiness.

The bedroom at Fournes was smaller and darker than their nest in Comines. It had a big, brass-knobbed bed with a mattress that sank under their weight, tossing them into its centre, as though embracing them.

Hitler locked the bedroom door, after making several fumbling attempts. Marie cast aside her clothes and every remaining scrap of maidenly modesty. Drunk as much on the sunshine, the music and the dancing as the coarse, red wine, she made it plain she was more than ready for love.

She leaped on to the bed and, smiling an invitation, struck one of the sultry poses she had seen on the French postcards so beloved of the soldiers. Marie sprawled, hands behind her head, breasts jutting and legs spread lewdly.

When she looked at her lover, her smile melted. Still fully dressed, he was busily rummaging in his pack. He pulled out a piece of board and a tobacco tin, and placed them on a wooden chair.

Still he paid her no attention. Tears ran down Marie's cheeks as, totally absorbed, he took rolls of paper from the pack and pinned them to the board. Had romance melted away like the sun in a summer storm?

Hitler took sticks of charcoal from the tin. With a rush of elation, Marie understood. Hitler the artist was about to immortalise her. When he turned towards Marie, she saw his excitement hadn't diminished.

On this fiesta day, her lover had made yet another departure from his strange and unbending self.

The man who drew or painted only landscapes and buildings, was today intent on capturing the sexuality of a living, breathing and totally nude woman. And that woman was Marie LeBrun.

When Hitler spoke, his irregular breathing betrayed his excitement: He gruffly commanded: "Hold that pose. Don't move a muscle."

Hitler sat on the chair, balanced the board across his knees, and began sketching with bold, fluent strokes. He traced the lush, adolescent curves, the thrust of her breasts, the long, elegant legs that met in a luxuriant bush.

He asked Marie for other, lascivious poses. Hitler had discovered a new and powerful sexual stimulus. As he worked, he breathed increasingly heavily and the one-eyed snake in his trousers seemed eager to burst free.

Marie, nipples stiff with desire, turned on her side for yet another saucy pose. But this time Hitler threw aside his charcoal and tore off his uniform. Marie thrilled as she saw his rampant erection.

The girls in the fields were wrong. Adolf Hitler was indeed a man like any other. He was about to prove he could do a straight fuck like the best of them.

There was no foreplay. Hitler stormed the girl's body like an assaulting infantry battalion. The savage attack was over within a minute.

Afterwards, her lover still heavy upon her, Marie felt a glow of triumph. She had at last aroused Dolphie with her body alone. There had been no need for the usual disturbing play-acting.

With her woman's instinct, she knew that this was The Time. And when Lady Scarlet failed to arrive the following month, Marie was certain.

It remained only to tell the wonderful news to Dolphie.

With a sudden premonition, Marie felt afraid.

❋

At Bethlehem Farm, Marie pulled the blankets from her head and breathed the dank air of reality. Her warm memories melted into glacial misery.

As shadows danced on the cellar's walls, she remembered the terrible day she told her man he was going to be the father of their child.

Marie timed her fateful announcement with care. They were lying, relaxed after their new-style love-making in the bedroom at Fournes. Hitler, for once, was silent.

Marie had rehearsed her speech a dozen times. Hopefully, he would gather her into his arms, cover her with kisses and start to plan their future. Only the last part of that dream came true.

And the future planned by an incandescently angry Adolf Hitler had led her to this frightening tomb on this night of death, destruction and disgrace.

Hitler erupted in fury at the news that Marie was pregnant. He called her a whore and shouted that she was a rock in his road to glory. She was a threat to Hitler's New World.

At one point, he snatched up his bayonet, threatening to plunge it into her guilty belly. His blue eyes blazed, fuelled by an inner furnace of rage. Marie feared for her life and that of their child.

She didn't even bother to undress at their next rendezvous. She knew the days of love-making were over. Marie sat numbly and silently on the edge of the bed as Hitler outlined his plan.

No girl could have imagined the nightmare he had in store for her. Hitler ordered his lover to become a whore.

He told her he would take her to Bethlehem Farm on the eve of a battle.

Then he would leave her alone to await the arrival of the attacking troops. If she survived, she was to seize any opportunity to sleep with the enemy.

Later, Hitler said, his voice bereft of emotion, she must tell some—at present faceless—Tommy that Dolphie's precious baby was his.

Hitler's plan was scarcely credible. When Marie realised its full implication, she shrieked with horror and despair. Downstairs in the café, the soldiers nudged one another knowingly.

One shouted boozily: "They're at it again! Is anyone keeping score?"

Back at the farm, as Marie wept helplessly in her Spartan bed, the guns suddenly fell silent.

Now it was to begin.

❋

June 7, 1917

In a British front line trench, confronting the dark silhouette of Messines Ridge, the ominous silence reached deep inside Sergeant Ernie Cornish. It froze his guts to ice.

He and the other men from the Ninth North Kents knew the end of the barrage was the prelude to an attack. Soon whistles would blow, summoning them "over the top" of the parapet and into No-Man's Land.

The order came: "Fix bayonets!" Steel clattered on steel.

The infantrymen knew they may be minutes from death or, worse, mutilation. Ernie fumbled in the tunic pocket over his heart and brought out a photograph of his "best girl", Maud Waterman.

He couldn't make out her features in the darkness, so he ran his fingers over the familiar cracked and well-worn surface of the snap. Ernie always went through this good-luck ritual before going into battle.

He slid the picture back into his pocket muttering: "Look after me, girl."

To the sergeant's left, a man was reciting the Lord's Prayer over and over again. Another was retching over the duckboards at the bottom of the trench. The private to his right was urinating for the dozenth time.

Over in the enemy lines, 400 metres away, the Germans were puzzled by the silence and inactivity. The British guns had stopped firing at 02.50 hours. Since then, nothing.

Why didn't the Tommies come?

The Germans sent a series of flares, high over the battlefield, to try to find the answer to this puzzle. But the British remained stolidly in their trenches.

More flares soared above the enemy lines, where machine-gunners waited, fingers on triggers. The expected slaughter of the British didn't happen.

Ernie and his men, mouths dry, hearts pounding, with a bullet "up the spout" of their Lee Enfield rifles, also waited. This battle was to be very different from those that had gone before.

That difference lay in dripping galleries, deep under their boots, in the rich, Flanders soil.

Ernie took his mind off the impending battle by thinking of his sweetheart back in Blighty. He remembered Maud as she had looked when they last parted.

She stood, shy, virginal and wreathed in steam on the platform at Southdown station. Maud smiled through her tears as she desperately clutched a soaked handkerchief.

So many boys had left from this platform to go to war, never to return. Ernie remembered the vows ever to be faithful he and Maud had made that day. Lovers made similar promises daily across war-torn Europe.

Ernie felt a stab of guilt, remembering his infidelities in the soldiers' brothel behind the lines in "Pop". He put his hand over the pocket where he kept Maud's photograph and whispered a plea for forgiveness.

Perhaps the next person to see her picture would be a soldier going through his pockets as he lay lifeless on the battlefield. He remembered the Tommies' joke about the Royal Army Medical Corps.

The soldiers said the regiment's initials stood for "Rob All My Comrades". This sometimes turned out to be only half a joke.

Ernie had written Maud's name, and the address of the Big House where she worked, on the back of her photograph. Perhaps some kind soldier would send it on to her.

Time ticked past. German officers consulted their watches and scratched their heads. It had been a full ten minutes since the British guns had fallen silent.

German intelligence had reported that the Tommies were massing for an attack. Yet still they were staying in their trenches.

Why didn't they come?

More questioning flares lit up the sky.

Ernie could see Fritz was getting the wind up. He looked up at the lights and prayed to the God of his Sunday School days that, when the time came, he would lead his men with courage.

They had never known how close he had come to cracking in past battles. In Ernie's unbending Edwardian culture, being a coward was far, far worse than being a corpse.

The sergeant and his men continued to stand, bayonets fixed, as tightly wound as watch springs.

Ernie looked up at the ridge's highest point. This spot, marked on the officers' maps as Spanbroekmolen, was to be the Ninth's objective this summer morning. How many men would die to capture this map reference?

Beneath the Tommies lay another, lethal world. Only minutes earlier, sweating miners of the 171st. Tunnelling company had emerged from a gallery, driven deep underground. Their job was done.

These mud-spattered sappers had survived gas, floods and cave-ins. They had sometimes fought desperate, hand-to-hand battles with the Germans deep underground

Now they squeezed silently past the Ninth Kents on their way to the comparative safety of the reserve trenches.

The miners left behind them a legacy of death for the Hun. That legacy was about to explode in a series of mighty, volcanic eruptions.

Earlier, Allied officers from along the front had been summoned to headquarters and issued with synchronised watches. Now they stood in the trenches with their men, watching the hands approaching zero hour—3.10 a.m.

Down the line from Ernie, the attack was being orchestrated by 51-year-old General Frederick, the 10th. Earl of Cavan and head of X1V Corps.

The General, dug out of retirement when war broke out, was proving to be one of the most brilliant leaders on the Western Front. Now he stood, gold hunter in hand, in the "firing dug-out".

The General's was the only voice to break the silence as he chanted the final count-down: "One minute . . . 45 seconds . . . 30 . . . 15 . . . 10 . . . five . . . four . . . three . . . two . . . one . . . GO!"

The veteran general unleashed a heart-stopping, lung-sucking cataclysm. The top of Messines Ridge erupted into an 800-foot, 3,000 degree C, pillar of fire and earth. Front-line enemy troops were vaporised.

A British chaplain, watching the gigantic mine explosions, crossed himself and gasped: "The earth has opened and swallowed them up."

Dazed, Ernie hauled himself up a ladder and peered over the parapet of the trench. The terrible truth dawned on him.

The Spanbroekmolen mine, consisting of 41 tonnes of ammonal buried 88 feet below the enemy trenches, had failed to explode. The Ninth's objective was still intact. And so was the enemy.

Ernie and his comrades were facing the dreaded combination of barbed wire and machine-guns. He climbed down into the trench, and his Army training immediately over-rode any instinct of self-preservation.

Although the Germans were waiting, the young sergeant knew it was his duty to carry out the orders given to him earlier: "Whether the mine goes off or not, you will attack."

The whistles blew and Ernie shouted: "Come on, lads! What's the matter with you? Do you want to live forever?" He climbed the ladder, propped against the trench wall, and plunged into No-Man's Land.

Ernie's men, heavily laden with rifles, equipment and ammunition, trotted stolidly after their sergeant, bayonets glinting in the light of flares and German distress rockets.

The enemy, as usual, was holding his fire until the Tommies came close enough to mow down. The British barrage roared once more, trying to obliterate what remained of the opposition.

The German artillery in the rear, as though awakening from a bad dream, thundered a reply.

Suddenly, 15 seconds late, the Spanbroekmolen mine at last exploded. The earth shook and blast, mighty as the Devil's breath, caught the Ninth Kents helpless in the open.

Ernie was plucked into the air, as though by a giant hand, and tossed into a shell-hole. He lay for a minute or two, ears ringing, body turned to jelly. Then, shakily, he crawled out and looked around him.

The tardy British mine had claimed some of the first British casualties in the Battle of the Messines Ridge. Dead and wounded lay strewn about the battle-field. Ernie picked his way among them, ignoring pleas for help from the injured men, as he had been ordered.

He gathered together a group of survivors and led them towards the column of dust and smoke. When they reached their objective, the men gazed in awe at a gigantic hole, measuring 250 feet in diameter and 40 feet deep.

There were no Fritzes left to oppose the Tommies as they arrived at the lip of the gaping chasm, later named Lone Tree Crater.

Ernie learned later that he had taken part in a great victory. Allied troops, following a creeping barrage, encountered little resistance as they surged forward on a nine-mile front.

It took them just three hours to take the whole of the ridge, newly disfigured by a series of huge mine craters.

Two great mines still lay beneath the battlefield, their locations later lost in the chaos of war. One exploded harmlessly during a thunderstorm on July 17, 1955.

The other was to change history.

But on June 7, 1917, Ernie and his comrades exultantly drove the Germans farther and farther back. The Tommies whooped and shouted, unaccustomed success going to their heads like wine.

Ernie led his jubilant band down the far side of the ridge, where Marie cowered fearfully beneath the ruined farm-house. When the mines exploded, the stone walls of the cellar shuddered and wept tears of moisture.

Overhead, Marie heard an outbuilding crash to the ground, and part of the farm-house roof tumbled on to the kitchen floor.

In the cellar, the light from the oil lamp shivered and guttered. Marie in her whore's night-dress, bed rocking, thought this must be how the world would end for sinners such as herself.

But Death refused to come and ease her suffering.

The British barrage strode like a rampaging giant across the wounded ridge. Miraculously, it passed by Bethlehem farm without obliterating the remaining buildings.

For a while, silence fell like a shroud over the battle-field. Then Marie faintly heard rifle shots and English voices screaming and shouting.

It was all happening just as Dolphie had predicted.

Her time had come. The girl slipped out of bed, wrapping a blanket round her shoulders. Then, blushing hotly, although she was alone in the cellar, she relieved herself in the bucket in the corner.

Marie picked up a tin mug, lying on the floor, and dipped it into the churn. The water tasted old and dusty, but Marie gulped it gratefully.

She looked at the bread and sausage Hitler had left on the table. But, at the thought of food, her stomach threatened to betray her.

Moving like an automaton, Marie washed her face and combed as much of the dust as she could from her dark hair. She looked down with dismay at her blatant night-dress, with its rosebuds embroidered on the neck and hem.

It was crumpled and stained in dark patches with the sweat of her terror. What man could fancy a girl wearing this rag? It was no longer any use for its lewd purpose

The girl shrugged the blanket to the floor and slipped off the night-dress. She stood for a moment, nude and shivering, before plucking up the courage to sluice her body with the remaining water.

Marie towelled herself dry on the rough blanket. She went, barefoot, to the table, across which her remaining lingerie was draped. Marie picked up the transparent black slip and pulled it over her head.

The garment only served to make her look more naked.

The cold of the cellar hardened her nipples, and they pushed the thin material out shamelessly. The garment's plunging neckline ensured that most of her firm young breasts were on display. And her pubic hair revealed itself as a dark shadow.

The petticoat's daring hemline bared her long legs and most of her thighs. Marie sat on the stool and pulled on her black silk stockings, securing them with the frilly lace garters, decorated with rose-buds.

Finally, she looked down at herself. Dolphie would have smiled his approval at her appearance. Marie felt a brief glow of satisfaction at the thought. She was being a bad girl for him and for him alone.

Who would have thought that Marie LeBrun, a regular churchgoer in her native Seboncourt and daughter of a respectable butcher and Freemason, could have come to this?

Shame on her. Today she looked just what she had become—a tart.

It just remained for Marie to carry out the next part of Hitler's plan.

The girl started with alarm as booted footsteps clomped across the kitchen floor above her head. Seconds later, an authoritative English voice shouted roughly down the open hatch:

"If there's anyone down there, come out NOW, with your hands up. I'm holding a grenade, and I'll be tossing it down in just ten seconds. What's it to be, Fritz?"

Marie screamed in terror.

The voice said wonderingly: "Jesus Christ, it's a woman! Here Johnny, take hold of this Mills bomb for a minute. The pin's out, so don't let go of the lever whatever you do.

"You stay here and chuck that thing at any Hun who happens to be passing. I'm going down to see who's hiding in the cellar."

The girl stood wordlessly, hands modestly held over groin and breasts, as a pair of dusty boots appeared at the top of the ladder. She watched as puttees, followed by khaki trousers, then a British uniform tunic appeared through the hatch.

Finally, Marie could make out the soldier's face under its steel helmet as he climbed down the remaining rungs into the cellar. His jaw was clenched and his eyes still had the fever of battle in them.

Sergeant Ernie Cornish had never seen anything like the golden vision in the fitful lamplight. He stared in open amazement, and Marie LeBrun, still shielding herself with her hands, modestly lowered her eyes.

The spell was broken when another face appeared at the entrance to the trap door. The second soldier gaped at the girl's semi-nakedness.

He exclaimed: "Fuckin' hell, Sarge, look what the good Lord 'as sent us! Spoils o' war." A few seconds later, another booted foot appeared on the top rung of the ladder.

Ernie shouted with all the authority of his three stripes: "Piss off, corporal! Go and chuck that Mills bomb somewhere useful. I'll handle this."

Sergeant Ernie Cornish walked slowly towards Marie LeBrun.

Hitler's plan was working perfectly.

CHAPTER 15

Tuesday, September 5, 2000

There was silence in the yellow Porsche as it snarled its power through the Flanders lanes. Both men stared through the fly-spattered windscreen, lost in turbulent thoughts.

Arthur Burfield felt himself transformed into what he considered to be his real self, powerful neo-Nazi Andre Lecroix. He would soon be commanding other, lesser mortals to the trivial duty of taking photographs.

He may soon have very much bigger fish to fry. Andre Lecroix planned to play Martin Bormann to Adam Cornish's Adolf Hitler. He would be the man closest to the new Fuhrer's power and money.

Bormann, the old Fuhrer's deputy and confidante, had long been Arthur's great hero. The coarse-mannered Nazi of the shadows had virtually ruled the Reich's vast empire with his pen.

With deadly ink, he dispatched millions of Jews and "sub-human Slavs" to slave labour and death camps. No-one—except Adolf Hitler himself—had been safe from Martin Bormann.

This Nazi was the most lethal bureaucrat in history. As Hitler's private secretary and keeper of his diary, Bormann was the Fuhrer's gate-keeper. He was in a unique position to regulate access to Hitler, and thus curb the power of the top Nazis.

Arthur wanted to be just like Bormann. The Nazi secretary had been so close to Hitler that he had acted as a witness at the Fuhrer's wedding to Eva Braun, as the Soviet Army closed in on the Berlin bunker.

Bormann had melted away before the Red hordes overwhelmed the devastated German capital. There had been many reported sightings of him over the years. By now, most people believed he had perished.

In fact, there had even been some "evidence" found of his demise, allegedly while he was escaping from the bunker.

But Arthur was convinced someone as clever as his hero would have kept a successful escape route up his sleeve. Bormann's plan must surely have included releasing a shoal of red herrings.

As the peaceful fields of Flanders sped past the Porsche, Arthur decided he would become a worthy successor to Hitler's Machiavellian secretary. Adam could do the strutting, but he would do the ruling.

His pen would build a New World Order, free from the malign influence of Jews and Reds. Cattle trains, packed with inferior humanity, would roll again. The camps would kill on a grand scale, this time using modern, green technology.

Arthur had long planned to build his Fourth Reich power base by spinning a web of spies. No-one would be safe from the betrayals of their neighbours and friends. Knowledge was power. Knowledge was fear.

Of course, like Bormann, Arthur would expect to be suitably rewarded for his expertise and loyalty. When you have power, money inevitably follows. He would make sure he was Adam's closest confidante.

The new Fuhrer would develop a warm, nostalgic affection for his old photographer buddy from their days at the Kentish World. Adam would soon find him indispensable.

Arthur chuckled as he saw a blue-overalled farm labourer on the road ahead, stolidly pedalling home on his bicycle for his lunch. The photographer aimed the Porsche at the man, driving him into a ditch.

He glanced in the rear-view mirror, and saw the labourer, crawling out of the mud and shaking his fist at him. The photographer's mood changed. Soon people would never even dare to raise their eyes in his presence.

Arthur savagely jammed on the brakes and thrust the car into reverse. The rear bumper ended just inches from the man. He jumped for his life . . . back into the water-filled ditch.

The photographer slipped the car into first gear and, as he resumed his journey, realised that Adam had broken his long silence. The reporter was looking back over his shoulder and laughing.

Adam, putting his dreams to one side, said gleefully: "Soon they'll all be dancing to our tune, eh, Arthur?"

Arthur, realising the significance of the remark, felt a glow of satisfaction. Adam obviously realised that Arthur was a mate on the same wavelength as himself.

He replied: "Not 'alf, Adam. We'll soon be leading 'em quite a dance."

Satisfaction turned to excitement as Adam expressed his thoughts for the first time since they had left Marguerite Vonneste and her grand-daughter, Anne-Marie.

Adam queried: "What on earth was my grandmother doing snuggling up to Adolf Hitler? Looking at the photograph, they were obviously more than 'just good friends'.

"I've been trying to work out where I might come into this scenario. And I've come to the conclusion there's a distinct possibility that I might make it into the history books."

Arthur remained diplomatically silent, keeping his eyes on the lane. Adam went on: "That girl in the old crone's book was definitely my French grandmother, Marie LeBrun. There is a photo of her in Ernie's family album.

"There can be no mistake. I must delve deeper into this affair. It was definitely the Frog bitch my grandfather, Ernie, married in the First World War. This could turn out to be quite a story.

"I think I told you before, Arthur, that this slag pissed off and left Ernie literally holding the baby—my father, Albert. She never even came back to see her grandson—me."

Adam's eyes blazed like the furnaces of Auschwitz as he declared: "She must be dead by now. I hope she is burning in hell. I'll give her a pasting in my film script for her sins, I can tell you."

Arthur looked across at his passenger and was shocked by the molten anger distorting Adam's face and reflected in his eyes He saw shades of the old Fuhrer.

At that instant, he was finally convinced in his own mind that Adam Cornish was Hitler's grandson.

The Bormann-in-waiting decided that, from now on, Adam would have to be handled very carefully indeed. But the die wasn't yet cast. Arthur reminded himself there was a vital test Adam Cornish had yet to pass.

As the Flanders fields flashed past, pieces of the jigsaw were falling into place in Adam's head. Ernie had married Marie Lebrun because he thought she was expecting his baby.

But was she? Today, Adam had just learned she had been the mistress of none other than Adolf Hitler himself.

Was Ernie tricked into marriage by Marie when she was already pregnant by the Fuhrer-to-be? Is that why she had deserted his grandfather so quickly after coming to England? Had she gone in search of her German lover?

Why had Arthur Burfield taken him for that revelation in Comines today? Was it to give a clue to Adam about the man of destiny he really was?

Who exactly was this photographer he thought he knew so well? Was Arthur Burfield part of some deep plot?

Questions whirled like Dervishes through the writer's head.

Adam had always known instinctively he was someone special. But at this moment, Adam Ernest Cornish was convinced he was indeed capable of turning his fantasies into fact.

Already, he relished the taste of revenge.

Adam imagined himself as the all-powerful Fuhrer, spreading terror like poison gas across a world-wide Fourth Reich. He would finish what his grandfather had begun.

No-one would feel safe—even for a micro-second— during his rule. He swore to himself he would learn his grandfather's lessons and prove a worthy successor. But there would be no death in a bunker for him.

When Adam spoke to Arthur, he had the steel of a new authority in his voice: "The old woman said I had the Fuhrer's eyes. She was certain of it. Would you agree with her?"

Arthur, Bormann-like, was careful in choosing his words. Although he was sure the man sitting next to him was the kin of Adolf Hitler, it wouldn't do to commit himself just yet.

On the other hand, it would do him no harm to ingratiate himself with his future master.

Adam thrilled at the new note of respect in the photographer's voice as he steered the Porsche down a winding lane towards a distant clump of trees.

Arthur said: "I would say that your eyes are very similar to those of our late, beloved Fuhrer, Adolf Hitler.

"Had that photograph been in colour, I'm sure there would have been no doubt. I expect you have been told many times that your eyes are a particularly striking shade of blue.

"I can now reveal that I am taking you to a place where you can prove you are indeed the Blood of the Fuhrer. Within the hour, you will undergo a test, set by Adolf Hitler himself, for this purpose.

"If you pass this trial, which has been awaiting the Fuhrer's rightful heir for many years, it will be the privilege of myself and thousands like me to serve you."

Arthur turned the car into yet another by-way, this one wide enough only for a single farm cart. He went on: "In such a case, I am honoured to lead you on this first step of your path to glory . . . to see you pick up the Fuhrer's torch."

Adam, sitting straight-backed in the car's passenger seat, his face a mask of arrogance, interrupted Arthur's obsequious rambling.

"Who the bloody hell *are* you, Arthur? It's obvious you're not the friendly photographer I've known all these years on the Kentish World. What game are you playing?"

Arthur began to reply: "Well, it's like this, old chap . . ."

Adam interrupted again, this time angrily: "Let me tell you now, the days when I was *your 'old chap'* are gone forever. After I have taken and passed this so-called test, you will address me as 'Fuhrer'.

"When we are alone together, because we were once colleagues, you may become more relaxed and address me simply as 'sir' or 'my Leader'."

Arthur, white with shock at the reprimand, failed to check his rear-view mirror. So he didn't see a black Range Rover slowly turn into the track behind them and park behind a screen of bushes.

"Yes, my Leader, I beg you to accept my apologies. Please don't think I lack respect. My real name is Andre Lacroix and I come from here in Flanders. I am a loyal National Socialist, as are my father, Wilfred, and my adopted brother Jacques.

"They are eager to meet you today, and my brother is said to have a historic story to tell. They will also officially announce that Adam Cornish is the true blood of the Fuhrer, if . . . er . . . I mean *when* you pass the Hitler test.

"This is to be the Nazis' long-awaited day of destiny. My Leader, I am sure in my heart that you are of The Blood. What happens here in Flanders within the next hour will shake the world and leave it trembling.

"My family and I and our many comrades ask only to assist you in your great mission."

Adam, reporter's antenna twitching, demanded: "Why were you posing as an English photographer on a local paper for all those years? Did you already know I was possibly Adolf Hitler's illegitimate grandson?"

Arthur stuttered in his haste to ingratiate himself: "We have evidence that made us strongly suspect this might be the case. Today, I am sure, is just a matter of confirmation.

"For years, it has been my job to protect you against dark forces who might seek to harm one of The Blood. I watched over you and kept you safe.

"Now comes your moment of destiny. We are approaching the place where you will perform your first historic act."

A black-bellied cloud, lurking over the distant mound of Mount Kemmel, suddenly blotted out the sun. Large drops of rain coursed down the Porsche's windscreen.

It was as though the sky were weeping for the ghostly armies buried in the fields below. Arthur switched on the windscreen wipers as the car approached a large sign by the side of the track.

Adam, peering through the rain, read:

"Hill 40. Bavarian Wood.
"Frauenlob mine-shaft and German trenches.
"Museum and canteen.
"Hitler served here with the 16th. R.I.R."

A schoolroom blackboard was propped next to the sign. Its chalked message, beginning to dissolve in the wet, announced in English Dutch, French and German that the historical site was closed indefinitely.

Arthur pulled into a small, roadside car park, formed by levelling a few furrows of a nearby cornfield.

Two modest Belgian Peugeots were already there. When the photographer parked the bright yellow Porsche beside them, it looked as though an exotic beast were sleeping amid dreary cattle.

Adam eased himself out of the car and, ignoring the downpour, slowly looked around. He felt in his bones that this was Hitler's sacred place. It was eerily silent. No birds sang in the nearby wood.

He turned towards the west where Mount Kemmel, once the scene of bitter fighting, was wearing a widow's veil of mist. A few hundred yards from where Adam stood, was a tiny war cemetery.

The gravestones showed white as Brussels lace against the brown velvet of the tilled fields surrounding them.

To the north, the lane continued down a gentle slope. A hundred yards farther on, a modest stone memorial to a fallen soldier sat sadly beside the road.

The lane wound past a farm on the right, and then headed towards the distant spires and Cloth Hall tower of Ypres.

Finally, Adam turned to his right and faced the "shrine", the Bayernwald—Bavarian Wood—itself. This was where his grandfather had fought so valiantly.

Adam instinctively felt that Hitler's heroic shade must haunt these dripping trees and bushes.

Standing in front of the wood, as though on guard, was a strange house. Here, deep in the Flanders countryside, was a Swiss chalet. The eccentric building, surrounded by an unkempt hedge, had an air of deep neglect.

Its paint was peeling and its windows were unwashed. Drooping curtains were grey with the grime of years. What had once been a lawn in front of the chalet was like a rough cow pasture.

Ranged along an uncut hedge, facing Ypres, were four poles, from which the flags of France, Britain, Belgium and Germany flapped dismally in the rain.

Arthur led Adam to the left of the house, down a cart-track which divided Bavarian Wood from the surrounding fields.

An old shell-case, hung from a frame, of the type rigged in the Great War as an alarm for gas attacks, stood next to two high wooden gates. These were flanked by substantial posts, surmounted by red turrets.

They gave the place the air of some sad and decayed Disneyland.

Scrawled in capital letters, on a large piece of cardboard, pinned to one of the gates, was the word "CLOSED". Arthur, ignoring the sign, pushed open one of the gates and gestured Adam to follow.

But the writer, raindrops streaming down his face like tears, didn't budge. He was listening to a new and compelling Voice, speaking to him from inside his head. It told him that, soon now, he would achieve the greatness that was his destiny.

Arthur, puzzled, again beckoned to Adam. The bearded writer stepped past the "Disneyland" gates into his new life.

He paused to look at the bizarre scene inside a cluttered courtyard. Rusting shell-cases formed a neat pyramid, next to a waterless fish-pond. Rotting army socks were pegged to a washing line.

There was a large picture window at the back of the Swiss house. Adam saw dusty exhibits peeping from within. A door, labelled "WC", was ajar, revealing a primitive earth closet.

At the far side of the courtyard, a pointing finger sign, nailed to a stump of wood, indicated: "To the trenches and mine-shaft". Beyond that, a flooded WW1 crater glinted sombrely in the rain, its water like the pitted steel of an old bayonet.

So this dismal scene, Hitler's haunted and sacred place, was to be the cradle of Adam's new empire.

Arthur grasped Adam's arm and pointed to a small, brick-built canteen, partly shielded by trees and brambles, to the left of the gates. A chimney on the moss-encrusted tiles of its roof puffed fragrant clouds of wood smoke.

There were flickers of movement behind cobweb-festooned windows. The photographer, anxious for Adam to enter the building, grasped his sleeve.

The writer brusquely shrugged him off. He stood silently, rain darkening the shoulders of his jacket, drinking in the atmosphere.

Adam knew from his research that this unremarkable tangle of trees and bushes, because of its shape, used to be called Axle Wood. It was renamed Bavarian Wood to mark the valour of Hitler's Munich-based regiment.

This was where Hitler won his Iron Cross, Second Class, during the bitter fighting early in the war. It was here, too, that he received his one and only promotion—to humble *gefreiter*.

One book Adam found in the Southdown public library, said Hitler had planned to build a giant and imposing statue of himself here, proclaiming the "millennium of the Third Reich".

It was to Bavarian Wood, still scarred by the old German trenches in which he had once served, that the conquering Fuhrer hurried soon after the fall of Belgium in 1940.

Adam made his late grandfather a silent promise that his statue would one day rise in glittering white stone from among these trees. It would be hailed by an adoring National Socialist multitude led, of course, by himself.

The writer tensed as a shadow moved in the bushes by the mine-crater. He relaxed as a wild goose lifted from the water, wings beating powerfully. Flying low, it vanished like a ghost into the mist.

Arthur said deferentially: "They are waiting for us, sir. They have been expecting you for several hours."

He led Adam to the door of the canteen, which he pulled open. The oil-starved hinges shrieked in protest, and a blast of warm air hit them.

Inside, two men were sitting on straight-backed wooden chairs, drawn close to an old army stove. This glowed with heat, and there was a neat pile of logs stacked nearby.

The stove's pipe pierced the smoke-stained ceiling. The place smelled of wood smoke, rot and acrid Belgian cigarettes. Everything had a light covering of dust.

Adam, his wet clothes beginning to steam, looked round with interest as the men in the canteen remained silently staring at him.

The bar was made of two old trestle tables, pushed together. This was loaded with a rich variety of Belgian beers, and ranks of glasses of dubious hygiene. More dusty bottles lined rows of shelves behind the bar.

A pheasant hung from a nail driven into a wall, and sausages, drooping in coils from the ceiling, had garnered a rich, nicotine patina.

A splash of colour was provided by copies of World War One paintings by Adolf Hitler, depicting local scenes— Messines Church" and a long-since obliterated trench called "The Hollow Way".

There was also a framed black and white photograph of Hitler, pointing out places of interest to his aides, during his visit to Bavarian Wood in 1940.

The museum shelves were a disorganised clutter of unlabelled artifacts. Bayonets, shell-case art, British and German water bottles, gas respirators and old beer and wine bottles jostled for space with a broken-down trench pump and rusty grenade cases.

Arthur felt the time had come to introduce to Adam the two men, still sitting silently in this strange canteen-cum-museum.

The photographer nodded to the younger of the two. This was a man fleshing out in middle age, time making grey inroads into a shock of dark hair.

He had a mild, scholarly air. The man's face, flushed with the heat, indicated a sensitive nature. His rumpled jacket, with leather patches on the sleeves, and baggy corduroy trousers could have been stolen from a jumble sale.

The man climbed slowly to his feet and regarded Adam shrewdly and respectfully.

Arthur told Adam: "This, sir, is my adopted brother, Jacques. He is the owner and keeper of this sacred ground. Jacques, too, is a true and loyal National Socialist. He has waited many years for this meeting."

Jacques bowed his head respectfully. He opened the lid of the stove and threw in three logs before seating himself again

Arthur now turned to the other man whom, Adam noticed for the first time, was fiercely clutching a metal box in his lap. He appeared to be in his eighties, but the eyes in his heavily-lined face were sharp and alert.

The old man, grey hair cropped close to his skull, was wearing a leather jacket, a black shirt, and riding breeches. He exuded an air of military and arrogant authority.

Arthur told Adam: "I have the privilege, sir, to introduce you to my father, Wilfred Lacroix. He served valiantly with the Nazi liberators of Flanders during the war, and has kept the National Socialist faith alive during these wilderness years."

Wilfred Lacroix remained seated, eyes shrewdly evaluating the visitor. Adam felt a twinge of anger at the implied disrespect. He snapped: "Why don't you get off your arse in my presence, old man?"

The writer's blue eyes flashed a warning, and there was a sharp intake of breath from Arthur. Lacroix calmly remained seated. Then he raised the box in both hands, as though holding aloft the chalice at Holy Communion.

He told Adam: "Before I stand for you, I have to know you are truly of The Blood. This box, entrusted to me by Adolf Hitler himself, will tell me if this is the case or not.

285

"Having told you this, you now know part of our holy secret." Lacroix reached under his jacket and produced a World War Two Luger pistol. Adam, Arthur and Jacques froze like children playing the game of statues.

The old man went on: "It must be obvious that, if you do not prove to be our new fuhrer, you must be silenced. And that means for ever. I shall do it here and now. We hear the vultures are gathering and you may well be one of them."

Jacques rose unobtrusively to his feet and moved to block the door. Wilfred addressed his adopted son, almost conversationally: "Yesterday was a sunny day, was it not, Jacques?"

"Yes, father."

"Have you acted as ordered?"

"Yes, father. I placed the box in the sun for several hours in a safe and secure place. It is now fully charged."

The veteran Nazi rose. Adam saw that, although a little bent with age, he was lean, muscular and still more than six feet tall. He pushed the pistol into his belt and walked stiffly to the bar.

Wilfred pushed aside bottles and glasses and placed the metal box reverently in the dust. He crooked a finger at Adam, who found himself obediently walking towards him.

The Nazi said: "Now we will see whether I shall either stand to attention before you, or shoot you down like a dog. Pick up this box and push aside the shutter on its lid. Behind the shutter you will see a lens.

"You will look directly into this, at a distance of approximately three feet, for three minutes. I will time this on my watch. If you are of The Blood, the box will open, for it is constructed to recognise an eye inherited from the Fuhrer.

"I do not know exactly what the box contains. But I do know that, inside it, Adolf Hitler has left the key to the Fourth Reich for his successor."

Wilfred Lecroix, the deep creases in his face etched black by the shadows, drew the Luger, pointed it at Adam's head and clicked off the safety catch. With his free hand, he pulled an old silver watch from his pocket and studied it intently.

The writer trembled as he picked up the box and slid back the cover. Wilfred's watch ticked away the seconds as Adam stared, with his vivid blue eyes, into the exposed lens.

Logs sighed and collapsed in the stove. Rain tapped like the Grim Reaper on the windows.

The lid of the box sprang open, the tiny click sounding like a clap of thunder in the tense atmosphere of the canteen.

Wilfred lowered the gun and stowed it away. He stood stiffly to attention and raised his arm in the Nazi salute.

He barked: "Heil Hitler!"

Arthur and Jacques also saluted, and echoed: "Heil Hitler!"

None of the men glimpsed a shadow passing outside one of the canteen's grime-encrusted windows.

Wilfred shouted: "Welcome to the new Fuhrer! I am at your service for what is left of my life. Adolf Hitler has commanded that myself and my son, Andre, must now leave. Jacques will remain.

"*Mein Fuhrer,* what is inside Hitler's box is, at present, for your eyes only. He has commanded that Jacques should be present to tell you a secret."

Wilfred marched out of the canteen, followed by Arthur Burfield. Their footsteps squelched into the distance.

Down by the mine-crater, another wild goose rose and skimmed the water.

Adam and Jacques peered at the folded paper in the open box. Jacques bowed deferentially and gestured for the bearded writer to take it.

The museum owner averted his eyes as Adam unfolded what he saw with awe was a sheet of Hitler's personal notepaper.

He read:

"To whom it may concern,

"The fact that you have managed to open this device means that you are honoured by having the Blood of the Fuhrer in your veins.

"Possessing my precious blood is a heavy responsibility. For I now appoint you the chosen one, who will carry on my great work. I hereby give you both permission and the means to create a Fourth Reich in my name.

"The man who keeps the museum at Bavarian Wood, in Wytschaete, Flanders—Jacques Deberte—will have seen you open this box and read this note. Therefore, he will know you are the new messiah of National Socialism.

"I order him to tell you the secret which is the key to untold wealth and power. You will use this to appoint yourself Fuhrer in my name. You will build a world of which I, Adolf Hitler, would be proud. This will be a true, Aryan world, free of the canker of Jews, Communists and Freemasons.

"Let nothing and nobody get in your way. This holy crusade demands that you will be as ruthless as I.

"Heil, new Fuhrer!

"Adolf Hitler"

Andre was deathly pale. He shivered, in spite of the warmth of the stove. It was time, after all these years, to tell his great secret. Would he be again struck dumb by its horror? Would he be expendable after its telling?

Would he now be signing his own death warrant?

Adam folded the Fuhrer's letter reverently into its original creases, placed it back in the box and snapped the lid shut.

The shabby reporter, for so long the butt of office jokes, the man everyone overlooked, was now the new Fuhrer. Adolf Hitler himself had appointed him and granted him untold wealth and power.

Soon, just as Adam had always dreamed, the world would indeed dance to his tune. He straightened his back and fixed Jacques with those fateful blue eyes.

Adam barked: "I am now the Fuhrer! I command you to tell me the secret which Adolf Hitler, in his great wisdom, says will enable me to build a National Socialist world.

"Before you speak, you will hand me a beer, and then keep more coming. My thirst is now your thirst. I'll down them straight from the bottle. I wouldn't let a dog drink from those filthy glasses."

Jacques handed Adam a beer and a bottle opener, wiping the neck of the bottle with his handkerchief.

The dam of memory broke after all those years, and words came pouring out.

"I was in the wood and I saw it all. I didn't tell Wilfred what I witnessed, even though he broke my arm. It was terrible, terrible. A young boy should never see such things."

Jacques' voice broke. He put his hands over his face and sobbed. Adam drained half his bottle of beer in two huge gulps.

"Blood. Blood. It was everywhere. The dead were covered in it . . ."

Adam drained the bottle and gestured for another. He snapped impatiently: "Stop burbling, man, and pull yourself together. What is this secret of yours? Speak up now—your old Fuhrer and your new Fuhrer demand it!"

With a huge effort, Jacques choked back his tears. He looked waveringly at Adam, whose beard glistened with spilt beer. Then, voice hoarse with emotion, Jacques at last described what he had seen that fateful day at Bavarian Wood.

"The secret, my Fuhrer, lies beneath our feet. It is the secret of the Frauenlob. It is deep in water and blood. All those men died to seal their lips.

"The Jews carried crate after crate of heavy material from trucks. S.S. men stored these in the mine-shaft. I could hear the soldiers saying there must be treasure in those crates—probably gold.

"This was a deadly secret, my Fuhrer. First, I saw the Jews shot, then the soldiers and, finally, the officer in charge. They capped the shaft. There was blood . . . blood . . . I was afterwards struck dumb."

Adam, his eyes fixed on the museum's owner's ashen face, gestured for yet another beer. He took a deep swig and ordered: "Continue."

Jacques went on: "After everyone was wiped out, I continued to hide in the wood. I didn't want to die if soldiers came. I was the only one left who had seen what had been going on.

"Sure enough, more S.S. men arrived. There was also a car with a big-wig, who had a moustache and a monocle. I recognised him from pictures in the newspapers as Heinrich Himmler himself.

"He ordered the soldiers to uncap the mine-shaft, throw the bodies down, and then reseal it. I waited until long after all these men had gone before trying to run home. I was caught on the way by Wilfred.

"But I told him nothing. I have not spoken of this ever since. I . . ."

Adam interrupted: "This must remain a secret for now, known to only a select few. Go and find Wilfred and Arthur Burfield, or whatever-his-name-is. We have much to discuss."

Five minutes later, Wilfred and Arthur stood respectfully before Adam. Jacques was slumped on his chair, his inflamed eyes fixed unseeingly on the stove.

This was the biggest story of Adam's life, and he couldn't resist a touch of drama. He announced: "I have personally found Hitler's legendary treasure. It is beneath us as I speak . . . stored in the Frauenlob.

"That is the Fuhrer's great secret. To reveal it without my permission is to sentence yourselves to death."

Arthur Burford whispered, as though hidden ears were listening: "I and my father and brother will guard this secret with our lives. So the story of the Jewish gold was true. We are the first to find it. It's all ours."

Wilfred, hands clenched into fists to stop them shaking, added: "It is *not* ours—it belongs to the new Reich. The treasure lies beneath many gallons of water. It will not be easy to retrieve.

"Fortunately, my old Fuhrer, Hitler, with his usual foresight and genius, provided me with the money for such a project. First, we must buy powerful pumps to drain the shaft and its galleries. Then we must haul out the material.

"For all of this, unfortunately, we must recruit labour. I will personally see to it that every one of these men keeps his mouth shut. Perhaps, when we are in power, we will still their lips forever."

Jacques turned a tear-stained face towards his adopted father and stammered: "Father, I have told my secret as instructed. Now I ask you to tell me *yours*. This question has caused me untold agony over the years.

"I lie in bed at night wondering, 'What has happened to my real parents, Gilberte and Roger? Why was I taken from them and given to you?' I never told you of my pain over this matter because I thought you would be angry with me.

"But I still see their loving faces. Sometimes, I imagine we are all together again in our happy home in Voormezele. Where are they? Will I ever see them again, father?"

Wilfred, preoccupied with thoughts of riches and the task ahead, waved a dismissive hand. He roared: "Now is not the time to concern ourselves with such trivia!"

The usually mild-mannered Jacque's reaction startled the men in the canteen. He gave a piteous scream and leaped to his feet with such violence that his chair crashed to the floor.

"Where ARE they? I MUST know! What has happened to mama and poppa? For years I have done your bidding without asking a single question. I DEMAND to know this one thing!"

The old Nazi's face turned to hardened steel. "Seeing as you have DEMANDED the truth, you shall have it—plain and unvarnished. It will be interesting to see how you enjoy it.

"Adolf Hitler himself gave me implicit instructions about disposing of your parents. He told me to send them to Auschwitz with a note to the commandant asking him to make sure they never came back.

"So they went up the chimneys with the Jews and other n'er-do-wells, my little son. So don't bother me any more with your foolish questions. We have the Fuhrer's work to do."

Jacques screamed again, like a fox in a trap. He ran from the canteen and stumbled blindly into the weeping trees and bushes of Bavarian Wood.

He started in terror as a hand gripped his shoulder and forced him to a standstill. An educated English voice whispered in his ear: "Take it easy, Jacques. I am a friend. Come with me and we'll have a little chat.

"We have something in common.

"It's called revenge."

CHAPTER 16

July 14, 1917

Ernie was back in "Pop" for a few days respite from the trenches. But, at this moment, the weary young veteran was not in his cosy room over the Café de Ville. He was marching alone through the town's darkened streets to keep a rendezvous with a nightmare.

A few minutes earlier, he had crept quietly from his snug bed and the warm body of Marie. She lay, as if asleep, curled gracefully round the comfort of a pillow. Child-like, she had a thumb in her mouth.

While he was washing and shaving in the ice-cold water from a pitcher on the bedroom's wash-stand, Ernie glanced at the girl and, with a jolt of unease, noticed a trickle of tears down her cheeks.

He pulled on his uniform and walked as quietly as his Army boots would allow, down the café's stairs. When he reached the fourth one, he heard the girl beginning to sob

Minutes after Marie heard the café door close, she threw back the bedclothes, pulled a chamber pot from beneath the bed, and was violently sick. This had become her daily early-morning ritual.

As he marched through the night, Ernie wondered about those tears. What had caused them? Bad dreams? Memories of the bloody battle of Messines? He felt a stab of guilt as he steeled himself to ask a further question: "Was it something more personal?"

Was Marie an innocent girl he had made to whore for him? She seemed willing enough to set their bed a-dance. But was she play-acting to keep him as her protector in this alien and uncertain world?

Ernie's boot-steps echoed from the sleeping houses. He wondered whether he had subconsciously used the girl's body as a means of exorcising the memory of those thousands of other bodies he had seen, lying torn and bloated on the battlefields.

Some instinct told Ernie that, for all her wantonness in bed, Marie had built an invisible barrier between them, as impenetrable as the stone ramparts of nearby Ypres. Marie had given him her body, but not her heart.

Did that heart belong to another? Was that why she wept alone? If there were a lost lover, who could he be? Was he English, German, French or Flemish? Was he better in bed than Ernie?

The sergeant made a determined effort to stop this self-torture. He told himself he had probably saved Marie's life at Messines. Now he was providing her with protection and a *cushy*—comfortable—billet that many another girl out here would envy.

He came to a halt before Poperinge's town hall, and all thoughts of Marie fled. For it was here, in a few minutes, he would face his dark horror.

Sergeant Ernest Frederick Cornish believed he was about to commit cold-blooded murder.

He marched through the building's open gates into a court-yard. Ernie joined three other men of the Ninth Kents, huddled, shivering into their great-coats and clutching rifles.

One of them handed Ernie an extra Lee Enfield he was carrying. The four soldiers gazed across the yard to where lights burned behind barred windows. In that room, two young men were spending their last minutes on earth.

The sergeant and his three privates were that morning forming a firing squad. They were waiting for the first streaks of dawn to lighten the sky before doing this dreaded duty.

The squad personally knew the condemned soldiers. At 16 years old, these Tommies were little more than children, having lied about their age in their zeal to join up. But their patriotic fervour quickly turned to terror when, after only two weeks in Flanders, the battalion was ordered up the line for an attack.

The two terrified boys wept in the ranks as the soldiers trudged to the starting-off point. On the way, they passed the mangled bodies of men, mules and horses.

Bloodied, wounded soldiers limped down the shell-battered road in the opposite direction. The menacing growling of the German guns grew steadily louder. Shells began to blow gaps in the Kents' ranks.

Finally the boys, minds numbed and befuddled, did what Ernie and most other Tommies often came to within a heart-beat of doing themselves . . . they broke and ran.

Ernie shouted after them, but his voice was drowned as the British barrage opened up. When the soldiers didn't return, he had to report their defection. Then the military justice machine ground into action.

For the brass-hats knew just how near the brink of breakdown many of the men in the trenches were. Panic could spread like a virulent epidemic. Some of the French had already refused to fight. Examples had to be made.

The military police—the hated "Red Caps"—caught up with the youngsters four miles behind the lines. The deserters were crouched, shivering and hungry, in a roofless barn.

The two lads were brought back and charged with cowardice. The fact that they were, at 16 years old, officially too young to serve overseas, didn't save them.

Ernie and the whole battalion were paraded yesterday and the two soldiers, shaking uncontrollably, were hauled before them. The boys were made to suffer a ritual humiliation.

Their caps were snatched off by a sergeant, and every insignia of the Ninth Kents was roughly ripped from their uniforms. Then, in a posh, expensively-educated voice, an immaculately turned-out captain read out the guilty verdict of the court martial which had tried them.

He told how the two soldiers had run away, letting down their comrades just as they were about to go into action. The officer added that many of those comrades had died bravely while facing the enemy.

The assembled troops listened silently. The captain then told the battalion the men would be shot at dawn the following day.

The condemned soldiers were members of Ernie's platoon. So he placed himself on the firing squad and ordered the others to draw lots for the hated duty.

Now, in the pre-dawn cold, Ernie and the other three men shuffled restlessly as execution time drew near. These veterans had seen countless men die, but not like this. Not British soldiers shot down by British soldiers.

The sergeant decided to steady the squad. He told them in a low voice: "Now lads, I don't like this any more than you do. But it's a job that's got to be done. We are soldiers of the Ninth. So we obey orders.

"We've always done our duty. Don't forget these men were prepared to drop us in the shit when we were about to fight for our lives."

The three men stopped fidgeting as they listened to Ernie. But, as though drawn by a magnet, their eyes kept returning to those barred, golden-lit windows.

The Tommies knew a padre had been with the condemned men all night. Fat lot of good his bloody prayers would do them. Better by far the rum given to those poor lads to dull the edge of their terror.

For the hundredth time, the firing squad peered into the dark sky. Ernie made another attempt at distracting them. He said softly: "When they took our rifles away, they loaded them at random. Three have live rounds up the spout and the other a blank."

One of privates spoke for the first time: "That just goes to show that those bloody brass-hats behind the lines have never been on the business end of a Lee-Enfield. Otherwise they would have known the difference between the kick of a live round and the fart from a blank."

Ernie ignored him and went on: "Now, pay attention. In a few minutes they're going to bring out the poor sods. They will then be blindfolded, and the medical officer will pin a piece of white cloth over each man's heart.

"Meanwhile, I suppose, the padre will keep on saying his prayers. Watch the officer. He will raise his arm and, when he drops it, he will remain silent. That is your signal to fire.

"Now, this is what I want to happen then. Smithy and Jones will take the man on their left. Me and Dusty will take the one on the right. Smithy will aim at the man's heart and Jones at his head.

"I will aim at our bloke's head and Dusty will fire at his heart. Job done. Imagine you're shooting at a bloody great Hun, coming towards you with a fucking great bayonet."

As the sergeant finished speaking, the faintest touch of grey brushed the eastern sky. A door slammed open at the building opposite, and light spilled into the court-yard.

Ernie said: "This is it, lads. Fall into a smart line. Remember where I told you to aim. It'll all be over in a few minutes. Stop worrying—it's better than going over the top At least nobody's shooting at *you.*"

A sad procession filed into the yard. The prisoners looked young enough to have been caught stealing apples from a farmer's orchard. They were incapable of walking, either through drink or fear.

Each was dragged along by a Red Cap on either side of him. Two more M.P.s appeared, carrying homely-looking kitchen chairs. The padre, robes flapping in the breeze of a new day, murmured a benediction.

The medical officer, clearly preferring to be tending to the wounded down at his aid post on the Menin Road, stationed himself in a corner of the yard and stood, fiddling with his stethoscope.

The same immaculate captain, who had publicly disgraced the deserters yesterday, prepared to direct the final act of the tragedy.

The boys, both sobbing and with their trousers soiled, were bound into the chairs. MPs tied on blindfolds, and the doctor strolled to the men and pinned white targets over their hearts.

Ernie said in a hoarse, near-whisper: "It's our turn. Remember where I told you to fire." The Tommies raised their rifles to their shoulders, thumbed off the safety catches, instinctively squeezed first pressure on their triggers, and took aim.

The officer raised his arm and, almost immediately, let it fall. Ernie felt the familiar kick of a live round as he squeezed the trigger. Three rounds of 303 calibre small arms ammunition slammed into the prisoners.

To the sergeant's horror, Ernie saw his man was groaning and twitching in his bonds. The captain marched smartly across, drew his revolver and despatched the prisoner with a shot to the head. It was the classic *coup de grace.*

The M.O. walked to the bodies, applied his stethoscope to the ruined chests, and nodded to the other officer.

Sergeant Cornish felt numbed by the enormity of what he had done. But he kept his voice steady as he barked "Slope arms! Stand properly to attention there, Smithy! Officers on parade, squad—dis-miss!"

The three Tommies obeyed by long-ingrained habit, turning smartly to the right and giving butt salutes on their rifles. Then they walked slowly and wordlessly into the newly-awakening town.

Ernie stood impassively, watching them go. He knew the men would make for an early-morning café and do their best to achieve alcoholic oblivion. No military policeman, knowing what these men had just done, would dare disturb them.

Two soldiers removed the bodies from the chairs and placed them into two rough wooden coffins. It was over.

Ernie marched smartly into the street. Suddenly, to the bemusement of early-rising passers-by, he broke into a galloping run, as though the Kaiser himself and the Legions of the Damned were hot on his heels.

The studs on his ammunition boots clattered over the cobbles as he raced through the town square and down Gasthuisstraat.

The men of the Ninth would have stared in disbelief had they seen the tears pouring down the cheeks of their tough sergeant as he ran into Talbot House and clattered up the stairs to the first floor.

Ernie, chest heaving, thundered on the door marked "Chaplain's Room". It was opened by the Rev. Tubby Clayton, Army greatcoat draped over his shoulders to keep out the early-morning chill.

Beneath this, he was wearing flannelette striped pyjamas and carpet slippers. Tubby's trade-mark monocle was firmly in place. He took a brief look at the distraught sergeant and said: "Come in, my boy. It looks as though we need to have a chat."

Ernie stepped into the room, wiping his eyes with a large, khaki handkerchief. The padre pretended not to notice, and indicated the chair opposite his paper-strewn desk. Ernie slumped into it.

Diplomatically, Tubby remained silent while the sergeant composed himself. Outside the window, birds were busy orchestrating the dawn chorus. He pulled open the bottom drawer of his desk and produced a lemonade bottle filled with rum.

Tubby poured a generous tot into a soldier's-issue mug. He pushed it across the desk to Ernie, who picked it up in both hands. The sergeant took two great gulps, gagging on the raw spirit.

Tubby busied himself with the papers on his desk, looking up only to replenish Ernie's rum. Eventually, the sergeant's even breathing told the padre Ernie had calmed down. He put down his pen and gazed at him kindly.

During his time on the Western Front, Tubby had seen many a young man in this state, close to breaking point. This soldier, like many others, was sick in spirit. He needed the balm of healing words.

Ernie was the first to speak, his words tumbling out like Germans from a captured dug-out.

"Padre, I am guilty of rape and murder. I know God won't forgive me for doing these terrible things. What can I do, Padre? Any day now I may go to meet my Maker. Please help me . . . I don't know what's to become of me."

Before replying, Tubby poured more rum into Ernie's mug. This time he was careful to dole out a smaller, though still therapeutic, tot. This sergeant needed to keep his wits about him as he went through his crisis of conscience.

The padre gazed at the handsome, well-set-up n.c.o. Tubby saw a young lad, cruelly burdened by the responsibility of the three stripes on his arm. This boy should be at home, learning a peaceful trade and walking with his girl through sunlit meadows.

The war had made him an old man overnight. His face was deeply engraved with lines, like the scars of battle. But it was the sergeant's eyes that said it all . . . they were haunted, red-rimmed and reflected a thousand horrors.

Tubby bought time by polishing his monocle with his handkerchief. He was so moved by this soldier's anguish, he scarcely trusted himself to speak. At last, he said gently: "What is your name, my boy?"

"Ernie, sir—Ernie Cornish."

"Listen to me, Ernie. There is no sin anyone can commit that is unforgivable. God loves sinners who genuinely repent. So you must have no more worries on that score. He loves you and He always will."

Ernie sipped his rum and listened intently. Like all the Tommies in Tubby's Western Front "parish", he regarded the padre as a near-saint. Tubby decided to lance the boil festering on Ernie's soul.

- "This murder, Ernie . . . tell me about it."

- "I have just shot a man in cold blood, padre. Shot him dead. He was an Englishman, just like me. I killed him when he was all tied up. It was sheer, bloody murder, sir. There's no other word for it."

- "Ah, now I see. You were part of the firing squad that shot the two deserters this morning. Everyone in Pop knew about it. My window was open, and I heard the shots from here.

"You are a soldier, Ernie. A soldier has to do his duty. God knows that, my boy. He knows it better than we do. He also knows how hard it is at times to obey lawful orders.

"He forgave the Roman soldiers who killed him. They, too, were an execution squad. In His goodness and wisdom, He doesn't blame you for doing what a soldier must do. So there is no need to seek His forgiveness.

"I can tell you, Ernie, God wants you to be at peace. He has taken those two poor boys to Himself. You helped send them to a place where there is no more fighting and fear."

Ernie reached for his mug, but set it down again before the rum touched his lips. Tubby went on: "Now we come to the matter of the rape. I will need to know more about it if I am to give you my view on that, my boy.

"For things are not always what they seem. This is particularly so when one is upset or under stress."

This part of the conversation was harder for Ernie than bayoneting a Hun. His Edwardian Sunday School teachers could never have imagined him speaking about sex to a man of the cloth.

He began hesitantly: "There is this young girl called Marie, sir. I found her hiding in a cellar during the battle of Messines. She hardly had anything on, and I was tempted . . .

"I took her there and then, Padre, and I've been taking her ever since. I am living in sin with her here in Pop. I'm as good as raping her all the time. To make it worse, I have a best girl back in Blighty who's promised to me, sir."

303

Ernie covered his face with his hands. His voice was muffled as he added: "I have let them both down terribly, sir. They are both good girls. I'm nothing but a beast."

Tubby had heard this story in its various forms many times since he set up the Soldiers' House here in Pop. His heart went out to these lads, far from home, who lived on the brink of extinction.

Lonely Tommy . . . girl back in Blighty . . . willing girl out here with an eye to the main chance . . . the situation was as emotionally explosive as a Mills bomb.

It spoke of the soldiers' basic goodness that they were troubled by these lesser sins, dwarfed as they were by the great sin of the war.

He asked softly: "Was she—is she still—willing, Ernie? Do you physically have to force her? How is it you are still together after the battle?"

Ernie looked up, warmed by a shaft of hope. He replied: "She doesn't fight me at all. sir. I'm not making excuses, Padre, but she seems to egg me on. Sometimes I wonder why, for I'm as sure as can be that she doesn't truly love me.

"I keep thinking of my girl, Maud, who is sweet, innocent and trusts me. I want to stop this affair with Marie. But I can't. I don't love her. I just need her."

Tubby replaced the lemonade bottle into his desk drawer. He told Ernie: "Stop a moment and think before you drown in guilt. You're obviously a decent chap. When you came upon Marie, she happened to be half-naked. Was that an accident?

"She seemed to invite you to have sex with her. And that still appears to be the case. Now you have given the girl a roof over her head and a bit of security. You are obviously attracted to each other.

"This may be illicit sex, my boy, but it certainly isn't illegal. It's a long chalk from being rape. Yes, you are both sinning. But there are worse sins by far. As for Maud, that is something you will have to deal with down the road. You have enough on your plate for now.

"Drop in to see me any time you feel like it."

Tubby stood, stretching extravagantly to signal the chat was over. Soon more troubled souls would come knocking at his door.

Ernie, calm now and with a little colour returning to his cheeks, also stood. He said: "Thank you very much, Padre."

Tubby smiled and waved away the thanks. As Ernie opened the office door the padre called out: "Come back to Talbot House soon, Ernie, problems or not."

Ernie walked slowly and thoughtfully to the Café de Ville. He sank a couple of beers before climbing to the bedroom. Marie was sound asleep, looking like a schoolgirl exhausted by a picnic.

The sergeant stripped off his uniform and slipped carefully into bed. Before falling asleep, he whispered one of his boyhood Sunday School prayers.

October 20, 1917

They were dying in the mud for yet another accursed ridge. They called this one Passchendaele, named after a pile of rubble and brick dust, the corpse of a village sitting atop the rise.

Soon the name of Passchendaele would go down in history as the scene of the most bloody slaughter in the bloodiest war known to man

But to Ernie and his comrades, bogged down in a wilderness of sludge a few miles North-East of Ypres, this was simply another hell-hole.

To them, the road and fields to Passchendaele were paved with the bodies of British infantry. Men struggled forward through a sucking quagmire, burdened by heavy packs, weapons, ammunition, grenades and entrenching tools.

Ernie watched as soldiers struggled under the weight of Lewis machine-guns or ponderous reels of telephone wire. The mud constantly reached out with icy fingers to try to trap the Tommies.

The sergeant had seen men slip from narrow duckboard tracks and drown in the evil porridge. No-one stopped to help these lost souls. They knew that, if they did, they, too, would be dragged in and sink to their deaths.

Ernie and his men would trudge on, with averted eyes, through the constant downpour. There was no respite from the heaviest rain the area had known for 30 years.

Moving heavy guns and equipment became a labour of Hercules. Tanks, those wondrous new inventions, foundered helplessly.

Rain, rain, rain. Mud. Mud. Mud. These were as much the soldiers' enemy as the Hun.

It dominated their lives. They were up to their ears in it. It was in their eyes, mouths, noses, clothes and food. It was a glutinous burial ground for tens of thousands of their comrades.

There was a simple explanation for this watery hell. Shells from the big guns had destroyed the carefully-constructed drainage system that had once turned these Flemish marshes into fertile fields.

Far from the quagmire, in his cosy headquarters, the British Commander-in-Chief, Field Marshal Douglas Haig, saw the battle as an opportunity to break through to the coast and glory.

Ernie and his mates saw it as an odds-on chance of dying. Their world had shrunk to the few hundred desolate yards surrounding them. That distant ridge seemed as unattainable as Mars.

Haig, a dour Scottish cavalryman, believed German morale was about to crack. Sergeant Cornish and the mud-encrusted Tommies fighting this third battle of Ypres could have told him there was plenty of life left in Fritz.

His seemingly impregnable pill-boxes spat lethal streams of machine-gun bullets at the advancing troops. With Teutonic thoroughness, the Germans had worked out accurate arcs and interlinking fields of fire.

Shells and bullets raked the attackers day and night. The Germans, although also being slaughtered in great numbers, still had their tails up. As far as the beleaguered Tommies were concerned, Fritz was tucking into his sausages with gusto.

Ernie and two other survivors of the Ninth Kents—Smithy and Dusty—were sheltering from a savage German barrage in what passed in this water-logged desert as a trench.

It was a shallow shelter, scooped out of the mud below the lip of a flooded shell-hole. Floating in the poisonous brew beneath them were the bloated bodies of men, horses and mules. A dead hand protruded imploringly from one of the earthen walls.

Ernie made his men constantly clean the filth from their Lee-Enfields and keep the working parts covered with rags. A jammed weapon could be a man's death warrant.

The sergeant had taken the precaution of "borrowing" a Webley revolver and its holster from the body of a British captain. Ernie reasoned that, if his rifle should fail, he would still have something with which to fight.

Dusty instinctively ducked as an enemy 5.9 shell roared over, exploding behind the shell-hole in a geyser of mud and red-hot splinters. He brushed dirt from his shoulders and asked Ernie: "Aren't we due to be relieved by the Midshires tonight, sarge?"

Ernie looked at the weeping sky, now beginning to darken into night. "That's the story, Dusty. But we've heard that one before and nothing's happened. If the Midshires *do* come up, we can make our way back.

"But 'slow's' the word, and 'careful'. We haven't lived this long without learning how to take it steady. Follow me and you'll be all right. Don't want you ending up in a puddle, do we?"

The dusk was fitfully lit by gun flashes when relieving troops crept into the Ninth Kents' makeshift lines. Ernie slung his rifle on his shoulder and prepared to lead his men to the rear.

But Dusty had already jumped from the shell-hole and started to run along the slippery wooden slats. The tantalising prospect of hot tea, sizzling bacon and a dry spot to sleep had driven the sergeant's warnings from his head.

He had squelched only a short distance when a shell landed 20 yards to his right. Although the force of the explosion was partly absorbed by the mud, the soldier was caught by a piece of flying metal.

Dusty collapsed backwards on to the track. Ernie and Smithy saw that the shell splinter had ripped open Dusty from shoulder to groin. Blood mingled with the pouring rain.

At that moment, the Germans, alerted that the British were being relieved, opened a thunderous barrage.

Ernie, gesturing to Smithy to stay under cover, leaped over the lip of the shell-hole and ran through the shell-bursts, along the slippery timbers of the track, to where his wounded comrade lay, writhing and moaning.

Machine-gun bullets hissed round the sergeant, one actually plucking at his sleeve, as he hoisted the wounded man on to his shoulder and ran back to the comparative safety of the shell-hole.

He propped Dusty against the streaming mud wall. The injured man, eyes wide with terror, began to claw at his gaping wound with bloody, mud-covered hands.

Ernie reached for Dusty's shell dressing but, when he pressed it to the wound, it was impossible to hold back the red torrent. As the shock wore off and the pain began to bite, the wounded man screamed like an animal caught in a trap.

He fixed his eyes pitifully on those of his sergeant. He pleaded, panting with agony: "Shoot me, Sarge. For Christ's sake shoot me!"

Smithy watched with horror as Ernie slowly undid the flap of his holster and pulled out the revolver. He pressed it to Dusty's forehead and thumbed off the safety catch.

As Ernie's finger curled round the trigger, he suddenly had a vision of a twitching boy, tied to a chair, in the courtyard of Poperinge town hall. An officer was bending over him, holding a Webley.

Ernie slowly lowered the revolver, placed it in the hand of the mortally-wounded soldier and turned his back. He waited for the sound of a shot. But there was only silence, as even the artillery died away.

Ernie turned to see that Dusty's hand, still clutching the revolver, had fallen to his side. The sergeant gently took the weapon, and held his chum's hand. Dusty's eyes were clouding with death.

Suddenly, he smiled a happy and welcoming smile and called: "Mother!"

Ernie reached forward and closed the dead man's eyes. Another one of the lads had gone west. Not many of the old originals left now. Who would be next?

Smithy put his arm reassuringly round Ernie's shoulders. Rank didn't matter now. He said: "Ernie, old lad, there was nothing more you could have done for Dusty.

"What you did, bringing him back through all those shells and that machine-gun shit, deserves the Victoria Cross. I only hope some officer saw you. I'll write and tell his mum about it when we go into reserve."

Ernie was later decorated with a much lowlier award—the Military Medal. By then, medals didn't seem to matter.

CHAPTER 17

November 10, 2000

German martial music of the Great War echoed from loudspeakers hidden in the trees of Bavarian Wood. Today, there were no tourists to hear it. But the former curator of Hill 40's museum liked to play the stirring marches from a sense of nostalgia.

Jacques Deberte, still managing to look untidy while wearing the black uniform of an S.S. colonel, had little to do and much to think about. He sat, as in the days before the advent of Adam Cornish, in front of the canteen stove.

The Hill 40 site was due to be redeveloped into a multi-million-euro shrine to Adolf Hitler. Apart from the memorial and grandiose statue, there was to be a sophisticated new museum.

Until work started, Hill 40 was closed to the public. The historic military site was deserted except, as the more fanciful claimed, by unquiet ghosts from the past.

The Frauenlob mine-shaft and underground galleries had long since been pumped dry, and Hitler's treasure hauled away in heavily-guarded armoured trucks to secret locations.

Jacques, the former schoolmaster with a taste for history, had insisted that the pumps should carry on. He announced that the deeply-buried galleries would one day become part of the new museum complex.

Millions of pilgrims from all over the world would soon be flocking to the spot where Jacques' humble museum and crumbling trenches once hosted the odd visiting history buff, tour party or school group.

Now the shabby, smoky and shambolic museum in which he was sitting, and which was so close to his heart, was scheduled for demolition. Jacques' old, gently-studious world was fast disappearing.

Jacques stared, deep in thought, at the glowing stove. Since he had learned the terrible truth about his parents' fate, Jacques' mop of dark hair had turned completely grey.

From the moment of that heart-breaking revelation, his whole life had changed. He knew with certainty it would never be the same again.

The door scraped open, interrupting Jacques' reverie. Rod Russell, the image of the perfect Brown-shirt captain, stepped into the canteen. His former lank, long hair was clipped to military trimness and his uniform starched and pressed to razor-edged perfection.

Rod diplomatically left Jacques to his musings, busying himself by feeding logs into the stove. The British undercover agent pulled up a chair to the warmth and waited patiently for Jacques to acknowledge his presence.

Eventually, Rod decided to break the silence himself. Jacques looked up as the Englishman said in flawless Flemish: "Don't just sit and brood, my friend. Now is the time for action.

"I'm glad I was able to make you see sense when you were rightly so upset. You were wise to swallow your anger over your parents' murder and take my advice to wait for the moment to strike. Together, we will get back at the bastards.

"The English have a saying, 'Revenge is a dish better eaten cold'. Today, the Nazis are arrogant and stupid enough to believe you are still the dedicated National Socialist they brought you up to be.

"Any information you are able to glean as such, will be very valuable to us."

Jacques, no longer the mild-mannered academic, snarled: "Just tell me the most painful way to make those animals pay, Rod. I'll strangle them with my bare hands, if needs be. I'll . . ."

Rod interrupted gently: "No need to upset yourself all over again. Relax and listen to what I've got to say. I, too, am thirsting for revenge.

"The Nazis recently murdered my fiancée. Her name was Fabienne and she was beautiful. They poisoned her, Jacques, for reasons you don't need to know. We both have debts of blood to settle.

"Settle them we will. I promise you that. As I see it, we both have something to offer the other. You have entrée to information as a member of the Nazis' inner circle. I have all the resources we need for revenge.

"I act for the British Government. Believe me, they are as eager to exterminate these vermin as are you and I. They will supply whatever it takes to get the job done."

Jacques rose, walked over to Rod and placed his hand on his shoulder. He said: "In 1914, your country went to war to help my country. I am a historian and I never forget the lessons of the past.

"Now the time has come for an Englishman and a Belgian to fight together again. I must avenge my mother and my father, and stop the stain of National Socialism spreading over Belgium and beyond.

"I believe the solution may at this moment lie beneath our feet. I have a plan to send our enemies sky high. That is why I asked you to bring me an explosives expert. Is he here yet?"

Rod crossed his legs and leaned back in the chair before replying: "He is, Jacques. This man is the best. He is a major of the British Army's Royal Logistic Corps, and one of their elite Ammunition Technical Officers.

"John Walker is a hero of our country. He has been awarded the George Cross, a non-combatant equivalent of the renowned Victoria Cross.

"During a distinguished career, he has served in bomb disposal in Northern Ireland and Bosnia. Most important of all, Major Walker is an expert on First World War mining and explosives."

Rod went on: "Now we come to where you can help. Major Walker is at present staying in a safe house—a cottage we are renting in Zillebeke. We have fitted him out with a Brown-shirt lieutenant's uniform.

"This has English flashes on the sleeves, like mine. Once you have given him suitable accreditation, Major Walker will become operational and will help you with your secret plan."

Jacques, his voice now brisk, said: "Major Walker will become Lieutenant Jeremy Brown immediately. I will see to his papers today. Please ask him to come here tomorrow at 9 a.m."

The Belgian, eyes blazing, shouted: "Let us hope this man will enable us to wipe Fuhrer Cornish and the evil vermin of his Fourth Reich off the face of the earth! Murderers!"

Suddenly, the Englishman, ever sensitive to danger, put his finger his lips. In the time it takes to blink an eye, he had seen a shadow flit past the window. He whispered: "Wait here."

Rod eased the door open inch by inch, to lessen the sound. He slipped outside, where the recorded music was playing a spirited version of *Deutschland, Deutschland uber Alles.*

A rabbit, disturbed, hopped through the undergrowth. A bird fled, squawking, through the wood. All was not well.

Silence. Then Jacques heard the unmistakable sound of a pistol shot. Silence again.

When Rod returned, he appeared calm and unconcerned. He said: "See you tomorrow at 09.00 hours, Jacques. Meanwhile, keep your eyes peeled for unwanted guests."

November 11, 2000

The next morning, a watery sun gilded the trees of Axle Wood and shone over a muddy corn-field that was once No-Man's Land. Three men stood on the footpath running down the edge of the wood, looking towards Ypres.

They remained silent for a few minutes, remembering that here in Flanders, at 11 o'clock, 82 years ago, the guns of the Great War fell silent and the slaughter ended. In Ypres today, they were preparing for a solemn ceremony at the Menin Gate, the memorial to the Allied dead with no known graves.

On this spot below the Messines Ridge, where so many men had died, it was quiet as one of the many war graves that littered the old Salient. The three men gazed over the peaceful cornfield, its muddy expanse broken only by a clump of trees—the only sign of life in this place of death.

Jacques and Rod were introducing John Walker to the old battleground. The major, in his Nazi uniform, looked every inch a military man. He was thick-set, ramrod straight and towered 6ft. 3ins. tall.

Rod reflected on how Walker's height must be painfully inconvenient when exploring World War One shafts and tunnels. The British officer had florid features and sported a neat, toothbrush moustache.

The major's hazel eyes were sharply perceptive as he surveyed the terrain. He asked crisply: "Is this where the big parade will take place?"

Rod replied: This is where it will *begin.* Jacques says he has a plan to make sure it will end somewhat abruptly."

Jacques, his voice heavy with sarcasm, announced: "Prefabricated parts of a 700-foot-high mausoleum to the late lamented Fuhrer are at this very moment being created in secret locations by a team of architects, builders and sculptors.

"This structure is designed so that it can be assembled within a few weeks, thus having the greatest dramatic effect. It will, of course, be missing one essential element—the old Fuhrer's body. That almost certainly doesn't exist.

"Hitler himself drew up extensive plans for a grandiose mausoleum that would 'endure for at least 1,000 years'. He believed this would keep him alive in the minds of the German people for generations to come.

"He wanted to create a Mecca, where pilgrims could come to touch his tomb and be inspired. Gracing it will be a huge stone statue of Hitler. This will be transported here, piece by piece and assembled, ready for the glorious day of dedication."

Jacques went on: "Delegations of National Socialists from all over the world will gather for a triumphant march-past. Then the statue will be unveiled by the new Fuhrer.

"There will be banners flying and martial music playing . . . a latter-day, tub-thumping Nuremburg. The Nazis are only too aware that they have enemies, so they have been keeping the date of the ceremony a strict secret."

Jacques smiled cynically and went on: "As one of the Inner Circle, I can tell you that the big parade will take place on Hitler's birthday, April 20, next year. That gives us less than six months in which to act."

John Walker, by habit, ran a forefinger under his moustache. He said briskly: "Well, we'd better crack on then. I'd like to take a look underground, Jacques. The location of this shaft suggests that the front lines were pretty close together.

"So it would probably have been used by the Germans for counter-mining work. A lot of that went on. They would listen for us working and try to blow in our tunnels."

Jacques, impressed by the Major's expertise, replied: "You are perfectly correct . . . er . . . Jeremy. The combatants here were only about 100 metres apart."

The three men picked their way through the wood, skirting the restored concrete bunkers and trenches. Old corrugated "elephant iron" had been salvaged and used to cover part of the trench system.

This morning, no First World War marching songs echoed from the loudspeakers in the trees. Again, no birds sang. The silence was oppressive. The sun vanished behind an angry bank of clouds.

The three men involuntarily shivered at the sudden chill as they walked over the buried bones of a lost generation.

Jacques broke the silence by dropping into his well-worn tour guide patter: "The Germans dug the mine-shaft in 1916. It was sealed during the battle of Messines on June 7, 1917.

"We don't know if it was deliberately blocked by the retreating Germans, or whether an Allied shell blew in the top of the shaft. In any event, it lay hidden until I discovered it, quite by accident, in 1979."

Jacques dropped easily into the old lie: "I was out with my shotgun in these woods one day. A rabbit ran across my path and I took a quick pot-shot. But I managed only to wound it. I pursued the rabbit, meaning to put it out of its pain.

"It vanished into a hole. I returned to the museum, fetched a spade and started to try to dig the animal out. Suddenly, I broke through into what seemed to be a big, dark hole.

"I told my adopted father, Wilfred, about what I had found. Together, we decided to investigate. We tried to find the depth of the hole by lowering down a piece of cord, 12 feet long, with a weight attached.

"This didn't reach the bottom of what turned out to be the Frauenlob shaft. We tried again, this time with 35 yards of cord. This still wasn't long enough. We never got to the bottom until the Fraulenlob was pumped dry fairly recently."

John asked: "So, just how deep did this shaft turn out to be?"

Jacques replied: "About 136 feet. My father and I dug around the shaft and discovered an old wooden floor and the collapsed walls of a surface structure. We even found a crane, used for hauling earth to the surface.

"Then we started restoring the old trenches, discovering such things as a concrete mortar emplacement and a first-aid post. Adolf Hitler served right here in Bavarian Wood.

"It was near this wood, during heavy fighting, that he won the Iron Cross Second Class and was promoted to *gefreiter*—a rank similar to that of the Americans' Private First Class. Hitler wrote a letter to his Munich landlady, Frau Popp, saying, 'It was a miracle I wasn't killed'.

"This was the place where, when Hitler arrived as the conquering hero in 1940, he told his Armaments Minister, Albert Speer, that he would build a towering tribute to his 'thousand-year Reich'."

As the entrance the mine-shaft came into view on the edge of the wood, the lie Jacques had told visitors for years, returned to haunt him. Like all the boys who fished in the mine crater, he had really known of the existence of the shaft all his life.

Memories of Frauenlob on that terrible day—July 14, 1944—had never ceased to awaken him, sweating with terror, in his bed at night.

As Jacques stood on this dank, November day with the two Englishmen, he thought he heard again the murderous rattle of Schmeissers and saw once more the piles of bodies and pools of blood.

He fancied he could even smell the smoke of the S.S. officer's cigar. Yes, he had known the mine-shaft only too well. The rabbit story was all fiction.

The three men came to the Frauenlob, her heart gently throbbing with the unceasing beat of nearby generators. John looked with a professional eye at the cables and the conduits snaking into the depths. He noted that the original steel ladder was still in place.

He asked Jacques: "What did you find when you pumped this out, apart from the gold?"

Jacques recoiled at the memory of the skull discovered by the S.S. during the war. He replied: "There were tools, bottles, boots and scraps of uniform. Much of the galleries had fallen in, and we had to shore them up.

"There would be a great deal more to do to make the underground workings safe enough for tourists to visit."

Then the Belgian told of his great plan. "But that will never happen if my scheme is put into operation. I thought we could burrow out under former No-Man's Land from the galleries, plant explosive and blow up the whole Nazi parade."

The Major said bluntly: "Impossible, old boy. We don't have the time or the manpower. Apart from the mining involved, it would take a battalion of men to cart a ton of explosive here.

"They certainly couldn't do that without being detected by the baddies.

"Sorry. What you suggest can't be done."

Jacques' world crashed around his ears. Tears of fury and frustration ran down his cheeks as he slowly led the other two back to the canteen.

It seemed nothing would stop the murderous bastards now.

CHAPTER 18

November 4, 1917

Hellelujah! The rain had stopped at last. The skies over Passchendaele were wiping away their tears for a heartbeat or two. But the ocean of mud still spread like an evil gruel over the desolate landscape. Shattered trunks of trees poked through it like dead men's fingers.

Ernie sat, up to his shins in the filthy water, in a makeshift trench gouged out of a series of shell-holes. He was spooning tepid bully-beef stew from his mess tin into a mouth numb with cold.

The veteran sergeant recognized the characteristic dull "plop" made by the shell even before the sentry sounded the gas alarm by beating his bayonet against a brass shell-case, suspended from a piece of rope.

Ernie lost precious seconds by spooning the last mouthful of the meal into his mouth before fumbling with frozen fingers for his respirator. The sentry's clamour went on and on as the sergeant discovered that the gas mask was firmly jammed in its case.

As Ernie struggled, he muttered the words of the Tommies' song:

"The bells of hell go ting-a-ling for you but not for me . . ."

By the time he had pulled out the respirator, a creeping cloud of gas had turned the buttons green on his tunic.

Worse, terribly and painfully worse, his eyes were blinded by poker-hot tears and his lungs filled with fire. So Ernie never saw the explosion on the muddy parapet of the trench, which buried him into an even greater darkness.

Minutes later, two privates of the Ninth Kents climbed over the muddy mess left by the shell-burst. One of them, Smithy, shouted: "Look over here, Bert! I think it's somebody . . . I can see 'is boot stickin' out. Give us a hand. Smartly now!"

The two soldiers dug frantically into the mud with their entrenching tools. Soon they uncovered Ernie's mud-encrusted face. Smithy gasped: "Blimey! It's our sarge. Help me tug 'im out! Christ Almighty. There's blood everywhere. Shout for the medics while I get this shit out of 'is nose and mouth."

Bert began yelling the mantra, only too familiar to every soldier on the Western Front: "Stretch-bearer! Stretcher-bearer! Over here, chums! Over here!"

Ernie's pals propped him against the slimy wall of the makeshift trench. His head lolled back, sightless eyes staring at the grey Flanders sky. Blood soaked the front of his muddy, khaki tunic. The German barrage relentlessly thundered on.

Smithy pulled the first-aid dressing from inside his tunic and tried to staunch the blood pouring from Ernie's chest. The two privates crouched over their sergeant as though their frail flesh and blood could shield him from further harm.

"Stretcher-bearer! Stretch-bearer! Over here! Over here!"

At last! Four weary medics, one an elderly corporal, clambered into the trench and, with difficulty, lifted the wounded man on to a stretcher. Smithy pulled off his greatcoat and covered his sergeant.

He said sternly to the bearers: "No goin' through 'is pockets, mind. I've heard all about you thieving bastards. R.A.M.C.—Royal Army Medical Corps—Rob All My Comrades, more like!"

The medics, old "sweats" from before the war, and regimental bandsmen when out of the line, ignored Smithy. They'd heard it all before. They lit Woodbine cigarettes before struggling to lift the loaded stretcher over the trench's parapet. Smithy's belligerence melted away.

He called out imploringly: "'E's goin' to be all right, ain't he? 'E'll pull through, won't 'e, chums? It's our sarge you've got there, and he's a real good 'un."

The corporal, chest bright with medals from past conflicts, pulled Smithy's greatcoat and Ernie's tunic aside and peered professionally at the wound. He told Smithy, who was close to tears: "I've seen worse.

"I give this one evens. A lot depends on what Fritz has to say on our little trip back. Something seems to be upsetting him today. Can't stop. The quicker we get there, the better for your sarge."

A whizzbang shell burst behind the trench, spattering the soldiers with mud. The corporal blew his nose on his finger and said calmly: "Blimey, the sausages must have disagreed with old Fritz."

The medics set down their burden among the other loaded stretchers and Ernie came round to a world of darkness and pain. He was a frightened child again. "Oh, God! Oh, sweet Jesus! I can't see. Somebody help me, please. Please!

323

"I can't stand this. I'm dying. Our Father, who art in heaven . . . Mummy! I'm hurting so bad. It's dark here. I'm frightened, Mum."

The corporal stretcher-bearer reached into his pack, produced a bandage and, with surprising gentleness, bound it over Ernie's eyes. He lit another Woodbine, and placed it between the sergeant's lips.

He crouched and spoke reassuringly to the wounded man: "Don't upset yourself, chum. You'll be as good as new in a coupla days. The docs will patch you up so that you have peepers like a hawk. Then you'll go marching home to your dear old mum. You'll be her hero soldier boy. I swear it on my mother's grave."

The corporal squeezed Ernie's shoulder, signalled to his three companions, and they set off with their stretcher once more for the front line. Ernie slipped into merciful blackness.

Days passed in a blur of agony and fear. Once, Ernie was conscious of being lifted into what seemed to be an ambulance. He went on a journey, where every bump in the road made him and other unseen sufferers scream until raw throats were even rawer. Another time, a choking mask was clamped over his mouth and nose and he swirled into a dizzying pit of oblivion.

He awoke in a bed whose sheets felt crisp and smelled clean. Ernie could detect the sharp tang of carbolic and the cloying scent of decay and death.

He came to dread the sound of a trolley, clanking down the ward and stopping at every bed. Its journey was punctuated by screams and pleadings. When it came to him, cool hands tore away his dressings and he, in his turn, cried out. New dressings were bound in place and the trolley clanked away. Until the next time.

Sergeant Ernie Cornish, Military Medal, fervently wished to die. But they wouldn't allow him that small mercy.

He came to recognise the voices around him. During the worst times, a girl with a soft, Irish accent sat next to him, holding his hand and murmuring words of comfort. Sometimes, she recited strange-sounding but comforting Catholic prayers.

Behind the bandage covering his eyes, the soldier pictured this nurse as one of the golden-haloed angels whose pictures shimmered in the pages of his Children's Bible.

One day, Ernie's angel performed a miracle.

It was heralded by the everyday sound of her brisk footsteps, stopping at his bedside. There was the usual "clank" as she set down a bowl on his locker. Ernie heard the crackle of the nurse's starched apron and detected the faint scent of lavender as she bent over him.

With heightened hearing because of his blindness, Ernie heard her dip something into the water. Then the nurse began gently to bathe his eyes. Dip . . . bathe . . . dip . . . bathe.

This morning she was more persistent than usual. Ernie heard the nurse whispering a prayer as she worked. Finally, she dabbed his eyes dry. Slowly, unbelievably, the mist began to clear.

The face of the young nurse bending over him swam into focus. She had a healthy blush to her cheeks, tentatively smiling lips and deeply concerned blue eyes.

She had, indeed, the face of an angel.

Ernie gasped: "My God, you're beautiful." His newly-seeing eyes filled with tears. So did those of the girl, her Catholic prayers answered. She reached out and, once more, clasped his hand. Nurse and patient were moved beyond words.

The nurse, whom Ernie later learned was called Kathleen, watched happily as her favourite patient daily gained strength.

Soon, a captain medical officer arrived to explain to Ernie that he was still too frail to withstand the journey back to England.

But, the officer told him cheerfully, Ernie was officially in the "evacuation zone". He would soon be strong enough to be loaded on to a train and then a hospital ship. It was just a matter of being patient.

After the doctor left, Ernie leaned back on his pillow and absorbed the significance of the captain's words.

Home. Mother. Father. Southdown. No mud. No death. No danger. Maud. Maud! Christ Almighty—Maud!

. . . .

November 1917

Marie LeBrun stood like a wraith in the November mist. Still as a statue on the pavement opposite Talbot House, Poperinge, she watched the soldiers come and go. In one hand, she clutched a crumpled piece of paper and, in the other, a tear-soaked, lace-trimmed handkerchief.

Some of the Tommies whistled and waved to her. One of them, catching sight of the girl's stricken face, muttered: "Steer well clear. That one looks like trouble."

A thick-set, middle-aged soldier, sergeant-major's crowns bright on his sleeves, back rigid, a pace-stick clasped under one arm, came marching smartly down the road.

Marie felt reassured by his mature years and air of authority. She made a quick decision, and darted across the road. The French girl clutched at the sergeant-major's sleeve and pleaded: "Sir! Sir! I implore you to spare me a moment. Please."

The soldier, who had a daughter about Marie's age, looked down at her from beneath the stiff, vertical peak of his cap. He said, gruffly but kindly: "Now, miss, you shouldn't be doing this sort of thing—especially in the street in broad daylight. Go home to your mum and dad, that's my advice. I wouldn't like to see anything nasty happen to you. Now, run along."

The warrant officer, one of the few surviving pre-war regular soldiers from the ranks of what the Kaiser had sneeringly called "this contemptible little British army", tried to shake Marie's hand from his arm. But she clung on desperately, thrusting her scrap of paper at him.

She gasped: "My boy-friend gave me this, sir. He said to bring it here if he didn't come back. It's a message for the priest, sir."

The sergeant-major, who could make strong men quail with a single glare, visibly softened as he read the note. Then he thrust out his stick, barring the way of a passing private and roared: "You, there—you sad apology for a soldier! Accompany this young lady to the padre, *toot sweet.*"

He stood in the hall of the Soldiers' House and watched the couple until they disappeared round a bend in the staircase.

Once out of sight, the private relaxed and gave Marie a cheeky grin. "Blimey, miss, I can't believe old Iron Drawers knows a pretty girl like you. He's a bit of a dark horse, he is."

The soldier knocked at a door labelled "Chaplain's Room". There was a cheery invitation to enter, and he poked his head round the door and announced: "A young lady to see you, Reverend."

Duty done, the private gently pushed Marie into the Rev. Tubby Clayton's sanctum and hurried away to join in a game of housey-housey.

Tubby, sitting behind his cluttered desk, looked at the distraught girl standing hesitantly before him. He gestured for her to sit down, and gave her time to compose herself by polishing his monocle.

Marie placed the scrap of paper on his desk and waited anxiously. Tubby's eyes went immediately to the name at the bottom of the note . . . "Ernest Cornish—Sergeant, 1/9th North Kents". He knew this man.

So this was the French girl who'd caused Ernie all the soul-searching. Today, she didn't look to be in good emotional shape herself. Tubby read the careful, copperplate writing, taught in all the schools of Ernie's generation:

Dear Reverend,

I am very sorry to trouble you. This is Marie LeBrun, the girl I told you about. Because you are reading this, I know she needs your help. I have probably gone West. Now she has no-one. As far as I know, I was all she had.

I have been using this innocent girl in a sinful way, may God forgive me. I took the liberty of telling her, before I left for the Front that, if she didn't hear from me for some time, to take this note to you. You would know what to do.

Please give her a helping hand, sir. She is a good girl. God bless you. Say a prayer for me, wherever I have ended up.

Your obedient servant—Ernest Cornish, Sergeant, 1/9th North Kents.

Tubby laid the note on his desk. There was a knock on the door. He ignored it. Another—more insistent. He ignored that, too. This matter was more important than anything else in his busy life at the moment. Tubby had God's work to do.

He polished his monocle again and screwed it into his right eye before saying softly to Marie: "If Ernie has made the Great Sacrifice, I'm here to help. It is my Christian duty. What can I do for you, Marie LeBrun?"

Marie said simply: "I am with child, Father."

Tubby tried not to look shocked. He asked: "Did Ernie know?" Marie wordlessly shook her head.

"Please don't take offence, I must ask you this. Are you sure the child is his?"

Marie couldn't speak the lie aloud. She nodded and covered her eyes with her hands. The girl felt she was drowning in a whirlpool of sin. "Oh, Dolphie, Dolphie, what have you done to me?"

Tubby thought for a while, tapping a pencil on the desk. Then he reached for the field telephone, rigged for him as a favour by some kind signaller. He cranked the handle and, after some preliminary chat, was put through to the officer he sought.

The chaplain proceeded to call in yet another favour. Whatever the Rev. Tubby Clayton wanted, the sainted Tubby Clayton was given—from a harmonium to confidential military information. He began to scribble on a pad, the receiver pressed to his ear. Then he boomed his thanks and cut the connection.

The padre beamed at the nervous girl sitting before him and told her: "Capital news, Marie. Top hole! Your sergeant is alive and kicking. He's a bit frayed round the edges, but is definitely on the mend. Better still, Ernie isn't too far from here. The good Lord, aided by my friend the Colonel, has laid on some transport. So we're going on a journey."

An hour later, a lordly, chauffeur-driven staff car, with Tubby and Marie sitting in the back, drew up in the drive of a rambling country house, with a line of mud-spattered ambulances parked in its forecourt. Tubby explained that this was known among the military as a "stationary hospital".

The couple walked into the hospital's lobby, which throbbed with controlled chaos. A grey-haired, sturdily-built nursing sister, crackling with efficiency, approached, introduced herself and barked: "Follow me. Don't stay with the patient for more than ten minutes. He's quite poorly."

Marie's coat was unbuttoned, and the sister cast a sharp, professional eye over her. "I see somebody could be in for a surprise. I haven't had time to warn the sergeant of your visit."

She bustled away, setting a scorchingly rapid "light infantry" pace. The sister led Tubby and Marie through a tangle of stretchers, limping and bandaged soldiers and swiftly-gliding nurses. Marie pulled her coat tightly around her.

They found Ernie walking slowly along a lengthy ward lined—Nightingale style—with neat beds on each side. He was leaning heavily against a pretty young nurse. The sister blocked the sight of Tubby and Marie with her ample body before announcing: "You have visitors, sergeant. Nurse, sit him down and remain here in case he requires assistance."

Nurse Kathleen replied in her soft, Irish brogue: "Yes, sister. We were just finished anyway, and are on our way to the sergeant's bed. He has done well today with his walking."

A doctor called urgently to the sister from the end of the ward. She marched rapidly towards him. A good nurse *never* runs. Kathleen led Ernie to his nearby bed and helped him to sit. He glanced up and saw Marie for the first time. Her coat had fallen open again, revealing the tell-tale bulge.

Sergeant Ernie Cornish looked as though he had unexpectedly been caught in a Hun barrage. Kathleen, who had already summed up the situation, stood ready for any dramas that might occur.

Ernie, his voice trembling, asked Marie: "Are you?"

"Yes."

Tubby sat on the bed and broke the ensuing emotion-charged silence by saying: "I have a plan. Take the weight off your feet, Marie, while you and Ernie listen to it."

. . . .

December 1, 1917

Smithy, both hands pushing his sergeant's backside firmly heavenwards, silently blasphemed as he manoeuvred Ernie up the steps leading to the attic of Talbot House. From above, Bert grasped Ernie's wrists and dragged him into the chapel.

The sergeant, looking round, saw that everything was prepared for today's unprecedented event. This was to be Tubby's first wedding in Talbot House. But, instead of the joyous pealing of bells, there was the distant, malignant thunder of guns. Other things were comfortingly familiar. The concert party corporal, *sans* Woodbine, played a selection of well-loved hymns on the harmonium.

The roughly-hewn wooden pews were packed with the bridegroom's chums from the Ninth Kents. They had scraped the mud of the trenches from their uniforms and boots, and polished their buttons and brasses to a parade-ground shine.

Padre and troops were savouring the ceremony as a nostalgic trip down Blighty's Memory Lane. The joyful joining in holy matrimony of Ernie Cornish and Marie LeBrun was reassuringly similar to the weddings celebrated in their own parish churches.

Tubby, too, had risen to the occasion with a smart, military turn-out. His surplice and clerical collar were snowy-white and his boots shone like twin black mirrors. He smiled benignly when the groom, his face etched with pain and supported by best man Smithy, limped in front of him.

With a flourish, the corporal broke into the Wedding March. Marie and Bert, who had volunteered to give the bride away, negotiated the stairs and walked, arm-in-arm, up the aisle. Marie was wearing a flowing white dress, generously cut to hide her burgeoning secret, and expertly sewn by Sister Therese, a middle-aged nun from a nearby convent.

The good sister, whose severe demeanour and frosty expression belied a warm heart, was a good friend of Tubby's. He was the only person in Pop who knew the nun was German-born. Surrendering to the padre's gentle urging, Sister Therese had agreed to take this pregnant girl under her wing. The nun little knew the vital role she was to play in Marie's life in the turbulent years ahead.

The bride's face was modestly covered by a yellowing veil of Brussels lace, lent by yet another of Tubby's contacts. She carried a posy of flowers, gathered fresh that morning from the garden at Talbot House. There was a liberal sprinkling of poppies which, defying this brutal war, grew in profusion in the surrounding fields. The bride looked stunningly beautiful.

A lance-corporal nudged his neighbor and whispered: "Blimey! The sarge has got himself a bit of all right there. Let's hope he's got a Blighty one. Good luck to 'em both and God bless 'em."

Tubby dropped easily into the old ritual: "Dearly beloved, we are gathered here today . . ."

After the ceremony, he added a private prayer of his own: "Lord, bless these Thine children, keep them safe and forgive them their small trespasses." The chaplain little thought that the bride and groom were also silently praying.

Marie, lips moving: entreated: "Holy Mary, mother of God, forgive me, a sinner . . . and please keep my Dolphie safe."

Ernie prayed: "God forgive me. Maud, forgive me. Mother and father, forgive me."

As the notes of the harmonium died away, everyone clattered downstairs to the hop store. Trestle tables groaned with goodies, donated from dozens of Tommies' parcels from home. Tubby unscrewed his monocle so that he could turn a blind eye to the bottles of beer and stone jars of issue rum that had magically appeared. Soon, faces became flushed and voices were raised in raucous bonhomie. Trenches, mud and death faded from the revellers' memories.

After the wedding feast had roared on for an hour, Tubby and Sister Therese decided that pregnant bride and wounded groom were in no condition to celebrate further. The padre walked over to the middle-aged sergeant-major, at that moment tipping the last dregs of rum from a jar down his throat, and said: "Your voice is louder than mine. Could you call the troops to order and announce that the happy couple are about to retire?"

The warrant officer roared: "Pay attention, you lot! Mr. and Mrs. Cornish have had enough of you noisy layabouts. They want to go to bed for a nice rest."

A barrage of ribald laughter and catcalls greeted the sergeant-major's announcement. Then the soldiers cheered as Marie and Ernie, arm-in-arm, left the barn.

A large room in Talbot House, overlooking the garden, had been prepared as the bridal suite. Two Army-issue beds had been pushed together. Tubby gently tugged Ernie from his bride and led him into the bedroom. Sister Therese whisked Marie into the privacy of an adjoining room.

Tubby told the sergeant, who was ashen with pain: "No need to talk about the birds and the bees, Ernie—I think you are both past all that. Just don't indulge in any undue exertion. Marie will be here in a minute. She's just having a little womanly chat with Sister Therese."

Ernie suddenly thrust a letter into Tubby's hand. He said: "Read this, Padre. Then please post it yourself. I don't want it to go through the censor." Tubby took the single sheet of paper from the envelope and read:

"My dear Maud,

"I'm afraid this will come as something of a shock. Today I got married to a French girl out here. She is having a baby, so I must do what is right. Please forgive me. I wouldn't have knowingly hurt you for worlds.
"My wound is still a bit of a nuisance but, otherwise, I am in the pink. I hope you are well, too. I'm really sorry to have let you down.

"Yours faithfully—Ernie."

Tubby, lost for words, tucked the letter into one of the top pockets of his tunic. Then he shook hands with Ernie and bade him "God bless".

In the room next door, Sister Therese was also looking shaken. Marie, too, had asked a startling favour. She had thrust a letter into the nun's hand, pleading breathlessly: "Please read this, sister. If you know any possible way to send it on, I will be eternally grateful to you. You are my only hope. I pray you may know a way of getting my letter to the other side of the lines."

Sister Therese had seen much of life and considered herself unshockable. But she was staggered when, after slipping on a pair of steel-rimmed spectacles, she read the address on the envelope: *"Gefreiter Adolf Hitler, Iron Cross Second Class, 16 R.I.R., German Army."*

The nun's eyes widened still more when she took out the letter and began to read:

"Dearest, darling Dolphie,

"I am missing you terribly. I have today married an Englander, as you commanded. Do you smile at my obedience? Are you pleased with me because your plan is working so well?

"Our beautiful baby—I know it will be a boy—will be born early in the Spring. I only wish you could be there to see him. Perhaps one day you will meet your son. I am sure he will have your wonderful blue eyes.

"I can't wait for the war to end so that I can be with you once again. Whatever happens, my heart is yours for ever.

"All my love—Your Marie."

Sister Therese asked Marie: "Are you sure about this, little one? Really, really sure?"

"As sure as God is in His heaven, sister."

"Then I will try to do this for you. May the good Lord forgive us both."

The nun tucked Marie's letter into the folds of her black habit. She led the girl from the room, knocked gently on the door of the "bridal suite" and entered. When the newly-weds were sitting demurely, side by side on the beds, Tubby addressed them:

"I am told Ernie will be going home to England just before Christmas. The Sister and I believe it wouldn't be wise for Marie, in her condition, to have all the trauma of travelling to a strange land. It would be better for Ernie to get settled and for his wife and child to join him later.

"That means Marie will have her baby here. Sister Therese, who is a member of a medical Order, has made all the necessary arrangements to look after her at the convent.

"When mother and baby are deemed strong enough, I will arrange for them to be dispatched to England to join Ernie. That will be a joyous occasion to look forward to."

Sister Therese coughed discreetly and said to Tubby: "I think we should leave now, Father. I fear the festivities downstairs may have reached the stage where a strict eye and a firm hand is necessary."

She turned to Ernie and said sternly: "Remember your wound, sergeant. You must go back to the hospital in the morning, and we don't want any complaints about your condition from the doctors and nurses, do we?"

Chaplain and nun clattered downstairs.

Ernie turned and, wincing with pain, took Marie in his arms and kissed her passionately. After a couple of heartbeats, she pushed him gently away. Marie admonished: "Remember what the Sister said about your poor wound, *cherie*."

Ernie gingerly lowered himself on to his back on the lumpy eiderdown. He told himself: "It's still there—that bloody, fucking barrier between us. I can feel it now we're married more than ever. It is as though she is hiding a secret from me.

"Will it always be like this with us?"

. . . .

336

CHAPTER 19

November 12, 2000

It wasn't much of a funeral at Hill 40 for the Nazi Rod had surprised spying from the woods. The Flanders morning provided an appropriate grey shroud of drizzle and mist.

Rod Russell whistled a jaunty tune as he stuffed mud-encrusted clips of World War One small arms ammunition from a nearby stack into the pockets of the corpse. The dead storm-trooper, shaven-headed, bare arms heavily tattooed, shone with moisture as though sweating heavily.

Jacques Deberte instinctively crossed himself as Rod and John Walker picked up the body by its arms and legs and tossed it into the flooded mine crater. The muddy water bubbled and swirled before settling into its normal placid self.

Seconds later, a duck descended on the water and began to paddle happily. The three men stood for a moment, watching the bird.

John ran a finger under his moustache and said: "You did well there, Captain, creeping up on the nosey bastard. There's a bit of the old commando in you yet. A bullet in the back of the neck is just what he deserved.

"He's nothing but a bag of bones now. Can't do anybody any harm."

Rod brushed mud splashes from his immaculate uniform. He stared worriedly at the dripping trees, naked of both leaves and birds. He said: "That 'bag of bones' may already have done a great deal of harm, major.

"The bastard had set up a pretty sophisticated listening post in the bushes. He had a directional radio facility for eavesdropping on distant conversations. There was a transmitter, too.

"The big question is . . . had our friend already passed on details of my conversation with Jacques before I despatched him. If he had, we are in big trouble. His friends will come looking for us, pronto. Eventually, they'll come looking for him anyway."

The major, conscious of being the senior man here, briskly shrugged off all pessimistic thoughts. He barked: "They may or may not be on to us, Captain. We have no way of knowing.

"So our only course of action is to be vigilant and carry on. We have our duty to do, and this is obviously a vital mission."

Jacques, still crushed by the news that his plan to blow up the Nazis' parade was unworkable, said hesitantly: "How can we carry on? You told me it would take a ton of explosive, in the first place, to . . ."

John interrupted: "I've since inspected down below and had a few thoughts. There is a long shot we can take. Hell of a gamble, but it's better than sitting on our arses and letting them get away with it."

The major impatiently wiped raindrops from his forehead. He turned to Rod and went on: "Meanwhile, captain, I have a chore for you." He delved into a tunic pocket and brought out a piece of paper.

He said: "Here is a shopping list of things I want from England. Ring this number, and you won't have any trouble. Stress that we need all this yesterday. No need to worry about Customs and all that rubbish."

Rod ran his eye quickly down the list, stopping in surprise at the final item. He exclaimed: "A dog! You want a dog, Major! The military stuff I can understand. But what's this about a dog?"

John said impatiently: "Just get on with it, man. All will become clear, soon enough."

He turned to Jacques: "Have you still got that old crane at the mine-shaft?"

"Yes, sir"

"Get it working by tomorrow. I want picks, shovels and a wheelbarrow. There's work to be done and we must get on with it. Our efforts will probably be for nothing, but we won't think about that.

"Meanwhile, the enemy will miss their tattooed friend, even if they're not on to us straight away. Captain, you're first for guard duty. Get yourself a hidey hole and watch over us. I take it you're armed?"

"Yes, sir."

"If anyone comes poking around, do what you did to the last one. Clear?"

"Yes, sir. Perfectly, sir."

"Jacques, come with me. We're going to take another look down the shaft."

November 12, 2000

Adam Cornish worked on the principle that it would benefit nobody if he denied himself the good things of life. After all, he had paid his dues all these years by living frugally in a Southdown attic.

So now Adam was doing himself proud. He had come to Flanders with his retinue to oversee the final details of his great parade. The ex-reporter had requisitioned luxurious quarters in a hotel overlooking the Yser river, in the pleasant town of Dixmuide.

The Fuhrer knew he occupied an historic spot, very special to the Belgians. This was where their little army fought the Germans to a standstill in '14-'18.

The opposing armies faced one another across this narrow strip of water. At the scene of some of the fiercest fighting, there were now carefully-restored "Trenches of Death", with a small war museum.

More importantly from Adam's point of view, Dixmuide is a rallying place for international Nazis. It is fitting that he should choose this place to plan the greatest National Socialist rally of all time.

The British Fuhrer had given great thought to setting up his personal office in what had once been the hotel's grand ballroom.

His vast desk, made from solid mahogany, was hand-crafted by English cabinet-makers. They had also created a conference table, capable of accommodating a small army of top brass.

The finest craftsmen in Germany had made and upholstered matching chairs. The office was lit by priceless antique chandeliers looted, in the best Nazi tradition, from a chateau on the Loire.

Amid this splendour, Adam was careful to remind visitors and supplicants that he was, at heart, a simple man with a simple mission. His life was dedicated to spreading National Socialism across the globe.

His grand strategy was charted on a huge wall map of the world. This was spotlighted and carefully placed to be the second thing visitors saw after meeting him in his *sanctum sanctorum.*

Forests of swastika flags blossomed in dozens of countries. More lay in a tray, ready to record future conquests. The former Royal Air Force acting corporal rarely looked at this map himself. He secretly found it difficult to comprehend.

These days Adam, like the first Fuhrer, favoured a simple, austere uniform. He wore a plain khaki gabardine jacket and black trousers, with a crisp, white shirt and black tie.

On his breast was the ribbon of the Nationalist Socialist Order of Honour. Adam was the only holder of this, his Reich's highest award, which he himself had invented.

Adam didn't share his grandfather's teetotal and vegetarian tastes. There was a heavy, 200-year-old French sideboard against one wall, containing everything from his favourite Belgium Duval beer to rare wines.

The hands of an ornate French antique clock on the marble fireplace melodiously chimed the morning hour of eleven. In a nearby kitchen, dozens of guinea fowls were fragrantly roasting.

The humbler cooks were preparing mountains of vegetables and plunging them into saucepans. Others were creating cloyingly sweet desserts, just the way the Fuhrer liked them. This was lunch for the Nazi hierarchy.

Other chefs were already at work on tonight's customary six-course gourmet banquet. Expensive wines were being chilled or uncorked.

After the feasting would come the revels. Curtains would be drawn and all but the most senior Nazis expelled from the dining-room. Naked beauties, trafficked from Eastern Europe, would be whipped in, pawed over and debauched.

Adam's genitals tingled at the prospect of the cruel games. But first, there was work to be done. He was in the early stages of planning the April 20 ceremony at Wytschaete.

A number of trestle tables were set up in his office. On these, experts had created a *papier-mache* landscape of

Hill 40 area in precise detail. Every tree, every bush, every tussock of grass was meticulously recorded,

There was a knock on one of the oak double-doors. Adam pretended to be concentrating on his wall map before shouting: "Come in!" Arthur Burfield poked his head round the door and announced: "Your packages have arrived, Fuhrer."

Adam nodded, and three men entered, carrying heavy parcels. They set them down gently before departing. Arthur remained, unsheathing an ornamental S.S. dagger from its scabbard.

The Fuhrer eagerly stood over his secretary as Burfield slit open the packages and unpacked exquisitely-made model soldiers and bandsmen, each carefully cocooned in tissue paper. This was the most expensive set of toy soldiers every made.

Adam produced a finely-detailed lay-out of the parade, and the two men began the long process of setting out the storm-troopers in marching ranks. The Fuhrer spent a delicious ten minutes studying a specially-sculpted model of himself.

It was perfect in every detail. The features were an exact replica of his own, right down to those startlingly blue eyes.

Adam carefully placed his likeness on the miniature parade ground, marching proudly at the head of his legions.

Millions of TV viewers round the world would see Fuhrer Adam Cornish in all his glory. He believed he would present an impressive martial figure, having already secretly rehearsed his old R.A.F. marching and drill movements in the hotel garden.

Arthur saluted and departed to his beloved paperwork, leaving Adam to play. He was immersed in shuffling the trombonists to the front rank of the first marching band when there was another knock on the door.

Arthur Burfield entered timidly, his expression one of intense anxiety. He said: "Please excuse me, Fuhrer, but I feel I must bring a matter of extreme importance to your attention.

"It may be nothing, but I feel . . ."

Adam snapped: "If it may be nothing, stop bothering me. Can't you see I'm busy?"

Arthur, trembling with frustration, persisted: "My Fuhrer, I would like to warn you of a situation of possible danger . . ."

Adam picked up a full bottle of Duval, standing ready at his elbow, and flung it with a crash of shattering glass into the fireplace. His face turned an angry shade of scarlet and his eyes blazed.

He roared at Arthur: "Warn? Warn? What sort of nonsense are you spouting now? We have the world's most elite soldiers guarding us, plus my own S.A.S.-trained bodyguards.

"Piss off and stop wasting my time. You're turning into an old woman, and there's no place for old women on my staff."

It was a naked threat. The former photographer turned pale and almost ran from the room. But he was determined to deal with the matter, with or without his leader's express backing.

Arthur Burfield, like his hero, Martin Bormann, had a finely-tuned antenna for trouble. And at the present moment, it was twitching with a vengeance.

He returned to his office, where genial photographer Arthur Burfield morphed into arrogant S.S Colonel Andre Lacroix. He straightened his expensively-tailored black jacket before seating himself in the leather-upholstered swivel chair behind his executive-sized desk.

Colonel Lacroix picked up the phone and ordered: "Send Captain Schuemaker to me . . . and tell him to double." He drummed his fingers on the desk for three minutes, when there was a knock on his door.

The Colonel barked: "Enter", and pretended to be scribbling, head bent, over some papers. He left the captain, ruddy-faced as a farmer with overdeveloped muscles bulging under his uniform, waiting for long minutes.

Eventually, Andre looked up and snarled: "You're too slow. Stand to attention and salute your superior officer. Don't you know *anything?*"

Startled, the man obeyed. He scarcely recognised this peremptory, rule-book colonel as the boozer who downed matey drinks with him every night in the hotel bar.

Lacroix slowly melted back into Burfield. He reached into the bottom drawer of the desk and produced a bottle of Scotch and two glasses. He filled these to the brim and said affably: "Sit down, Hans, I've a job for you.

"I want you to make a discreet check on something. You are to report back to me, and me alone. Understood?" Schuemaker, still in shock, took a sip of the proffered whisky and nodded warily.

Burfield continued: Within the last 24 hours, our communications centre received a signal from a covert listening post situated at Hill 40. This is a very sensitive location for various confidential reasons.

"The Hill 40 operator sent the message, 'Activity at Frauenlob mine-shaft. Deberte is with two unidentified officers. I think I hear the word 'explosives' . . .'

"The worrying thing is that the transmission was suddenly terminated. We haven't heard since from our man.

At present, the site is mothballed. Deberte, as the caretaker, might occasionally take a stroll there.

"But who were these other two men? Were they really talking about explosives? If so, why? What is happening at Hill 40? Find out for me, Captain. Above all, keep this matter just between the two of us."

November 12, 2000

Captain Hans Schuemaker was an hour too late to catch the intense activity at Frauenlob that afternoon. By the time he arrived, the woods appeared deserted. The officer picked a lair with care, choosing a spot behind a screen of bushes. With the aid of binoculars, Schuemaker had an uninterrupted view of the mine-shaft.

He reached into his rucksack and pulled out sophisticated electronic equipment, similar to that used by his late predecessor. He had just turned on the directional receiver when some soldier's instinct made him spin round.

"Goodbye, nasty little Nazi," Rod said softly as he pulled the trigger of his automatic. The sound of the shot broke the eerie silence of the old battleground.

Back in Diksmuide, Arthur Burfield leaned over the shoulder of a radio operator in the communications centre. He asked impatiently: "Anything from Hill 40 yet?"

The operator shook his head. He pushed one earphone aside so that he could hear Arthur better and said: "There should have been a routine signal by now, establishing contact."

Hill 40 remained silent. Arthur was now torn between sparking the Fuhrer's wrath by insisting on telling him his misgivings, or ignoring the Leader and taking further action on his own initiative.

This second path, which he had never before chosen, was fraught with danger. Which of the two choices was the worse minefield? It was a decision that shouldn't be rushed.

"Keep listening," he ordered the radio man, and stomped off to his quarters to wrestle with the dilemma.

In the Fuhrer's office nearby, Adam continued to play with his toy soldiers.

Deep in the Frauenlob, Jacques and John, wearing hard hats with miners' lamps and dressed in grubby blue overalls, were busy digging. Wilkie, a liver and white English Springer Spaniel, was happily gnawing at what looked like an ancient human femur.

The dog, which had been lowered down the mine-shaft by the newly-constructed crane, together with the major's boxes, seemed unaffected by the dank, claustrophobic conditions.

The two men, sweating heavily, kept glancing apprehensively at the walls and ceiling of the sap they were digging out. They were carefully shoring it up with timbers, smuggled in under cover of darkness.

The major paused to ease his screaming muscles, his lanky body constantly cramped in these conditions. He sat with his back to the wall and thought of the brave men, soldiers like himself, who once toiled in these lethal tunnels.

He told Jacques: "Not exactly the Ritz down here. But those `14-`18 miners were at least safe from the shells and bullets above. It was hard graft, digging out galleries and saps, filling sandbags with soil, and cranking the spoil to the surface.

"Of course, they could, at any time, meet the enemy face-to-face down here and fight to the death."

Had Major John Walker been a fanciful man, he might have wondered how many souls of departed soldiers wandered the galleries of the Frauenlob. But he was of a practical sapper breed. The two men resumed work.

The going became easier after they had removed the debris and mud of the initial cave-in. Eventually, they broke into the cluttered space of the original sap, still intact a lifetime after being abandoned.

It extended for a good distance under the battlefield, ending in a wall of mud.

John whistled and called: "Wilkie, here boy!" The Springer, tail thrashing, ran up to him. The major ordered: "Find! Find, boy!"

The dog proceeded to sniff the end of the sap inch by inch, growing more and more excited. Suddenly, Wilkie sat down, still as a statue, nose pointing at the wall.

John patted him on the head and gave him a tennis ball from his pocket. Wilkie, duty done, trotted away with his reward.

The major said to Jacques: "Time for a rendez-vous with the captain, and a sit-rep."

"Sit-rep?"

"It's Army-speak for 'situation report'. We now have something to report to Rod. The dog has smelled explosive. He is never wrong. I hope Rod has nothing to report to us."

The two men climbed the steel ladder to the surface and cranked up Wilkie. John turned towards the wood, where he knew Rod would be watching. He placed his right hand on his head, fingers arched—the Army sign for "group on me".

Minutes later, the three men were sitting in the museum canteen. John turned to Rod and said: "You first, captain. Has anything happened on your front?"

Rod replied: "I'm afraid so, sir. We have another funeral to arrange. I know for sure this one didn't have time to transmit. But two men going missing will soon get the Nazis' alarm bells ringing."

John said: "From now on, we must behave as though under constant surveillance. We are lucky to have already taken our stuff underground unobserved. Now we must come and go only during the hours of darkness.

"We must assume the Nazis are now suspicious and will send more watchers. Give them nothing to see. Jacques here can take his usual strolls about the place. Any conversations must take place down below.

"We must be armed at all times. I'm calling this Danger State Red. Watch out! Be alert! Our lives depend on it. Jacques, crack open those bottles of Duval, there's a good chap."

The Major took a deep swig of beer before continuing: Now for my news: You can come off watch for this, Rod. I will assume they can't yet have put a new man in place.

"I'll lay it all out for you chaps. Don't get too excited. I have already told you I am taking a very long shot. If this were a horse running in the Derby, I wouldn't even risk tuppence on it.

"When I surveyed the old No-Man's land, where the parade is to take place, I correctly assumed the 1914—18 lines would have been reasonably close together.

"This means both sides would have sapped out in attempts to place explosive under each other's trenches. It was hell down there. They would pause from time to time, and listen intently for noise of the others working.

"Sometimes, one or the other side would locate the other's sap and blow it up with counter mines. It needed only a modest charge to achieve this. The Germans, for example, would use some 500 to 600 kilos of *Westfalite* powdered explosive.

"This is similar to Ammonal, which the British used on the Western Front. It was, in fact, the explosive in the chain of 19 great mines which raised the curtain on the Battle of Messines on June 7, 1917. These mines contained up to 41 tonnes of the stuff."

Jacques pounced on the statistic, saying: "So any one of these would have the punch needed to blow the parade to smithereens."

John drained his beer and opened another bottle. He said: "Exactly. This is where we go into the realms of fantasy, as far as I am concerned. Somewhere in this area is the mine from 1917 that didn't go off. It's still buried.

"Today, the dog indicated that there was explosive at the end of the sap we were excavating. This could be just a small anti-sapping cache. Or, beating odds of several million to one, it could lead to the lost British mine."

Rod asked: "If we found the stuff after all these years, would it still go bang?"

John answered cautiously: "Possibly. In those boxes I ordered from England, there is kit that, if the Ammonal is still o.k, will help to vaporise Adam and his crew.

"For example, when lightning set off another lost '14-'18 mine in July, 1955, you could have put a couple of double-decker buses in the hole that it made. This could still be lethal stuff."

Wilkie began to paw at the canteen door. Time for a walk. Rod set down his empty beer bottle and said to the dog: "O.k., let's go and have a look at the wood. You've done your duty for today."

As the Irish Guards captain stepped outside, it began to rain fat, sad drops. He shouted to the two men: "Funeral time, gents. We don't want the next Nazi falling over his late mate."

Minutes later, the water of the mine-crater and its resident duck embraced yet another casualty of Hill 40.

The rain ran in rivulets down the windows of the hotel by the Yser in Dixmuide. But Adam, absorbed in constantly arranging and rearranging his toy soldiers, was oblivious to the weather and everything else. Arthur Burfield knew better than to disturb the Fuhrer again.

The colonel had made his decision. It was a milk-and-water one, but better than nothing . . . and far better than bringing the wrath of his boss crashing down on him. He had decided to post a series of watchers at Hill 40 . . . but only during the hours of daylight.

If anything was happening at the normally-deserted site, it would be too dark to see, Arthur Burfield lamely reassured himself. He pushed the existence of infra-red sights to the back of his mind.

So he was only half disobeying orders. He still felt all was not well.

Where had his two watchers got to, he wondered? It was possible they had become bored peering for so many hours at a deserted mine-shaft, and had slid off to the nearest cafe. That's what Adam's slack storm-troopers would tend to do.

They were nothing but yobs with no discipline. Not like his father's generation. Arthur sent for yet another watcher, whom he briefed for the next day. This was going to take a whole team. He hoped they could keep their mouths shut.

The Fuhrer must never find out.

December 3, 2000

For the last few nights, John Walker had felt it a justifiable risk to pull off his night sentry. There had been no Nazi in the bushes during the hours of darkness so far. If the enemy posted one during the day, there would be nothing to see at Frauenlob.

Besides, extra hands were desperately needed as work progressed in the dripping sap beneath former no-man's land. They were wheel-barrowing excavated soil and piling it at the end of another gallery, so that no trace of their work showed above the surface.

John, Rod and Jacques sat on their haunches, eating cheese sandwiches and drinking coffee from flasks. They must be well out under No-Man's land, because they were now chopping away tree roots.

Wilkie was playing with a German boot. The team had built up quite a collection of souvenirs, including an empty wine bottle, a pick-axe head and a heavily-rusted bayonet.

The three men finished their supper and began again clearing the sap. Although no-one dared to say it, every shovel-full they dug out added to their gloom. This backbreaking work, it seemed, would almost certainly lead to a dead end.

The major was hacking at yet another root when Wilkie suddenly dropped the boot and began to sniff excitedly at the fall of soil blocking the sap. The three men stopped work and watched the dog.

Tail thrashing, Wilkie suddenly sat as though at a silent command, nose quivering.

John felt in his pocket and handed the dog another tennis ball. The major and the other two diggers resumed work with building excitement. Within ten minutes, the lamps on their helmets revealed that they were breaking into a large chamber.

Wilkie leaped through the gap and started running enthusiastically over a huge pile of orange bags. These were intact, neatly stacked and glistening with damp. A Tommy's helmet topped the pile, a symbol of work accomplished.

This was John Walker's Aladdin's cave; his Shangri La. He said, almost reverently: "Ammonal. Plenty of it. We've found the lost mine, chaps. Pity I couldn't have put money on it."

The major widened the gap and stepped into the British gallery, where no human had set foot since early summer, 1917. Even before he examined the explosive, he knew it was as deadly as the day it had left the factory in Blighty.

The airless conditions underground would have preserved the Ammonal so that it could fight another day. That day would soon be coming.

CHAPTER 20

April 20, 2001

The luminous hands of John Walker's watch showed that Hitler's birthday was two minutes old. This was the day the major planned murder on a large scale.

Thunder rumbled like ghostly artillery over the Messines ridge. But John, Rod and Jacques were deaf to the approaching storm. The three men, resplendent in their Nazi uniforms, were deep in the sap below ground.

The major prepared to orchestrate the final act of the drama. He pointed to the sacks of explosive piled in the cavern, their orange surfaces gleaming in the light of the miner's helmets.

John said: "Technically, we're going to set this Ammonal off, exactly as they would have in 1917. This lot is, as I have already explained, as lethal as the day the Tommies left it here.

"The airtight conditions underground have seen to that. What we need to set the mine off is a donor charge, otherwise known as a demolition charge, and a detonator."

John reached into one of the boxes at his feet and, like a conjuror pulling a rabbit from a hat, produced a piece of modern army kit. He explained: "This is an L2 electric detonator."

He delved into the box and brought out another "rabbit". The major announced, as though lecturing a class: "I am now holding a demolition charge. This consists of six pounds of what we military types call PE4—Plastic Explosive No. 4.

"Watch carefully. I am now embedding the detonator into the plastic explosive." John brushed his finger under his moustache and went on: We have now taken the first step towards making our big bang.

"If General Plumer is looking down today, he will be proud of us. We will soon have completed his stated task of altering the local geography. The last of the good general's mines will go up, and the enemy will again have been defeated."

Overhead, the rain began to weep over the old battlefield, drenching the temporary city of tents that housed the sleeping army of Nazis. In one of the canvas shelters, Sergeant Wayne Durrant, the sentry detailed for the daylight shift at Hill 40, stirred uneasily.

In his hotel bedroom in Dixmuide, Arthur Burfield tossed and turned restlessly. His built-in antenna shrieked danger.

Down the Frauenlob, the major reached into a crate and produced a drum of twin-flex cable. Deftly, he used a pair of electrician's pliers to bare the twin wires before connecting one end of the cable to the detonator.

The major's final exhibit was a green box, approximately the size of a paperback book. He held it up for Jacques and Rod to see. He continued: "This, gentlemen, is known as a Shrike exploder.

"After the required length of cable has been unrolled from the drum, I shall connect the far end to the Shrike. This will be the final part of the explosive chain.

"Now, pay particular attention. For, if I am knocked out today, one of you will have to take over and make the bang. So you must know how to set up this all-important Shrike."

Jacques and Rod huddled over the exploder as John went through a well-rehearsed drill. He told them: "First, you test the circuit by pressing this button. A green light will tell you the cable is connected to the detonator.

"Next, press the charging button, here. This should produce a flashing red light. The Shrike is capable of firing charges on four circuits. In this case, we will need only one, which I am calling Charge One.

"When you are happy with everything, you will simultaneously press the circuit button and the fire button designated for Charge One. The Ammonal will explode, ruining Adam Cornish's whole day.

"The mine is perfectly placed. It is slap, bang under the middle of the parade. We couldn't have planned it any better. Any questions?"

Jacques and Rod, imagining a volcanic upheaval of earth and human beings, remained silent.

John beamed: "Good! Now all three of us know how the whole thing works. So, if we get into a scrap, we shall have three chances of making the kill."

He pointed to the stacked Ammonal, surmounted by the detonator and plastic explosive charge, and went on: "When this lot blows, we don't want it to take us with it. So we shall proceed to put a safe distance between the explosive and ourselves.

"We must be behind substantial cover to shield us from the blast. Now, as you should all know, good reconnaissance wins battles. I have already taken a look round and identified a safe hidey-hole.

"Just 20 yards from the canteen, is a narrow, metalled lane. If you turn right, it takes you to Voormezele village. But we shall turn left. That way, the lane runs for about a mile before joining the Messines-Wytschaete road.

"To the left of the lane, there is Bavarian Wood and the flooded mine crater. To the right, are fields. About half a mile down the lane, on the left-hand side, is a derelict cottage and poultry farm."

The major paused, looking keenly at the other two to make sure his briefing was sinking in. Satisfied, John continued: "This disused farm is surrounded by a substantially-built dry stone wall.

"We will take up our position behind this. We shall be well out of sight of the Nazis and safe from the blast. Any questions?"

Again, Rod and Jacques remained silent. There was nothing left to say. The major, a true professional, had obviously done his homework well. Moisture dripped on to their helmets and they shivered in the clammy dampness.

The major pointed to the cable, saying: "Now we will reel this out, under cover of darkness, to the old chicken farm. I'll guide the cable. You two will conceal it as best you can as we go along.

"Waterproof capes at the ready. Let's move!"

The three men climbed the Frauenlob's steel ladder to the surface. The rain had stopped, but the air was heavily-laden with an approaching storm. Lightning flashed above the martyred city of Ypres.

The stage was set for the day's drama.

Rod said: "You two start work. I'm going for a quick look round, and then I'll join you." He slipped like a wraith into the misty darkness of Bavarian Wood.

John started paying out the cable from the drum. Jacques followed, smearing it with mud before burying it in the rich, Flemish soil. Where the ground was hard, he covered the cable with leaves and pieces of fern.

After 20 minutes, Rod rejoined them. John looked at him questioningly and Rod shook his head, whispering: "Nothing Nobody about."

They reached the lane and the major was paying out the cable into a ditch on the left-hand side. The three men were halfway to the poultry farm when they saw headlights approaching.

John tossed the reel of cable smartly into the ditch, shouted: "Attention!" and gave a stiff-armed salute. A lorry, packed with Brown-shirts chanting a Nazi marching song, roared past on its way to Hill 40.

After the truck disappeared, the darkness seemed blacker than ever. Thunder rumbled closer.

The three men worked at a feverish pace, paying out and concealing the cable. With a sense of relief, they reached the old poultry farm, and crouched behind the wall.

Rod shaded a pencil torch with his hand as John made the final connections and tested the circuit. The major was rewarded by a green light, followed by a flashing red. It would now take only the pressure of two fingertips to unleash the cataclysm.

John pulled his waterproof cape tightly round him. He told Jacques and Rod: "They're obviously up and about. We daren't risk being seen, so we'll lie low here until zero hour."

He glanced once more at his watch, adding: "Now it's just a matter of timing. I've worked out when they will all be strutting their Nazi stuff in the middle of the big field.

"Then I'll set the Ammonal off. The explosion will break the surface in a big way, and it will be, 'Goodnight nurse' to Cornish and his crew."

The rain began coming down like stair rods. The three men huddled behind the wall. Just feet away, lorry after lorry, packed with storm-troopers, raced down the road.

In the former 1914-18 No-Man's land, Nazis began striking their tents and clearing the ground for the parade. Film, radio and television crews arrived, setting up antennas and unpacking complex equipment.

In Dixmuide, as the Fuhrer slept, a deeply-worried, Arthur Burfield, eyes bloodshot after a sleepless night, addressed a platoon of elite S.S. troopers, drawn up on the road outside the hotel.

This morning, Arthur Burfield was most emphatically in S.S.Colonel Andre Lacroix mode. He paced up and down a line of men, glaring at them from under the glistening peak of his officer's cap.

Burfield shouted: "Pay attention and listen to me carefully. You have a vital duty today . . . nothing less than protecting the person of our Fuhrer. I have reason to believe he could be in great danger."

Arthur knew that to admit he was worried simply by "a funny feeling something is wrong" would make him lose all credibility with this expressionless line of black-uniformed men.

He went on dramatically: "You will go immediately to Hill 40 and place a ring of steel round Bavarian Wood and the parade ground. No-one must enter the area without your permission.

"Be ruthless. Check their credentials to the last comma and full stop. Make a thorough search of the wood. Arrest any suspicious intruder. Brook no arguments.

"Be vigilant. Be careful. Such an intruder could be armed and highly trained. We have many enemies. They are resourceful. They are determined. We must regard ourselves and, especially our Fuhrer, as targets today.

"We rely on you to keep us safe . . . and, if necessary, to wreak vengeance on our enemies. Your transport is here. Do your duty. Heil Cornish!"

The S.S. men snapped to attention, returned the salute and dismissed. They climbed into a waiting truck, its engine idling. It then sped off into the reluctantly lightening dawn. Arthur walked slowly into the hotel and pushed open the door of the communications centre.

He leaned over the shoulder of the operator, detailed to stay in touch with the watcher, soon due on duty at Hill 40. The man, headphones clamped to his ears, gestured that nothing had been received.

Adam's faithful deputy had a queasy premonition that he may already be too late.

Back at Hill 40, Sergeant Wayne Durrant was on the move, rubbing the sleep from his eyes. He was on his way to check a snare he had set for rabbits, while playing truant from his sentry duties.

Several boring and uneventful days ago, the sergeant decided to extract some small profit from the wild goose chase on which that old fart Lacroix had sent him. He had already snared three plump rabbits, which a hotel chef had cooked and shared with him.

Durrant decided that, if he'd caught another rabbit this morning, he would have it made into a pie. As he tramped dreamily through the rain-soaked long grass by the Frauenlob, the sergeant could almost smell the appetising aroma that would waft from the crust when he cut into it.

Suddenly, the sergeant's reverie was shattered. His foot caught in something, sending him crashing to the ground. Cursing, Durrant raised himself to his knees. He glimpsed the cause of his fall—a cable, snaking through the grass.

The storm-trooper crouched and examined it. The cable, wet with rain, looked brand new. In one direction, it led towards the road. He tugged the cable from the ground and decided to follow it in the other direction.

The buried cable led him directly to the mouth of the Frauenlob mine-shaft. Durrant decided the wire must be a power cable belonging to one of the many TV crews.

They were probably doing a moody shoot underground. He stood with the wet flex in his hand, pondering this mundane explanation. As such, the wire was not worth bothering with.

The sergeant smiled as another thought struck him. This television cable could be used to earn a few Brownie points with Old Twisted-Knickers Lacroix.

By reporting this non-find, and hamming it up a little, he would show the colonel that he, Sergeant Wayne Durrant, was alert and on the ball. When the whole thing came to nothing, he would still be in Lacroix's good books.

Durrant decided to save his titbit for later. He would give it maximum impact by waiting until the parade was ready for the off. Then he would get on to his radio and cause a hell of an alarm. This would raise a laugh in the sergeant's mess tonight.

But now Sergeant Durrant had something more important to do. He walked into the wood, inspected the snare and was delighted to find the still-warm body of a rabbit. The animal was twitching as he released it from the wire noose.

So the day at Hill 40 started with a small death.

Wayne Durrant lay on the edge of the wood, just like a small boy called Jacques Leberte had lain there nearly 57 years before. Durrant, just like young Jacques, was playing the wag—stealing some time off. He, too, was fascinated as he watched the Nazis.

Hundreds of men were milling about in the bare cornfield that was once a killing ground. Storm-troopers

360

bore the standards of many nations. Musicians' instruments gleamed like gold coins against the dark velvet of the threatening storm.

An S.S. sergeant-major, easily topping six-foot nine inches, was roaring invective as he tried to make order of the chaos. Gradually, the men were formed into ranks and then into divisions.

The storm broke with a vengeance. Lightning forked across former No-Man's land, vivid against the deep-bellied clouds. The fury of the thunderclaps made men cower as though under attack.

Durrant saw a limousine, flanked by motor-cyclist out-riders, draw up in the lane next to the rain-soaked parade ground. It was time.

He hurried to his lair in the bushes and switched on his radio. He said into the microphone: "This is Sergeant Durrant at Hill 40. There is something serious to report. I have just discovered a newly-laid cable near the mine-shaft."

There was severe crackling as lightning racked the woods and storm-trooper-packed field. The lone tree at its centre was silhouetted like an evil sentinel.

In the communications room in the Dixmuide hotel, Durrant's voice came intermittently between bursts of static: "It may be nothing . . . feel . . . should be reported . . . Colonel Lacroix . . . as . . . urgency . . ."

Arthur Burfield, wearing the radio operator's earphones, snatched the microphone. He had stayed behind, instinctively expecting a message from Bavarian Wood, when the Fuhrer's cavalcade swept off.

He snapped: "Stay where you are. S.S. men will be with you within minutes. You will show them the exact location of this cable."

Durrant heard nothing but heavy static.

Burfield said to the Dixmuide operator: "Switch to the Hill 40 S.S. platoon's channel. Quickly, man!" The operator fiddled briefly with the controls and reported: "The electrical storm is getting worse, Colonel. It is blotting out communications."

Sergeant Durrant watched as Fuhrer Adam Cornish, surrounded by his bodyguards, climbed out of the limousine. The Fuhrer contemptuously thrust aside a mackintosh proffered by one of the S.S. men. Within seconds, his uniform was soaked.

The massed bands broke into a medley of patriotic songs from around the Fourth Reich, beginning with Land of Hope and Glory. Adam looked round, puzzled by the absence of his shadow, Arthur Burfield.

He felt as though he had lost his right arm. After glancing at his watch, the Fuhrer told his staff officers: "We'll give the Colonel three minutes. Then we will have to start without him. Millions are waiting on us."

At that moment, Burfield abandoned all attempts at establishing communication with Hill 40. He ran outside the hotel into the deluge and roughly thrust a motor-cyclist from his machine.

He sparked the motor-cycle into life and roared off towards Hill 40, rain streaming down his face like giant tears. His instincts were never wrong. This could be trouble, terrible, terrible trouble.

If his worst fears were confirmed, Arthur Burfield knew he may have only a matter of minutes in which to act.

Bile stung the back of his throat as he twisted the throttle open and raced through the lanes towards the great parade. Thunder, almost overhead, drowned the sound of the motor-cycle's engine as it roared through Voormezele.

At Hill 40, Adam had lost patience waiting for his *eminence grise.* He announced: "We can't hang around any longer. I only hope Burfield has a good excuse. Otherwise, he'll be out of a job."

The bands fell as silent and gazed at Hitler's stone statue, draped in its giant Nazi flag. The Fuhrer strode towards the head of the parade. TV and film cameramen, cameras hooded against the rain, watched through their viewfinders as he unhurriedly took his place.

There was a dramatic crack of thunder, like the salute of an artillery piece. Then the bands struck up an old Nazi marching song, the words of which the storm-troopers had been made to learn by heart.

The S.S. sergeant-major roared: "Parade . . . parade . . . quick march!" Banners flying, bands playing, storm-troopers goose-stepping, it was as if a pre-war Nuremburg rally had risen from the grave.

Racing up the lane towards the clamour of martial music, Arthur Burfield ran head-on into his own "ring of steel". An S.S. corporal, unslinging his automatic weapon, stepped into the road and held up his hand for the motor-cyclist to halt.

Burfield barked: "I'm Colonel Lacroix, you idiot! Get on your walkie-talkie. If that doesn't work, pass the word for as many of you as possible to assemble at the Frauenlob. At the double! This is a matter of life or death!"

The former photographer felt the destiny of the Fourth Reich lay in his hands. He rode his motor-cycle round the edge of the parade ground, where he saw the marchers were well into their stride.

Several yards ahead of the columns was the lone, rain-soaked figure of Fuhrer Adam Cornish, head up, back straight, looking every inch the dignified grandson of

Adolf Hitler. His old R.A.F. drill instructor would have been proud of him.

By the time Burfield reached the mine-shaft, half a dozen S.S. men had gathered there. More ran to join them.

Sergeant Wayne Durrant, looking deeply apprehensive, crawled out of his woodland lair, marched smartly over and stood to attention in front of his chief.

He said: "I'll show you the cable immediately, sir." He led the group to where the uncovered wire lay gleaming among the ferns and grass.

Burfield ordered his S.S. men: "Split into two groups. Each will follow this cable in a different direction to see where it leads. I understand the walkie-talkies are working. Keep in touch. Be prepared to neutralise any threat. Go!"

He and six of the S.S. troopers broke into a run as they followed the cable towards the road. The other black-uniformed men climbed down the gleaming, wet ladder into the mine-shaft.

Behind the wall of the poultry farm, John Walker decided zero hour had come. He pressed the button to test the circuit and was rewarded by a green light. Pressure on the second button resulted in a flashing red.

Rod and Jacques watched, as though hypnotised, as the Major reached out to press both buttons at once.

Down the lane, the martial music was competing with deafening claps of thunder. Lightning spotlighted a sea of Flanders mud as the storm-troopers splashed through the worsening storm.

The first bullet took Major John Walker M.C. in the right eye. He slumped to the ground, his blood mingling with the mud and weeds. The major's hand moved feebly towards the firing button, twitched once, then fell motionless.

The S.S. men and Arthur Burfield, leaning over the stone wall, unloosed a burst of automatic fire. Rod's hand was also just inches from the Shrike when his chest blossomed into great crimson petals. His body slumped over that of the major.

Burfield's eyes widened with surprise when he recognised the third member of the group behind the wall. He shouted to his men: "That one is a fucking traitor. You, put a couple of bullets into his belly. I want him to die slowly."

The S.S. trooper obediently fired two shots into Jacques, who fell on to his back, eyes rolling in agony. Torrential rain poured into his gaping mouth, stifling his shrieks.

Down in the Frauenlob, the second S.S. party discovered a cache of torches at the foot of the shaft. They followed the cable to the excavated sap.

The S.S. men inched their way warily along the narrow tunnel. Suddenly, they stopped, stunned by the sight of an Aladdin's cave piled high with explosive.

A sergeant was the first to recover from the shock. He stepped forward and gingerly began to examine the bags of Ammonal and the explosive charge.

The sergeant wasn't an expert at this sort of thing, and his hand shook as he leaned forward and managed to disconnect the cable from the detonator.

Above the sap, the rally was reaching its climax. Rank upon rank of storm-troopers was drawn up, standing stiffly to attention. Adam Cornish moved slowly forward, to where Adolf Hitler's statue loomed, draped in its swastika flag.

Trumpeters broke into a fanfare as their new Fuhrer, blue eyes ablaze with pride, reached for the golden cord to unveil this soaring memorial to his grandfather, the old Fuhrer.

In that split second, history repeated itself. Just as in 1955, a bolt of lightning leaped from the black clouds. It struck the lone tree in No-Man's Land, secretly standing guard over the lost Messines mine.

The tree stood out starkly in an explosion of light in the middle of the parade ground. It was as though a heavenly searchlight had been turned on to the hundreds of men, the Fuhrer and the great bulk of the statue.

In a nano-second, a charge of electricity snapped down the wet tree, picked up an ancient copper wire and sizzled into the bowels of the earth.

It streaked along the old 1914-18 Tommies' gallery. The electricity fizzed into the chamber where the S.S. men were still standing in wonderment. It arrived at the stack of Ammonal.

The S.S. sergeant had rendered harmless the modern PE4 explosive and detonator. But he had failed to see that, deep in the gloom of the chamber, the old World War One detonator was still in place.

The electricity reached for it greedily . . .

The surface of the old battlefield heaved like a giant awakening under a blanket. A mighty mountain of earth thundered towards the lowering sky. The British mine, just as its forebears had done in the summer of 1917, vaporised all that stood in its way.

If the chaplain, who had watched the awesome sight of the mines exploding in the Great War, had been there today, he would have again crossed himself.

The apocalyptic explosion, later reported to be heard as far away as London, finally faded into a chain of echoes. The downpour softened. Gentle raindrops fell into the raw and gaping crater, now the grave of the Fourth Reich.

Down the road, among the weeds of the old poultry farm, it bathed the bodies of Major John Walker GC, Captain Hamish Sinclair MC and Jacques Leberte.

On the other side of the stone wall by the poultry farm, Arthur Burfield and his S.S. troopers stood in the lane, stunned by the giant blast and staring speechlessly at the angry sky over Hill 40.

Sunday, July 8, 2001

In a modest, semi-detached house, nestling snugly into a newly-built South London estate, a telephone chirped. Maya Cornish, an attractive, middle-aged blonde, was busy in the kitchen when she heard the sound. She wiped her floury hands on her apron.

Maya shushed her two lively, blue-eyed youngsters—a tousle-headed boy, Adam, and a brunette, gamin-featured girl, Marie—her husband had insisted on giving them "family names". She reached for the instrument on the kitchen wall.

But, before Maya could lift the phone, her husband, Grant Cornish, came in from the garden.

Grant, a mildly-successful local estate agent, had the beginnings of a comfortable middle-aged spread bulging over his gardening trousers. His thinning, dark hair was streaked with grey and his puffy face spoke of a close acquaintance with alcohol.

Grant's only outstanding feature, and the one that had first attracted Maya to him at a college disco, was the startling blue of his eyes. Grant gestured that he would take the call, at the same time miming drinking a cup of tea.

Maya obediently switched on the electric kettle, set out a mug and poured in milk. She didn't want to spark another one of her husband's scary rages.

Grant put the phone to his ear. A bluff voice with a hint of a country accent said: "Good morning, Mr. Cornish. You don't know me, but . . ."

Annoyed at being disturbed on a Sunday morning by what he surmised was yet another double-glazing salesman, Grant snarled: "Who the hell is this? Are you trying to sell something?

"He mimicked, 'You may not know me,' and I certainly don't want to know you . . ."

The caller interrupted: "Just hold it there, Mr. Cornish. I am not a salesman. I was a good friend and comrade-in-arms of your late father, Adam Cornish. I commiserate with you in your sad loss.

"I now have something vitally important to tell you that will change your life forever. Are you listening?"

Maya proffered the mug of tea and looked questioningly at her husband. He stood, clutching the phone tightly. He ignored his wife and whispered: "Who ARE you?"

The caller became authoritative and snapped: "Never mind who I am, Cornish. If you behave sensibly, you will find out later. Suffice to say I am worth listening to. Shall I go on?"

Grant, his mouth and throat dry, croaked: "Please do. Say what you have to."

At the other end of the line Arthur Burfield told Adam's son: "You have seen and heard that your father was very publicly murdered. The whole world was shocked at the death of our Fuhrer.

"I can now tell you that your father left you a legacy. Yes, there is money, and plenty of it. But the most important part of your inheritance will enable you to change the course of history.

"I will be in touch."

Before Grant could reply, the call was abruptly terminated. For a long time, he stood with the receiver still pressed to his ear.

His vividly blue eyes were shining with a strange fervour Maya had never seen before.

THE END

ABOUT THE AUTHOR

Frank Durham is a veteran journalist, who has travelled the world searching out exclusive stories. These range from movie star interviews in Hollywood, to reporting Royal Marine commandos in action. Durham's by-lined work has been published in leading newspapers and magazines in countless countries.

In the course of his travels, he has come across many dramatic, intriguing and hitherto untold stories. These form the basis for a projected series of "faction" novels, the first of which is *The White Crow*. He has already begun work on his second book, *Spawn of Evil*.

Durham was born in inner London and raised in Harrow, North West London. Aged 18, he was drafted into the Royal Air Force, and trained as a Russian linguist during the Cold War.

He uses his Russian skill when making frequent trips to Kiev in the Ukraine, where the International Order of St. Stanislas—in which he holds the rank of Commander's Cross—helps the orphans and disadvantaged boys of a military academy.

Durham has edited newspapers and magazines. He founded an international features agency in Fleet Street, which he later sold to become a globe-trotting freelance, Now he is concentrating on writing books.

He is single, and lives in Sevenoaks, Kent, England.

Lightning Source UK Ltd.
Milton Keynes UK
UKOW050344091211

183453UK00001B/3/P